Powerful & Proud

KATE HEWITT

First Published in Great Britain 2017
By Mills & Boon, an imprint of HarperCollins*Publishers*
1 London Bridge Street, London, SE1 9GF

POWERFUL & PROUD © 2017 Harlequin Books S. A.

Beneath The Veil Of Paradise, *In The Heat Of The Spotlight* and *His Brand Of Passion* were first published in Great Britain by Harlequin (UK) Limited.

Beneath The Veil Of Paradise © 2012 Kate Hewitt
In The Heat Of The Spotlight © 2013 Kate Hewitt
His Brand Of Passion © 2013 Kate Hewitt

ISBN: 978-0-263-92970-6

05-0717

Kate Hewitt discovered her first Mills & Boon romance on a trip to England when she was thirteen, and she's continued to read them ever since. She wrote her first story at the age of five, simply because her older brother had written one and she thought she could do it too. That story was one sentence long—fortunately they've become a bit more detailed as she's grown older. She has written plays, short stories and magazine serials for many years, but writing romance remains her first love. Besides writing, she enjoys reading, travelling and learning to knit.

After marrying the man of her dreams—her older brother's childhood friend—she lived in England for six years, and now resides in Connecticut with her husband, her three young children, and the possibility of one day getting a dog.

Kate loves to hear from readers—you can contact her through her website: www.kate-hewitt.com.

BENEATH THE
VEIL OF PARADISE

BY
KATE HEWITT

CHAPTER ONE

Was she ever going to start painting?

The woman had been sitting and staring at the blank canvas for the better part of an hour. Chase Bryant had been watching her, nursing his drink at the ocean-side bar and wondering if she'd ever actually put brush to paper, or canvas, as the case might be.

She didn't.

She was fussy; he could see that straight off. She was in a luxury resort on a remote island in the Caribbean, and her tan capris had knife-edge pleats. Her pale-blue polo shirt looked like she'd ironed it an hour ago. He wondered what she did to relax. If she relaxed. Considering her attitude in their current location, he doubted it.

Still, there was something intriguing about the determined if rather stiff set of her shoulders, the compressed line of her mouth. She wasn't particularly pretty—well, not his kind of pretty anyway, which he fully admitted was lush, curvy blondes. This woman was tall, just a few inches under his own six feet, and angular. He could see the jut of her collarbone, the sharp points of her elbows. She had a narrow face, a forbidding expression, and even her hairstyle was severe, a blunt bob of near black that looked like she trimmed it with nail scissors every week. Its razor-straight edge swung by the strong line of her jaw as she moved.

He'd been watching her since she arrived, her canvas and paints under one arm. She'd set her stuff up on the beach a little way off from the bar, close enough so he could watch her while he sipped his sparkling water. No beers for him on this trip, unfortunately.

She'd been very meticulous about it all, arranging the collapsible easel, the box of paints, the little three-legged stool. Moving everything around until it was all just so, and she was on a beach. In the Caribbean. She looked like she was about to teach an evening art class for over-sixties.

Still he waited. He wondered if she was any good. She had a gorgeous view to paint—the aquamarine sea, a stretch of spun-sugar sand. There weren't even many people to block the view; the resort wasn't just luxurious, it was elite and discreet. He should know. His family owned it. And right now he needed discreet.

She finished arranging everything and sat on the stool, staring out to the sea, her posture perfect, back ramrod-straight. For half an hour. It would have been boring except that he could see her face, and how emotions flickered across it like shadows on water. He couldn't exactly decipher what the emotions were, but she clearly wasn't thinking happy thoughts.

The sun had begun its languorous descent towards the sea, and he decided she must be waiting for the sunset. They were spectacular here; he'd seen three of them already. He liked watching the sun set, felt there was something poetic and apt about all that intense beauty over in an instant. He watched now as the sun slipped lower, its long rays causing the placid surface of the sea to shimmer with a thousand lights, the sky ablaze with myriad streaks of colour, everything from magenta to turquoise to gold.

And still she just sat there.

For the first time Chase felt an actual flicker of annoyance. She'd dragged everything out here; obviously she'd intended to paint something. So why wasn't she doing it? Was she afraid? More likely a perfectionist. And, damn it, he knew now that life was too short to wait for the perfect moment, or even an OK moment. Sometimes you just had to wade into the mire and do it. Live while you could.

Pushing away his drink, he rose from his stool and headed over to Miss Fussy.

Millie did not enjoy feeling like a fool. And it felt foolish and, worse, pathetic, sitting here on a gorgeous beach staring at a blank canvas when she'd obviously come to paint.

She just didn't want to any more.

It had been a stupid idea anyway, the kind of thing you read about in self-help books or women's magazines. She'd read one on the plane to St Julian's, something about being kind to yourself. Whatever. The article had described how a woman had taken up gardening after her divorce and had ended up starting her own landscaping business. Lived her dream after years of marital unhappiness. Inspirational. Impossible. Millie turned away from the canvas.

And found herself staring straight at a man's muscled six-pack abs. She looked up and saw a dark-haired Adonis smiling down at her.

'I've heard about watching paint dry, but this is ridiculous.'

Perfect, a smart ass. Millie rose from her stool so she was nearly eye-level. 'As you can see, there's no paint.'

'What are you waiting for?'

'Inspiration,' she answered and gave him a pointed look. 'I'm not finding any here.'

If she'd been trying to offend or at least annoy him, she'd failed. He just laughed, slow and easy, and gave her a thorough once-over with his dark bedroom eyes.

Millie stood taut and still, starting to get angry. She hated guys like this one: gorgeous, flirtatious, and utterly arrogant. Three strikes against him, as far as she was concerned.

His gaze finally travelled up to her face, and she was surprised and discomfited to see a flicker of what almost looked like sympathy there. 'So really,' he asked, dropping the flirt, 'why haven't you painted anything?'

'It's none of your business.'

'Obviously. But I'm curious. I've been watching you from the bar for nearly an hour. You spent a long time on the set-up, but you've been staring into space for thirty minutes.'

'What are you, some kind of stalker?'

'Nope. Just bored out of my mind.'

She stared at him; tried to figure him out. She'd taken him for a cheap charmer but there was something strangely sincere about the way he spoke. Like he really was curious. And really bored.

Something in the way he waited with those dark eyes and that little half-smile made her answer reluctantly, 'I just couldn't do it.'

'It's been a while?'

'Something like that.' She reached over and started to pack up the paints. No point pretending anything was going to happen today. Or any day. Her painting days were long gone.

He picked up her easel and collapsed it in one neat movement before handing it back. 'May I buy you a drink?'

She liked the 'may', but she still shook her head. 'No thanks.' She hadn't had a drink alone with a man in two years. Hadn't done anything in two years but breathe and work and try to survive. This guy wasn't about to make her change her ways.

'You sure?'

She turned to him and folded her arms as she surveyed

him. He really was annoyingly attractive: warm brown eyes, short dark hair, a chiseled jaw and those nice abs. His board shorts rode low on his hips, and his legs were long and powerful. 'Why,' she asked, 'are you even asking? I'd bet a hundred bucks I'm not your usual type.' Just like he wasn't hers.

'Typecast me already?'

'Easily.'

His mouth quirked slightly. 'Well, you're right, you're not my usual type. Way too tall and, you know—' he gestured around her face, making Millie stiffen '—severe. What's with the hair?'

'The hair?' Instinctively and shamefully she reached up to touch her bobbed hair. 'What about it?'

'It's scary. Like, Morticia Addams scary.'

'Morticia *Addams*? Of the Addams Family? She had long hair.' She could not believe they were discussing her hair, and in relation to a television show.

'Did she? Well, maybe I'm thinking of someone else. Somebody with hair like yours. Really sharp-cut.' He made a chopping motion along his own jaw.

'You're being ridiculous. And offensive.' Yet strangely she found herself smiling. She liked his honesty.

He raised his eyebrows. 'So, dinner?'

'I thought it was a drink.'

'Based on the fact that you're still talking to me, I upped the ante.'

She laughed, reluctant, rusty, yet still a laugh. This annoying, arrogant, attractive man amused her somehow. When was the last time she'd actually laughed, had felt like laughing? And she was on holiday—admittedly enforced, but she had a whole week to kill. Seven days was looking like a long time from here. Why not amuse herself? Why not prove she really was moving on, just like her boss Jack had urged her to do? She gave a little decisive nod. 'OK, to the drink only.'

'Are you *haggling*?'

Interest flared; deals she could do. 'What's your counter offer?'

He cocked his head, his gaze sweeping slowly over her once more. And she reacted to that gaze, a painful mix of attraction and alarm. Dread and desire. Hot and cold. A welter of emotions that penetrated her numbness, made her *feel*.

'Drink, dinner, and a walk on the beach.'

Awareness pulsed with an electric jolt low in her belly. 'You were supposed to offer something less, not more.'

His slow, wicked smile curled her toes—and other parts of her person, parts that hadn't curled in a long time. 'I know.'

She hesitated. She should back off, tell him to forget it, yet somehow now that felt like failure. She could handle him. She needed to be able to handle him.

'Fine.' She was agreeing because it was a challenge, not because she wanted to. She liked to set herself little challenges, tests of emotional and physical endurance: *I can jog three miles in eighteen-and-a-half minutes and not even be out of breath. I can look at this photo album for half an hour and not cry.*

Smiling, he reached for the canvas she clutched to her chest. 'Let me carry that for you.'

'Chivalrous of you, but there's no need.' She strode over to the rubbish bin on the edge of the beach and tossed the canvas straight in. The paints, easel and stool followed.

She didn't look at him as she did it, but she felt herself flush. She was just being practical, but she could see how it might seem kind of…severe.

'You are one scary lady.'

She glanced at him, eyebrows raised, everything prickling. 'Are you still talking about my hair?'

'The whole package. But don't worry, I like it.' He grinned and she glared.

'I wasn't worried.'

'The thing I like about you,' he said as he strolled towards the bar, 'is you're so easy to rile.'

Millie had no answer to that one. She *was* acting touchy, but she felt touchy. She didn't do beaches, or bars, or dates. She didn't relax. For the last two years she had done nothing but work, and sunbathing on the beach with a paperback and MP3 player was akin to having her fingernails pulled out one by one. At least that wouldn't take a whole week.

The man—she realised she didn't even know his name—had led her through the beach-side bar to an artful arrangement of tables right on the sand. Each one was shaded by its own umbrella, with comfortable, cushioned chairs and a perfect view of the sea.

The waiter snapped right to attention, so Millie guessed the man was known around here. Probably a big spender. Trust-fund baby or bond trader? Did it matter?

'What's your name?' she asked as she sat across from him. He was gazing out at the sea with a strangely focused look. The orange streaks were like vivid ribbons across the sky. He snapped his attention back to her.

'Chase.'

'Chase.' She gave a short laugh. 'Sounds appropriate.'

'Actually, I don't generally do much chasing.' He gave her a slow, oh-so-sexy smile that had annoyance flaring through her even as her toes—and other parts—curled again.

'Charming, Chase. Do you practise that in the mirror?'

'Practise what?'

'Your smile.'

He laughed and leaned back in his chair. 'Nope, never. But it must be a pretty nice smile, if you think I practise.' He eyed her consideringly. 'Although, the more likely possibility is that you just think you I'm an arrogant ass who's far too full of himself.'

Now she laughed in surprise. She hadn't expected him to be so honest. 'And I could probably tell you what you think of me.'

He arched one eyebrow. 'And that is?'

'Uptight, prissy know-it-all who doesn't know how to have a good time.' As soon as she said the words, she regretted them. This wasn't a conversation she wanted to have.

'Actually, I don't think that.' He remained relaxed, but his gaze swept over her searchingly, making Millie feel weirdly revealed. 'Admittedly, on the surface, yes, I see it. Totally, to a tee. But underneath…' She rolled her eyes, waiting for the come-on. Everything was a chat-up line to a guy like this. 'You seem sad.'

She tensed mid-eye-roll, her gaze arrowing on him. A little smile played around his mouth, drawing attention to those full, sculpted lips. Lips that were lush enough to belong to a woman, yet still seemed intensely masculine. And it was those lips that had so softly issued that scathing indictment. *You seem sad.*

'I don't know what you're talking about.' As far as comebacks went, it sucked. And her voice sounded horribly brittle. But Millie didn't have anything better. Averting her eyes, she slipped out her smart phone and punched in a few numbers. Chase watched her without speaking, yet she felt something from him. Something dark, knowing and totally unexpected.

'What's your name?' he finally asked and, knowing she was being rude, she didn't look up from her phone.

'Millie Lang.' No work emails. Damn.

'What's that short for? Millicent? Mildred?'

She finally glanced up, saw him still studying her. 'Camilla.'

'Camilla,' he repeated, savouring the syllables, drawing them out with a sensual consideration that didn't seem forced or fake. 'I like it.' He gestured to her phone. 'So what's going on in the real world, Camilla? Your stock portfolio sound? Work managing without you?'

She flushed and put her phone away. She'd just been about to check NASDAQ. For the fifth time today. 'Everything ship-shape. And please don't call me Camilla.'

'You prefer Millie?'

'Clearly.'

He laughed. 'This is going to be a fun evening, I can tell.'

Her flush intensified, swept down her body. What a mistake this was—a stupid, stupid mistake. Had she actually thought she could do this—have dinner, have fun, *flirt*? All ridiculous.

'Maybe I should just go.' She half-rose from her chair, but Chase stopped her with one hand on her wrist. The touch of his fingers, long, lean and cool against that tender skin, felt like a bomb going off inside her body. Not just the usual tingle of attraction, the shower of sparks that was your body's basic reaction to a good-looking guy. No, a *bomb*. She jerked her hand away, heard her breath come out in a rush. 'Don't—'

'Whoa.' He held his hands up in front of him. 'Sorry, my mistake.' But he didn't look sorry. He looked like he knew exactly what she'd just experienced. 'I meant what I said, Millie. It's going to be a fun evening. I like a challenge.'

'Oh, please.' His stupid comment made her feel safe. She wanted this Chase to be exactly what she'd thought he was: attractive, arrogant and utterly unthreatening.

Chase grinned. 'I knew you'd expect me to say that.' And, just like that, she was back to wondering. Millie snatched up a menu.

'Shall we order?'

'Drinks first.'

'I'll have a glass of Chardonnay with ice, please.'

'That sounds about right,' he murmured and rose from

the table. Millie watched him walk to the bar, her gaze glued to his easy, long-limbed stride. Yes, she was staring at his butt. He looked good in board shorts.

By sheer force of will she dragged her gaze away from him and stared down at her phone. Why couldn't she have one work crisis? She'd had a dozen a day when she was in the office. Of course she knew why; she just didn't like it. Jack had insisted she take a week's holiday with no interruptions or furtive tele-commuting. She hadn't taken any in two years, and new company policy—supposedly for the health of its employees—demanded that you use at least half of your paid leave in one year.

What a ridiculous policy.

She *wanted* to work. She'd been working twelve-, fourteen- and sometimes even sixteen-hour days for two years and screeching to a halt to come here was making her very, very twitchy.

'Here you go.' Chase had returned to the table and placed a glass of wine in front of her. Millie eyed his own drink warily; it looked like soda.

'What are you drinking?'

'Some kind of cola.' He shrugged. 'It's cold, at least.'

'Do you have a drinking problem?' she asked abruptly and he laughed.

'Good idea, let's skip right to the important stuff. No, I don't. I'm just not drinking right now.' He took a sip of his soda, eyeing her thoughtfully. Millie held his gaze. All right, asking that had been a bit abrupt and even weird, but she'd forgotten how to do chit-chat.

'So, Millie, where are you from?'

'New York City.'

'I suppose I should have guessed that.'

'Oh, really?' She bristled. Again. 'You seem to think you have me figured out.'

'No, but I tend to be observant. And you definitely have that hard city gloss.'

'Where are you from, then?'

He gave her one of his toe-curling smiles. His eyes, Millie thought distantly, were so warm. She wanted to curl up in them, which was a nonsensical thought. 'I'm from New York too.'

'I suppose I could have guessed that.'

He laughed, a low, rich chuckle. 'How?'

'You've got that over-privileged, city-boy veneer,' she responded sweetly, to which he winced with theatrical ex-aggeration.

'Ouch.'

'At least now we understand each other.'

'Do we?' he asked softly and Millie focused on her drink. *Sip. Stare at the ice cubes bobbing in the liquid. Don't look at him.* 'Why are you so prickly?'

'I'm not.' It was a knee-jerk response. She *was* being prickly. She hadn't engaged with a man in any sense in far too long and she didn't know how to start now. *Why* had she agreed to this? She took another sip of wine, let the bubbles crisp on her tongue. 'Sorry,' she said after a moment. 'I'm not usually quite this bitchy.'

'I bring out the best in you?'

'I suppose you do.' She met his gaze, meaning to smile with self-deprecating wryness, but somehow her lips froze in something more like a grimace. He was gazing at her with a sudden intentness that made her breath dry and her heart start to pound. She wanted him to be light, wry, *shallow*. He wasn't being any of those things right now. And, even when he had been, she had a horrible feeling he'd simply done it by choice.

'So why are you on St Julian's?' he asked.

'Holiday, of course.'

'You don't seem like the type to holiday willingly.'

Which was all too true, but she didn't like him knowing it, or knowing anything. 'Oh?' she asked, glad to hear she was hitting that self-deprecating note she'd tried for earlier. 'And you know me so well?'

He leaned forward, suddenly predatory. 'I think I do.'

Her heart still pounding, Millie leaned back as if she actually felt relaxed and arched an eyebrow. 'How is that?'

'Let's see.' He leaned back too, sprawled in his chair in a manner so casually relaxed and yet also innately powerful, even in an ocean-side bar wearing board shorts. 'You're a lawyer, or else you're in finance.' He glanced at her, considering, and Millie froze. 'Finance, I'd say, something demanding but also elite. Hedge-fund manager, maybe?'

Damn it. How the hell did he know that? She said nothing.

'You work long hours, of course,' Chase continued, clearly warming to this little game. 'And you live in a high-rise building, full-service, on— Let's see. The Upper East Side? But near the subway, so you can get to work in under twenty minutes. Although you try to jog to work at least two mornings a week.' Now he arched an eyebrow, a little smile playing about his mouth. 'How am I doing so far?'

'Terrible,' Millie informed him shortly. She was seething inside, seething with the pain of someone knowing her at all, even just the basics. And she hated that he'd been able to guess it, read her as easily as a book. What else could he find out about her just by his so-called powers of observation? 'I run to work three mornings a week, not two, and I live in midtown.'

Chase grinned. 'I must be slipping.'

'Anyway,' Millie said, 'I could guess the same kinds of things about you.'

'OK, shoot.'

She eyed him just as he had her, trying to gain a little

time to assemble her thoughts. She had no idea what he did or where he lived. She could guess, but that was all it would be—a guess. Taking a breath, she began. 'I think you work in some pseudo-creative field, like IT or advertising.'

'*Pseudo*-creative?' Chase interjected, nearly spluttering his soda. 'You really are tough, Camilla.'

'Millie,' she reminded him shortly. Only Rob had called her Camilla. 'You live in Chelsea or Soho, in one of those deluxe bachelor loft apartments. A converted warehouse with views of the river and zero charm.'

'That is so stereotypical, it hurts.'

'With a great room that's fantastic for parties, top-of-the-line leather sofas, a huge TV and a high-tech kitchen full of gadgets you never use.'

He shook his head slowly, his gaze fastened on hers. He smiled, almost looking sorry for her. 'Totally wrong.'

She folded her arms. Strange how her observations of him made her feel exposed. 'Oh? How so?'

'All right, you might be right about the loft apartment, but it's in Tribeca—and my television is mid-size, thank you very much.'

'And the leather sofas?'

'Leather cleans very easily, or so my cleaning lady tells me.' She rolled her eyes. 'And I'll have you know I do use my kitchen, quite often. I find cooking relaxing.'

She eyed him uncertainly. 'You do not.'

'I do. But I bet you don't cook. You buy a bagel on the way to work, skip lunch and eat a bowl of cereal standing by the sink for dinner.'

It was just a little too close to the truth and it sounded unbelievably pathetic. Suddenly Millie wanted to stop this little game. Desperately. 'I order take-out on occasion as well,' she told him, trying for breezy. 'So what do you do, anyway?'

'I'm an architect. Does that count as pseudo-creative?'

'Definitely.' She was being incredibly harsh, but she was afraid to be anything else. This man exposed her in a way that felt like peeling back her skin—painful and messy. This date was over.

'As entertaining as this has been, I think I'll go.' She drained her glass of wine and half-rose from her chair, only to be stopped by Chase wrapping his fingers around her wrist, just as he had before—and, just as before, she reacted, an explosion of senses inside her.

'Scared, Millie?'

'Scared?' she repeated as contemptuously as she could. 'Of what—you?'

'Of us.'

'There is no *us*.'

'There's been an *us* since the moment you agreed to a drink, dinner and a walk on the beach,' he informed her with silky softness. 'And so far we've just had our drink.'

'Let me go,' she said flatly, her lips numb, her whole body buzzing.

Chase held up both hands, his gaze still holding hers as if they were joined by a live wire. 'I already did.'

And so he had. She was standing there like a complete idiot, acting as if she were trapped, when the only thing imprisoning her was her own fear. This man guessed way too much.

She couldn't walk away now. Admitting defeat was not an option. And if she could handle this, handle him as she'd assured herself she could, then wouldn't that be saying something? Wouldn't that be a way of proving to herself, as well as him, that she had nothing either to hide or fear?

She dropped back down into her chair and gave him a quick, cool smile. 'I'm not scared.'

Something like approval lit his eyes, making Millie feel

stupidly, ridiculously gratified. Better to get through this
evening as quickly as possible.

'So shall we order?'

'Oh no, we're not eating here,' Chase informed her. Millie
stared at him, nonplussed. He smiled, slow, easy and completely in control. 'We'll eat somewhere more private.'

CHAPTER TWO

'MORE private?' Millie's voice rose in a screech as she stared at him, two angry blotches of colour appearing high on her cheeks. He should be annoyed by now, Chase mused. He should be way past annoyed. The woman was a nutcase. Or at least very high-maintenance. But he wasn't annoyed, not remotely. He'd enjoyed their little exchange, liked that she gave as good as she got. And he was intrigued by something underneath that hard gloss—something real and deep and alive. He just wasn't sure what it was, or what he wanted to do with it.

But first, dinner. 'Relax. I'm not about to about to abduct you, as interesting as that possibility may be.'

'Not funny.'

She held herself completely rigid, her face still flushed with anger. He'd had no idea his change of dinner plans would provoke such a reaction—no; he had. Of course he had. He just hadn't realised he'd enjoy it so much. Underneath the overly ironed blouse her chest rose and fell in agitated breaths, making him suspect all that creaseless cotton hid some slender but interesting curves. 'You're right, it's not funny,' he agreed with as much genuine contrition as he could muster. 'We barely know each other, and I didn't intend to make you feel vulnerable.'

She rolled her eyes. 'We're not on some mandatory course

for creating a safe work environment, Chase. You can skip the PC double-speak.'

He laughed, loving it. Loving that she didn't play games, not even innocent ones. 'OK. Fine. By more private, I meant a room in the resort. Chaperoned by wait staff and totally safe. If you're feeling, you know, threatened.'

'I have not felt threatened by you for an instant,' Millie replied, and Chase leaned forward.

'Are you sure about that?' he asked softly, knowing he was pressing her in ways she didn't want to be pressed. He'd seen that shadow of vulnerability in her eyes, felt the sudden, chilly withdrawal as her armour went up. He knew the tactics because he'd used them himself.

It's not good news, Chase. I'm sorry.

Hell, yeah, he'd used them.

She stared at him for a moment, held his gaze long enough so he could see the warm brown of her eyes. Yes, *warm*. Like dark honey or rum, and the only warm thing about her. So far.

'Threatened is the wrong word,' she finally said, and from the starkness of her tone he knew she was speaking in total truth. 'You do make me uncomfortable, though.'

'Do I?'

She gave him a thin-lipped smile. 'I don't think anyone likes being told that it's obvious she eats a bowl of cereal by the sink for dinner.'

Ouch. Put like that, he realised it was insulting. 'I wouldn't say obvious.' Although he sort of would.

'Only because you're so perceptive, I suppose?' she shot back, and he grinned.

'So shall we go somewhere more private so you can continue to be uncomfortable?'

'What an appealing proposition.'

'It appeals to me,' he said truthfully, and she gave a little shake of her head.

'Honestly? What do you see in me?' She sounded curious, but also that thing he dreaded: vulnerable. She really didn't know the answer, and hell if he did either.

'What do you see in me?' he asked back.

She chewed her lip, her eyes shadowing once more. 'You made me laugh for the first time in—a long time.'

He had the strange feeling she'd been about to give him a specific number. *Since when?* 'That's a lot of pressure.'

Her eyes widened, flaring with warmth again. 'Why?'

'Because of course now I have to make you laugh again.'

And for a second he thought he might get a laugh right then and there, and something rose in his chest, an airy bubble of hope and happiness that made absolutely no sense. Still he felt it, rising him high and dizzily higher even though he didn't move. He grinned. Again, simply because he couldn't help it.

She shook her head. 'I'm not that easy.'

'This conversation just took a *very* interesting turn.'

'I meant *laughing*,' she protested, and then she did laugh, one ridiculously un-ladylike hiccup of joy that had her clapping her hand over her mouth.

'There it is,' Chase said softly. He felt a deep and strangely primal satisfaction, the kind he usually only felt when he'd nailed an architectural design. He'd made her laugh. Twice.

She stared at him, her hand still clapped over her mouth, her eyes wide, warm and soft—if eyes could even be considered soft. Chase felt a stirring deep inside—low down, yes, he felt that basic attraction, but something else. Something not quite so low down and far more alarming, caused by this hard woman with the soft eyes.

'You changed the deal,' she told him, dropping her hand,

all businesslike and brisk again. 'You said dinner here, in the restaurant.'

'I did not,' Chase countered swiftly. 'You just didn't read the fine print.'

He thought she might laugh again, but she didn't. He had a feeling she suppressed it, didn't want to give him the power of making her laugh three times. And it did feel like power, heady and addictive. He wanted more.

'I don't remember signing,' she said. 'And verbal agreements aren't legally binding.'

He leaned back in his chair, amazed at how alive he felt. How invigorated. He hadn't felt this kind of dazzling, creative energy in months. Eight months and six days, to be precise.

'All right, then,' he said. 'You can go.' He felt his heart thud at the thought that she might actually rise from the table and walk down the beach out of his life. Yet he also knew he had to level the playing field. She needed to be here because she wanted to be here, and she had to admit it. He didn't know why it was so important; he just felt it—that gut instinct that told him something was going on here that was more than a meal.

She chewed her lip again and he could tell by the little worry marks in its lush fullness—her lips were another soft part of her—that this was a habit. Her lashes swept downwards, hiding her eyes, but he could still read her. Easily.

She wanted to walk, but she also didn't, and that was aggravating her to no end.

She looked up, eyes clear and wide once more, any emotion safely hidden. 'Fine. We'll go somewhere more private.' And, without waiting for him, she rose from the table.

Chase rose too, anticipation firing through him. He wasn't even sure what he was looking forward to—just being with her, or something else? She was so not his type, and yet he couldn't deny that deep jolt of awareness, the flash of lust. And not just a flash, not just lust either. She attracted and intrigued him on too many levels.

Smiling, he rose from the table and led the way out of the beach-side bar and towards the resort.

Millie followed Chase into the resort, the soaring space cool and dim compared to the beach. She felt neither cool nor dim; everything inside her was light and heat. It scared her, feeling this. Wanting him. Because, yes, she knew she wanted him. Not just desire, simple attraction, a biological response or scientific law. *Want*.

She hadn't touched a man in two years. Longer, really, because she couldn't actually remember the last time she and Rob had made love. It had bothered her at first, the not knowing. She'd lain in bed night after endless nights scouring her brain for a fragment of a memory. Something to remind her of how she'd lain sated and happy in her husband's arms. She hadn't come up with anything, because it had been too long.

Now it wasn't the past that was holding her in thrall; it was the present. The future. Just what did she want to happen tonight?

'This way,' Chase murmured, and Millie followed him into a lift. The space was big enough, all wood-panelled luxury, but it still felt airless and small. He was still only wearing board shorts. Was he going to spend the whole evening shirtless? Could she stand it?

Millie cleared her throat, the sound seeming as loud as a gunshot, and Chase gave her a lazy sideways smile. He knew what she was thinking. Feeling. Knew, with that awful arrogance, that she was attracted to him even if she didn't like it. And she didn't like it, although she couldn't really say why.

It had been two years. Surely it was time to move on, to accept and heal and go forward?

She shook her head, impatient with herself. Dinner with someone like Chase was not going forward. If anything, it was going backwards, because he was too much like Rob. He was, Millie thought, more like Rob than Rob himself. He was her husband as her husband had always wanted to be: powerful, rich, commanding. He was Rob on steroids.

Exactly what she didn't want.

'Slow down there, Millie.'

Her gaze snapped to his, saw the remnant of that lazy smile. 'What—?'

'Your mind is going a mile a minute. I can practically see the smoke coming out of your ears.'

She frowned, wanting to deny it. 'It's just dinner.'

Chase said nothing, but his smile deepened. Millie felt a weird, shivery sensation straight through her bones that he wasn't responding because he didn't agree with her. It wasn't just dinner. It was something else, something scary.

But what?

'Here we are.' The lift doors swooshed open and Chase led her down a corridor and then out onto a terrace. A private terrace. They were completely alone, no wait staff in sight.

Millie didn't feel vulnerable, threatened or scared. No, she felt *terrified*. What was she doing here? Why had she agreed to dinner with this irritating and intriguing man? And why did she feel that jolt of electric awareness, that kick of excitement, every time she so much as looked at him? She felt more alive now than she had since Rob's death, maybe even since before that—a long time before that.

She walked slowly to the railing and laid one hand on the wrought-iron, still warm from the now-sinking sun. The vivid sunset had slipped into a twilit indigo, the sea a dark, tranquil mirror beneath.

'We missed the best part,' Chase murmured, coming to stand next to her.

'Do you think so?' Millie kept her gaze on the darkening sky. 'This part is more beautiful to me.'

Chase cocked his head, and Millie turned to see his speculative gaze slide over her. 'Somehow that doesn't surprise me,' he said, and reached out to tuck a strand of hair behind her ear. Millie felt as if he'd just dusted her with sparks, jabbed her with little jolts of electricity. Her cheek and ear throbbed, her physical response so intense it felt almost painful.

Did he feel it? Could it be possible that he reacted to her the way she did to him? The thought short-circuited her brain. It was quite literally mind-blowing.

She turned away from him, back to the sunset. 'Everybody likes the vibrant colours of a sunset,' she said, trying to keep her voice light. 'All that magenta and orange—gorgeous but gaudy, like an old broad with too much make-up.'

'I'll agree with you that the moment after is more your style. Understated elegance. Quiet sophistication.'

'And which do you prefer? The moment before or after?'

Chase didn't answer, and Millie felt as if the very air had suddenly become heavy with expectation. It filled her lungs, weighed them down; she was breathless.

'Before,' he finally said. 'Then there's always something to look forward to.'

Millie didn't think they were talking about sunsets any more. She glanced at Chase and saw him staring pensively at the sky, now deepening to black. The sun and all its gaudy traces had disappeared completely.

'So tell me,' she said, turning away from the railing, 'how did you arrange a private terrace so quickly? Or do you keep one reserved on standby, just in case you meet a woman?'

He laughed, a rich, throaty chuckle. This man enjoyed

life. It shouldn't surprise her; she'd labelled him a hedonist straight off. Yet she didn't feel prissily judgmental of that enjoyment right now. She felt—yes, she really did—*jealous*.

'Full disclosure?'

'Always.'

He reached for a blue button-down shirt that had been laid on one of the chairs. He'd thought of everything, and possessed the power to see it done. Millie watched him button up his shirt with long, lean fingers, the gloriously sculpted muscles of his chest disappearing under the crisp cotton.

'My family owns this resort.'

She jerked her rather admiring gaze from the vicinity of his chest to his face. 'Ah.' There was, she knew, a wealth of understanding in that single syllable. So, architect *and* trust-fund baby. She'd suspected something like that. He had the assurance that came only from growing up rich and entitled. She should be relieved; she wanted him to be what she'd thought he was, absolutely no more and maybe even less. So why, gazing at him now, did she feel the tiniest bit disappointed, like he'd let her down?

Like she actually wanted him to be different?

'Yes. Ah.' He smiled wryly, and she had a feeling he'd guessed her entire thought process, not for the first time this evening.

'That must be handy.'

'It has its benefits.' He spoke neutrally, without the usual flippant lightness and Millie felt a little dart of curiosity. For the first time Chase looked tense, his jaw a little bunched, his expression a little set. He didn't smile as he pulled out a chair for her at the cozy table for two and flickered with candlelight in the twilit darkness.

Millie's mind was, as usual, working overtime. 'The Bryant family owns this resort.'

'Bingo.'

'My company manages their assets.' That was how she'd ended up here, waiting out her week of enforced holiday, indolent luxury. Jack had suggested it.

'And you have a rule about mixing business with pleasure?'

'The point is moot. I don't handle their account.'

'Well, that's a relief.' He spoke with an edge she hadn't heard since she'd met him. Clearly his family and its wealth raised his hackles.

'So you're one of the Bryants,' she said, knowing instinctively such a remark would annoy him. 'Which one?'

'You know my family?'

'Who doesn't?' The Bryants littered the New York tabloids and society pages, not that she read either. But you couldn't so much as check your email without coming across a news blurb or scandalous headline. Had she read about Chase? Probably, if she'd paid attention to such things. There were three Bryant boys, as far as she remembered, and they were all players.

'I'm the youngest son,' Chase said tautly. He leaned back in his chair, deliberately relaxed in his body if not his voice. 'My older brother Aaron runs the property arm of Bryant Enterprises. My middle brother Luke runs the retail.'

'And you do your own thing.'

'Yes.'

That dart of curiosity sharpened into a direct stab. Why didn't Chase work for the family company? 'There's no Bryant Architecture, is there?'

His mouth thinned. 'Definitely not.'

'So what made you leave the family fold?'

'We're getting personal, then?'

'Are we?'

'Why did you throw out your canvas?'

Startled, she stared at him, saw his sly, silky little smile. 'I asked you first.'

'I don't like taking orders. And you?'

'I don't like painting.'

He stared at her; she stared back. A stand-off. So she wasn't the only one with secrets. 'Interesting,' he finally mused. He poured them both sparkling water. 'You don't like painting, but you decided to drag all that paraphernalia to the beach and set up your little artist's studio right there on the sand?'

She shrugged. 'I used to like it, when I was younger.' A lot younger and definitely less jaded. 'I thought I might like to try it again.'

'What changed your mind?'

Another shrug. She could talk about this. This didn't have to be personal or revealing. She wouldn't let it be. 'I just wasn't feeling it.'

'You don't seem like the type to rely on feelings.'

She smiled thinly. 'Still typecasting me, Chase?'

He laughed, an admitted defeat. 'Sorry.'

'It's OK. I play to type.'

'On purpose.'

She eyed him uneasily. Perhaps this was personal after all. And definitely revealing. 'Maybe.'

'Which means you aren't what you seem,' Chase said softly, 'are you?'

'I'm exactly what I seem.' She sounded defensive. *Great.*

'You *want* to be exactly what you seem,' he clarified. 'Which is why you play it that way.'

She felt a lick of anger, which was better than the dizzying combination of terror and lust he'd been stirring up inside her. 'What did you do, dust off your psychology textbook?'

He laughed and held up his hands. 'Guilty. I'm bored on this holiday, what can I say?'

And, just like that, he'd defused the tension that had been thickening in the air, tightening inside her. Yet Millie could not escape the feeling—the certainty—that he'd chosen to do it, that he'd backed off because he'd wanted to, not because of what she wanted.

One person at this table was calling the shots and it wasn't her.

'So.' She breathed through her nose, trying to hide the fact that her heart was beating hard. She wanted to take a big, dizzying gulp of air, but she didn't. Wouldn't. 'If you're so bored, why are you on holiday?'

'Doctor's orders.'

She blinked, not sure if he was joking. 'How's that?'

'The stress was getting to me.'

He didn't look stressed. He looked infuriatingly relaxed, arrogantly in control. 'The holiday must be working.'

'Seems to be.' He sounded insouciant, yet deliberately so. He was hiding something, Millie thought. She'd tried to strike that note of breeziness too many times not to recognise its falseness.

'So are we actually going to eat?' He hadn't pressed her, so she wouldn't press him. Another deal, this one silently made.

'Your wish is my command.'

Within seconds a waiter appeared at the table with a tray of food. Millie watched as he ladled freshly grilled snapper in lime juice and coconut rice on her plate. It smelled heavenly.

She waited until he'd served Chase and departed once more before saying dryly, 'Nice service. Being one of the Bryant boys has its perks, it seems.'

'Sometimes.' Again that even tone.

'Are you staying at the resort?'

'I have my own villa.' He stressed the 'own' only a little, but Millie guessed it was a sore point. Had he worked for what he had? He was probably too proud to tell her. She wouldn't ask.

She took a bite of her fish. It tasted heavenly too, an explosion of tart and tender on her tongue. She swallowed and saw Chase looking at her. Just looking, no deliberate, heavy-lidded languor, and yet she felt her body respond, like an antenna tuned to some cerebral frequency. Everything jumped to alert, came alive.

It had been so *long*.

She took another bite.

'So why are you on holiday, Millie?'

Why did the way he said her name sound intimate? She swallowed the fish. 'Doctor's orders.'

'Really?'

'Well, no. Boss's. I haven't taken any holiday in a while.'

'How long?'

That bite of fish seemed to lodge in her chest, its exquisite tenderness now as tough as old leather. Finally, with an audible and embarrassing gulp, she managed, 'Two years.'

Chase cocked his head and continued just looking. How much did he *see*? 'That's a long time,' he finally said, and she nodded.

'So he told me.'

'But you didn't want to take any holiday?'

'It's obvious, I suppose.'

'Pretty much.'

She stabbed a bit of rice with her fork. 'I like to work.'

'So *are* you a hedge-fund manager?'

'Got it in one.'

'And you like it?'

Instinctively '*of course I do*' rose to her lips, yet somehow the words didn't come. She couldn't get them out, as if someone had pressed a hand over her mouth and kept her from speaking. So she just stared and swallowed and felt herself flush.

Why had he even asked? she wondered irritably. Obviously she liked it, since she worked so hard.

'I see,' Chase said quietly, knowingly, and a sudden, blinding fury rose up in her, obliterating any remaining sense and opening her mouth.

'You don't see anything.' She sounded savage. Incensed. And, even worse, she *was*. Why did this stupid man make her feel so much? Reveal so much?

'Maybe not,' Chase agreed. He didn't sound riled in the least. Millie let out a shuddering breath. This date had been such a bad idea.

'OK, now it's your turn.'

She blinked. 'What?'

'You get to ask me a personal question. Only fair, right?'

Another blink. She hadn't expected that. 'Why do you hate being one of the Bryants?'

Now he blinked. 'Hate is a strong word.'

'So it is.'

'I never said I hated it.'

'You didn't need to.' She took a sip of water, her hand steady, her breath thankfully even. 'You're not the only one who can read people, you know.'

'You can read me?' Chase leaned forward, his eyes glinting in the candlelight. She saw the golden-brown stubble on his jaw, could almost feel its sandpaper roughness under her fingers. She breathed in the scent of him, part musk, part sun, pure male. 'What am I thinking now?' he asked, a steely, softly worded challenge. Millie didn't dare answer.

She knew what she was thinking. She was thinking about taking that hard jaw between her hands and angling her lips over his. His lips would be soft but firm, commanding and drawing deep from her. And she would give, she would surrender that long-held part of herself in just one kiss. She knew it, felt it bone-deep, soul-deep, which was ridiculous, because she barely knew this man. Yet in the space of an hour or two he'd drawn more from her than anyone had since her husband's death, or even before. He'd seen more, glimpsed her sadness and subterfuge like no one else could or had. Not even the parents who adored her, the sister she called a best friend. No one had seen through her smoke and mirrors. No one but Chase.

And he was a *stranger*.

A stranger who could kiss her quite senseless.

'I don't know what you're thinking,' she said and looked away.

Chase laughed softly, no more than an exhalation of breath. 'Coward.'

And yes, maybe she was a coward, but then he was too. Because Millie knew the only reason Chase had turned provocative on her was because he didn't want to answer her question about his family.

She pushed her plate away, her appetite gone even though her meal was only half-finished. 'How about that walk on the beach?'

He arched an eyebrow. 'You're done?'

She was *so* done. The sooner she ended this evening, the better. The only reason she wasn't bailing on the walk was her pride. Even now, when she felt uncomfortable, exposed and even angry, she was determined to handle this. Handle him. 'It was delicious,' she said. 'But I've had enough.'

'No pun intended, I'm sure.'

She curved her lips into a smile. 'You can read into that whatever you like.'

'All right, Millie,' Chase said, uncoiling from his chair like a lazy serpent about to strike. 'Let's walk.'

He reached for her hand and unthinkingly, *stupidly*, Millie let him take it.

As soon as his fingers wrapped over hers, she felt that explosion inside her again and she knew she was lost.

CHAPTER THREE

CHASE felt Millie's fingers tense in his even as a buzz travelled all the way up his arm. Her fingers felt fragile, slender bone encased in tender skin. A sudden need to protect her rose in him, a caveman's howl. Clearly it was some kind of evolutionary instinct, because if there was one woman who didn't need protecting, it was Camilla Lang.

He thought she might jerk her hand away from his, and he was pretty sure she wanted to, but she didn't. Didn't want to show weakness, most likely. He smiled and took full advantage, tightening his hold, drawing her close. She tensed some more.

This woman was *prickly*. And Chase had a sneaking suspicion she had issues, definitely with a capital I. Bad relationship or broken heart; maybe something darker and more difficult. Who knew? He sure as hell didn't want to. Didn't he have enough to deal with, with his own issues? Those had a capital I too. And he had no intention of sharing them with Millie.

Even so he drew her from the table, still holding her hand, and away from the terrace, down the lift, through the resort, all the way outside. He threaded his way through the tables of the beach-side restaurant and bar, straight onto the sand. She held his hand the whole time, not speaking, not pulling away, but clearly not all that pleased about it either.

There they were, holding hands alone in the dark.

The wind rattled the leaves of the palm trees overhead and he could hear the gentle *shoosh* of the waves lapping against the shore. The resort and its patrons seemed far away, their voices barely a murmur, the night soft and dark all around them. Millie pulled her hand from his, a not-so-gentle tug.

'Let's walk.'

'Sounds good.'

Silently they walked down the beach, the sand silky and cool under their bare feet. Lights of a pleasure yacht glimmered in the distance, and from far away Chase heard the husky laugh of a woman intent on being seduced.

Not like Millie. She walked next to him, her back ramrod-straight, her capris and blouse still relentlessly unwrinkled. She looked like she was walking the plank.

He nearly stopped right there in the sand. What the *hell* was he doing here, with a woman like her? Didn't he have better ways to spend his time?

'What?' She turned to him, and in the glimmer of moonlight he saw those warm, soft eyes, shadowed with a vulnerability he knew she thought she was hiding.

'What do you mean, *what*?'

'You're thinking something.'

'I'm always thinking something. Most people are.'

She shook her head, shadows deepening in her eyes. 'No, I mean…' She paused, biting her lip, teeth digging into those worry marks once more. If she didn't let up, she'd have a scar. 'You're regretting this, aren't you? This whole stupid date.'

He stopped, faced her full-on. 'Aren't you?'

She let go of her lip to give him the smallest of smiles. 'That's a given, don't you think?'

Did it have to be? How had they fallen into these roles so quickly, so easily? He wanted to break free. He didn't want to be a flippant playboy to her uptight workaholic. He had a sudden, mad urge to push her down into the sand, to see her clothes wrinkled and dirty, her face smudged and sandy, her lips swollen and kissed…

Good grief.

Chase took a step back, raking a hand through his hair. 'We're pretty different, Millie.'

'Thank God for that.'

He couldn't muster a laugh. He had too many emotions inside him: longing and lust, irritation and irrational fear. What an unholy mix. He'd asked her out because it had seemed fun, *amusing*, but it was starting to feel way too intense. And he didn't need any more intense. He took a breath and let it out slowly. 'Maybe we should call it a night.'

She blinked, her face immediately blanking, as if her mind were pressing delete. Inwardly Chase cursed. He didn't want to hurt her, but he knew in that moment he had.

'Millie—'

'Fine.' Her back straighter than ever, she started down the beach away from the resort. He watched her for a second, exasperated with her stubbornness and annoyed by his own clumsy handling of the situation.

'Aren't you staying at the resort?'

'I'm finishing our walk.'

He let out a huff of laughter. He *liked* this woman, issues and all. 'I didn't realise we'd set a distance on it.'

'More than ten seconds.' She didn't look back once.

She was far enough away that he had to shout. 'It was more like five minutes.'

'Clearly you have very little stamina.'

There was more truth in that then he'd ever care to admit. 'Millie.' He didn't shout this time, but he knew she heard anyway. He saw it in the tensing of her shoulders, the half-second stumble in her stride. 'Come back here.'

'Why should I?'

'On second thought, I'll come to you.' Quickly he strode down the beach, leaving deep footprints in the damp sand, until he reached her. The wind had mussed her hair just a little bit, so the razor edges were softened, blurred. Without even thinking what he was doing or wondering if it was a good idea, Chase reached out and slid his hands along her jaw bone, cupping her face as he drew her to him. Her skin felt like cool silk, cold silk, icy even. Yet so very, unbearably soft. Eyes and lips and skin, all soft. What about her, Chase wondered, was actually hard?

She was close enough to kiss, another inch would do it, yet he didn't. She didn't resist, didn't do anything. She was like a deer caught in the headlights, a rabbit in a snare. Trapped. Terrified.

'Sorry,' he breathed against her mouth, close enough so he could imagine the taste of her. She'd taste crisp and clean, like the white wine she'd drunk, except it would be just her. Essence of Camilla.

She jerked back a mere half-inch. 'Sorry for what?'

'For acting like a jerk.'

Her lips quirked in the tiniest of smiles. 'To which point of the evening are you referring?'

'All right, wise-ass. I was talking about two minutes ago, when I said we should call it a night.' He stroked his thumb over the fullness of her lower lip, because he just couldn't help himself, and felt her tremble. 'I don't think I was too much of a jerk before that.'

Millie didn't answer. Chase saw that her lips were parted, her pupils dilated. *Desire.* The brief moment of tenderness suddenly flared into something untamed and urgent. Chase felt a groan catch in his chest, his body harden in undeniable and instinctive response. His hands tightened as they cradled her face, yet neither of them moved. It was almost as if they were paralysed, both afraid—no, terrified—to close the mere inch that separated them, cross that chasm.

Because Chase knew it wouldn't be your average kiss. And he was in no position for anything else.

With one quick jerk of her head, Millie slid out of his grasp and stepped backwards. 'Thanks for the apology,' she said, her voice as cool as ever. 'But it's not needed. It was interesting to get to know you, Chase, but I think we've fulfilled both sides of the deal.' She smiled without humour, and Chase couldn't stand the sudden bleakness in her eyes. Damn it, they were meant to be *soft*. 'Good night,' she said and headed back down the beach.

Millie walked without looking where she was going or caring. She just wanted to get away from Chase.

What had just happened?

He'd almost kissed her. She'd almost let him. In that moment when his hands had slid along her skin, cradling her face like she was something to be cherished and treasured, she'd wanted him to. Desperately. She would have let him do anything then, and thank goodness he hadn't, thank God he'd hesitated and she'd somehow found the strength to pull away.

The last thing she needed was to get involved with a man like Chase Bryant.

She left the beach behind and wound her way through the palm trees to the other side of the resort. She'd go in the front entrance and up to her room, and with any luck she wouldn't see Chase again all week. It was a big place, and he'd told her he was staying at his villa.

So why did that thought fill her with not just disappointment, but desolation? It was ridiculous to feel so lost without a shallow stranger she'd met a couple of hours ago. Absolutely absurd.

Clearly what this evening had shown her, Millie decided

as she swiped her key-card and entered the sumptuous suite Jack had insisted she book for the week, was that she was ready to move on. Start dating, have some kind of relationship.

Just not with a man like Chase Bryant.

The words echoed through her, making her pause in stripping off her clothes and turning on the shower. *A man like Chase Bryant.* She'd pigeon-holed Chase from the moment she'd met him, yet he'd surprised her at every turn. Just what kind of man *was* he?

A man who asked pressing questions and told her things about herself nobody else knew. Who turned flippant just when she needed him to. Whose simple touch set off an explosion inside her, yet who kept himself from kissing her even when she was so clearly aching for his caress.

A man who made her very, very uncomfortable.

Was that the kind of man she didn't want to get involved with?

Hell, yes.

She wished she could dismiss him, as she'd fully intended to do when she'd first met him: spoiled and shallow playboy, completely non-threatening. That was the man she'd agreed to have dinner with, not the man he *was*, who had set her pulse racing and tangled her emotions into knots. A man who touched her on too many levels.

Was that what she didn't want? Getting involved with someone who had the power to see her as she really was, to hurt her?

Well, *duh*. Obviously she didn't want to get hurt. Who did? And surely she'd already had her life's share of grief Millie stepped into the shower, the water streaming over her even as her thoughts swirled in confusing circles.

Her mind was telling her all that, but her body was singing a very different tune. Her body wanted his touch. Her mouth wanted to know his kiss. Every bit of her ached with a longing for fulfilment she thought she'd forever suppressed.

She let out a shudder and leaned her head against the shower tile as the water streamed over her.

She could stay analytical about this. So she didn't want to get hurt. She didn't have to. How much she cared—how much she gave—was in her control. And here she was—and Chase was—on a tropical island for a single week, neither of them with very much to do…

Why not?

Why not what?

She dumped too much shampoo into the palm of her hand and scrubbed her hair, fingernails raking her scalp as if she could wash these tempting and terrible thoughts right out of her mind.

Just what was she contemplating?

A week-long affair with Chase Bryant. A fling. A cheap, sordid, sexual transaction.

She scrubbed harder.

She didn't do flings. Of course she didn't. Her husband had been her only lover. Yet here she was, thinking about it. Wondering how Chase would taste, how he would hold her. What it would feel like, to be in his arms. To surrender herself, just a little bit of herself, because even if he sensed she had secrets she wasn't going to tell them to him. She just wanted that physical release, that momentary connection. The opportunity to forget. When Chase had been about to kiss her, she hadn't been able to think about anything else. All thoughts and memories had fled, leaving her nothing but blissful sensation.

She wanted that again. *More*.

Millie rinsed off and turned off the shower. She could control this. She could satiate this hunger that had opened up inside her and prove to herself and everyone else that she'd moved on.

She just needed to tell Chase.

Chase watched the poker-straight figure march down the beach as if in step with an invisible army and wondered why on earth Millie was looking for him. For there could be no mistaking her intent; she'd arrowed in on him like a laser beam. What, he wondered, was with all the military references going through his mind?

Clearly Millie Lang was on the attack.

And he was quite enjoying the anticipation of an invasion. He sat back on his heels on the deck of his sailboat, the water lapping gently against its sides, the sun a balm on his back. Millie marched closer.

Chase had no idea what she wanted. He'd stopped trying to untangle his thoughts about their date last night, from the almost-kiss he hadn't acted on, to the hurt that had flashed in her eyes to the fact it had taken him three hours to fall asleep, with Millie's soft eyes still dancing through his mind. Definitely better not to think about any of it.

'There you are.'

'Looking for me?'

She stood on the beach, feet planted in the sand, hands on hips, a look of resolute determination on her face. 'As a matter of fact, I am.'

'I'm intrigued.' He stood up, wincing a little at the ache in his joints. He couldn't ignore the pain any more. She watched him, eyes narrowed, and he smiled. He could ignore it. He would. 'So, what's on your mind, scary lady?'

Her mouth twitched in a suppressed smile, and then she was back to being serious. 'Is this your boat?'

He glanced back at the sailboat, doing an exaggerated double-take. 'What—this?'

'Very funny.'

'Yep, it's my boat.'

'Did you sail here?'

He laughed, reluctantly, because once he might have. Not any more. He didn't trust himself out on the sea alone. 'No, I flew in a plane like most people. I keep the boat moored here, though.'

'I suppose the Bryants are a big sailing family and you started at the yacht club when you were a baby.'

He heard an edge to her voice that he recognised. She hadn't grown up rich, suspected the proverbial silver spoon. 'More like a toddler,' he said, shrugging. 'Do you sail?'

Lips pressed together. 'No.'

'You should try it.'

She glanced at him suspiciously. 'Why?'

'Because it's fun. And freeing. And I'd like to see you out on the water, your hair blowing away from your face.' She'd look softer then, he thought. Happier too, maybe.

'You would, huh?'

'Yeah. I would.'

'Well, you already told me how you felt about my haircut.'

He chuckled. 'True. Feel free to let me know if there's anything you don't like about my appearance.'

She eyed him up and down deliberately, and Chase felt a lick of excitement low in his belly. He liked that slow, considering look. Millie Lang was checking him out. 'I will,' she said slowly, 'but there isn't anything yet.'

'No?' He felt it again, that licking flame firing him up inside. Was Millie *flirting*? What had changed since last night, when she'd been as sharp and jagged as a handful of splinters? When he'd let her walk away because he told himself it was better—or at least easier—that way.

And then hadn't stopped thinking about her all night.

'Come aboard,' he said, and stretched out a hand. She

eyed it warily, and then with a deep breath like she was about to go underwater she took it and clambered onto the boat.

It was a small sailboat, just thirty-two feet long with one cabin underneath. He'd bought it with his first bonus and sailed halfway around the world on it, back when he'd been a hotshot. Now he cruised in the shallows, like some seventy year old pensioner with a bad case of gout and a dodgy heart. No risks. No stress. No fun.

'It's…nice,' Millie said, and he knew she didn't know a thing about boats. Who cared? He liked seeing her on deck, even if her clothes were still way too wrinkle-free. Today she wore a red-and-white-striped top and crisp navy-blue capris. Very nautical. Very boring. Yet he was intrigued by the way the boat-neck of her top revealed the hard, angular line of her collarbone. He wanted to run his fingers along that ridge of bone, discover if her skin was as icily soft as it had been last night.

'I could take you out some time,' he said. 'On the boat.' Why was she here? He stepped closer to her, inhaled the scent of her, something clean and citrusy. Breathed deep.

She turned to him, her hair sweeping along her jaw, and his gaze was caught by the angles of her jaw and shoulder, hard and soft. Her top had slipped a little, and he could see the strap of her bra: beige lace. No sexy lingerie for this lady, yet he still felt himself go hard.

'You could,' she said slowly, and he knew she was gearing up to say something—but what?

He folded his arms, adopted a casual pose. 'So?'

'So what?'

'Why are you here, Millie?'

Again that trapped look, chin tilted with defiance. This woman was all contradiction. 'Do you mind?'

'Not a bit.' And that was the truth.

She turned away, rubbing her arms as if she were cold. 'How long are you on this island, anyway?'

'A week, give or take.'

'You're not sure?'

'I'm being flexible.'

'And then you go back to New York?'

'That's the plan.' This was starting to feel like an interrogation. He didn't mind, but he wondered what she was getting at.

'I've never come across you in New York,' she said, almost to herself, and Chase just about kept himself from rolling his eyes.

'It's a pretty big city.'

She turned to face him. 'And we move in completely different circles.'

'Seems like it.'

'So there's no chance we'd see each other again.'

Maybe he should start feeling offended. But he didn't; he just felt like smiling. Laughing. Why did he enjoy her prickliness so much? 'Is that what you're afraid of?'

She met his gaze squarely. 'I'd prefer it if we didn't.'

He rubbed his jaw. 'If that's what you'd prefer, why are you on my boat?'

'I meant after. After this week.' Her words seemed heavy with meaning, but he still didn't get it.

'OK. I think I can manage that.' Even if he wasn't sure he wanted to.

'It would be easier,' she said, sounding almost earnest now. 'For me.'

Now he was really confused. 'Millie, I have no idea what you're talking about.'

'I know.' She pressed her lips together, gave a decisive nod. OK, Chase thought, here it comes. 'I'm attracted to you. You probably know that.'

He lifted one shoulder in a shrug that could mean anything. He didn't want to ruin this moment by agreeing or disagreeing; he just wanted her to keep talking.

'And I think you're attracted to me. Sort of.'

She looked so pathetically and yet endearingly vulnerable that Chase had to keep himself from reaching for her. What he would do when he had her in his arms, he wasn't completely sure. He did know one thing. 'I'm attracted to you, Millie. More than I'd ever expect.'

She let out a short laugh. 'Because I'm not your usual type.'

'No, you're not. Does that matter?' He wasn't even sure what he was asking. Where was she going with this conversation?

'No, I don't think it does.' She didn't sound completely sure.

'But, trust me, I am.' If she risked a glance downwards, she'd know.

'Well. Good.'

'Glad we're on the same page.'

She let out a breath and looked straight in his eyes. Vulnerability and strength, hard and soft. 'I hope we are.'

'Maybe we'd find out if you clued me into where this conversation is going.'

'Fine.' She took a deep breath, plunged. 'I want to sleep with you.'

CHAPTER FOUR

To HIS credit, Chase's jaw didn't drop. He didn't laugh or raise his eyebrows or even blink. He just stared at her, expressionless, and Millie felt herself flush.

She'd decided on the straightforward approach because, really, what else could she do? She didn't flirt. She couldn't play the seductress, and in any case she knew instinctively that Chase would see through any gauzy ploys. No, all she had was a straight shot, and she'd fired it. Direct hit.

'OK,' Chase finally said, letting out a breath. 'That's… good to know.'

She gave a shaky huff of laughter. 'I'm glad you think so.'

He rubbed his jaw, the movement inherently sexy. She could see the rippling muscled six-pack of his abs, the glint of sun on his stubble, his strong arms and lean fingers. Yes, she was definitely attracted to him. 'So,' he said. 'What brought this about?'

Of course he'd start asking questions. Most guys would take what she said at face value and drop their pants. Not Chase. She should have realised this wasn't going to be simple.

She shifted her weight, tried to act at least somewhat nonchalant. 'What do you mean?'

'Why me?'

'You're here, you're interested and I'm attracted to you.'

He arched an eyebrow. 'I take it this isn't your normal behaviour?'

She swallowed, kept his stare. 'No, not exactly.'

'So why now?'

How much truth to tell? She decided to fire another straight shot. 'Look, I don't want to get into messy details. This isn't about emotion, or getting to know each other, or anything like that.'

'I appreciate your candour.'

'Good.' She felt that flush creep back. This had seemed like such a good idea last night, when she couldn't forget how much she'd wanted him to kiss her. When having a fling with Chase Bryant had seemed like the perfect way to move on from the spectres of her failed life. To forget, at least for a little while.

From here it wasn't looking so good.

'So?' she finally prompted, a definite edge to her voice.

'Well, I'm flattered.' Chase leaned over the boat to haul in some kind of rope. Millie waited, everything inside her tensing. He straightened, tossing the rope into a neat coil on the deck. 'But I'm not that easy a lay.'

She blinked, tried desperately to arrange her face into some sort of blankness. 'Oh? You could have fooled me.'

He looked almost amused. 'Now what gave you the impression that I was a man-whore, Miss Scary?'

'I didn't mean that.' Her face, Millie suspected, was bright red. 'I only meant you asked me out last night and so you must be…you know…open.'

'Open?' Now he really seemed amused.

'To a—a no-strings type of…' She trailed off, unwilling to put any of it in words. Affair? Fling? *Relationship?*

'Thing?' Chase supplied helpfully, and she nodded, bizarrely grateful.

'Yes. Thing.'

'Interesting.' He reached for another rope, and Millie felt the boat rock under her feet.

'So do you think you could give me your answer?' she asked, trying not to sound impatient. Or desperate.

'An answer,' Chase mused, and Millie gritted her teeth. He was tormenting her. On purpose.

'Yes, Chase. An answer.'

'As to whether I'll sleep with you.'

She heard the grinding screech as she gritted her teeth even harder. 'Yes.'

He smiled as he coiled another rope on the deck. 'The short answer is yes.'

She let out a quick, silent breath. 'And the long answer?'

'We'll do it on my terms.'

He turned to her, completely relaxed, utterly in control. Millie felt her heart flip over in her chest. It wasn't exactly a pleasant sensation. So, Chase would sleep with her. She would sleep with him. They would have sex.

Her body tingled. Her heart hammered and her mouth dried. Just what she had started here? And how would it finish?

'Relax, Millie. I'm not about to drop my pants.'

Even if that was what she'd wanted from him originally: a simple, quick, easy transaction. Now she didn't know what she wanted. She swallowed, tried to ease the dryness in her throat.

'So what are your terms?'

'Don't worry, I'll keep you informed as we go along.'

Too late Millie realised they were moving. They'd gone about twenty feet from the shore and Chase was doing something with the sails or rigging or whatever was on this wretched boat. She didn't know the first thing about sailing.

'What—what are you doing?' she demanded.

'Sailing.'

'But I don't—'

'I told you I wanted to see you on my boat,' Chase said with an easy smile. 'With your hair blowing away from your face.'

'But—'

'My terms, Millie.' His smile widened. Millie suppressed a short and violent curse. Just what had she got herself into? 'Relax,' he said. 'You could even enjoy yourself.'

'That *was* kind of the point,' she muttered, and he laughed.

'Glad to hear it.'

She watched Chase let out the sail, the white cloth snapping in the brisk breeze. They were quite far out from the shore now, far enough for Millie to feel a sudden pulse of alarm. She was alone on a boat in the middle—well, *sort* of the middle—of the Caribbean with a man. With Chase.

She didn't feel frightened, or even nervous. She felt… alert. Aware. *Alive.*

'OK,' she said, taking a step towards him. 'So where are we going?'

'Do we need a destination?'

'I'm kind of goal-oriented.'

'So I've noticed.'

Her hair was blowing in the breeze, but not away from her face. In it. Strands stuck to her lips and with an impatient sigh she brushed it away. Chase grinned in approval.

'There.'

'What?' she asked irritably. 'Is this some kind of weird fetish you have? Women and hair?'

'I just like seeing you look a bit more relaxed. More natural.' He paused, as if weighing his words. 'Soft.'

'Don't.' The single word came out sharp, a cut. 'Don't,' she said again, and this time it was a warning.

'What?'

'Don't—don't try to change me. This isn't about that.'

She couldn't stand it if he thought he was on some wretched mercy mission, making her relax and enjoy life. He had no idea. No clue whatsoever.

'What *is* it about?' Chase asked calmly. 'Sex?'

'Yes. I thought I made that clear.'

'You did.' Just as calmly he strode towards the sail and started doing something with it. Millie couldn't tell what. 'And I made it clear this would be on my terms. Watch out.'

'What—?'

She saw something heavy and wooden swing straight towards her face and then Chase's hands were on her shoulders, pulling her out of the way. She collided with his chest, her back coming against that bare, hard muscle. Her heart thudded and his hands felt hot on her shoulders, his thumbs touching the bare skin near her collarbone.

'What was that?' she asked shakily.

'The boom. I had to tack.'

'Tack?'

'Change direction. I should have warned you, but all this sex talk was distracting me.'

She had no answer to that. All she could think about was how warm and heavy his hands felt on her shoulders, how he'd only have to move his thumbs an inch or two to brush the tops of her breasts. How she wanted him to.

'We're good now,' he said, dropping his hands. 'We should have a pretty nice run. Let's sit down.'

Numbly Millie followed him to a cushioned bench in the back of the boat. Chase reached into a cooler and took out a bottle of sparkling water, offering it to her before he took one himself.

'Cheers. Sorry I don't have champagne to toast this momentous occasion.'

'So why don't you drink, exactly?'

'More doctor's orders. Reduce stress.' He spoke with that

deliberate lightness again. He wasn't telling her the truth, or at least not the whole truth.

Millie swallowed and took a sip of water. Her thoughts were racing as fast as the boat that skimmed lightly over the aquamarine sea onto an unknown horizon. *What was going to happen here?*

'So. Tell me more about these terms of yours.'

'The first one is I decide when we do the deed. And where. And how.'

She swallowed. 'That's asking for a lot of control.'

'I know. And I'm not asking. I'm telling.'

The bottle felt slippery in her hands. 'I'm not really comfortable with that.'

'OK.' He shrugged, everything so easy.

'What do you mean, OK?'

'The deal's off, then. No sex.'

She bit her lip. 'I didn't mean that.'

Another shrug. 'You want to sleep with me, you agree to my terms.'

'You make it sound so—cold.'

'No, Scary, you're doing that all on your own. You're the one who wants to have some hurried grope and then brush yourself off and move on with life.'

'I never said that.'

'Am I wrong?'

She looked away. 'It wouldn't have to be *hurried*.'

'What is this, some milestone? First time you'll have had sex since you broke up with your long-time boyfriend?'

She kept her gaze on the sea, frills of white amidst the endless blue. 'No.'

'Divorce?'

'No.'

He sighed. 'Something, though, right?'

'Maybe.'

'Fine. You don't want to tell me. No messy details.'

'That's right.'

'But I'm telling you I'm not interested in some soulless, sordid transaction. If you want that, hire an escort service. Or go hang out in the bar for a little while longer. Someone will pay or play.'

She blinked and set her jaw. 'As tempting as that sounds, I'm not interested.'

'Why not?'

'Because—' She hesitated. She felt as if he were stripping away her defences, and yet she didn't know how he was doing it. She kept darting around to cover her bases, but they were already gone. 'Because I don't want that.'

He leaned forward, his voice a soft, seductive whisper. 'What do you want, Millie?'

Reluctantly, she dragged her gaze towards him. His eyes glittered gold and the wind ruffled his hair. He looked completely gorgeous and so utterly sure. 'I want you.'

He held her gaze, triumph blazing in his eyes, a smile curving his mouth. *Damn it.* Why had she said that? Admitted so much?

'And I want you,' he told her in a low, lazy murmur. 'Rather a lot. But I want to be more than a milestone, and so we're doing this my way.'

More than a milestone. Already she was in over her head. She'd been so stupid, convincing herself that she could handle Chase, that he'd agree to some one-night stand. On the surface, he should have. But from the moment she'd met him he'd never been what she'd thought he was. What she wanted him to be.

So why had she pursued this? Why was she still here, still wanting to do this deal? Did she really want him that much?

Yes.

'Fine. We'll do it your way. But I want to know what that is first.'

His smile turned to a pie-eating grin. 'Nope.'

'Nope?'

'Nope. Information is given on a need-to-know basis only.'

Her fingers tightened on her bottle of water, her knuckles aching. 'I need to know, Chase.'

'I'll decide that.'

She could not believe how horribly autocratic and arrogant he was being. She could not believe she was taking it. Why on earth was she not telling him to piss off and take her back to the shore? Was there some sick, depraved little girl inside her who wanted to be told what to do?

Or did she just want him that much?

Yes, she did.

'Fine,' she said, forming the word through stiff lips. He nodded, no more. She took a sip of water to ease the dryness in her throat. 'So what now?' she asked once she'd swallowed and felt able to speak again.

'You take off your clothes.'

Her bottle of water slipped from her nerveless fingers and Chase reached forward to catch it.

'Easy there, Scary. I was joking. Right now we relax, enjoy the sun and sea. I'll let you know when clothes or lack thereof come into the equation.'

She shook her head slowly. 'Why are you doing this?'

'Doing what?'

'Toying with me.'

He arched an eyebrow. 'Is that what it feels like?'

'Pretty much.'

He didn't answer for a moment, just took a long swallow of water so she could see the brown column of his throat, the breadth of his chest tapering down to lean hips. He was beautiful. 'Well,' he finally said, his gaze meeting hers with too much knowledge, 'I suppose it's because you've been trying to toy with me.'

She took a startled step back. 'I have not.'

'Oh, really? You march over to my boat and practically demand to sleep with me. You think I'm just going to lie down and let you have your wicked way with me?'

'No…not exactly.'

'You think you can tell me how, when and where I'm going to have sex with you?'

'That's what you're trying to do with me!'

'Exactly. And I'm not going to be entered into your smart phone and then deleted when you're done. I'm not a hedge fund, Millie. I'm not an account or a client or a to-do item to tick off. And, more importantly, neither is what's between us.'

She felt as if he'd wrapped an iron band around her chest and *squeezed*. Breathing hurt. 'There's nothing between us.'

'That is bull and you know it.'

'What do you *want*, Chase?'

'You. Just like you want me. But I think we have very different definitions of just what that means.'

She dragged a breath into her constricted lungs. Spots danced before her eyes. She was in way over her head now; she was drowning and she had no idea how to save herself. 'I think we must,' she finally managed, and Chase just grinned.

Chase watched Millie process what he said and wondered if she was going to pass out. She'd gone seriously pale. And admittedly he'd laid it on pretty thick. He didn't even know why he was pushing so hard. He'd thought last night had been too intense, and yet today he'd upped the ante a hundred fold. He'd acted on instinct, telling her he was going to call the shots, not just because he didn't want to be her toy-boy but because he knew on a gut level she needed to

let go of that precious control. And he wanted to be the one
to make it happen.

As for what was *between* them… She was right. There
was nothing between them, not really.

Yet.

So what did he want?

He took another long swallow of water, desperate for a
cold beer. A distraction. He was scaring himself with all
this talk. Asking for more than he'd ever intended to want,
never mind have.

Maybe he was acting this way because ever since his diagnosis everything in life had felt important, urgent. Precious.
And if he felt a connection with a woman well, then, perhaps
he should just go for it. Take it as long and far as he could.

Except did he even know how long or far that could be.
He didn't have a lot of options here. A lot of freedom.

He was, Chase reflected, a lousy deal.

Yet Millie only wanted this week, and really that should
suit him perfectly. A week, he had.

A week, he would give.

And it would be the most incredible, intense week either
of them had ever experienced.

'You OK there, Scary?'

She glanced at him, still looking dazed. 'Are you doing
this on purpose?'

'What?'

'Pushing my buttons. Making me uncomfortable.'

He paused as if he had to think about it, which he didn't.
'Yes.'

She shook her head. 'OK, let me spell it out for you,
Chase. I don't want to be pushed. I don't want buttons to be
pressed. I want a week-long fling, some really great, mind-
blowing sex, and that's *it*. And, if you don't think you can

deliver, then maybe you should just take me back to shore right now.' She was trembling.

'Mind-blowing, huh?'

'Yes. Definitely.'

'I think I can deliver.'

'And nothing *more* than that,' she stressed, as if he didn't get it already.

'That's a problem.'

She blew out an impatient breath, pushing her hair behind her ears. She looked younger when she did that, although he guessed she was about his age, maybe a little younger. Mid-thirties, probably. 'Why is that a problem?'

'Because I don't think sex can be mind-blowing if a few buttons aren't pressed. In a manner of speaking, of course.'

She looked so disbelieving he almost winced. 'Are you telling me you haven't had cheap sex before? One-night stands? Flings?'

'No, I'm not saying that.' He'd had more than his share of all the above. He wasn't particularly proud of his past, standing on this side of it, but he'd own up to it.

'Then why are you insisting on something more now?'

He stretched his legs out in front of him, laced his hands behind his head. 'I suppose it depends on what you think of as more.'

'Stop talking in riddles.'

'OK, here it is, totally straight. We're both here for a week, right?'

'Right.'

'A week out of time, out of reality, and we'll never see each other again in New York or elsewhere. Yes?'

'Yes.'

'See, we *are* on the same page.'

'Spit it out,' she said, her teeth gritted, and he couldn't keep from grinning. He loved riling her.

'So you give me one week, and I give you mind-blowing sex. Deal?'

'I'm not signing until you tell me the fine print,' she said tautly, and he laughed aloud.

'You give me one week,' he repeated. He leaned forward, the urgency and excitement he felt coming out on his voice, his body. He felt it thrum between them with the pulse of an electric current. 'One week. Seven days. But you give me *everything*, Millie. You give me all of yourself, no holding back, no hiding. All in. And in return I give you mind-blowing.'

She stared at him silently for a long moment, her eyes wide, pupils dilated—with fear or desire? Probably both. Hell, he felt both. He couldn't believe he was doing this. He couldn't believe how much he wanted to.

'That,' she finally said, 'is a *lousy* deal.'

'You really think so?' He felt a tiny flicker of disappointment, but still that urgent hope. She was here. She was still talking, still wanting.

And, God knew, he wanted her. A lot.

'I told you I didn't want to get into messy emotional stuff. I don't want to *know* you, Chase.'

The flicker of disappointment deepened into actual hurt. He pushed it away. 'Except in the biblical sense, you mean.'

She let out a huff of exasperated breath. 'You're totally reneging on what we agreed on.'

'Nope. You are. My terms, remember?'

Her lips parted, realisation patently dawning. He waited. 'I thought you meant—well, the physical aspect of—of things. Like, maybe something a little bit kinky.' A beet-red blush washed over her face like a tide.

'We could go there if you like,' Chase offered. The prospect held an intriguing appeal. 'And I did say the when, where and how, it's true. But now I'm giving you some of those need-to-know details.'

She said nothing, just turned to stare out at the sea. They were in open water, the wind starting to die down. He should tack again, but he just waited. This moment was too important.

'I don't want to talk about my past,' she said slowly, forming each word with reluctance. 'I'll give myself in other ways, but not that.'

'That's kind of a big one.'

She turned to face him, and he felt as if a fist had struck his soul. She looked incredibly, unbearably bleak. 'Then you can take me back right now.'

Chase held her gaze, felt a twisting inside him. She was truly beautiful, he realised, but it was a stark, severe beauty, all clean angles and pure lines. And sadness. So much sadness. 'No need for that,' he said as lightly as he could. 'I agree.'

Her breath came out in a rush. 'Good.'

'So it's a deal?'

Her mouth trembled in an almost-smile. 'I guess it is.'

Chase stood up and walked towards the rigging. It was time to change direction. 'Then let our week begin.'

CHAPTER FIVE

MILLIE watched Chase steer the boat—he'd done something with the sail again—and tried to slow the hard beating of her heart. It was impossible.

She couldn't believe she had agreed. She couldn't believe she'd *wanted* to agree. They weren't her terms, not by a long shot, but maybe she could live with them. One week. No talking about the past. *Mind-blowing sex.*

Yes, she could live with them. Even if she felt a kind of numb terror at the thought of what lay ahead.

'So, are we going somewhere now?' she asked, rising from the bench to join him at the sail. This time she watched for the boom.

'Yep, land ahoy.' He pointed straight ahead to a crescent of sand amidst the water. It didn't look like much.

'What is that?'

'Our own version of *Survivor.*'

'You mean a deserted island?'

'I knew you were quick.'

'What are we going to do there?'

He gave her a knowing look. 'What do you think?' Millie gulped. Audibly. 'Relax, Millie. We're going to eat lunch.'

'Oh.' Another gulp. 'OK.'

'Although,' Chase mused as he navigated the boat towards that slice of beach, 'I almost think we should just do the nasty and get it over with, so you stop looking at me like I'm going to jump you at any second.'

She felt a flare of anticipation—and relief. 'Maybe that would be a good idea.'

Chase gave her another knowing look. 'I said almost.'

She folded her arms. 'Well, when are we going to—?'

'Need-to-know basis only,' Chase reminded her breezily. Then he was mooring the boat and the island—it really wasn't much—loomed before them.

He jumped out first, splashing through the shallows to moor the boat more securely, before turning to her and holding out his arms. 'Want to jump?'

She stood on the deck, one foot poised uncertainly on the railing, unsure just how she was going to get out of this thing. 'No, thank you.'

'I'll let it go this time, but remember our terms, Scary—you've got to give me everything.'

She stared at him, saw him looking both serious and smug, and then without warning or even thinking she took a flying leap from the boat and landed right on top of him. With a startled *'Oof!'* Chase fell back into the sea, pulling her with him. She was soaked instantly, and she felt the hard lines of his body press into her own soft curves. Excitement and awareness flared like rockets inside of her, obliterating thought.

Then through the sudden haze of her own desire she saw that Chase was wincing in what could only be pain. Mortification replaced lust and she tried to clamber off him. 'Did I hurt you—?'

'No.' He held her still on top of him and sucked in a breath. 'Surprised me, though.' He adjusted his arms around her, sliding his palms down her back so her hips rocked against his. 'Not that I mind.'

The water lapped around them, salty and warm. Her face

was inches from Chase's and she could see droplets of water clinging to his cheek and lips. Unable to resist touching him—and, really, why should she resist now?—she put the tip of her finger to one of the drops on Chase's cheek. He sucked in another breath, his gaze holding hers like a vise. Daringly, Millie touched another droplet on his lips. His mouth felt soft and warm, hard and cool all at the same time. Sensation zinged through her, frying her senses. Just one little touch and she was already drowning in a sea of desire.

Chase hadn't moved, just kept his hands on her hips, cradling her with aching closeness. She felt the hard thrust of his arousal against her thighs and instinctively shifted, though whether to bring him closer or farther away she didn't even know. Couldn't think.

The moment spun out and Millie felt the breath dry in her lungs as she waited for him to move.

And then he did.

'So.' Slowly, smiling, he eased her off him. 'Lunch.'

So they weren't going to go for it right then. She felt a bewildering mixture of disappointment and relief. Of course, he *had* said he preferred the moment before rather than after. There was still so much to look forward to.

Millie struggled up from of the water, watching as Chase rose out of the ocean like some archaic deity, water streaming in rivulets off the taut muscles of his back. He sluiced the water from his face and hair and then turned to her. 'You got a suit under there?'

'A suit?' She glanced down at the now-soaked striped top and capris her secretary had ordered her as part of her holiday wear. She hadn't had time to go shopping. 'Umm… No.'

'Shame. I was looking forward to seeing you in a string bikini.'

'I don't own a string bikini.'

'Let me guess—sensible one-piece.'

'I burn easily.'

'Remind me to apply another layer of sunscreen on you after lunch. But first, we dive.'

'Dive?' she repeated incredulously. 'But I just told you I don't have a swimsuit.'

Chase shrugged. 'You'll have to swim in your underwear. Or naked, if you prefer.'

'*What?*' This came out in a screech. Chase raised his eyebrows.

'Millie, we *are* going to sleep together, right? See each other naked? Touch each other in all those intimate places? Bring each other screaming to ecstasy?'

She was blushing. Like fire. *Way* too many details. 'That doesn't mean I want you to see me in my underwear in broad daylight,' she managed.

'Maybe I've decided to make love to you in broad daylight.' He pointed to the slender strip of sand. 'Maybe right there on that beach.'

Millie followed the direction of his pointing finger and could already see the two of them there on the beach, bodies naked, sandy and entwined. She could imagine it all too easily, no matter that she still felt shy about taking off her clothes. 'Even so,' she muttered. 'It's different.'

Chase let out a long-suffering sigh. 'So you want to swim in your clothes?'

'No.' She recrossed her arms, shifted her weight. She didn't know what she wanted. She'd agreed to this, she'd known it would be uncomfortable, and yet some bizarre and perverse part of herself still wanted it. Wanted him. Wanted the intimacy with him, even if she felt sick with nerves.

But if she really did want it why was she still resisting? Why was she fighting Chase on every little point? They'd already established he wasn't going to ask her about her past. They wouldn't see each other after this week.

They were going to have sex.

'Fine.' In one abrupt movement she slid her wet top over her head and kicked her way out of her capris. The clothes bobbed and floated on the surface of the sea, and belatedly she realised they were the only clothes she had here. She didn't relish the prospect of walking down the resort beach in her undies. Lifting her chin, she glared at him. 'Satisfied?'

'I wouldn't say I'm *satisfied*,' Chase said slowly, his gaze wandering over her in leisurely perusal. 'But pleased, yes.'

Millie shivered even though the air was sultry. She felt ridiculous standing there in her bra and panties, both a sensible, boring beige, even though Chase was only wearing a pair of shorts. They were both near-naked and yet…

When had someone last seen her this close to bare? A man? Rob, of course. Rob was the *only* man who had seen her in her underwear, besides her obstetrician. The thought was both absurd and excruciating.

Standing there under Chase's scrutiny, she was agonisingly conscious of all her faults. She was too skinny, due to the black-coffee breakfasts and skipped lunches. Her appetite had fallen off a cliff since the accident. And, while supermodels looked good stick-thin, Millie knew she didn't. Her hip bones were sharp and she'd dwindled down to an A-cup. And then of course there were the stretch marks, just two silver lines below her belly button—would he notice those? Would he ask?

No questions about her past. She'd remind him if necessary, and often.

Chase smiled and reached into the boat, bringing out two dive-masks. Millie eyed them dubiously.

'Why are we diving, anyway? I thought we were eating lunch.'

'We have to catch it first.'

Her jaw dropped. 'You have got to be kidding me.'

He arched an eyebrow. 'Do I look like a kidder?'

'Well, since you asked...'

'Seriously, it's easy. We're looking for conch—you know the big, pink shells? The pretty ones?' She nodded. 'We'll find a couple of those, I'll pry out the meat and we'll have conch salad. Delicious.'

'Raw?'

'Haven't you ever eaten sushi?'

'Only in a Michelin-starred restaurant in Soho.'

'Live a little, Millie.'

She frowned. 'I don't want to get food poisoning.'

'The lime juice in the dressing has enough acid to kill any nasties,' he assured her. 'I've eaten this loads of times.'

And just like that she could imagine him here, looking so easy and relaxed, with the kind of curvy blonde he usually dated. *She'd* have a string bikini. Or maybe she'd go bare. Either way Millie felt ridiculous standing there in her underwear, having no idea what to do. And, worse, she felt jealous.

Chase tossed her a mask. 'Look for the shells. We only need one or two.'

Dubiously she put the mask on. This was so out of her comfort zone, which was precisely why Chase had chosen to do it. When he'd said lunch she'd envisioned a picnic on the boat, gourmet finger-food and linen napkins. As if.

Still, she wouldn't give Chase the satisfaction of seeing just how uncomfortable she was. Squaring her shoulders, she adjusted her mask and followed Chase into the water. He was already cutting easily through the placid sea and with a deep breath Millie put her face in the water and gazed down into another world.

Rainbow-coloured fish darted in the shoals and amidst the rocks, prettier than any she'd seen in an aquarium. The sea water was incredibly clear, so the whole ocean floor seemed to open up in front of her, stretching on endlessly. Her lungs started to burn and she lifted her head to take a breath.

'You OK?' Chase had lifted his head too, and was glancing at her in concern.

'I'm fine.' She felt a strange stirring inside that he'd asked, something between gratitude and affection, that he was worried. He might be pushing her, but he wasn't going to let her fall.

And she wouldn't let herself either.

Chase kicked forward. 'Let's swim a little farther out.'

She followed him out into deeper water, and they swam and dove in silent synchronicity, the whole exercise surprisingly relaxing, until she finally saw a conch, pearly pink and luminescent, nestled against a rock. Taking a deep breath, she dove down and reached for it, her hand curving around its smooth shell as she kicked upwards to the surface.

Chase was waiting for her as she broke through. 'I got one!' Her voice rang out like an excited child's, and she gave him an all-too-sloppy grin.

'It's always a thrill. I got one too. That should be enough.'

They headed back to shore and Millie sat on the beach and watched while Chase retrieved a knife, cutting board and a few limes and shallots from the boat.

'You come prepared.'

'It's a quick, easy meal. But delicious.'

The sun dried her off, leaving salt on her skin as she sat with her elbows on her knees and watched him at work. She should have known he wouldn't let her sit back and do nothing for very long. Giving her a sideway glance, he beckoned her over.

'You can help.'

'You want me to slice some limes?' she asked hopefully, and he grinned.

'I thought you'd like a challenge. You can clean the conch.'

Bleh. Still, she wasn't going to argue. She eyed her wet tee-shirt drying on the boat, conscious that she was still only in her bra and pants. At least they were both sturdy and definitely not see-through. Chase caught her glance and shook his head.

'Your unmentionables are more modest than some of the bikinis I've seen, you know.'

'I'll bet.'

'Come on, Scary. You can do this.' He handed her a knife and instructed her on how to insert, twist and bring out the entire conch. Grimacing, Millie tried, and finally succeeded on her third try.

'Well done. Now we just need to fillet it. I'll do that, if you like.'

'Please.'

'You slice the limes.'

They worked in companionable silence for a moment, the sun warm on their backs. When everything had been sliced and diced, Chase fetched a wooden bowl from the boat and tossed it all together. He divided the salad between two plates and presented one to Millie with a courtly flourish.

'Your lunch, madam.'

'Thank you very much.' She took a bite, her eyes widening in surprise at how tasty it truly was. Chase smiled smugly.

'Told you.'

'Don't rub it in.' Unthinkingly she nudged him with her foot, a playful kick, and Chase raised his eyebrows. Too late Millie realised it could have looked like she was flirting. But she hadn't been, not intentionally anyway. She'd just been... enjoying herself.

And when was the last time she'd done that?

'A penny for your thoughts,' Chase said lightly. 'Or how about a bottle cap? I don't actually have any spare change.'

She glanced up and realised she'd been frowning. 'This is delicious, but it does seem a pity to eat such beautiful creatures.'

'They are pretty,' Chase agreed. 'They're actually endangered in US waters. But don't worry, they're still plentiful here. And the resort monitors the conch population around the island to make sure it never falls too low.'

'How eco-friendly of them. Is that a Bryant policy?'

He shrugged. 'A Chase Bryant policy. And economically friendly as well. If we don't conserve the island, there's no resort.'

Her salad finished, Millie propped her chin on her hands. 'But I thought you don't have anything to do with the resort.'

'Not really. But I'm interested in environmental policy, so...' He shrugged, but Millie wasn't fooled.

'Something happened?'

He tensed, and although it was barely noticeable Millie still felt it. Curiosity and a surprising compassion unfurled inside her. What had gone wrong between Chase and his family?

A second's pause was all it took for him to regain his usual lightness. 'Do I need to invoke the "no talking about the past" clause of our contract?'

'That was my past. Not yours.'

'I assumed it went both ways.'

She smiled sweetly. 'Fine print.'

Chase polished off the last mouthful of his meal before collecting their dishes and tossing them back into the boat. 'Fine. I was a bit of a reckless youth, made a few significant mistakes, and my father decided he'd rather I had nothing to do with the family business.' He shrugged, as if it were such ancient history that none of it mattered any more. 'So I went my own way, and am happy as a clam. Or a conch.'

Millie gazed at him, sensing the cracks in his armour.

He was just a little too deliberate with his light tone, and his story was far too simple. She wasn't about to press him, though. She'd been the one to insist that this week wasn't about emotional honesty or intimacy. But then, what *was* it about? It had been half a day already and they hadn't even kissed.

Yet she'd relaxed and enjoyed herself more than she'd ever thought possible.

'Come on,' Chase said, standing up and reaching a hand down to her. 'Let's explore the island.'

'That should take all of two minutes.'

'You'd be surprised.'

He hauled her to her feet, his strong, warm hand encasing hers, his fingers sliding over hers, skin on skin. Millie nearly shivered from the jolts that raced up and down her arm at that simple touch. When they did have sex, it was going to be amazing.

Mind-blowing.

Her heart slammed against her ribs as the realisation hit her again. Was she ready for this? Did she have any choice?

'Stop hyperventilating,' Chase said mildly. 'If it sets you at ease, I prefer a bed, or at least a comfortable surface. A beach seems romantic, but the sand can get into all sorts of inconvenient places.'

'You've tried it?' Millie tried not to feel nettled. *Jealous.* She'd never had sex on a beach.

'Once or twice,' Chase answered with a shrug. He was leading her away from the boat, towards a small grove of palm trees. 'Trust me, it's overrated.'

Millie's mind buzzed. OK, a bed. What bed? Her bed at the resort? At his villa? How were they going to *do* this? Well, obviously she knew *how*, but how without it being completely awkward or embarrassing? She hadn't had sex in over two years and then only ever with one man. What on earth had she been thinking, suggesting a fling? She was the least flingy person she knew.

She also knew it was way too late to be thinking this way. She should have considered all the uncomfortable practicalities before she'd made the suggestion to Chase. Before they'd agreed on a deal.

Before she'd suddenly realised just what this all meant, and that there was no such thing as simple sex.

Yet, even though she *was* hyperventilating, she knew she didn't want to back out. She wanted Chase.

Did his sailboat have a bed?

'Yes,' Chase called back and Millie skidded to a halt right there in the trees.

'What do you mean, *yes*?'

He stopped and turned, so aggravatingly amused. 'Yes, the sailboat has a bed.'

Her jaw dropped. 'Did I say that out loud?'

'No, but I could follow your thought process from here. I hate to say it, but you're kind of predictable.'

'You didn't expect me to jump on top of you from the boat,' Millie pointed out, and Chase cocked his head.

'True. I like when you surprise me.'

She'd liked it too. She'd liked feeling his hard body under hers. She'd enjoyed touching him. Just thinking about it now made her blood heat and her body pulse. Why was she waiting for him to kiss her? What if she kissed him?

'Don't get ahead of yourself there,' Chase murmured. 'Our first kiss needs to be special.'

She let out a most inelegant snort. 'What are you, a mind reader?'

'You were staring at my lips like they were the latest stock market report. It didn't take a huge amount of mental ability to guess what you were thinking.'

Disgruntled, she tugged her hand from his. 'So where are we going, exactly?'

Chase took her hand back, folding her fingers in his once more. 'I'll show you.'

They walked through the palms for a few more minutes, wending their way through the drooping fronds, the ground sandy beneath their feet. Then Chase stopped, slipping his arm around Millie's waist to draw her to his side. He did it so easily, so assuredly, that she didn't even think about any awkwardness as her leg lay warm against his, his fingers splayed along her hip.

'Look.'

She looked and saw a perfect little pool right there in the middle of the trees, a tiny jewel-like oasis, its surface as calm as a mirror. Millie knelt down and cupped the water with two hands; it was clear and cool. She glanced up at Chase. 'It's fresh?'

'Yep, fed by an underground spring, I think.' She shook her head in wonder, amazed that such a tiny island would have a source of fresh water. 'Drink,' Chase said. 'I've drunk it before, it tastes great. You could sell it for five bucks a bottle in the city.'

She took a sip, suddenly self-conscious at how Chase was watching her. When had taking a drink of water become sensual? Provocative?

'You know what the most amazing thing is, though?' he said, and she sat back on her heels.

'What?'

'You've been walking around in your underwear for most of the day and you haven't even noticed.'

She let out an embarrassed little laugh. 'And, now that you've reminded me, I'm going to notice.'

He grinned. 'Actually, what I was really going to say is that a couple of hundred years ago there were some ship-

wrecked sailors on a little atoll just a few hundred yards
away, without any fresh water. They didn't discover this
place and they died of thirst.'

She dropped her hands. 'That's awful.'

'I know. If they'd just tried swimming around a little bit,
or even making a raft or something, they might have survived.' He shook his head. 'But they were just too scared.'

Millie narrowed her eyes. 'And I'm supposed to make the
connection, right?'

He stared at her in exaggerated innocence. 'Connection?'

She stood up. 'If those sailors had just been a little more
adventurous, they would have survived. Really lived. All
they had to do was swim a little farther than they were comfortable with.'

'I don't think they could swim at all, actually. Most sailors back then couldn't.'

She folded her arms. 'I don't need the morality tale.'

'It was obvious, huh?'

'Like a sledgehammer.'

'And I made the whole thing up to boot.'

She let out a huff of outraged laughter. 'You did?'

'No, I didn't. It's actually true. Well, a legend around
here anyway.' He grinned and Millie didn't know whether
to throttle him or kiss him. She felt like doing both, at the
same time.

'You're unbelievable.'

'So I've been told.'

His gaze rested on her like a heavy, palpable thing, assessing, understanding. Knowing. She drew a breath.

'Look, Chase, I know I'm uptight and you think I need
to relax. I probably seem like a joke to you.'

'You don't,' Chase said quietly. 'I promise you, Millie,
this is no joke.'

She looked away, discomfited by the sudden intensity in

his voice. 'I don't want to be your project,' she said quietly. 'The reckless playboy teaches the uptight workaholic how to relax and have fun. Shows her how to really live.' She bit her lip hard, surprised by the sudden catch of tears in her throat. 'That isn't what I want from you.'

Chase took a step closer to her. 'Then maybe you should tell me what you do want.'

She forced herself to meet his gaze. 'Mind-blowing sex, remember?'

'I remember. And I remember the deal we made. One week, and you give me everything.'

He'd come closer, close enough so she could feel the heat of him, inhaled the scent that she was starting to realise was just Chase. Sun and musk and male. She drew a shaky breath. 'I don't know how much I have to give.'

He touched her chin with her hand, his fingers like a whisper against her skin. 'Someone hurt you. I get that. But this can be different, Millie.'

She shook her head, swallowed the hot lump of tears. 'No one hurt me, Chase. Not the way you think.'

'No questions about the past, I know,' he said, the hint of a smile in his voice. 'And this week isn't meant to be some lesson. It's just us—enjoying each other.'

Her breath came out in a soft hiss. 'OK.'

He stroked her cheek, and she had to fight not to close her eyes and surrender to that little caress. 'And I enjoy seeing you open up like a flower in the sun. I like seeing your face surprised by a smile.'

'Don't.'

'Is that scary, Millie? Is that out of your comfort zone?'

She swallowed. 'Yes.'

His other hand came up to cradle her face, just as he had last night. Had it only been last night? She felt as if she'd known this man for years. And he knew her.

'How long has it been,' he asked, 'since you were happy?'

'Two years.' The answer slipped out before she could think better of it. 'But really longer. Two years since I've known.' She stared at him, knowing he was drawing more from her than she'd ever intended to give, and also knowing that she wanted to give it. One week. For one week she wanted intimacy. Physical, emotional, intense. All of it. *All in*.

Chase was gazing back at her, his expression both tender and fierce, and then slowly, deliberately, he dipped his head and brushed his lips with her own.

A soft sigh of surrender escaped her as her lips parted underneath his. His lips were all the things she'd thought they would be: soft, hard, cool, warm. And so achingly gentle.

He brushed his lips across hers a second and third time, like a greeting. Then he touched his tongue to the corner of her mouth, and then the other corner, as if he were asking her how she was. A wordless conversation of mouths. Her lips parted wider, accepting. *I'm good.*

He deepened the kiss, his hands tightening as they cradled her face, and Millie's hands came up to bunch on the bare skin of his shoulders. Yet even as sensation swirled through her another part of her was stepping back and analysing everything.

His hands felt bigger than Rob's. His body was harder. His kiss was more demanding and yet more gentle at the same time. More assured. Yet could she even remember the last time she and Rob had kissed? That last day, all she'd had were harsh words, impatient sighs…

She hadn't even said goodbye.

Chase lifted his head, pulling back a little bit so Millie blinked in surprise. 'Your lack of response is a bit of a buzzkill, you know.'

'What?' She gaped like a fish. 'I wasn't—'

'No,' Chase agreed, 'you weren't. It started off rather nicely, but then you went somewhere else in your head.' She couldn't deny it, and his gaze narrowed. 'What were you thinking about, Millie?' She swallowed, said nothing. 'You were thinking about some other guy, weren't you?'

'No!' Millie protested, then bit her lip. She couldn't lie, not to Chase. 'I couldn't help it.'

For the first time since she'd seen him, he looked angry. Or maybe even hurt. Emotion flashed in his eyes like thunder and then he deliberately relaxed. 'I know you think too much. You've got to turn off that big brain of yours, Millie.'

'I know.' Did she ever. The whole reason she'd embarked on this fling of theirs was to keep herself from thinking. Remembering. Tormenting herself with guilty regrets.

'Let's go back to the boat,' Chase said. 'We should get back to St Julian's before dark.'

Silently Millie followed him back through the grove to the slender beach and then onto the boat. Chase didn't so much as look back at her once, or help her onto the boat. Any warmth between them seemed to have evaporated. Millie fetched her clothes, now thankfully dry but stiff as a board and caked with salt, and clutched them to her. She stood uncertainly on the deck while Chase set the boat free from its moorings, his movements taut with suppressed energy—or emotion? Was he angry with her?

'Is there somewhere I can change?'

'Don't bother.' He didn't even look at her as he reached for another line.

'What?' She didn't like seeing Chase this way, the hard lines of his face transformed into harshness—or maybe just indifference. Gone was the charming, charismatic man she'd come to like—and trust. 'I don't want to walk into the resort in my underwear,' she said, trying to joke, but Chase turned to her with a dangerously bland expression.

'You can put your clothes on after.'

'After?'

'After we have sex. That's what you wanted, isn't it, Millie? No messy emotions or entanglements, no getting to know each other.' He spread his arms wide, a cool smile curling his mouth. 'Well, here we are. Alone in an ocean, and there's a perfectly good bed in the cabin below. No reason not to hop to it.'

Millie stared, swallowed. 'You mean now?'

'Right now.' He jerked a thumb in direction of the ladder that led below deck. 'Let's go.'

CHAPTER SIX

WHAT the hell was he doing? Being a total bastard, judging by the look of shocked horror on Millie's face. But he was angry, even if he shouldn't be. The thought of Millie thinking of some other jerk while he was pouring his soul into that kiss filled him with a blind rage.

'Well?' Chase arched an eyebrow and put his hands on his hips. 'What are you waiting for?'

Her teeth sank into those worry marks on her lower lip. She clutched her clothes tighter to her chest. 'Somehow, with the way you're looking at me, I don't think it's going to be mind-blowing.'

'Leave that to me.'

She shook her head. 'I don't like angry sex.'

He gave her a level look. 'I'm not angry.' He wasn't, he realised with a flash of cringing insight. He was hurt. He hadn't expected to care so much, so quickly.

Millie gave just as level a look back, even as her eyes flashed fire. He might not be angry, but she was. Well, fine. Bring it on.

'All right.' She lifted her chin a notch, her eyes still flashing, and stalked past him to the ladder. Chase watched her descend below deck, her body taut and quivering with tension. Or maybe anger, or even fear.

Did it matter? Wasn't this what she wanted, a quick bout

of meaningless sex? She could get him out of her system, or so she undoubtedly hoped.

And maybe he'd get her out of his. He'd spent the afternoon coaxing smiles from her even as he enjoyed himself more than he'd ever thought possible. Every smile, every laugh, had felt like a discovery. A victory.

He thought they were building something—admittedly something fragile and temporary, but *still*. Something. And the whole time she'd been thinking of some stupid ex.

'Are you coming?' she called from below, her voice as taut as her body had been.

Chase's mouth curved grimly at the unwitting *double entendre*. 'You'd better believe it.'

He hauled himself down the ladder and saw that Millie stood in front of the double bed. She turned to him, her chest heaving, her nipples visible beneath the thin, silky material of her bra. She arched her eyebrows and curved her mouth in a horrible rictus smile.

'All right, Chase. Let's see what you've got.'

He swallowed, acid churning in his gut. How had they got here? The afternoon had been full of tenderness and teasing, and now they were acting like they hated each other.

Millie's eyes glittered and he knew she wouldn't back down. She never backed down from a challenge; he'd learned that already.

And hell if he'd back down either. She was the one who had said she didn't want to get to know him. Wasn't interested in emotional anything. Right now, right here, he could give her what she wanted. The only thing she wanted.

And, damn it, he'd want it too.

'Take off your bra.' A pulse beat hard in the hollow of her throat but she undid it and tossed it to the floor. Her breasts were small and round, high and firm. Perfect. Chase swallowed. 'And the rest.' She glared at him as she kicked off her underwear, her chin still tilted high.

'Is this what you call foreplay?'

He almost laughed. She was magnificent. Naked, proud, defiant, *strong*. He shook his head. 'I just like to see what I get in this deal of ours.'

'Only fair I get the same opportunity, then.'

He arched an eyebrow, aroused in spite of the anger. Or maybe because of it. Hell, he didn't know anything any more. 'What are you saying, Scary?'

'Take off your pants.'

He did.

They stared at each other almost in grim silence, both of them totally naked, nothing between them. The air seemed to crackle with the tension, with the expectation.

Hell.

What now?

Millie folded her arms. Waited. Chase felt like a circus seal, or a damn monkey. She clearly expected him to *perform*.

He hadn't wanted it to be this way. He'd wanted to gain her trust, even her affection, and help her to lose control in the most amazing way possible. Right now she was clinging to that precious control with her french-manicured fingernails and it was slipping crazily away from him.

He didn't want this.

He wasn't going to back down.

'Get on the bed.'

She gave him a little smirk, almost as if he were being *so* predictable, and lay on the bed. She even put her hands behind her head as if she were incredibly relaxed, but she was trembling.

Damn.

Again Chase hesitated. *Don't do this.* He didn't want to

ruin what they had by losing her trust, affection, *everything*, in a bout of absurdly unsexy sex. Except who was he kidding? They didn't *have* anything.

This was all they had—this, right here on the bed.

'Let me tell you,' Millie drawled, her hands still laced behind her head, 'this is turning out to be the worst sexual encounter of my life, and forget about mind-blowing.'

Chase saw that she still trembled.

He sat on the edge of the bed and slowly ran his hand from the arch of her foot along her calf to behind her knee, his fingers instinctively seeking further, finding the soft, smooth skin of her inner thigh. More softness. He felt her muscles tense and quiver beneath his touch. Her breath hitched.

'I'm not going to play this game,' he said quietly and she stared at him, her whole body going rigid.

'This was *your* idea.'

'Yeah, I'll grant you that. But you went for it because this is what you want.'

'You think *this* is what I want?'

'There's no emotional intimacy or getting to know you in this scenario, is there?' He slid his hand higher, savouring the sweet softness of her thigh. Another couple of inches would be even sweeter.

She stared at him, mesmerised, trapped. He stilled his hand. 'You know I'm right, Millie.'

In answer she reached up, lacing her fingers behind his head, and pulled him down for a hungry, open-mouthed kiss. Her tongue delved inside and she arched upwards, pressing her body against him.

Shock short-circuited Chase's brain for a second. Then his libido ramped up and he kissed her back just as hungrily with an instinct he was helpless to repress—even as he acknowledged this wasn't what he wanted. He didn't even think it was what Millie wanted, not deep down. She was trying to stay in control, seizing it desperately, and he couldn't let her.

But then her hand wrapped around him and he stopped thinking about what he couldn't do. His body was telling him what he could.

'Millie.' Her name was a groan against her mouth and he reached up to try to remove her death grip on the back of his head. *'Wait...'*

But she didn't want to wait. She was all over him, eager, urgent, desperate, making him feel the same way. His self-control was slipping away. How did a man argue for a more emotional experience when the woman beneath him was determined to drive him wild? For the feel of Millie's hands on him, her legs hooked around his hips as she angled upwards, was making him crazy. Through the fog of his own lust he tried to remember where he'd put the condoms.

'Quickly...' Millie whispered, her voice a ragged whimper, and Chase stilled. He heard too much desperation and even sadness in her voice, and he didn't want that. No matter how much his body screamed otherwise.

'Millie.' He pushed away from her a little bit, enough to see her pale, dazed face. 'Let's hold on a moment, shall we?' he said unevenly, even though his greatest desire at that point was to forget emotion and sensitivity, and even a condom, and just drive right into her.

'No, I don't want...' Her face went a shade paler, and then she lurched upwards. 'I think I'm going to be sick.' In one abrupt movement she rolled off the bed and raced to the head. Chase listened to her retching into the toilet in a kind of stunned disbelief.

This was starting to feel like the worst sexual encounter of his life too. He reached for his shorts and pulled them on, grabbed a spare tee-shirt from the drawer and waited on the edge of the bed.

A few minutes later a pale and shaky-looking Millie emerged. From somewhere Chase found a smile. 'I don't think that was because of the conch.'

She gave him a rather wobbly smile back, although her eyes were dark with pain. 'No, it wasn't.' Somehow the anger, tension and even the desperation of moments before had evaporated, but Chase didn't know what was left. He felt bewildered, like someone had skipped ahead in the scene selection on a DVD. He was clearly missing some plot points to this story.

'Here.' He handed her the tee-shirt and she slipped it on. Her hair was tousled, the shirt falling to mid-thigh. With a little sigh she sat on the edge of the bed, about as far away from him as possible.

'Sorry about that.'

'To which part of the evening are you referring?' he quipped, parroting her own words from last night back to her.

Millie gave a tiny, tired smile and leaned her head against the wall. She closed her eyes and with a pang of remorse Chase saw how exhausted she looked. Today had been quite the rollercoaster.

'To the part where I threw up in your bathroom a few minutes ago.'

'On a boat it's called a head.'

'Whatever.' She opened her eyes. 'That was another buzz-kill, I suspect.'

'To say the least.' They stared at each other, unspeaking, but Chase was surprised at how *un*-awkward it seemed. Maybe you got to a point with a person where things didn't seem so embarrassing or strange. If so, he'd got to that point pretty quickly with Millie. 'You want to tell me what's going on?'

'Remember the no-talking clause?'

'That clause was voided when you threw up. I was about six seconds from being inside you, Millie.'

She bit her lip and he reached over and gently touched those worry marks. 'You're going to get a scar from doing that if you don't cut it out.'

She sighed and shook her head. 'Maybe this whole thing was a bad idea, Chase.'

He felt a lurch of what could only be alarm. He didn't like feeling it. At this point, he should be agreeing with her. This *was* a bad idea. Neither of them needed the kind of mind games this week seemed to play on them. He'd convinced himself he wanted intense, but this? This was way too much.

Yet even so he heard himself saying, 'Why do you say that?'

'Because I'm not ready.'

She'd felt pretty ready beneath him. With effort Chase yanked his thoughts from that unhelpful direction. 'Ready?' he repeated.

'For this. A fling, an affair, whatever you want to call it. I wanted to be ready, I wanted to move on, but I don't know if I can. I can't stop thinking—' She stopped abruptly, shook her head.

It was no more than he'd already guessed, yet he didn't like hearing it. Didn't like thinking that some guy still owned her heart and mind so much he couldn't even get a toe-in. Jealousy. That was what he felt, pure and simple. Determinedly Chase pushed it away. 'We went about this all wrong, Scary,' he said. 'And that was my fault. I'm sorry.'

Surprise flashed across her features, like the first beam of sunlight after a downpour. 'For what?'

'For getting angry. I didn't like the fact that you were thinking of whatever guy did a number on you when I was kissing you.' He smiled wryly. 'It's kind of an insult to, you know, my masculinity.'

'Sorry.'

'It's OK. I should have got over it. Instead I pushed you—and myself—in a direction I had no intention of going.'

Her mouth curved in the faintest of smiles. 'Angry sex, huh?'

'It's really not that great.'

'Kind of like sex on a beach.'

'Exactly. Both overrated.' He sighed and raked his hand through his hair. 'Look, let's hit rewind on this evening. Go back on deck and forget this happened.'

'Well,' she said, sounding almost mischievous, 'I don't think I'm going to forget the sight of you naked in a hurry.'

Chase grinned. 'Me neither, Scary. Me neither.' Still smiling, he reached for her hand and felt a clean sweep of thankfulness when she took it. How bizarre that all that tension, anger and hurt had melted and reformed into something else. Something deeper and truer. Friendship.

'I hope,' Millie said as he led her from the cabin, 'we're not diving for dinner.'

'Definitely not.' He felt himself warm from the inside out, and he gave her hand a squeeze before helping her up the ladder.

Millie walked to the cushioned bench in the back of the boat on wobbly legs. She felt exhausted, both emotionally and physically, by the events of the day and especially the last hour. Chase Bryant was putting her through the wringer. Or maybe she was doing it to herself, by trying to have the desperate, mindless sex she'd thought she wanted until her body had rebelled and thrown up a whole lot of conch.

Chase was right, of course. It wasn't the conch that had made her sick. It was the memories. She couldn't turn her brain off, as much as she wanted to. Couldn't stop remembering, regretting. She'd wanted to have this fling so she could forget, but it wasn't happening that way at all. It was making things worse. Chase was opening up things inside her, stirring to life everything she'd wanted to be forgotten and buried, *gone*.

She watched as he set sail, part of her mind admiring the lean strength of his tanned, muscled body even as the rest whirled and spun in confusion. She hadn't expected him to become so angry earlier. And she hadn't expected him to be so understanding just then.

For a moment there on the bed, the cabin silent except for the draw and sigh of their own breathing, she'd actually wanted to tell him things. Confide all her confusion, sadness and guilt. But that would mean telling him about Rob. About Charlotte. And she never spoke about Charlotte. Even now the pain ripped through her, all too fresh even though it had been two years. Two years since the phone call that had torn her world apart, taken everyone she loved.

Shouldn't two years be enough time for the scars to heal? To finally feel ready to move on?

She felt the cushion dip beneath her and blinked to see Chase sitting next to her. She'd been so lost in her own miserable thoughts she hadn't seen him coming.

He touched her mouth and even now, after everything that had and hadn't happened, she felt that quiver of awareness, the remnant of desire. 'Scars, Scary. I'm serious.'

She let out a trembling little laugh. 'It's hard to stop something you're not even aware you're doing.'

'What deep thoughts are making you bite your lip?'

'They're not particularly deep.' She turned a little bit away from him, forcing him to drop his hand. 'Are we heading back to the resort?'

'No. To my villa.'

She turned back to him, felt a frisson of—what? Not fear. Not excitement. No, this felt strange and suddenly she knew why. She felt hope. Even after the absolute disaster below deck, Chase was giving her—*them*—a second chance.

'What are we going to do there?'

He regarded her speculatively for a moment. 'I'm going to cook for you while you soak in my jacuzzi. Then we're going to eat the fantastic meal I've whipped up, watch a movie, maybe have a glass of wine. Or sparkling water, as the case may be.'

'That sounds surprisingly relaxing.'

'Glad you think so.'

'And then?'

'And then we'll go to sleep in my very comfortable, king-sized bed and I'll hold you all night long.'

He spoke breezily enough, yet Millie heard the heartfelt sincerity underneath the lightness, and she felt tears sting her eyes. She blinked hard.

'Why are you being so nice to me?'

'Hasn't a man been nice to you before, Millie?' He spoke quietly, as if he felt sad for her. She shook her head.

'Don't pity me, Chase. I've—I've had a perfectly fine relationship before.'

'That sounds incredibly boring and unromantic, but OK. Good for you.'

She let out a trembling laugh. He *never* let up, but then neither did she. 'This doesn't sound very intense, though,' she told him. 'I thought this week was all about excitement.'

'There are different kinds of intense. And I think a quiet evening at home will be intense enough for you.'

He rose from the bench and Millie watched as he steered the boat, one hand on the tiller. The wind ruffled his short hair, his eyes narrowed against the setting sun. He paused, his hand still on the tiller, to watch the glorious descent of that orb of fire towards the now-placid sea. Shock jolted through her because for a moment Chase looked like she felt. Desperate. Sad. Longing to hope.

Then he straightened his shoulders and turned back to her with a smile, all lightness restored. 'Almost there.'

Half an hour later Millie was soaking in the most opulent tub she'd ever seen, huge, sunken and made of black marble. Chase had filled it right to the top with steaming water, half a bottle of bubble bath, and then left not one but two thick, fluffy towels on the side. Then with a smile and a salute he'd closed the door and gone to cook dinner.

When, Millie wondered, had she ever felt so incredibly pampered? So *loved*?

She froze, even in all that hot, fragrant water. *Don't even think that,* she told herself. *Don't go there.* The dreaded L-word. She'd loved Rob. She'd loved Charlotte. And here she was, two years later, heartbroken and alone.

She slipped beneath the foaming water and scrubbed the sand from her hair. The thoughts from her mind. She wanted to enjoy this evening, all the lovely things Chase had promised her. It had been so long since she'd had anything like this.

Since she'd felt anything like this.

Don't think. One week. That was all they had, all she wanted to have. One week of enjoyment, of fun and, yes, of sex. Despite today's disaster they could still have it. Enjoy it.

And then walk away. Move on, just like she wanted to, because anything else—anything real or lasting—was way too frightening. She'd loved once. Lost once. And it wasn't going to happen again.

One week suited her perfectly. One intense, wonderful week.

When Millie came out of the bathroom she saw, to her surprise, her suitcase laid out by the bed. How on earth had Chase been able to get into her room and take her stuff?

The answer was obvious: he was a Bryant. For a little while there she'd forgotten; he'd just been Chase. Annoyance and affection warred within her. It was nice to have her clothes, but it was a little *too* thoughtful. Sighing, she discarded her towel and reached for one of the boring outfits her secretary had chosen, this one a beige linen dress with short sleeves and no shape. She glanced down at it and gave a grimace of disgust. She wished, suddenly and fiercely, that she owned something sexy.

But then she'd never owned anything sexy. She and Rob hadn't been about sexy. Their sex life had been good enough, certainly, but they had both been so focused. There had been no time or inclination for sexy or silly or fun.

Everything that Chase was.

Was that why she'd chosen him for her first fling? Because, despite initial appearances, he was utterly unlike her husband?

Her thoughts felt too tangled to separate or understand. And maybe, like Chase said, she was over-thinking this. Straightening the boring dress, Millie headed out into the rest of the villa.

It was a gorgeous house, made of a natural stone that blended into its beach-side surroundings, the inside all soaring space and light. She found Chase in the gourmet kitchen that flowed seamlessly into the villa's main living space with scattered leather sofas and a huge picture-window framing an expanse of sand and sky.

'That smells delicious.'

'Chicken with pineapple and mango salsa,' Chase informed her, whipping a dish cloth from his shoulder to wipe something up on the granite work surface. Millie felt her heart—or something—squeeze at the sight of him. He'd changed into a worn blue tee-shirt and faded jeans, and he

looked so natural and relaxed standing there, different bowls
and pans around him, the smells of fruit and spice in the air.

She and Rob had never cooked. They'd eaten takeaway
every night or ready-made meals from the gourmet super-
market. Why cook, Rob had used to say, if you don't have
to? And she had agreed. After a ten-hour day at work, the
last thing she felt like doing was making a meal. And they'd
both been proud of the way Charlotte, at only two years old,
would eat all the things they ate. Brie and smoked salmon.
Spicy curries and pad thai. She'd loved it all.

A knot of emotion lodged in Millie's throat. Why was
she thinking about Charlotte? She never did. She'd closed
that part of herself off, shut up in a box marked *'do not
open'*. Ever.

Yet here she was, memories springing unbidden into her
mind, filling up her heart.

'Millie?' Chase was glancing at her, eyes narrowed. 'You
OK there, Scary?'

She nodded. Sniffed. How stupidly revealing of her, but
she couldn't help it. She'd thought she could handle this
week, but already she was finding she couldn't. She was
thinking too much. Feeling too much. She'd thought Chase
would make her forget, but instead he was helping her to
remember.

'That bath was wonderful,' she said, in a deliberate and
obvious effort to change the subject. 'I could live in it for
a week.'

'The water might get a bit cold.' Chase reached for a
couple of green chilies and began dicing them with practised ease.

'Fair point.' She took a breath and decided she needed
to get on firmer footing. Find a little distance. 'As nice as
it is to wear my own clothes, I'm not sure how they got in
your bedroom.'

'A very nice bell hop drove them over while you were in the tub.'

'Don't you think you could have asked?'

He glanced up, eyebrows arched. 'Are we still going over this? My terms, remember?'

'You can't keep throwing that at me every time I object to something, Chase.'

'And that is because…?'

She blew out an exasperated breath. 'It's not fair.'

'True.'

'So?'

'We're not playing baseball, Millie. Or Parcheesi. There are no rules.'

She folded her arms. 'Are you on some huge power trip? Is that what this is about?'

'Does it seem like it?' He sounded genuinely curious, and Millie was compelled to an unwilling honesty.

'No, which is why I don't get it. I still don't really get what you want, Chase. Most men would take the sex and run.'

'Has that been your experience?'

'Don't go there. No questions about the past.'

'I told you what I wanted. One week.'

'One intense, all-in week.'

'Only kind that works for me.'

'Why?'

Chase didn't answer for a moment. He concentrated on his cooking, taking out some pieces of chicken from the bowl of marinade and tossing them into a pan shimmering with hot oil. Millie listened to the sizzle and spat as they cooked, a delicious aroma wafting up from the pan.

'Why not?' he finally said and flipped the chicken. 'I know it's easier and simpler on the surface, Millie, just to skim life. Don't dig too deeply. Don't feel too much. I've been there. That's most of my misspent youth.'

She swallowed, knowing he was right. Easier, simpler and safer. 'But now?'

'I want something more. I want the whole *carpe diem* thing. Seize life. Suck the marrow from its bones.'

'For one week.'

'Yep. That's about the size of it.'

'And you decide to do this with me?' She couldn't keep the disbelief from her voice. 'When you must know I'm the exact opposite of all that?'

He gave her a decidedly roguish smile. 'That makes it more fun. And all the more reason why it has to be on my terms. Otherwise we'd never get anywhere.'

Millie shook her head. How could she argue with him? How could she explain that she was afraid one week with Chase might be enough to peel back all her protective layers, leave her bare, exposed and hurting? She didn't want to admit the possibility even to herself.

She slid onto a stool and braced her elbows on the counter. 'So what made you change your mind? To stop skimming?'

He poured the rest of the marinade on top of the chicken, stirring it slowly. 'I think I might take this opportunity to invoke part B of the no-talking-about-the-past clause, which details that I don't have to talk about it either.'

'You have something to hide?'

She almost missed the dark flash in his eyes. She knew he was touchy about his family, but he'd told her the basics about that. Was there something else? Something he didn't want her to know?

'Not really,' he said, taking the lid off a pan of rice and spooning some onto two plates warming on the hob. 'Just some things I'd rather not talk about.'

'What about your youth was so misspent?'

'You trying to get to *know* me?'

'Maybe.'

He shrugged. 'Just the usual, really, for a spoiled rich kid. Expelled from half a dozen boarding schools, crashed my father's Maserati. The final straw was sleeping with his girl-friend.' He spoke so very nonchalantly, yet Millie sensed a thread of self-protectiveness in his voice. Maybe even hurt.

'That's pretty misspent.'

'Yeah, well, I like to do things right.' Now he ladled the chicken in its fragrant sauce over the rice, and Millie had to admit it all looked delicious. The man could cook.

'And what made you change? I assume you're not crash-ing Maseratis now?'

'Only the odd one here or there.'

'Seriously.'

'You want me to be serious?' He let out a long-suffering sigh and handed her a plate. 'In that case, I need sustenance.'

They sat in a dining alcove, the floor-to-ceiling windows giving an endless view of the ocean darkening to damson under a twilit sky.

'Your favourite part of the day,' Chase said softly, and a thrill ran through her—a thrill at the thought that this man was starting to *know* her. And that she liked it.

How terrifying.

'So?' Millie said, attempting to banish that thrill. 'Why the change?'

Chase speared a piece of chicken. 'Remember I told you my father decided he didn't want me in the family business?'

'That was, I assume, after the girlfriend incident?'

'Correct. That, of course, just made me more determined to be as bad as I could be.'

'How old were you?'

'Seventeen.'

Millie felt a surprising tug of sympathy for the teenaged Chase. Normally she'd just roll her eyes at even the thought of some spoiled rich kid going through cars and women at a break-neck speed, but when she knew it was Chase… When she knew he wasn't shallow or spoiled, had more depth than most people she met… Well, it felt different. She felt different.

'So you were super-bad, then?'

'More of the same, really. Parties, cars, women, drink. Some recreational drug use I'm definitely not proud of.' He still spoke lightly, but she saw shadows in his eyes. Felt them in her heart. What a sad, empty life. And her life, in a totally different way, had been sad and empty too. *Still was*.

'So what was your life-changing moment?'

He gave her a speculative glance. 'This is getting pretty personal.'

She swallowed and decided not to dissemble. 'I know.'

Chase speared another bit of chicken and chewed slowly before answering. 'My father died. I was finishing college, I'd been studying architecture more for the hell of it than anything else. I was still pretty much a waste of space.' He paused, and Millie almost reached out to him, touched him, even just a hand on his arm. She stopped herself and Chase continued.

'I found out from his will that he'd legally disowned me from inheriting anything. Cut me out completely. It was what he'd threatened to do years before, but I guess I didn't really believe he meant it until then. And, while I have to admit I was pretty disappointed that I wouldn't be getting any of his money, I felt something worse.' He glanced away, his expression shuttering. 'Disappointment. Disappointment in myself, and how little I'd made of my life.'

Then Millie couldn't stop herself. *All in, right?* She reached across the table and touched Chase's hand, just a whisper of her fingers against his, but it was big for her and she thought he knew that. He glanced down at their touching hands and then looked up, smiling wryly.

'Not that inspiring a story, really.'

'Actually, it is. You recognised your mistakes and did something about them. Most people don't get that far.'

'Did you?'

The blunt question startled her. All this intimacy and sharing was great until he turned the tables on her. She withdrew her hand. 'Maybe, in a manner of speaking.' She paused, her fingers clenching into an involuntary fist. 'But it was too late.'

'Why was it too late, Millie?' She shook her head. She'd said too much. 'All these secrets,' Chase said lightly. 'You know it only makes you more intriguing, right? Sexier too. And it makes me want to find out what you're hiding.'

'Trust me, it's not sexy. Or intriguing. It's just…' She let out a breath. 'Sad. In a lot of different ways. And the reason I don't want to tell you is because you'll look at me differently.'

'Would that be a bad thing?'

'Yes, it would.' She liked the way Chase teased her. Riled her. Yes, he made her uncomfortable, but he also made her feel real and alive. He didn't tiptoe around her feelings, didn't tinge every smile with pity or uncertainty. Didn't look at her like she was a walking tragedy.

The way everyone else did.

Maybe *that* was what had attracted her to him in the first place—the fact that he didn't really know her at all. And yet, Millie had to acknowledge, he did know her. The real her. He just didn't know what had happened in her life.

And she liked it that way.

Yet how could he really know her, without knowing that?

Tired of the tangle of her thoughts, she rose from the table. 'Didn't you say something about a movie?'

Fifteen minutes later, after friendly bickering about whether to see an action flick or worthy drama, they settled on a DVD. Chase sat down on the sofa and before Millie could debate where to sit he pulled her down next to him, fit her snugly next to him and draped his arm around her shoulders. Millie tensed for just a second and then relaxed into Chase's easy embrace. Why was she fighting this? The weight of his arm and the solid strength of his body felt good.

She tried to pay attention to the movie—the worthy drama she had insisted upon—but she was so tired that her eyelids were drooping halfway through. She must have dozed off, for some time later she stirred to find herself being scooped up in Chase's arms.

'I can't believe I sat through something with subtitles so you could fall asleep on me,' Chase said, and there was so much affection in his voice that Millie curled naturally into the warmth of him, putting her arms around his neck.

'Time for bed, Scary,' he muttered, and she heard a catch in his voice. As he carried her through the villa to the bedroom in the back, Millie had the sleepy, hazy thought that there was nowhere else she'd rather be. In Chase's house. In Chase's arms. Going to Chase's bed.

CHAPTER SEVEN

MILLIE woke early, just as dawn was sliding its first pale fingers across the floor. She always woke early; quarter to five was usual. Yet, instead of bolting upright and practically sprinting to the shower, she woke slowly, languorously, stretching before she rolled over, propping herself up on one elbow to gaze at Chase.

He was fast asleep, his hair rumpled, his breathing slow and even. He looked gorgeous, and since he was asleep she let herself study him: the strong, stubbly angle of his jaw; the sweep of golden-brown lashes against his cheek. His lips were lush and full, his nose straight. The dawn light caught the golden glints in his close-cropped hair. Her gaze slid lower. He'd taken off his shirt. She'd seen his chest already, of course. He'd practically been shirtless the whole time she'd known him. Yet now she could study the perfect, muscled form; the sprinkling of dark-brown hair that veed lower, broad shoulders tapering to lean hips. The sheet was rucked about those hips, and she couldn't tell what he was wearing underneath. Dared she peek?

'Boxers, Scary.'

Her gaze flew back to his face. He was blinking sleep from his eyes and giving her the slowest, sexiest smile Millie had ever seen. Her heart juddered in her chest but she didn't try to dissemble.

'I was wondering. You seem like the type to sleep in the buff.'

'Nope, I'm strictly a boxers man. Sleeping naked can create all sorts of awkward situations, like when your cleaning lady arrives a bit earlier than you expected.'

Her mouth curved. 'You seem to have experienced a lot of awkward situations.'

'It certainly makes life a bit more interesting.'

'I'll take your word on it.'

He reached out and touched her hair, his fingers threading through it. 'Your hair's not so scary when you've slept on it.'

'It's probably a mess.'

'I like it.' He tucked a strand behind her ear, then trailed his fingers along her cheek before resting his thumb on the fullness of her lower lip. 'Those worry marks look a little better.'

'Do they?' Her heart had started the slow, thudding beat of expectation. They were both in a bed. Nearly naked. Had Chase removed her dress last night? She couldn't remember, but she was wearing one of his tee-shirts. And nothing underneath.

Surely now…?

'As enticing a prospect as that is, I think we'll have breakfast first,' Chase said, and Millie let out a huff of breath.

'Stop reading my mind.'

'It's too easy. Every thought is reflected in your eyes.'

'Not every thought,' Millie objected. She knew she had some secrets and she wanted to keep it that way.

Didn't she?

'More than you think,' Chase said softly, and he drew her towards him for a lingering kiss. It was the kind of kiss you had *after* you made love, slow and sated. It didn't have the urgency she expected, that she *felt*. Because today was day three of her week's holiday and since she'd met Chase time had started slipping by all too fast.

'Soon,' Chase murmured against her lips and she groaned.

'*Stop* that.'

'Actually, I think you kind of like it.'

She didn't answer, because she knew he was right, even if the way he read her so easily was seriously annoying. She liked being *known*. 'What are we doing today?' she asked as she followed him out of the bedroom into the kitchen. Sunlight poured through the picture windows and Chase, still only wearing boxers, was reaching for the coffee grinder. Within seconds the wonderful aroma of freshly ground beans was wafting through the air.

'I thought you could decide that,' he said as he poured the ground beans into the coffee maker.

'Me?'

'Yes, you. You're not just along for the ride, you know.'

'I sort of thought I was. Your terms, remember?'

'Exactly. And my terms state that today you decide what we do. Of course, I have the right to veto any and all suggestions.'

'Oh, I see. Thanks for making that clear.'

'No problem.'

What *did* she want to do today? As Chase got out fresh melon and papaya and began slicing both, Millie considered. What did she want to do with *Chase*?

'I want to paint you.'

He paused, a mug in each hand, eyebrow arched. 'Too bad your paints are in the rubbish bin, then.'

'I can draw you,' Millie said firmly, surprised by how certain she felt. 'I brought charcoals too. They're in my suitcase.'

'So you've changed your mind about the painting thing?'

'Technically I won't be painting.'

'You are such a literalist.'

'Yes,' Millie said quietly, and it felt like a confession. 'I've changed my mind.'

Chase stared at her long and hard, and the moment unfurled, stretched between them into something that pulsed with both life and hope.

'OK,' he said. 'Breakfast, and then you can draw. I assume you'd prefer a nude model?'

She laughed and shook her head. 'You can keep your boxers on. For now.'

After a breakfast of coffee, fresh fruit and eggs Chase scrambled while Millie sat at the table and imagined just how she would sketch him, she fetched her paper and charcoals and they headed outside.

The day was warm, the sun already hot, although a fresh breeze blew off the sea. Millie had changed into a polo shirt and capris, and Chase had, on her instruction, put on a tee-shirt and shorts.

'Are you sure you don't want me nude?' he said, sounding disappointed, and Millie shook her head.

'Far too distracting.'

'Well, that's something at least.'

'Just try to act natural.'

He gave an exaggerated sigh. 'Whenever someone says that, you can't act natural any more.'

'Try.'

'I bet you're a real ball-breaker at work.'

'That,' Millie informed him, 'is a horrible, sexist term.'

'But you are, right?' He positioned himself on the sand, hands stretched out behind him, legs in front. 'This OK?'

'Perfect.' She found a comfortable spot just a little bit away and laid the sketch pad across her knees. After staring at Chase this morning, she realised how much she wanted to draw him, to capture the ease and joy of his body and face so she could remember it always.

So she could have something of him even when this week was over.

She swallowed, also realising just how much she was starting to care for him. Forty-eight hours—forty-eight *intense* hours—were changing how she felt. Changing *her*.

'You going to put pencil to paper this time, Scary?'

'Yes.' Swallowing, she looked down at her paper, began to roughly sketch the shape of him.

'So you haven't been doing the art thing for a while,' Chase remarked, gazing out to the sea so she should capture his profile. 'Why did you stop?'

Millie hesitated. She knew she should remind him about the no-talking rule, but it seemed kind of pointless to keep at it now. She didn't even want to. She could still control what she told him. 'Life happened,' she said. 'I got too busy and drawing seemed kind of a silly pastime.' And totally out of sync with her and Rob's focused, career-driven lives.

'And then you finally took a holiday and thought you might like to try again?'

'Basically.'

'So why did you throw out the paints when I first met you?'

'All these questions,' Millie said lightly. 'You are *so* violating our agreement, Chase.'

'But you're answering them,' he pointed out. 'For once.'

She didn't speak for a moment, just sketched faster and faster, the feel and look of him emerging from her charcoal. 'I didn't like how obvious it seemed,' she finally said. 'Like I was trying to *find* myself or something.'

'Were you?'

She glanced up, the sketch book momentarily forgotten. 'I'm not lost,' she said sharply. 'I'm not *broken*.'

'You're not?' He still spoke mildly, yet she felt that spurt of rage anyway. Her fingers tightened around the charcoal.

'No.'

'Because I think you are.'

Shock had her fingers slackening again, and the charcoal fell to the ground. 'How dare—?'

'Why do you think you're here, Millie?' He turned to gaze at her and she saw a blaze of emotion lighting his eyes. 'Why do you think you were willing to have this crazy, intense week? And not just willing, but needing it?'

'I don't *need* it.'

'Liar.'

She shook her head, hating that he saw through her. Hating that she didn't have the strength to deny it any longer. She *was* lost. Broken. And she needed this week with him; she needed *him*.

And he knew it.

He kept his gaze on her, assessing, knowing, and she hated that too. The raw honesty between them in this moment felt more exposing and intimate than lying naked on a bed with him had yesterday.

She reached for the dropped charcoal, her fingers closing around it even though she knew she wouldn't draw any more. She couldn't. She stared blindly at the sketch pad, her mind spinning, her heart thudding.

'Our session is finished, I presume?' Chase drawled, and Millie nodded jerkily. 'And now you're going to go all haughty on me, aren't you? The Millie Lang armour goes up, and you get all scary and severe.'

'You're the one who calls me scary,' Millie said through numb lips. Every instinct in her was telling her to *run*. Save herself, or as much of herself as she could. How had she let it get this far? Chase had been so clever at seducing her into an emotional intimacy she had never intended to give or reveal. Damn it, all she'd wanted was *sex*.

And they still hadn't had it.

Maybe it was time to rectify that situation.

'I'm not going to go scary on you,' she told him, clutching her sketch pad to her chest. 'But you did say I could decide what we did today, and now I've decided.'

'And it's not sketching?' Chase still looked relaxed, still had his hands stretched out behind him like he was enjoying a nice morning in the sun.

'No, it's not.' Her voice still rang out, strident, aggressive. It sounded strong, even if she didn't feel it. 'I'll tell you what it is.'

'I bet I could guess…' Chase murmured and, furious that he still seemed to know her so well, she cut across him.

'It's sex. I want to have sex with you.'

Chase regarded her with lazy amusement, although he was far from feeling either lazy or amused. He knew Millie felt vulnerable and exposed, but damn it so did he. He hadn't meant to say any of that. Lost? Broken? He could have been talking about himself. What the hell had he been thinking, getting that honest? That *real*?

He hadn't been thinking at all. He'd just been acting on instinct, allowing the deep within him to call to the deep within her. And for a few charged seconds he knew they'd connected in a way that was far more powerful than anything they could do on a bed—or whatever surface they chose.

'You want to have sex with me,' Chase repeated. 'Sometimes, Millie, you have a one-track mind.'

'I'm serious, Chase. The whole reason we're having this stupid fling is—'

'Now our fling is stupid? I'm offended.'

'You know what I mean. I started this because—'

'*You* started it?'

'Stop interrupting me!'

'Because I'm the one who walked up to you on that beach, sweetheart. *And* asked you out.'

'I'm the one who suggested we sleep together.'

'I'll concede that point, but that's the only shot you're going to call.'

She stared at him, her face white, her lips bloodless. What had scared her so much? The fact that he saw her need, or that she sensed his own? And how did she think sex was going to solve anything?

On second thought…

'OK, Scary.' Chase rose from the beach, turning his face so Millie didn't see him grimace at the throbbing ache of his joints. It was getting worse. The new medication wasn't helping as much as he'd hoped. Hell, he was as broken as she was. He just hid it better.

'OK?' she repeated uncertainly, the wind blowing her hair into tangles even as she clutched the sketch pad to her chest like it was a body shield.

'OK, we'll have sex. I think we've had a fair amount of anticipation, don't you?'

'Yes.' She sounded uncertain. He wasn't surprised. She hadn't expected him to agree—well, guess what? Sex was probably the only place where he could make her let go of that all-too-precious control. Break the barriers she surrounded herself with, force her to be exposed and empty; only then could she be covered and filled.

Is that what you really want?

Yes. Certainty blazed through him, surprising him. He didn't know more than that, wouldn't look farther. *No more questions*.

Time to act.

'Come on,' he said, and reached a hand down to her. She

took it gingerly, her eyes so heartbreakingly wide, her teeth sunk deep into her lower lip.

'Where are we going?'

'I told you I prefer to make love on a bed, right?'

'Yes…'

'Cold feet?' he jibed softly, knowing she'd rise to that easy bait.

'No! Of course not!'

'Of course not,' he agreed. Yet her hand was icy-cold and her slender fingers felt like bird bones in his.

He led her back inside, through the house and then right to his bedroom door. Turned to her as he still held that icy, trembling hand. 'You're scared.'

She opened her mouth to deny it, then stopped. 'Yes.'

'You're thinking too much.'

'I know.'

'I think,' Chase murmured, 'I know a way to make you to stop thinking.' He kicked open the door and pulled her into the bedroom.

Millie felt weirdly numb as she followed Chase into the bedroom. It looked the same as it had a few hours earlier, when they'd lain in that nice, wide bed and talked and teased each other.

It *felt* totally different now.

Her heart was thudding so hard it hurt. Her mouth was dry. Her legs felt like jelly. She didn't think she'd ever felt this nervous before. Fizzing with both fear and a glorious anticipation. She wanted this, even if it scared her senseless.

Chase turned to her, his expression serious. Thoughtful. She closed her eyes and tipped her head back, waited for him to take over. Make her stop thinking.

He didn't do anything. She opened her eyes. 'What are you waiting for?'

He smiled. 'Sorry, Scary, this isn't the Chase Bryant Show.'

'You want me to do something?'

'I know you'd rather I just did everything, but since when have I ever let you have it easy?'

She let out a trembling huff of laughter. 'Sorry. It's… It's been a long time.'

'I kind of figured that out.'

She closed her eyes again, this time in embarrassment. With her eyes closed, she couldn't see him but she felt him step closer, felt the whisper of his fingers as he brushed her cheek, tucked her hair behind her ear. 'Telling you to relax isn't going to do a thing, is it?' She shook her head, felt Chase's hesitation. 'You sure you want to do this, Millie? You know you could back out now. I wouldn't— Well, yeah, I'd mind, but I'd understand. This is big for you. And scary. I get that.'

A hot lump of emotion lodged in her throat. Speaking was impossible. She just shook her head, eyes still closed. She heard Chase's soft breathing, felt his fingers gently brush her cheek again.

Finally she opened her eyes. He looked so concerned and tender as he gazed down at her that her heart seemed to seize up. Her emotions were fully engaged, much more than she'd ever intended or wanted. And, even though it terrified her, she knew bone-deep that she really *did* want this. She craved it. Not just the physical release, but the emotional intensity. *Intimacy.* How scary was that?

'I might not be doing much,' she whispered, 'but I'm not trying to leave, am I?'

'No. You're not. And thank God for that.' Slowly, deliberately, he drew her towards him, his hands cradling her face. Her heart pounded. This was it. He was going to kiss her, and then…

'Stop *thinking*, Scary.'

'I can't help it,' she groaned. 'I can't turn my mind off.'

'I realise.'

'I want to turn it off, Chase. I want to forget. I want to forget everything.' Her mouth was a whisper away from his. He gazed down at her, his eyes warm and soft with compassion as his thumbs stroked her jaw bone.

'But then you'll just have to remember again.'

'Just for a little while. I want to forget for a little while.' She drew in a shaky breath. 'Please. Make me forget. Make me forget everything.'

He smiled faintly even though she saw a shadow of concern in his eyes. 'That's kind of a tall order.'

'You're the only one who can.' And she knew she spoke the truth. '*Please*. Whatever it takes.'

In answer he kissed her, his lips brushing hers once, twice, as if getting the sense of her before he suddenly delved deep and she felt that kiss straight down to her soul. Shocks of pleasure and excitement sizzled along her nerve endings and she surrendered to that kiss, kissing him back, hands curling around his shoulders, nails digging in.

Yet even as she surrendered her mind took a step back. She started thinking. It was as if that kiss had taken over every part of her body and mind except that one dark corner where the memories crouched, waited till she was vulnerable to attack.

You never kissed Rob like this.

You shouted at him before he left for the last time.

You didn't kiss Charlotte goodbye. You didn't even look at her.

'*Easy*, Millie.' She opened her eyes and realised she'd been standing rigid, her nails like claws in Chase's shoulders.

'I'm sorry.'

'So am I.' Gently he unhooked her hands from his shoulders. 'You were doing some serious thinking there.' Chase stared at her for a moment, and then he took her by the hand and led her to the bed. He stripped off his shirt and dropped his shorts. Millie blinked. She'd seen him naked yesterday, but he was still magnificent. Beautiful, everything taut and sculpted and golden-brown.

'Now I'm naked,' he said.

'Clearly.'

'You still have your clothes on.'

'I'm aware.'

'I'm going to take them off.'

Her heart turned over. 'OK,' she said. He'd seen her naked yesterday, but that had been her choice. Her action. Now, as she stood still and he reached for the buttons on her shirt, she knew it was his. She'd just relinquished a little bit of control, just as he wanted her to. As she wanted to, even if it was so incredibly hard.

Deftly Chase's fingers undid the buttons on her polo shirt. 'Raise your arms,' he said, and she did. He slipped the shirt over her head, tossed it aside. Millie glanced down at the plain white cotton bra she wore; the straps were frayed. *Why* had she never indulged in sexy underwear? 'We'll leave that on for now,' Chase said, his mouth quirking in a small smile. 'I kind of like it.'

She practically snorted in disbelief. 'You like my old, plain white bra?'

'I know; weird, huh? But I've seen plenty of push-up monstrosities. This doesn't pretend or hide.' He touched her chin, tilting her face so she had to meet his gaze. 'Unlike you.'

'My *bra* is more honest than I am?' she huffed.

'Pretty much,' he said, and undid the snap on her capris. Millie's breath caught in her chest as Chase slid them down her legs. His touch was feather-light and swift, hardly a practised caress. And yet she felt as if she burned where his fingers had so briefly touched her. He sank to his knees as he balanced her with one hand while he used the other to help her out of the capris, then tossed them over with the shirt.

She was in her underwear. Again.

And he was naked, on his knees in front of her.

She tried not to gulp too loudly as she gazed down at him, all burnished, sleek muscle. Slowly, so slowly, he slid his hands up her legs and then held her by the hips, his palms seeming to burn right through the thin cotton of her underwear as his fingers slid over her butt. She let out a stifled cry as he brought his mouth close to the juncture of her thighs and she tensed, anticipating his touch, fearing the intensity of her own response. But he didn't touch her, just let his breath fan over her, and that was enough.

Her knees buckled.

She *felt* Chase's smile and he stood up. 'Better,' he said, and she let out a wobbly laugh. Sensation fizzed inside her. The fear lessened, replaced by a warm, honeyed desire.

Then her mind started going into hyperdrive again, memories, thoughts and fears tumbling around like a washer on spin cycle.

'Stop thinking.'

'I *can't.*'

'Then I'll have to help you.'

'Yes.' *Please.*

Wordlessly he tugged her hand and led her to the bed. Her mind was still spinning relentlessly, and she had a sudden picture of her bed back in New York, her and Rob's bed, all hospital corners and starched duvet, and how she'd sank onto it when the phone had rung, and the police had told her there had been an accident...

'Lie down.'

'OK.' She felt only relief that he was interrupting her thoughts. She wanted to stop thinking. Stop analysing. Stop remembering so much. Why did being with Chase make her remember? She'd spent two years trying *not* to think, and now the thoughts came fast and thick, unstoppable.

She needed Chase to stop them.

She lay on the bed and he knelt over her. Millie felt herself tense. 'What are you—?'

'Trust me.'

And she knew she did trust him. Amazingly. Implicitly. Yet that thought was scary too. Chase reached for something above her head, and she saw he'd taken the satin pillow-case from the pillow.

He took the pillow-case off the other pillow and Millie waited, arousal and uncertainty warring within her.

'Care to tell me what's going on?' she asked as lightly as she could.

Chase slowly slid his hand from her shoulder to her palm, lacing her fingers with his own as he raised her hand above her head.

'I'm tying you up.'

'What?' She thought he was joking. Of course he was joking. Then she realised he'd done it, and her hand was tied to the bed post with a satin pillow-case. She stared at him with wide eyes, totally shocked. Chase simply knelt there, smiling faintly, his eyes dark and serious. Waiting.

Waiting for her permission.

She drew in a deep, shuddering breath, her whole body intensely, unbearably aware. She had no room for thoughts. She said nothing.

He bent down and kissed her deeply on the mouth, another soul-stirring kiss that had her arching instinctively towards him.

And then he tied up her other hand. She lay there, her hands tied above her head, her body completely open to his caress.

Vulnerable.

This felt far more intense than anything that had happened so far between them, and she knew why Chase was doing it.

He was taking everything from her. Taking it all, so he could give.

All in.

Slowly Chase slid his hands across her tummy, over her breasts, reaching behind to unhook her bra. 'Sorry,' he whispered. 'I do like it, but it had to go eventually.'

She still couldn't speak. Especially not when he tossed the bra onto the floor and bent his head to her breasts, his tongue flicking lightly over her nipples. She arched again, her head thrown back, pleasure streaking through her like lightning—but still the thoughts.

My breasts are too small.

Rob never liked them.

I don't deserve a man like this.

'Still thinking, huh?' He lifted his head and looked at her, his voice wry even as his eyes blazed.

'Sorry,' she whispered. She wanted him to help her forget, but maybe she couldn't forget unless she first released the memories. *Shared* them.

The most terrifying thought of all.

'Don't be sorry.'

'I want to stop thinking so much. Remembering.'

'I know you do.'

'Help me,' she implored. 'Help me, Chase.'

He gazed at her, his face suffused with both tenderness and desire. What a heady combination. She felt more for him in that moment then she ever had before, and then he took another pillow-case, folded it in half and placed it over her eyes. Millie gasped aloud. Chase waited, the pillow-case folded over her eyes but not tied.

She blinked, shocked and yet knowing she needed this.

Chase was helping her, helping her in a way she'd never have expected. It was strange and scary, yet amazingly *right*.

'OK?' he asked softly and she nodded. He tied the blindfold around her eyes.

Millie lay there, trying to adjust to this new reality. Her world had shrunk to the feel, sound and scent of Chase. Her mind had no room save for the sense of him. Her body tensed in a kind of exquisite anticipation, waiting for his touch. Wondering where he would touch her, every nerve taut with glorious expectation as she lay there, helpless, *hopeful* and utterly in his control.

And then she felt his mouth between her thighs, right on the centre of her, and she let out a shudder of shocked pleasure. She had not expected *that*.

Her body writhed beneath him and she felt a pleasure so intense it was akin to pain as her body surged towards a climax. '*Chase*,' she gasped, his name a sob. And then he stopped, taking her to the brink and no further, and she ached with the loss of him. 'Chase,' she said again, and this time it was a plea.

She could hear his breathing, ragged and uneven, and his knees pressed on the outside of her thighs. She felt his heat, knew he was right above her. Where would he touch her next?

She let out a long shudder, every sense sizzling with excitement.

And then he began to touch her, a blitz of caresses that had her so focused on the sensation she could not form so much as a single coherent thought. First a butterfly brush of a kiss on her wrist. A blizzard of kisses on her throat. Then he kissed her deeply on the mouth and she responded, straining against the bonds that had brought her to this moment. He kissed her everywhere, light, teasing kisses, deep-throated demands, bites, licks and nibbles. She cried beneath him, first out of pleasure and amazement and then something deeper.

Something inside her started to break.

She'd told him she wasn't broken, and she hadn't been. She'd been holding herself together, only just, her soul and heart a maze of hairline cracks and fissures. And now, under Chase, she shattered.

Pain and pleasure, joy and sorrow, erupted from the depths of her being in helpless cries that became wrenching sobs, her whole body shaking with the force of them even as she lay there, splayed open to him, everything exposed. Everything vulnerable.

'Millie,' he said, and his voice was full of love.

'Yes,' she choked. 'Yes, Chase, *now*.'

Distantly she heard the rip of foil and knew Chase would finally be inside her. She'd never wanted anything so much, and yet she still gave a cry of surprise and joy when she felt him slide inside, fill her up.

She'd been so *empty*.

His arms came around her and Chase freed her so she enfolded her body around his, drawing him deeper inside as she buried her face in his neck and sobbed through her climax.

Chase surged inside her, deeper and deeper, and with his arms around her, holding her tightly and tenderly to him, he brought them both home.

CHAPTER EIGHT

CHASE felt his heart race as he held Millie in his arms and she sobbed as if her own heart were breaking.

God help him. God help them both. He'd never expected sex between them to be like *that*. Mind-blowing indeed. He was completely and utterly spent, emotionally, physically, everything.

Millie pressed her face against his neck, her body shaking with the force of her emotion. Chase didn't speak, knew there were no words. He just stroked her back, her hair, wiped the tears from her cheeks with his thumbs.

Millie's sobs began to subside into snuffles and hiccups, and she curled herself into him, as if she wanted to be as close to him as possible, her legs across his, her arm around his waist, her head still buried against his neck.

Chase held her, cradled her closer, even as part of him was distantly acknowledging that this had been one *hell* of a mistake.

She lifted her face from his neck and gazed up at him with rain-washed eyes. She looked so unbearably open; she'd dropped all the armour and masks. Nothing hid her from him any more, and he really wasn't sure how he felt about that. He shifted so he could hold her a bit more loosely, waiting for her to speak.

'I want to tell you,' she said quietly, hesitantly. 'I want to—to talk about my past.'

He didn't think he wanted to hear it. Chase adjusted her more securely against him, knowing she needed that. She needed him, God help them both.

'OK,' he said.

Millie glanced down, ran her hand down the length of his bare chest. Even now he reacted, felt the shower of sparks her touch created in him. He wanted to dismiss it as mere chemistry, but he knew he couldn't.

'My husband died two years ago,' Millie said, and everything, *everything* in him shrivelled.

Damn.

'I'm sorry,' he said quietly. He'd suspected some heartbreak; of course he had. How could he not? Sadness seeped from her pores. But a husband? A *widow*? He thought of all his light, deprecating jokes and inwardly winced.

Outwardly he ran his hand up and down her back, strokes meant to soothe and comfort even as his mind seethed.

'What happened?' he asked eventually, because for all her wanting to tell him everything she'd lapsed into silence.

'He died in a car accident. On the Cross Bronx expressway. A collision with an eighteen-wheeler. They think the driver fell asleep at the wheel.'

Chase swallowed. He couldn't think of anything more to say, so he just held her.

'I didn't tell you because for the last two years it's completely defined me. Everyone I know looks at me like I'm a walking tragedy.' Which she was. 'No one knows what to say to me, so they either ignore me or apologise. I hate it.'

He identified all too much with everything she said, albeit for a different reason. But he knew there was more she wasn't telling him.

'And then I feel guilty for thinking that way. Like I want to be happy, even when I know I never can be.'

'Everyone wants to be happy,' Chase said. 'You can be happy again, Millie.' But not with him. Now, he knew, was not the time to remind her they only had one week together. Four more days after this.

'I liked the fact that you didn't know,' she said quietly. 'That you treated me normally. I almost—I almost felt normal.'

'And then you felt guilty for feeling normal,' Chase supplied. What a depressing cycle.

'Yes, I suppose,' Millie said slowly. 'But more than that.' She stopped again and he knew he would have to prompt her. Coax the heartbreaking story with all its drama and tragedy out of her bit by bit.

But he didn't think he had the energy. That probably made him an incredibly shallow bastard, but he couldn't help it. He'd had his own share of depressing drama, tragedy and pain. He wasn't sure he could take Millie's.

And he knew she couldn't take his.

'We had a good marriage,' she finally said. 'I loved him.' And what was he supposed to say to *that*? She bowed her head, her hair brushing his bare chest. 'And I know no marriage, no relationship is perfect, but I look back and I see all the mistakes I made. We both made,' she allowed, her voice a throaty whisper, and Chase just let her talk. He didn't have much to offer her. He hadn't had too many serious relationships, and he'd never come close to marriage.

Yet.

Why the *hell* had he thought that?

'We grew apart,' Millie said after a moment. 'Because… because of different things. And the day he died I was sharp with him. I don't even remember what we argued about, isn't that stupid? But I didn't— I didn't kiss them—

him—goodbye. I don't think I even *said* goodbye. And Charlotte…' Her voice caught and Chase pulled her closer. He still didn't say anything. He had nothing to offer her in this moment, and he knew it. Maybe she did too.

After a ragged moment Millie slipped from his arms. He let her go, watched from the bed as she scooped up her clothes and headed towards the bathroom. 'I'm going to take a shower,' she said, her back to him so he could see all the delicate knobs of her spine, the slender dip of her waist and curve of her hip.

'OK,' Chase said, and as she closed the bathroom door he felt a shaming wave of relief.

Millie turned the knobs on the shower and rested her head on the cool tile. Her heart had stopped its thunderous racing and for a second she wondered if it still beat at all. After feeling so painfully, gloriously alive, she now felt dead inside. Numb and lifeless with disappointment.

So Chase didn't really want intense. Not the kind of intense she'd been offering as she'd lain in his arms and tried to tell him her story. Even as he put his arms around her, went through the motions, she'd felt the coldness of his emotional withdrawal. She'd violated the terms of their agreement— the terms *she* had made—and he didn't like it. Didn't want to go that deep or far.

Stupid, *stupid* her.

Drawing a shaky breath, she stepped into the shower, let the water stream over her and wash away the traces of her tears. She'd cried after the accident, of course. She'd done the counselling and the support groups and even *journalled*. But she'd never cried like that. She'd never given so much, so freely, and stupidly it made her want more. It made her want to tell him everything, about her marriage, the accident, *Charlotte*.

But within thirty seconds of speaking she'd realised Chase didn't want to know. He wasn't the only one who could read people.

Another shuddering breath and she reached for the shampoo. At least now she understood the terms: no talking about the past. Chase was all about the physical intimacy, having her melt in his arms, but the emotional stuff? Not so much. He'd liked pushing her but he didn't like the results. Well, she got that now. And it was just as well, because even if for a few shattering seconds she'd wanted to tell him everything, had maybe even thought she *loved* him, she understood now that wasn't where this was going. And when rationality had returned she'd known she didn't even want to go there. She'd loved and lost once. She wasn't going to attempt it again, and especially not with a man who was only in it for a week.

By the time she'd showered and dressed, Millie felt more herself. She'd found that icy control, and she was glad. She stepped out of the bathroom, saw the late-afternoon sun slant across the empty bed. They'd skipped lunch and, despite the emotional tornado she'd been sucked into all afternoon, she was hungry. Her stomach growled.

She wandered out to the kitchen and saw Chase talking on his mobile. She waited, far enough way so she couldn't eavesdrop, and a few seconds later he disconnected the call and gave her a quick, breezy smile.

'Good shower?'

'Fine. I'm starving, though.'

'I'm glad to hear it. I just made reservations at Straw Hat on Anguilla.'

'Anguilla? How far away is that?'

'An hour in my boat.'

'OK.' Maybe escaping the island would be a good thing. The door bell rang, and Millie watched as Chase went to answer it. She felt like everything was on fast forward, plans put in motion before she could even think.

'What's that?' she asked when he came back with several shopping bags with the resort's swirly logo on the side.

'A couple of dresses. I thought you might like something new.'

She gazed at him levelly. 'I have a whole suitcase of new clothes.'

Chase just shrugged. 'I don't think your wardrobe runs to fun and flirty.'

'Maybe I don't want *fun and flirty*.'

He sighed. 'Don't wear them if you don't want to, Millie. I just thought it might be nice for our big date.'

'Oh? So this is a big date?'

He narrowed his gaze. 'What's with you?'

'Nothing.' Somehow everything had changed between them, and not for the better. Chase wasn't as light and laughing as he'd used to be, as she *needed* him to be. He was tense and touchy, even if he was trying to act like he wasn't. And so was she.

'Fine. I'll take a look.' She reached for the bags and caught Chase's bemused look. 'Thank you,' she added, belatedly and ungraciously.

Chase's mouth quirked in a smile that seemed all too sad. 'No problem,' he said quietly, and she retreated to the bedroom.

Half an hour later she was on Chase's boat, wearing a shift dress of cinnamon-coloured silk as they cruised towards Anguilla.

Chase had shed his blazer and tie and rolled the sleeves up of his crisp white shirt to navigate the boat. He looked amazing.

They hadn't said much since the exchange in the kitchen, and the silence was making Millie twitchy. She wanted that fun, teasing banter back, the ease she'd felt in Chase's presence. She'd told him he'd made her uncomfortable, but it was nothing like this.

Moodily she stared out at the sea. The sun was already slipping towards the horizon. A third sunset. Only four more to go and their week would be over. And by mutual agreement, they would never see each other again.

Chase left the tiller to come and sit next to her, the wind ruffling his hair as he squinted into the dying sun. He didn't ask her what she was thinking, didn't say anything, and Millie knew he didn't want to know. He'd only pushed her when he thought she'd push back, not give in. It was the anticipation that had been fun for him, the moment before.

Not the moment after.

'So how come you have a villa on St Julian's if you didn't want to have anything to do with the Bryant business?' she asked when the silence had stretched on long enough to make her want to fidget.

Chase kept his gaze on the darkening sea. 'My grandfather bequeathed the island to my brothers and me, and my father couldn't do anything about it. As soon as I'd established myself I had the villa built. I hardly ever use it, actually, but it was a way to thumb my nose at my father—even if he was dead.'

'It must have hurt, to have him disinherit you,' Millie said quietly.

Chase shrugged. 'It didn't feel good.'

'What about your mother?'

'She died when I was twelve. Breast cancer.'

'I'm sorry.'

Another shrug. Clearly he didn't like talking about any of this, but at least he was giving answers. And Millie knew she wanted to know.

'And your brothers? Do you get along well with them?'

He sighed, raked a hand through his hair. 'More or less. Aaron is nice enough, but he views life as a game of Monopoly where he has all the money. Luke is my middle brother, and he's always been trying to prove himself. Total workaholic.'

'And where do you fit in?'

'Black sheep, basically, who only semi-made-good.'

'Are they married?'

'Nope, none of us seem eager to take the plunge.' He spoke evenly, almost lightly, but she still heard the warning. *Oh, fabulous.* So after this afternoon he thought she was going to go all doe-eyed on him, start dreaming of happily-ever-afters. She'd only done that for a *second*.

'And you get along?'

'More or less.'

It didn't sound like the best family situation. She was blessed to have parents and a sister who loved and supported her, but even they hadn't been able to break down her walls or keep her from hiding behind the rubble.

Only Chase had done that.

She let out a restless sigh, knowing she needed to stop thinking this way, wanting something from Chase he couldn't give. Ironic, really, that she'd assumed he was shallow, then believed he wasn't, only to discover he really was. And, while she'd wanted shallow before, she didn't want it now.

'And what about you? You have family around?' Chase asked.

'Parents and a sister.'

'Are you close with them?'

'Yes.' She paused, because even though she was close she hadn't told them as much about her marriage as she had Chase.

'Not that close, huh?' Chase said, sounding cynical, and

Millie shook her head. She couldn't bear for him to think that her family was like his, or that her life had been all sadness.

'No, actually, we are. My sister Zoe is fantastic. She stops by almost every week with my favourite snack, makes sure I'm not working too hard.'

'Your favourite snack?'

'Nachos with fake cheese.'

He let a short laugh. 'That is so low-brow. I was expecting dark chocolate or some exotic sorbet.'

'I don't play to type *that* much,' she said lightly, and for a moment everything was at it had been, the lightness, the fun. Then something shuttered in Chase's eyes and he turned away to gaze at the sea.

'We're almost there.' He rose and went to trim the sail as the lights of Anguilla loomed closer, shimmering on the surface of the tranquil sun-washed sea. They didn't speak as he moored the boat and then helped her onto the dock.

The restaurant was right on the sand, the terracotta-tile and white-stucco building one of a jumble along the beach. It felt surprisingly refreshing to be out of the rarefied atmosphere of St Julian's, to see people who weren't just wealthy guests. A rail-thin cat perched along the wall that lined the beach, and a few children played with a ball and stick in the dusky light.

Millie slowed her steps as she watched the children. One of the girls had a mop of dark curls. She looked to be about five years old, a little older than Charlotte would have been.

'Millie?' Chase reached for her hand and she realised she'd been just standing there, staring. Children had been invisible to her for two years; it was as if her brain knew she couldn't handle it and just blanked them out. She didn't see them in her building, in the street, in the park. It helped that her life was so work-focused; there weren't many children on Wall Street.

Yet she saw them now, saw them in all their round-cheeked innocence, and felt her raw and wounded heart give a death-defying squeeze.

'Millie,' Chase said again quietly and slowly she turned away from the raggedy little group. She wanted to rail at him, to beat her fists against his chest.

See? See what you did to me? I was fine before, I was surviving, and now you've opened up this need and hope in me and you don't even want it any more.

Swallowing, she lifted her chin and followed Chase into the restaurant. The place was a mix of funky Caribbean decor and fresh, well-prepared food. The waiter greeted Chase by name and ushered them to the best table in the restaurant, in a semi-secluded alcove.

'What's this? A huge ashtray?' Millie gestured to the rectangular box of sand in the middle of the table.

'Nope, just a little sand box to play with while we wait for our food.' He took a little spade lying next to the box and handed it to her with a glinting smile. 'Dig in.'

'Clearly meant for guests with short attention spans.' She scooped a bit of sand with the miniature spade and dumped it out again. 'So do you like being an architect?'

'All these questions.'

She glanced up sharply. 'It's called conversation, generally.' She heard an edge to her voice, knew he heard it too. So *now* he didn't like the questions.

Chase leaned back in his chair and took a sip of sparkling water. 'I like making things. I like having an idea and seeing it become a reality.'

'What firm do you work for?'

His mouth quirked upwards. 'Chase Bryant Designs.'

'Your own.'

'Yep, started it five years ago.' He spoke casually, but she heard a betraying note of pride in his voice. He'd made something of himself, and without help from his wealthy family. She wanted to tell him she admired that, that she was proud of him, but how stupid would that be? He'd just feel even more awkward. So she took a large gulp of wine, and then another, deciding that alcohol was a better option.

'Slow down there, Scary,' Chase said, eyeing her near-empty wine glass. 'Or I'll have to carry you home.'

'I'm not a lightweight.'

'No, indeed.' Now she heard an edge in his voice, and she pushed her wine glass away with a little sigh of irritation.

'Look, Chase, why don't you just come out and say it?'

He stilled. Stared. 'Say what?'

'You're done.'

'*I'm* done?'

'Yes. Ever since—' She paused, swallowed. 'It's obvious you've had your bout of intense sex and you're ready to move on. So maybe we should call it a day. A night. Whatever.' She grabbed her wine glass again and drained it, half-wishing she hadn't started this conversation.

Half-wishing even now he'd tell her she was wrong.

'You're the one who has been picking fights,' Chase said mildly. 'I bought you a dress and took you out to one of the best restaurants in the whole Caribbean. So, sorry, I don't get where you're coming from.'

She met his gaze squarely. 'You don't?' she asked quietly, no edge, no spite. Just raw honesty.

Chase held her gaze for a breathless beat and then glanced away. 'No, I don't,' he said quietly, and she felt that tiny tendril of hope she'd still been nurturing even without knowing it shrivel and die.

It hurt that, after all they'd experienced and shared, he wouldn't even own up to how things had changed. It hurt far too much.

She'd known this man for three days. Yet time had lost its

meaning in this surprising paradise; time had lost its meaning ever since she'd agreed to have this fling—this intense, intimate, all-in fling—with Chase.

For a second Millie almost rose from the table and walked out of the restaurant. She didn't need this. She didn't need Chase. Then the waiter came and they gave their orders, and the impulse passed, her strength fading away.

For it was weakness why she stayed. A weakness for him. That little tendril of hope might have withered and died, but its seed still remained in the stubborn soil of her heart, desperate to grow.

Chase watched the emotions—disappointment, hurt, sorrow—ripple across Millie's face like shadows on water, wishing he couldn't read her so easily. Wishing he wasn't screwing up so badly right now.

Nothing had been the same since the sex, and more importantly since the conversation after the sex. He'd pushed and pushed Millie, had wanted to see her lose that control, had wanted to be the one to make it happen. And when it had, and she'd taken a flying leap over that cliff, what had he done?

He'd backed away, and pretended he hadn't. Acted like he was still right there with her, flying through the air, when she knew he'd really high-tailed it in the other direction.

Coward. *Bastard.*

He took a sip of water and stared moodily around at the restaurant. He'd always enjoyed this place, found it fun and relaxing, but not this time. Now he didn't think anything would kick-start his mood. He wanted the fun back with Millie, the easy companionship they'd had. He hadn't even realised just how easy it had been, until now.

Now words tangled in his throat and he couldn't get any of it out. Couldn't even begin. What to say? *I'm sorry. I'm sorry I'm not there for you, when you thought I would be. When you wanted me to be and I just couldn't do it.*

Hell, this was all his fault. He should have listened to that cool, rational part of his brain that had told him to walk away from this woman before she drove him insane. Who said no to 'intense', no to a fling, no to anything with Millie Lang.

Instead he'd done the opposite, followed his libido and even his heart, and now he had no idea what to do. He hated seeing the deepening frown lines on Millie's face, the worry marks on her lip fresher and more raw than ever. As he watched a little bright-red pearl of blood appeared on her lower lip from where she'd bitten it.

Damn. Damn it to hell.

'Millie…' He reached over, placed his hand on hers. She looked up, eyes wide, teeth sunk into that lip. 'I'm sorry,' he said in a low voice. 'I've totally screwed this up.'

Tears filled those soft brown eyes and she blinked hard as she shook her head, teeth biting even deeper. 'No. I'm the one who screwed up. I shouldn't have said all that…after. That wasn't part of our deal.'

'I led you to it.'

She arched an eyebrow, somehow managed a smile. This woman was *strong*. 'By tying me up and blindfolding me?'

'Basically.'

'Have you ever done that kind of thing before?' she asked, curious, and he actually blushed.

'No.'

'Me neither.'

'Yeah, I pretty much figured that out.'

She let out a laugh that trembled just a little too much. 'Oh, Chase, I just want it back.'

He eyed her warily. 'Back?'

'You. Me. *Us.* I was having fun, you know, and that felt

really good.' She gave him a wobbly smile that felt like a dagger thrust to the heart. 'It felt amazing.'

And he knew she was right. It *had* felt amazing. More amazing than anything else he'd ever had or known. Why was he pushing it away?

Four more days.

'Come on,' he said roughly. He rose from the table, nearly knocking over their drinks as he threw down some bills. 'Let's get out of here.'

She rose also, taking his hand as he threaded his way through the table. 'Where are we going?'

'To a room. A room with a bed.'

'Or any convenient surface?' she murmured, and something close to fierce joy pulsed through him.

'That's about the size of it,' he agreed, and led her out into the night.

Millie didn't ask questions, didn't say anything at all as he led her away from the beach and towards the street. He hailed a cab, thanked God one screeched to the kerb in three seconds flat and then hauled her inside it.

Still no speaking. Would words break what was between them? Chase didn't know. Was afraid to find out. And yet he had words, so many words, words he needed to say and, more importantly, she needed to hear.

But, first, a room. A bed.

'Cap Juluca,' he told the cab driver, and Millie just arched an eyebrow. 'It's a resort here,' Chase explained, his voice still rough with want. 'I booked it in case we didn't feel like sailing back.'

And that was all that was said as they drove away from Meads Bay, down the coast, through the resort's gates, and then up to the main building. Chase kept hold of her hand as he checked in and then led her away from the main complex towards the private cove that housed their accommodation.

Millie skidded to a stop. 'A grass hut? Seriously?'

'A luxurious grass hut,' Chase said and tugged her inside.

Millie glanced around and he could see her taking in the polished mahogany floor, the comfortable rattan chairs, the gauzy mosquito netting. And the bed. A wide, low bed with linen sheets and soft pillows, the ocean lapping only metres away through the draped net curtains. The wind rustled through the woven grass that made up the roof and walls.

She turned to him. 'It's beautiful.'

'You're beautiful,' he said, a catch in his voice, and she shook her head.

'I don't need flattery, Chase. I know I'm not beautiful.' She sounded so matter-of-fact, it made his heart twist inside him.

'Why do you think you aren't beautiful?'

'Even you called me scary. And I know I'm not your usual type.' She let out a long, low breath. 'Look, I'm not asking for something from you that you're not willing to give. I promise.'

And he knew he'd driven her to that confession. Knew she thought he'd had cold feet and, hell, he *had*. Except now he felt his heart twist and turn inside him and he wanted her all over again, in his bed, in his life.

'Come here,' he murmured, and kissed her, slow and deep. She kissed him back, her hands fisting in his hair, her body pressed hard against his.

Somehow they made it to the bed, stumbling and tripping, shedding clothes. She pulled him down on top of her, hands sliding over skin, drawing him closer. 'I want to touch you,' she muttered against his throat, licking the salt from his skin. 'Last time I never got to touch you.'

And he wanted to be touched. He rolled over on his back, let out a shuddering sigh as he spread his arms wide, submitted to her desires. 'Touch me, Scary. Touch me all you want.'

She laughed and slowly ran her hand down his chest, across the smooth skin of his hip, and then wrapped her hand around his erection. 'All I want?'

'Hell, yes.'

She laughed again low in her throat, a seductress filled with power. He liked—no, he *loved*—seeing her this way, confident, strong, sensual. She kissed her way down his chest, lingering in certain places, blitzing quick caresses in others, and left his whole body on fire. His hands tangled in her hair as she moved lower.

'Millie…'

'You said all I want,' she reminded him huskily, and took him in her mouth.

Lord have mercy. He closed his eyes, all thought obliterating as she moved on him. All he could feel was Millie. All he could think was Millie.

Millie.

His hips jerked and he let out a cry; she moved so quickly he barely registered the change as she sank on top of him so he filled her up and she set the pace, her hands behind her, braced on his thighs. Chase didn't have much left in him. He grabbed hold of her hips and arched to meet her, his eyes closed, his head thrown back, everything in him a surrender.

A joy.

'Millie,' he said aloud, groaning her name. 'Millie.'

She came on top of him, her body tensing gloriously and then drooping over him as her hair brushed his cheek and she let out a long, well-satisfied sigh.

Chase let out another shuddering breath. This woman was going to kill him if she kept this up. He felt the thunder of his heart, and knew it was more of a danger than he ever really wanted to admit.

But it would be a wonderful way to die.

CHAPTER NINE

MILLIE gazed out at the ocean, little more than a *shooshing* of waves in the darkness. A tiny sliver of moonlight glinted off the dark waters. The air felt cool now, chilling her overheated skin. Chase had fallen asleep after they'd made love—no, *had sex*—and she'd dozed for a bit before, restless, she'd prowled out here and come to sit on the hard, cool sand by the shore, her knees drawn up to her chest.

The problem, she thought, was for her it *had* been making love. Love, that dreaded word, that fearful concept. She was falling in love with him and had a terrible feeling it was too late to stop the descent. And descent is what it was, straight down to hell, to that underworld of fear and guilt where every day you wondered if this would be your last one of happiness.

Plenty of people, she reminded herself, had second chances. Plenty of people were bereaved and moved on with life, found someone else to risk it all for. Plenty of people, but not her. She just didn't think she was made that way, couldn't imagine breaking her heart all over again.

And what about Chase? Even if he was interested in taking their fling past this week, he'd surely want more than she could give. Marriage, maybe even children. The thought had a shudder of both longing and terror ripping through her.

All foolish fairy-tales, anyway, because Chase wasn't interested in any of that. He'd wanted the fun back, just like she had wanted, but no more. And she got that now. They'd play by his rules from now on, and they would be her rules too.

'I wondered where you'd gone.'

Millie stiffened at the sound of Chase's sleep-husked voice. He made her think of rumpled bed covers and salty skin. The way she'd abandoned herself to him just a few hours ago and how she'd gloried in it.

'I couldn't sleep.'

She heard the whisper of sand as he came closer. 'No?'

'No. I'm afraid I'm a bit of an insomniac. Comes with the job, unfortunately.'

'Have you checked the stock market today?' Chase asked, only half-teasing, but Millie stiffened in sudden realisation.

She hadn't. She hadn't checked the stock market in over forty-eight hours. Good Lord.

'Of course,' she answered breezily, but it was a beat too late.

'Liar,' Chase said softly, and came to sit beside her, clad only in boxers, his bare thigh inches from her own. She'd been intimate with him in so many ways, yet the feel of his leg next to hers still gave her the shivers.

'If I haven't checked, it's only because I can't get reception on your boat.'

'You're a terrible liar, you know that? You haven't checked because you haven't thought of it, and that scares you more than anything.'

Millie said nothing. She was falling in love with him, and even though her body still tingled from where it had been joined to his she knew it was the last thing he wanted.

'The stock market will live without me for a few days.'

'I suppose the more relevant question is, will you live without it?'

She angled her head so she was half-facing him, but she

couldn't make out his expression in the darkness. 'I'm here, aren't I?'

'Why did you leave my bed?'

'Oh, is this some caveman thing? Or is it just playboy pride?'

'Playboy pride?'

'You know, you've got to be the one who walks away first.' She tried to keep her voice light and teasing—banter, damn it—but she knew she'd failed. Chase didn't answer, and when he finally spoke it was too soft, too sad.

'I'm not walking away, Millie.'

'Yet. You have four more days, remember, and I take contract violations very seriously.'

Chase didn't say anything and Millie felt herself start to go brittle. Keeping up her side of the bargain was exacting a high price. Why couldn't he play along? Wasn't that what he wanted?

'When did things start to go wrong with your husband?' *What?* Millie froze, stared straight ahead. 'Is that why you still feel guilty?'

She drew a strangled breath. 'Why are you asking me these things now?'

'Because I should have asked them before. When you wanted to tell me.'

'Should have,' she repeated, and Chase gave a little nod. 'I know.'

She shook her head, decisive now. Needing to be. 'Look, Chase, I fully admit I was kind of vulnerable after we—after we had sex.' It had been so much than just sex. So much more than what she'd thought she wanted. 'That was kind of the whole point of the exercise, wasn't it?' she added, still trying, desperately, to tease.

'Are you calling the best sex you've ever an *exercise*?'

The best sex she'd ever had. And she couldn't deny it,

because it was true. Even if it hadn't been just sex. 'You know what I mean.'

'I know I wanted you to lose control but then I didn't know what to do when you did. I'm sorry for that.'

'Yeah. Well.' She scooped up a handful of damp sand and let it trickle through her fingers. 'It doesn't really matter.'

'How can you say that?'

'Because it's true. That—that conversation was just a momentary weakness. I'm over it now.'

'I'm not.'

She felt the first prickle of annoyance. 'Why are you doing this? I thought you'd be relieved.'

'You were going to tell me something else, something more than what you'd already told me.'

'No, I wasn't.'

'The real reason you carry all this sadness around. The reason you can't let it go.'

She felt her heart freeze in her chest, so for a moment she couldn't breathe. Couldn't think. 'If I seem sad, it's because my husband and—because my husband died. I think that would be obvious.' She turned to glare at him, forced herself to keep that angry stare.

Chase looked levelly back, eyes slightly narrowed, thinking. Figuring her out. 'If you won't tell me,' he said quietly, 'then maybe I should guess.'

'*Guess*?'

'Just like I did with your apartment and job and whole lifestyle.'

'Don't.'

'I know I messed up, Millie, but I want to make it right now.'

'It's too late.' She hugged her knees to her chest, amazed that even in the Caribbean she felt cold. *Icy.* 'Why bother anyway, Chase? We only have a few more days together.'

He had no answer to that, and she didn't expect him to. He still only wanted a week.

Chase stared at Millie's taut profile and tried to order his thoughts. He had to get this right. For an instant he'd wondered if he should stop pushing her, but a deeper instinct told him she needed this. Regardless of what did or didn't happen between them, she needed this reckoning. This release.

The only trouble was, he had no idea what sorrow she was still hiding.

'So.' He let out a long, considering breath. 'You said you and your husband grew apart over different things.' No answer. He really didn't have a clue how to go about this. Mentally he reviewed the facts he knew about Millie Lang: she was a hedge-fund manager; she'd been married; her semi-estranged husband had died in a car accident two years ago. Those were the basics, but what else?

She bit her lip when she was anxious. She was obsessive about work. She'd mentioned someone named Charlotte…

Charlotte.

Her words just now came back to him, and gears clicked into place. *If I seem sad, it's because my husband and— because my husband died.*

Someone else had died in that accident. Someone, he suspected, named Charlotte.

'Was your husband having an affair?' he asked quietly and she stared at him in blatant surprise.

'Why on earth would you think that?'

'You said you grew apart.' He racked his brain. 'Over different things.'

'Not that far apart.'

'So what did you disagree on?'

'It doesn't matter.'

'That is so far from the truth, Millie, that it's almost funny.' He laid one hand on her wrist, felt the desperate flutter of her pulse under his fingers. 'It matters so much you made me promise not to talk about your past at all.'

'I *told* you about my past.'

'Not all of it.' Of that he was certain.

'Enough,' she whispered, and it was a confession. There was more. There was more she wasn't telling him and, while he might not need to know, she needed to tell. He knew that, knew it with the same instinctive certainty that he'd known how to make her come alive in his arms.

He decided to risk a shot in the dark. 'Why do you never talk about Charlotte?'

Her mouth gaped open silently; he would have found her expression funny in almost any other situation. Now he found it heartbreaking. She looked like he'd just punched her in the gut. Like he'd broken her heart.

'Don't,' she finally whispered, and there was so much pain in her voice he almost backed down. He almost took her in his arms and told her he wouldn't ask anything more if she'd just smile and tease him again.

'Charlotte died in the accident with your husband,' he said instead, and heard how raw his own voice sounded. This was hard for him too. 'Didn't she?'

Millie just gave a little shake of her head, her gaze unfocused, and Chase knew she was still asking him to stop. He wouldn't.

'Who was she, Millie? Someone important to you, obviously.' She said nothing, just set her jaw and stared out to sea. Chase's first thought was that Charlotte had been her husband's mistress. Someone Millie refused to talk about or acknowledge. But as he gazed at her set profile he realised that was totally off. He knew Millie better than that. Charlotte wasn't somebody she'd hated; she was somebody she'd *loved*. Millie didn't talk about emotion or affection, and certainly not love. And, if she was willing to talk about her husband's death but not Charlotte's, then this Charlotte had to be someone even more precious to her.

Then it came to him. And it was so obvious and awful that for a moment he couldn't speak. He pictured Millie only hours ago, naked above him, and remembered those two silvery lines that had wavered just under her navel. He was a guy, and he didn't know a lot about that kind of stuff, but he still knew what they were.

Stretch marks.

'Charlotte was your daughter, wasn't she?' he said quietly, and in answer Millie let out a soft cry and buried her face in her hands.

Chase felt his heart pound and his own throat tighten with emotion. 'She died in the accident with your husband.' Millie's shoulders shook and Chase felt his eyes sting. 'Oh, Millie. I'm sorry. I'm so sorry.' Then he pulled her into his arms, just the comfort of his embrace, because he didn't have any words. She didn't resist, just buried her face in the curve of his neck as her body shook with the force of her sobs.

He thought she'd cried before, when they'd made love. He thought he'd breached all of her defences then, but he knew now she'd clung to this last desperate barrier. Her sobs were torn from deep within her, the raw, guttural sounds of an animal in pain.

Chase stroked her back, her hair, murmured words he wasn't even aware he was saying. 'Sweetheart, it's OK to cry. Let yourself cry, Millie. Let yourself cry, my love.'

My love. Distantly the words penetrated the haze of his own feeling. He loved her. Of course he did. It didn't even surprise him. It felt too right for that.

Chase didn't know how long Millie cried, how long he sat there holding her in his arms, the night soft and dark all around them. Time ceased to matter.

Eventually, after minutes or hours, Millie pulled away from him and sniffed.

'Rob wanted me to get an abortion. That's when things started to go wrong.' Chase didn't speak, just gazed at her steadily, his hand folded over hers. He wasn't going through the motions this time. He was feeling it, all of it, and it *hurt*. Loving someone—feeling her pain—it hurt.

Millie let out a shuddering breath. 'We'd been dating since college, but we waited to get married. We wanted everything to be right—our careers established, to be able to buy our own apartment. We'd thought about kids, but decided not to try till later. Rob was a lawyer, and he was completely focused on his career, like I was on mine. We both liked it that way.' She stared at him almost fiercely, as if he had disagreed. 'We *did.*'

'I believe you,' he said quietly.

'Then I fell pregnant, several years before we planned on starting a family. I was thirty.' She fell silent, lost in memory, and Chase just stroked his fingers over hers, light little touches to remind her that he was here. He was listening. 'I was surprised,' she said slowly, 'but I was OK with it. It was a few years earlier than we'd planned, but...' She shrugged. 'I thought we'd adjust.'

'And your husband didn't?'

'Rob wanted to become partner before we had kids. It was really important to him, and I understood that. We'd had a plan, and he wanted to stick to it.' She glanced at him with wide, troubled eyes. 'Don't hate him.'

Don't hate him? Of course he hated him. He hated everything about the selfish bastard. Chase squeezed her hand. 'I think it's more important that you don't hate him.'

'I don't,' she said quickly. 'I never did. I felt...sad. And guilty, like it was my fault for changing the plan.'

'It takes two, you know.'

She gave a tiny, mirthless smile. 'I know. But it was creating a lot of stress in our marriage, and so… I agreed to have the abortion.'

Chase's fingers stilled on hers. This he hadn't expected. 'You did?'

She nodded, biting her lip hard as a single tear tracked its way down her cheek. 'I did. I'd convinced myself it was for the best. That our marriage was more important than—than a baby.' She glanced down at her lap, wiping away that one tear with her fingers. 'I couldn't go through it. I went to the appointment, and I sat in the waiting room, and when they called my name…I was literally sick.'

'You have a habit of doing that in tense situations.'

She let out a soft huff of shaky laughter. 'Emotional situations. When it comes to buying and selling stock I have nerves of steel.'

'I bet.'

'I went home and told Rob I couldn't do it. And he accepted that. He did.' She glanced up quickly. 'I'm not revising history, I promise. He wasn't a bad man. I loved him.'

Chase said nothing. He didn't trust himself to offer an opinion on Rob. 'And then she was born,' Millie said softly. 'And she was beautiful. I never thought I was particularly maternal, and in a lot of ways I wasn't. I never got the hang of breastfeeding, and I couldn't even fold up the stroller.' She gave a little shake of her head. 'That thing always defeated me.'

'There are more important things.'

'I know. And I loved her. I did.' She sounded like she was trying to convince him, and Chase had no idea why. He'd never doubt Millie's love for her child. She might hate talking about emotions, but she had them. She could love someone deeply—if she let herself. And if the person she loved let her.

'I went back to work when Charlotte was three weeks old,'

Millie said after a moment. She sounded subdued now, her voice flattening out. 'I had to. Hedge-fund managers don't get a lot of maternity leave. It's still a man's field. And I worked long hours—ten- and twelve-hour days. We had a nanny, Lucinda. She saw a hell of a lot more of Charlotte than I did.'

'That doesn't make you a bad mother.'

'No.' Millie was silent for a moment, her eyes reddened and puffy, her face set in its familiar determined lines. 'But if someone had told me that I would only have her for two years, if I had ever realised how short my time with her would be…' She paused, looking up at Chase with such bleakness that he fought not to cry himself. 'I would have quit my job in an instant. In a *heartbeat*.'

'No one ever knows that kind of thing,' he said quietly. His throat was so clogged his voice came out hoarse. 'No one can ever know how long they have.' He certainly didn't.

'I know. But I wish I had thought of it. I wish I had realised. I wish—' Her voice broke, and she forced herself to continue. 'I wish I had said goodbye when Rob took her out that day. They were going to a petting farm out on Long Island. And I had to go into the office—on a Saturday—and was in a tizz about some client's meltdown. So I pushed them both out the door and didn't look back once.'

'Oh, Millie.' He took her in his arms again, this time because he needed to touch her. He pressed his cheek against the warm silk of her hair and closed his eyes, then repeated his question. 'Why don't you ever talk about Charlotte?'

'I can't. Couldn't.' Her voice was muffled against his chest. 'My family understood, they waited for me to talk first, and I never did. People at work felt too awkward, so they said nothing. I went to all the counselling and support groups and just talked about Rob. I could talk about that, I could say all the right things. But Charlotte…' Her voice choked. 'God, I miss her so much.' And then she began to cry again, silent, shaking sobs. 'I want to move on, I want to be happy again, but I'm terrified,' she said through her tears. 'Terrified of forgetting her somehow, and terrified to lose someone again.' She dragged her arm across her eyes. 'I could never go through that heartache again.'

Chase felt as if her words were falling into the emptiness inside him, echoing through all that silence. *I could never.* 'Of course you couldn't,' he murmured, and as he continued to stroke her hair, her back, holding her so achingly close, he felt the hope that had been blooming inside him wither and die.

Millie stared at the sand, wiping her cheeks of the last of her tears. Her body felt weak and boneless with exhaustion. She'd never cried so much, not even when she'd first learned of her husband and daughter's deaths. Yet they had been good tears this time. Healing tears. Telling Chase about Charlotte had been like lancing a wound. Painful and necessary, and now afterwards, she felt a surprising and thankful relief.

She glanced up at him, felt a rush of love at his serious expression, his eyes shadowed with concern. She loved him. She loved him for making her laugh, but she loved him more for making her cry. He'd known she needed to. He knew her so well, had known her since he'd first crossed the beach to ask her why she wasn't painting.

'Thank you,' she said softly, and Chase gave a small smile and nodded. She reached over and laced her fingers with his. He squeezed her hand and that reassured her. She wasn't exactly sure what he was thinking, or if he was freaked out now, the way he had been when she'd first told him about Rob. She didn't know what the future could possibly hold.

After all this, did Chase still want to walk away in another few days? Did she?

Loving someone was painful, messy, hard. And wonderful. Life-sustaining. Now that she'd felt all that again, could she even think of living without it?

'Let's go back to bed,' Chase said, and tugged her gently to her feet. Millie followed him back into the hut, slid into bed and pulled the cool linen sheets over both their bodies.

For a single second they both lay there, not touching, and her heart felt suspended in her chest. Then Chase pulled her to him, tucking her body to curve around his, his arm around her waist, his fingers threaded with hers.

Millie felt all the tension, anxiety and sadness leave her body in a fast, flowing river, and all that was left was tiredness—and peace. She closed her eyes, her lips curving in a tiny smile of true contentment, and slept.

When she woke she was alone in bed, and sunlight filtered through the net curtains that blew in the ocean breeze. Millie rolled over in bed, blinked up at the grass roof as memories and emotions tumbled through her. Then she smiled.

She slipped on her discarded silk shift, because even though the cove they were in was private she didn't know how private. Then she stepped out of the hut onto the sun-warmed sand and went in search of Chase.

There weren't many places for him to go, unless he'd gone over to the main part of the resort to fetch them some breakfast. He wasn't on their little stretch of beach, or anywhere in sight. Deciding he must have gone for breakfast after all, she went to the separate enclosure that housed the bathroom facilities, including a sumptuous, sunken tub of blue-black granite. She'd just stepped into the little hut, a smile still on her face, when she stilled. Tried to process the sight in front of her.

Chase lay on the floor, his face the colour of chalk, unconscious.

CHAPTER TEN

MILLIE didn't know how long she stood there staring, her mind seeming to have frozen in shocked disbelief. Too long, but finally she moved forward, knelt down, and tried to feel his pulse with fingers too numb to feel anything.

Finally she was able to detect his pulse, but she had no idea if it was normal. It seemed thin and thready, but maybe all pulses did.

'Chase.' She touched his face; his skin felt clammy. Her stomach cramped. '*Chase.*'

Nothing.

What had happened? What was *wrong* with him?

Taking a shuddering breath, Millie rose from the cold stone floor of the hut and hurried back to their sleeping accommodation. She scrabbled through her handbag for her mobile phone, the phone she hadn't checked in days.

'Please...' she whispered, and breathed a silent prayer of relief when she saw the row of bars that indicated reception. Then she dialled 911. She realised she didn't even know if Anguilla had emergency services, or a 911 number, so when she heard someone answer she nearly wept.

The questions the operator fired at her made her brain freeze again.

'Where are you located?'

'A resort…' She scrambled to remember the name. 'Cap something.'

'Cap Juluca?'

'Yes.'

'Can you tell me what happened?'

'I don't know. I went into the bathroom and he was just lying there, unconscious. I—I can't wake him up.' Terror temporarily closed her throat as memories attacked her.

There's been an accident. Critical condition… Come immediately…

When she'd got to the hospital, it had been too late.

Now, as if from a great distance, she heard the woman on the other end of the line tell her an ambulance would be coming within ten minutes.

'Please go to the scene of the accident and wait.'

The scene of the accident. The words caused an instinctive, visceral response to rise up in her and she almost gagged. She could not believe this was happening again.

The stone was cold under her bare knees as she knelt by Chase, held his cold hand and waited for the ambulance to come. Once he stirred, eyelids fluttering, and hope rose like a wild thing inside her, beating with hard, desperate wings. Then he lapsed back into unconsciousness and she bit her lip so hard she tasted blood. In the distance she heard the mournful, urgent wail of the ambulance.

The next hour passed in a blur of shock and fear. Still unconscious, Chase was loaded into the ambulance. Millie went with him, tried to answer questions she had no idea about.

Does he have any medical conditions you know about?

Does he take any medications?

Does he have any allergies?

She couldn't answer a single one. She felt swamped with ignorance, drowning in it. She loved him, she loved him so much, yet in this moment she couldn't help him. She could do nothing…just as before.

At one point in that endless ride to the hospital Chase regained consciousness, his eyelids fluttering before he opened his eyes and focused blearily on her. Millie's heart leapt into her throat.

'Chase…'

He smiled and relief flooded through her. It was all going to be OK. Everything, him, *them*, was going to be all right. Then he glanced around and she saw comprehension come coldly to him. That joyous light winked out and he turned his head away from her. Millie put her hand over his; Chase moved his away. She swallowed, trying not to feel the sting of rejection. They were in an ambulance; everything was confused, nerve-wracking. It didn't mean anything.

She ended up sitting in the emergency waiting room, exhausted and chilled despite the sultry Caribbean air, waiting for someone to tell her something. Anything.

Finally a nurse came through the double door and clicked her way across the tile floor. 'Mr Bryant may see you now,' she said, and with murmured thanks Millie followed her back through those double doors and into a utilitarian hospital room. Chase was sitting up in the bed, his face pale but otherwise looking healthy. Looking like himself. Relief poured through her just at the sight of him, healthy, whole, safe.

'Chase.' She started forward, wanting to cling to him but hanging back because she still didn't know what had happened.

'Hello, Millie.'

'Did they find out what happened to you? I saw you on the bathroom floor and I was so scared—but you're all right?' She glanced at him as if checking for signs of— what? Chase wasn't saying anything. He wasn't even looking at her. 'Chase?' she asked uncertainly, her voice seeming to echo through the room, and finally he looked at her.

'I have leukaemia, Millie.'

'Wh-what?' The words felt like no more than a jumble of syllables, nonsensical. 'Did they just *tell* you that? Because surely they'd have to do all sorts of tests first?'

He shook his head, the movement one of impatience. 'I've known for eight months and…' He let out a weary breath. 'Nine days. I passed out this morning because I'm on a new medication that can cause dizziness. I had a dizzy spell and hit my head on the tub.'

Millie just blinked. Her mind was spinning in hopeless circles, still unable to make sense of what he'd said. 'You have leukaemia?' she finally asked, as if he hadn't just told her.

'Chronic myeloid leukaemia.'

She sank slowly into a chair, simply because her legs would no longer hold her. She stared at him, speechless, while he gazed back all too evenly. She could not tell what he was feeling, but she was pretty sure it wasn't good.

'I'm sorry,' she finally said, and he inclined his head in cool acknowledgement. 'Why…?' Her throat was so dry she had to wait a moment to swallow and be able to speak. 'Why didn't you tell me?'

'You can really ask me that?'

'You didn't want me to know?'

'Obviously.'

She recoiled a bit, hurt by the coolness in his tone. Why was he pushing her away *now*? 'I can understand that, Chase, but I thought— I thought after I'd—' She stopped, unwilling to articulate what she'd hoped and believed when he was gazing at her so evenly, so *unhelpfully*. 'Tell me more,' she finally whispered.

'More?'

'About the leukaemia.'

He shrugged. 'What do you want to know? It's leukae-mia, Millie. Bone cancer. I take a medication which keeps it under control but my symptoms had started getting worse, so my doctor switched to a different inhibitor. That's why I was on St Julian's—to see how the medication affected me before I returned to New York.'

'You should have told me,' she said quietly, knowing it was the wrong thing to say—or at least the wrong time to say it. Yet she couldn't help herself. She'd bared herself to him, body and soul, and he'd kept all his secrets and emo-tions tucked firmly away.

'There was no reason to tell you.'

'No *reason*? What kind of relationship can we have if—?'

'We don't have a relationship, Millie.'

Millie stared, her mouth still open, her heart starting to thud. She didn't like the way Chase was looking at her, with steely certainty. Gone was any remnant of the laughing, light-hearted man she'd come to love. 'Chase,' she said, her voice so low it reverberated in her chest. She felt the awful sting of tears.

'We've had our intense week.'

'Actually,' she managed, and now her throat ached with the effort of holding all that emotion back, 'we have three more days.'

'They're keeping me in hospital overnight, so we'll have to cut it short.'

'You're *reneging*?' she asked, trying desperately to man-age some levity, and for a second she thought she'd reached him, saw a lightening in his eyes and prayed silently for him to stop this. To see what they had and know that it was *good*.

'Consider our contract terminated,' he said flatly and looked away.

Millie stared at him and clenched her fists in helpless

anger. She couldn't fight this. And why should she? Chase
was keeping to their original terms. She was the one who
had changed, who now wanted more. So much more.

'How am I supposed to get back to St Julian's?'

He hesitated, and she knew he was debating whether to
tell her to charter a boat by herself. Then with a shrug he
said, 'I'll take you back tomorrow, if you want to stay at Cap
Juluca another night.'

'All right. Thank you.' She'd take it, because she wasn't
ready to walk away for good. She needed time to think, to
figure out her next move.

'It won't change anything, Millie,' he said, the words a
bleak warning, and she gazed at him coolly.

'Everything's already changed, Chase. But I think you
know that.'

In a numb fog of swirling despair she took a taxi back to the
resort and arranged to stay another night. She paused on the
threshold of the grass hut where they'd spent last night as
lovers. Her heart wrung like a rag at the sight of that low,
wide bed, the linen sheets now pulled tightly across, the
scattered clothes now folded neatly on a wooden chest. She
sank onto the bed, then sank her face into her hands. She
felt so much sorrow, yet she couldn't cry. She had no more
tears left; she'd given them all to Chase. They'd been tears
for her pain, yet now she felt a grief for his.

Leukaemia.

He'd known for eight months. And he'd been keeping it to
himself, of that Millie had no doubt. She wondered if even
his brothers knew. She imagined Chase keeping up that light,
laughing front even as he battled with his diagnosis. Had
his lightness been his refuge, his way of coping? Or had it
been his armour, the only way to keep prying people and
their awful pity at bay?

She knew how it went. She understood how it felt to be defined by pain, and she even understood why Chase hadn't told her.

Yet it was different now. *They* were different, because she'd broken down her own barriers with Chase's help, and now she needed to help him break down his own.

How?

Millie left the hut for the smooth expanse of sand. From their private cove she couldn't see another building or person, just a few sailboats bobbing on the aquamarine waves. It was a gorgeous afternoon, a cloudless blue sky and a bright lemon sun. The sand sparkled under its rays. She wished Chase were here, wanted to see him with his feet planted in the sand and his face tilted up to that healing sun. She didn't like to picture him in a hospital room in a paper gown, living with the reality of his disease.

Even now she fought that reality. How could he be sick, when he looked so healthy? When he brimmed with vitality and life? Yet even as she asked herself these pointless questions another part of her mind remembered how he'd winced when she'd landed on him from the boat; how he'd squinted into the sunset with a grim focus. How he'd told her he wanted to seize life, suck the marrow from its bones.

Now she understood why. He didn't know how long he had to do it.

Part of her shrank in terror from that thought. Part of her wanted to run away, to forget. She didn't need the pain of losing someone again. She didn't know if she could survive it.

And yet. She had to fight for it, because life simply wasn't worth living without him. Without the love he'd given and shown her. The love she felt straight through to her soul.

Millie took a deep, cleansing breath. So she'd fight. And

that meant fighting Chase. Which meant she needed to throw down her armour…and find some weapons.

Chase stared at the doctor who had come in to give him the news. What news, he didn't yet know, but he knew enough not to expect anything good. Living with chronic leukaemia was a slow descent into disability. Into death.

'Your blood work has come back,' she said, closing the door behind her. Chase braced himself. He had his bloods done routinely and he knew what numbers he needed to stay in the chronic phase. If—when—he moved up to the accelerated phase, his days starting looking very numbered.

'And?' he asked tersely, because she was still scanning the lab report and not actually giving him information.

'They look fairly good.'

What did that mean? 'Fairly good' wasn't great. It wasn't fabulous or terrific or any of the other words he would have preferred. 'Fairly?' he repeated.

'Your platelet count is around two-hundred thousand. Which, as you probably know, is stable.'

Not that stable. It had been higher two weeks ago, when he'd first switched to the new inhibitor. It was clearly dropping, and that was not good at all.

'When you return to New York you should get your blood work done again,' the doctor said, and Chase just kept himself from saying, *Well, duh.* 'And reassess the effectiveness of your prescription.'

Again, obvious. Chase leaned his head against the pillow and felt the dread he'd banished for nearly a week creep back. The dread he hadn't felt since he'd met Millie, and fallen in love with her prickly self.

He quickly banished the thought, steeled himself to live without the exact thing that had been bringing him joy. *Millie.* There was no way, absolutely no way at all, he could burden her with this. *I could never go through that heart-ache again.* She'd spoken in a moment of raw grief and re-membrance, but Chase knew she'd meant it with every fibre of her being. She might think she felt differently right now, but he knew she didn't really want this. Him. If she shackled herself to him, there was every chance she would go through that same heartache—and who even knew how soon.

He spent a restless night in the hospital; he'd always hated the sterile rooms, the antiseptic smell, the sense of sorrow that permeated the very air like some invisible, noxious gas. His thoughts kept him awake too, for his irritating brain—or maybe it was his even more contrary heart—kept remem-bering and reliving every second he'd spent with Millie over the last four days.

Four days. He'd known her for four damned days. There was no way he should be as cut up about losing her as he was. He barely knew her. A week ago—one single week—he hadn't even known she'd existed.

And yet, a life without her seemed like a sepia-toned pho-tograph, leached of colour and even life. He couldn't imagine it, even as he grimly acknowledged that that was just what he'd be doing this time tomorrow.

Morning came, storm clouds a violet smudge on the hori-zon. A storm was going to kick up, the nurse told him, which meant rough sailing from here to St Julian's. He debated calling it off, telling Millie he couldn't sail in this weather, but he wasn't about to back down now. Besides, if he knew Millie—which he knew he did—she wasn't going to give up without a fight. He'd seen how shocked she'd looked when he'd ended it yesterday, had known she'd been think-ing they'd have something after this week. And how could she not, after all they'd shared? She'd cried in his arms. He'd held her heart. And now he was breaking it, which made him a stupid, heartless jerk because he should have known from the first that this was a likely outcome.

He'd known he was a lousy deal, and yet he'd convinced himself that one week would work. Would be enough for a woman like Millie—or a man like him. And they could both walk away with their heart and souls intact.

Ha.

As he left the hospital, the sky still cloudless blue despite the gathering storm clouds on the horizon, Chase had a sudden, fierce hope that he could turn this around. The statistics for the long-term survival rate of CML were good. *Excellent*, his doctor had assured him as she'd handed him rafts of literature. Chase had hated even the titles: *Coping with CML; Accepting Your Diagnosis.* Talk about a buzz-kill. It had all felt incredibly negative, while putting a desperately positive spin on something that just sucked. Basically, what happened with CML or any disease? You degenerated and then you died. End of story.

And so this was the end of his and Millie's story, brief chapter that it had been.

I could never go through that heartache again.

Well, Chase thought, she wouldn't. He'd make sure of it.

He kept up all of his steely resolve until he actually saw Millie. She was waiting for him in the grass hut where they'd made love and just seeing her there reminded him of how she'd lain on top of him, how she'd taken him into herself. How he'd felt so good. So loved.

Now she sat on the edge of the bed, her face pale and set, her silk shift-dress hopelessly wrinkled which, considering the usual state of her clothes, had to be driving her crazy.

Except she didn't seem aware of it at all.

She stared at him with eyes the colour of her dress, brown, warm and soft, just like she was. How had he ever thought she was hard or severe? Scary, he'd called her, and it had turned into an endearment, but it just seemed silly now. She was softness, warmth and light. She was love.

'You've been biting your lip again.'

She touched the deep red marks in the lush softness of her mouth. 'Old habits die hard, I guess.'

Chase thought about making some quip back, but then decided he didn't want to do the banter. It wasn't going anywhere; they weren't. Except back to St Julian's, and on to New York. The rest of their lives apart.

'You ready to go?'

'Fortunately I didn't bring much.'

He didn't say anything, just took one look at the handbag she'd left at her feet. It was one of those bulky hold-all types and he reached for it. She flung out one fluttering hand.

'I can get it.'

Chase stiffened. 'I can manage a single bag, Millie. Despite how you saw me earlier, I'm perfectly—' Healthy? No. 'Fine.' For the moment.

'I know you are,' she said quietly. 'I wasn't saying that, Chase.'

'Let's go.'

She stared at him for a second, her eyes still so dark and soft, and just one look had Chase's steely resolve start to rust and crumble. He wanted to take her in his arms. No, he wanted her to take *him* in her arms. He wanted to cry in her arms like she had in his.

The thought appalled him.

'Coming?' he demanded tersely, and with a single nod she rose from the bed.

They didn't speak as they walked through the lush gardens of the resort, or in the cab the concierge called for them that took them back to where his boat was moored in Meads Bay. No words even as he helped her into the boat and set sail.

No, Millie waited until they were out on open water running towards St Julian's to begin her attack. And that was what it felt like, the same as when she'd begun her battle to sleep with him. Now she battled to stay.

'Did they do blood work in the hospital?'

'Some.'

'What were the results?'

Chase shaded his eyes against the sun, gazed at the thickening clouds boiling on the horizon, spreading out. Damn. The storm was moving faster than he'd anticipated. He was a confident sailor, but after a sleepless night spent in hospital, not to mention his reaction to his new meds, he wasn't thrilled about riding out a storm. Especially not with Millie.

'Chase?' she prompted softly and he sighed.

'I don't really want to talk about this, Millie.'

'Why not?'

'Because there's no point. We had our week and now we're finished.' He took a breath, made himself be harsh. 'You don't have any part of my life any more.'

'I'm not sure I had any part of your life.'

He didn't say anything, didn't even shrug. She was probably right, even if it hadn't felt that way to him. It felt like she'd had a huge part of his life, a huge part of his *self*, but he wasn't about to hand her that ammunition.

'Chase, I think you care for me.'

Again no response. Silence was easier. He kept staring out at the horizon, until he felt a hard shove in his shoulder. He turned, astonished, to see Millie glaring at him.

'*Don't* give me the silent treatment. That is so cowardly.'

He felt a bolt of sudden rage. 'Are you calling me a coward?'

'If the shoe fits.'

He opened his mouth to issue some scathing retort, but

none came. She was right. He *was* being a coward. 'I'm sorry,' he finally said. 'You're right.'

'Wait, you're actually agreeing with me?'

He sighed, not wanting to joke with her even as he craved it. Craved her. 'Millie…'

'Don't do this, Chase. Don't throw away what we have.'

'We don't have anything.'

'Now you're a coward *and* a liar.'

'Call me what you want.'

'Look me in the eye and tell me you don't care for me,' Millie ordered.

Obliging her would be the easiest way out of this. 'Millie, I don't care for you.'

'In the eye, I said.'

He'd been staring at her chin. Reluctantly he raised his gaze to those dark, soft eyes—and felt himself sink into their warmth. Damn it. He couldn't say it. He knew he couldn't. He swallowed. Stared. Said nothing.

Millie smiled. 'See? You do.'

Fine, he'd be honest. 'You're right, I do. It was an intense few days, and naturally that created feelings in both of us.'

'So now you're trying the "it's not real" route.'

'How can we know it's real?' Chase argued. 'We've been on an island paradise, Millie. We haven't seen each other in action, in our homes and jobs and lives. How do we even know this will stand the test of a stressful week, much less time?'

She bit her lip. 'Well, there's only one way to find that out.'

He'd walked right into that one. 'I don't want to.'

'What are you afraid of?'

Dying. Dying alone. 'Millie, you said yourself you didn't want to go through that heartache again. You couldn't.'

Her eyes widened, lips parting. 'Is that what this is about? You're protecting me?'

'I have a terminal disease, Millie. Death is, at some point, a certainty.'

'Guess what, Chase? I have a terminal disease too. It's called life, and death is also a certainty for me.'

He almost smiled at that one, but he shook his head instead. 'Don't be flippant. I'm serious.'

'So am I.' She took a breath, launched into her second line of attack. 'I did the research.'

'What, on your phone?'

'As a matter of fact, yes. The long-term survival rate for CML patients is eighty-seven percent.'

He'd read the same statistic, probably on the same encyclopaedia website. 'For those who have it detected early enough.'

'Did you?'

'Maybe.' The doctor had given him a good prognosis, but then his platelets had fallen and the first inhibitor had stopped working. He could be staring at an accelerated phase within the year, or even sooner. He could be in that other thirteen percent.

'And after five years of living with CML,' Millie continued steadily, 'the rate rises to ninety-three percent, which is the same kind of life expectancy as a person without CML. Stuff happens, Chase. Accidents, diseases, life. There are no guarantees.' Her voice wavered slightly. 'Trust me, I know that.'

'I know you do. Which is why I don't want you to go through it again.' He decided he needed to be brutal, even if it hurt both of them. 'Millie, if we were married, if we'd known each other and been in love with each other for years, then yes, I'd expect you there by my side. I'd want you there. But we've known each other five days. Five *days*. And, yes, they were intense—and I'll admit it, they were some of the best days of my life. But that's all they were. Days. And with that little history you don't shackle yourself to someone who is a losing proposition.'

She blinked. Bit her lip. 'Shouldn't I be the one to decide that?'

He sighed wearily. She was the strongest, most stubborn woman he'd ever met, and even though he admired her tenacity he couldn't cope with it any more. 'We can't talk about this any more.'

'We *can't*?'

'No.' Grimly he pointed to the sky. It had been a sweet, clear blue half an hour ago, but now those violet clouds had boiled right up over the boat. The brisk breeze that had them on a good run back to St Julian's was picking up into a dangerous wind. 'A storm's coming,' he said. 'We need to secure the boat and you need to get below.'

CHAPTER ELEVEN

MILLIE stared at the thunderous clouds overhead and felt her stomach freefall. This didn't look good. The intensity of their conversation evaporated in light of a far more intense reality.

'What do you want me to do?' she asked, and Chase didn't even look at her as he responded.

'Get down below.'

'But you'll need help up here.'

'Millie, you aren't an experienced sailor. Having you up here is more of a liability than a help.' He glanced at her and she saw real fear in his eyes. 'Get down below.'

Millie hesitated. 'I don't want you to be up here alone.'

'I assure you,' he said coldly, 'I am perfectly competent.'

'You know, always assuming I am making some reference to CML is really annoying,' she flashed back. 'I wouldn't want anyone up here alone, Chase. It's dangerous. And I can be very good at obeying instructions.'

His mouth *almost* quirked. Or so Millie hoped. 'You could have fooled me.'

'Tell me what to do.'

'I'm sure that's the last time I'll hear *that* phrase from your lips. All right, fine.' He let out a long breath. 'We need to secure the boat.'

'Batten down the hatches?'

'Exactly.'

'Um…what does that mean, exactly?'

Chase rolled his eyes. Millie smiled. Even though a storm was coming, even though they were at an emotional impasse, she still loved being with him. Loved how he could always make her smile.

'You can close all the portholes and stow any loose items in a safe place—there's a chest at the end of the bed. I'll pump the bilge dry.'

Millie had no idea what *that* meant, but she hurried to obey Chase's instructions. The first raindrops splattered against the porthole in the galley as she closed it. She threw a bunch of books and clothes in the fixed chest Chase had mentioned, and then went back on deck. The wind had picked up and Millie felt its bite. She thought vaguely of all the news reports of deadly tropical storms and hurricanes she'd read or listened to over the years and suppressed a shiver of apprehension. Judging by Chase's expression, they were in for a wild ride.

'What now?' Millie asked, raising her voice so Chase could hear her over the wind.

'You keep the bilge dry and I'll keep us steady so we take the waves on the bow. I've located our position and we're about twenty minutes off St Julian's. I don't want to get any closer until the winds die down. The last thing we want is to founder on the rocks.'

'Right.'

Chase showed her how to pump the bilge, and as the wind picked up and the waves began to crash over the bow they worked in silent and tandem focus. Millie was too intent on her job to feel the fear that lurked on the fringes of her mind. She was soaked and cold, the silk dress plastered to her body. Several times the boat rocked and she fell over, jarring hard. She looked back at Chase and saw him at the tiller, soaking wet and steady. Strong. Even in the midst of this fierce storm her heart swelled with love.

Millie didn't know how long they remained there, keeping the boat afloat and steady as the winds howled and the waves broke over the bow. At some point Millie realised she was needing to pump less and the boat wasn't rocking so much. The storm, she realised, had passed over them.

As the sea around them began to calm, Chase turned around to give Millie a tired smile. He looked haggard, the strong angles of his face and body almost gaunt with tension.

'We did it,' he said and Millie smiled.

'So we did.'

'Thank you.'

She nodded, her throat tightening. Now they were back to the argument that had seen them locked in battle, but at least she would fire the next shot. 'We seemed to weather that storm pretty well.'

Chase narrowed his eyes. 'I'd say so,' he agreed neutrally.

Millie took a breath. 'And if we can manage to do that, then—'

'We can weather the storms of life?' He rolled his eyes. 'Scary, are you really going to go there?'

She took a step towards him. 'I'll do whatever it takes, Chase.'

He gazed at her with a quiet kind of sorrow for a moment. 'I know you will. That's what worries me.' He sighed and stared out at the now-placid sea. 'Come below. We should change into dry clothes.'

Millie followed him below deck and changed into a spare tee-shirt and shorts of his while he did the same. Dry and tense with anticipation, she watched as he sat down on the edge of the bed and patted the empty space next to him. Not exactly the move of a seducer.

On jelly-like legs, Millie walked over and sat next to him.

Chase took her hand in his. Millie tried not to gulp. He was going to make her cry again, she thought numbly, and this time it wouldn't heal. It would hurt.

'Millie.'

'Don't give me the let-me-down-gently speech, Chase. We're both too tough for that.'

He gave her a small smile instead. 'You're right. You're strong, Millie, and incredibly stubborn.'

'Don't forget scary.'

'And severe. A lot of S-words there.' He sighed, sliding his fingers along hers, as if even now he just enjoyed the feel of her. 'You're tough enough to take the truth.'

She bristled, readied for battle. 'And which truth is that, Chase?'

'The truth that since my diagnosis my platelets have been falling. I'm still in the chronic phase of CML, but if you did your internet search then you know that once you hit the accelerated phase it's not good. In fact, it's really bad.'

'There are no guarantees in life, Chase.'

'No, but it's a guarantee that, once I hit that phase, there's no turning back. It's simply a matter of time until I have a blast crisis, and from then on my days are numbered. And those days are hard. We're talking chemo, radiation, hospice, a long, drawn-out sigh towards the end. It's not pretty.'

She swallowed, visions of Chase growing weak and frail filling her head. 'I know that.'

'Here's some more honesty,' he said quietly. 'We had a very intense time. You especially, in telling me about Charlotte and your husband. You hadn't talked like that or cried like that since the accident, and it's bound to make you feel differently about me.'

'You think my feelings aren't real?'

'I'm saying there's no time to test if they're real. We go back to New York and start dating and in a week, a month, who knows, I'm in the hospital and all bets are off. That's not fair, Millie.'

'I should be able to decide.'

'Are you telling me you actually want that?' Chase demanded. He almost sounded angry now. 'You're prepared to be my damn *care-giver* when you barely know me? Waste what could be the best years of your life on someone who's running out of time? Not to mention to go through the whole grief thing again?'

She swallowed. Said nothing. Because, when he put it as bleakly and baldly as that, it did sound absurd. And awful. And for a heart-wrenching moment she wasn't certain of anything; she knew Chase saw it in her face, heard it in her silence.

'See,' he said quietly, and he sounded pained, as if her silence had hurt him. 'It's not going to work, Millie.'

And Millie, her heart turning over and over inside her, was afraid he was right. 'I want it to work,' she whispered, and he squeezed her fingers.

'Let's just remember what we had.'

She swallowed, her throat too tight for her to speak. And then with a sad smile he let go of her hand and went back on deck.

Three days later Chase was travelling first-class back to New York. He gazed down at the blueprint he'd been working on, the blueprint that had completely, completely absorbed him a week ago, but all he could see was Millie. Millie's soft, dark eyes and sudden smile. Millie leaning over as she lay on top of him and kissed him, that severe hair he now loved—just like he loved all of her—brushing his bare chest.

Forget about it, he told himself, and resolutely banished the image—just as he'd done three minutes earlier. Sighing, he shoved the blueprint away and raked a hand through his hair. Those last hours with Millie had been horribly awkward and yet so precious. After they'd sailed back to St Julian's, he'd moored the boat and walked her through the resort. Neither of them had spoken. They'd both known it was over, and now there was just the mechanics of departure.

'I'll leave your clothes at the front desk,' Millie had said, for she'd still been wearing his tee-shirt and shorts.

'Forget about it.' His voice came out rough, rougher than he intended, because it hurt to speak. It hurt to think. It shouldn't have hurt so much, because it was what he wanted, yet it did. It hurt, absurdly, that she had so readily agreed.

She nodded slowly, then came to a stop in front of an outdoor roofed corridor. 'My room's down here.'

'OK.' He nodded, unable to manage anything more. She blinked at him.

'Chase...'

He knew he'd break if she said anything more. He'd break and then they'd start on a desolate path he had no intention of taking either of them down. 'Goodbye, Millie,' he said, and without thinking—because he needed to touch her, to taste her once more—he drew her in his arms and kissed her hard on the mouth, sealing the memory of her inside him. Then he turned and walked away quickly, without looking back.

Now Chase reached for the blueprint once more. It was of a university library in New Hampshire, and he didn't have the entrance right. He wanted soaring space without being grandiose, and of course the building—as with all his buildings—needed to be made of local and renewable materials. The colour of the oak he was using for the shelving reminded him of Millie's eyes.

Damn. He pushed the blueprint away once more. No point

in attempting to work. At least in sleep he wouldn't think of her.

He'd dream.

Several days later Chase sat in the office of his haematologist while she scanned the results of the battery of tests he'd undergone as soon as he'd returned to the city.

'The good news?' she said, looking up, and Chase nodded. 'Your levels are stable.'

'And the bad news?'

'They're a little lower than I would have liked, but there could be a lot of reasons for that.'

'Like the fact that the new medication isn't working?' Chase drawled, and his doctor, Rachel, gave him a wry smile.

'Chase, I know there is a tendency to expect the worst-case scenario in these situations, as a kind of self-protective measure.'

Spare him the psycho-babble. 'It's been my experience that the worst case is what often happens.' Like his mother getting breast cancer and dying within six weeks. Six *weeks*. Or his dad dying of a heart attack before they could reconcile, before Chase had even *considered* reconciling. He'd been so busy trying to show his dad how little he cared and he'd thought he had so much time. Time to prove himself. Time to say sorry for being such a screw-up.

And most of all like meeting Millie when it was too late, when his days were most likely numbered. Yeah, the worst case could happen. Most times it did.

'This is not the worst case,' Rachel said quietly. 'Trust me. This inhibitor isn't working as well as I'd like, it's true, but there's another one we can try. And, while your levels have dipped, they're not rocketing in the wrong direction.'

'But lowering levels is a sign of an accelerated phase,' Chase said, and it was not a question.

Rachel sighed. 'It can be, *if* you are exhibiting several other factors.'

'Such as?'

'There would be cytogenetic evolution with new abnormalities.'

'I don't even know what that means.'

'The point is, just because one medication isn't working doesn't mean you've become unresponsive to all therapies.'

'But it's not good.'

'I still maintain that we diagnosed CML at a very early stage, and the statistics are extremely positive for patients with your profile.'

'But, ultimately, I'm not a statistic.'

'No, you're not. But neither are you a worst-case scenario.'

Chase drummed his fingers on the arm rest of his chair. He hated not knowing. He hated feeling like a ticking time bomb about to explode.

'Live your life, Chase,' Rachel said quietly. 'Don't live it in fear of what might happen.'

'What will likely happen.'

'I'm not saying that.' She reached for her note pad. 'I'm writing you a prescription for a different inhibitor. We'll monitor your levels closely, once a week for the next month, and see how we go.'

'Great.' More doctor's appointments. More wondering. Rather belatedly Chase realised he was acting like a total ass. 'Sorry, Rachel. It hasn't been the greatest day.' Or week, since he'd walked off that plane and into his barren life.

Rachel smiled sympathetically. 'Work going OK?'

Chase fluttered his fingers in dismissal. 'Fine.'

'Personal relationships?'

He smiled thinly. 'What personal relationships?'

Rachel frowned. 'You need people to support you through this, Chase.'

That was exactly what he didn't need. He hadn't told anyone at work about his diagnosis. He hadn't even told his brothers, because he doubted they really wanted to know. The three of them hadn't exactly been there for each other since his parents had died.

No, he'd only told Millie.

'It's fine,' he assured his doctor, even though it felt like nothing in his life was fine. Everything, Chase thought moodily, sucked.

'I know a holiday can make you feel a little behind, Millie, but this is ridiculous.'

Millie glanced up from her computer monitor where she'd been scanning the closing prices of the Hong Kong Stock Exchange. She'd invested one of her client's assets in some new technology coming out of Asia, and it was looking good so far. Very good. So why wasn't she happier?

'You like me to work, Jack,' she said, glancing back at the screen.

Jack sighed. 'Not sixteen-hour days. I pride myself on a tough work ethic, but yours borders on obsessive. It's not good for you, Millie. You'll burn out. I've seen it happen. It's not pretty.'

'I'm fine, and I'm happiest working.' *Lies.*

'How was the holiday, anyway?'

It had been two weeks since she'd returned from St Julian's. Two long, lonely weeks where every moment when her brain wasn't fully occupied with work she'd caught herself thinking of Chase. Dreaming of him, his touch, his smile.

It wasn't real. It was just five incredible days, that's all.

She'd told herself that a hundred times already, and she still didn't believe it.

'Millie?'

Belatedly she realised she hadn't answered her boss. 'My holiday? Oh, you know…' She fluttered her fingers. *Amazing.* 'It was fine.'

'Everything's fine, huh?'

'Yep.'

'What did you do?'

'What do you ever do on a holiday?' *Dive for conch. Make love. Cry in someone's arms.* 'Sunbathe, swim…' She trailed off, her gaze determinedly still fixed on the screen.

'I always pegged you as more of an active holidayer. I figured you'd learn to scuba dive or parasail or something.'

'Nope.'

'Millie.' Jack put his hand on her desk, distracting her from her blind study of the screen. She glanced up and saw how paternally compassionate he looked. And Jack never looked paternal, or compassionate. He was too driven for that, just as she was.

Was trying to be.

'What is it, Jack?'

'You OK? I mean, really OK? I know with what happened… You know…the accident…' Besides a heartfelt 'I'm sorry' at Rob's and Charlotte's funerals, Jack hadn't talked about her bereavement. She'd been giving off clear don't-ask-me signals, and he'd obeyed them. Everyone had. Easier all round.

So why was he asking now?

She must really look like she was losing it.

'Thanks for asking, Jack,' Millie said quietly. 'But I'm… OK. I'll always carry that sadness with me, but it's not as bad as it once was. It gets better every day.' That much, at least, was true. Ever since she'd confessed and cried in Chase's arms, she'd felt lighter. Better. Grief never went away completely, but it was no longer the suffocating blanket that had smothered her for so long. She could breathe. She was free.

She didn't have Chase.

It wasn't real.

It *felt* real. Lying awake at night, remembering how he he'd touched her and made her smile, it felt all too heartbreakingly real.

'Well.' Jack cleared his throat. 'I'm glad you're OK. So stop the sixteen-hour days, OK?'

Millie just smiled and clicked her mouse to the next page of the report. She had no intention of stopping.

Stopping meant thinking, and thinking meant thinking of Chase. And there was no point in torturing herself any more than she had to.

A week later her sister Zoe phoned her during her supposed lunch hour—spent at her desk—and informed her she was coming by for dinner.

'I'm kind of busy, Zo.'

'Exactly. I thought you'd come back from this holiday a little more relaxed, Millie, but you're worse than ever.'

'Gee, thanks.'

'I'm serious. I'll be by at seven.'

Since it was Zoe, Millie agreed. Zoe had been the one person she'd felt she could be almost real with after the accident. Zoe knew there had been tension between her and Rob, although she didn't know the source. She'd understood Millie didn't want to talk about Charlotte, and she'd never pressed. She just came over and brought corn chips and fake cheese, made margaritas.

Zoe buzzed up promptly at seven; Millie had got in the door three minutes earlier. She was still in her power suit and spiked heels, and Zoe raised her eyebrows at the sight of her.

'Raar. I bet men find that get-up *so* sexy.'

'That is so not the point.'

Zoe dumped her bag of provisions on Millie's sleek and spotless granite worktop. 'I know, but men are such weaklings. I bet all your work colleagues have fantasies about you unbuttoning that silk blouse as you murmur stock prices.'

Millie let out an unwilling laugh. 'Zoe, you are outrageous.'

'I try. So.' Zoe took out a bag of tortilla chips and spread them on a pan. 'What happened in Hawaii?'

'I went to the Caribbean.'

'Right.' She reached in the bag for a tub of bright-orange cheese product. Yum. 'So what went down there, Mills? Because something did and I'll get it out of you eventually.'

'No, you won't.' Of that Millie was certain. She had far more self-control than her fun-loving sister did.

'Was it a man? Some hot island romance?'

Millie watched as Zoe squeezed the cheese all over the chips, and thought of Chase telling her how low-brow her snack of choice was. Even now the memory made her smile. 'Actually, it was.'

'What?' Zoe looked up, astonished, and squirted fake cheese across the kitchen right onto Millie's pristine white silk blouse.

'You are so paying for this dry-cleaning bill.'

'Done. And you are so telling me what happened.'

'There's not all that much to tell.' Millie dabbed ineffectually at the bright-orange stain. She was already regretting her impulse to confide in her sister. Talking about Chase hurt too much.

'Did you actually get it *on* with some *guy*?' Zoe asked, so incredulous that Millie had to smile.

'I did.'

'Was he hot?'

'Totally.'

'I am totally jealous.'

'You should be.'

'So it was a fling? A holiday romance?'

'Basically.' Millie tried for insouciant and failed miserably. She turned away under the pretext of running water onto a cloth to dab on her blouse, but really to hide the tears that had sprung unbidden in her eyes.

And of course she didn't fool Zoe.

'Oh, hon.' She put one hand on her shoulder. 'What happened?'

'It's complicated.'

'Knowing your history, I'd expect that.'

Millie sighed. 'Let me tell you, I am pretty tired of complicated. And I'm tired of sad.'

'I know you are,' Zoe murmured.

Millie swallowed, blinked and turned around. 'He had some issues.'

'Oh no, not a guy with issues. You're better off without him, trust me.'

Millie smiled wanly. Zoe was infamous for dating toe-rags who left her on some pathetic pretext of how being hurt by their ex-girlfriends, or their mothers, or their first-grade school teachers had made them commitment-phobic. 'Not like that.'

'Then how?'

'He…' She paused, not wanting to reveal Chase's condition. It wasn't her secret to share. 'It doesn't matter. The point is, he didn't want to continue it because he didn't want me to get hurt.'

'That is so lame.'

'He meant it, though,' Millie said quietly.

Zoe shoved the pan of cheese-covered tortilla chips in the oven. 'Oh, really? Because when a guy says something about how he doesn't want you to get hurt, what he really means is *he* doesn't want to get hurt.'

'No—' Millie stopped suddenly and Zoe planted her hands on her hips.

'Am I right, or am I right?'

Could it be possible? Chase had seemed so sincere, so sorrowfully heartfelt when he'd held her hand and told her the truth. Mentioned words like *care-giver* and *hospice* and *blast crisis*. And she'd believed him, because she wasn't stupid; a future with Chase was scary. And uncertain. And yet even now, weeks later, it still felt like her only hope.

What if he'd sent her away because *he* was afraid? Because he wanted to send her away before she walked away on her own? Because he thought she wouldn't handle it, wouldn't *want* to handle it?

'You might be right, Zo,' she said slowly. 'I just never thought of that.'

Zoe peered in the oven to check on their chips. 'For a financial genius,' she remarked, 'you can be kind of stupid about some things.'

Millie had to agree.

CHAPTER TWELVE

MILLIE straightened the tight-fitting black cocktail dress and threw her shoulders back. Show time.

It had taken nearly two months to track down Chase. She could have found him sooner; she'd found his office address on the internet and she could have shown up there any day of the week. But she wasn't about to blunder into battle; she needed to do this right. And it had taken her that long to figure out just how that could happen.

Now she stood on the threshold of the lobby of one of Manhattan's boutique museums, this one dedicated to Swedish modern art. The result was spare, clean lines, a soaring ceiling and a lot of funky sculpture. And Chase, who had designed the museum's new conservatory on the top floor, was in attendance at this opening night party.

Millie had been to plenty of parties in the city. Rob had liked to work the Manhattan social scene, often stating that he accomplished more in one evening at a party like this one than a week at the office. Millie had enjoyed the parties they'd attended for the most part, but she hadn't been to one in two years. And she'd never gone alone.

More importantly, she'd never gone to one with the sole intent of seducing the guest of honour.

She took a deep breath and scanned the crowd for Chase. Time to start putting her plan into action.

* * *

Chase gazed around at the milling guests in their tuxedos and cocktail dresses—all black, which was practically required at dos like these. Normally he liked working the charm, enjoying the hors d'oeuvres and the low-grade flirting, but he felt only weary of it tonight.

Hell, he'd been weary of it for the best part of three months since he'd left Millie—and his heart—on St Julian's.

That sounded like a song, he thought moodily. A bad one. He took a sip of champagne. By all accounts he should be happy. The new conservatory was a huge success in art and architectural circles and, even more importantly, the new inhibitor Rachel had prescribed him was actually working. For how long, of course, no one could say, but she was happy with his levels and he felt physically better than he had in months. He was even allowed to drink.

So why was he still so miserable?

'Hello, Chase.'

Chase turned slowly, disbelievingly, at the sound of that familiar voice. He blinked at the sight of Millie, *his* Millie, standing there so calm and cool, a flute of champagne held aloft.

'Aw, Scary, you changed your hair.'

Her lush mouth curved in the faintest of smiles. 'You didn't like it before.'

He took her in, *drank* her in, for despite her hair, which was now tousled and short, she looked so wonderfully the same. Same soft, dark eyes. Same lush mouth. Same straight, elegant figure clad in the kind of dress he'd expect her to wear—a black silk sheath with a straight neckline and cap sleeves, saved from severity by the way it highlighted every slender curve. His hands itched with the desire—the *need*—to touch her.

'How have you been, Chase?'

'Fine. Good. You?'

'The same, I'd say.' Her mouth quirked up at the corner, like she was teasing him. So he wasn't being the most sparkling conversationalist. All his energy was taken up with just looking at her. Memorising her. 'It's good to see you,' Millie said quietly and Chase nodded jerkily.

'You too.'

She raised one slender arm to gesture to the milling crowds, to the Manhattan skyline visible through the walls of glass. 'I like the space. Very open and modern.'

'Thanks.' He sounded like an idiot. A wooden idiot.

'I know you're the guest of honour here, but do you think you could be free for a drink at the end of the evening?' Vulnerability flashed in her eyes; he saw it, he felt it. 'For old times' sake.'

Chase knew it wasn't a good idea. What did he and Millie really have to say to each other? His new medication might be working, but he hadn't changed his mind about their future, or lack thereof. He was still a ticking time bomb.

And yet, one drink. Just to hear how she was. To be able to *look* at her. Nothing more. 'Sure.'

'Good.' Now he saw relief flash in her eyes, and he knew she still cared. Hell, so did he.

Maybe this was a bad idea.

'When will you be free?'

'I'm free now.' He'd already made his remarks, shaken the requisite number of hands. He was ready. *So* ready; maybe it would be better to just get this over with. Final closure.

Because that was what it really was, right?

'Well, let's go then.' And, turning around, Millie sashayed out of the conservatory. Chase followed.

They didn't speak in the lift on the way down, or out on the street when Millie raised one arm and had a cab coasting to the kerb within seconds. Chase didn't hear the address she gave as they climbed into the cab; he was too diverted by the sight of her long, stocking-clad legs. She was wearing *suspenders*, and he'd seen an inch of milky-white thigh as she slid across the seat.

His blood pressure was sky-rocketing. He could feel the hard thud of his heart, the adrenalin racing through his veins. He'd missed her. He'd missed her way too much. And he wanted her right now.

'Where are we going, out of interest?' His voice, thankfully, hit the wry note of amusement he was going for.

'My apartment.'

Brakes screeched in his mind. 'What?'

She gave him a far too innocent smile. 'Why waste twenty bucks on two glasses of wine in a noisy, crowded bar? This is much more civilised.'

And much more dangerous. Was Millie *playing* him? He'd always thought her too blunt to be sneaky, but maybe not. What did she want out of this evening?

What did he?

They didn't say anything more until the cab came to a stop outside a luxury high-rise near the UN complex. Chase reached for his wallet but Millie had already swiped her card.

'My treat,' she murmured and, swallowing hard, he followed her out of the taxi and into the lobby of her building, all black marble and tinted mirrors.

She fluttered her fingers at the doorman and then ushered him into the lift. Tension was coiling in Chase's body, seeking release. Something was going on here, some kind of plan of Millie's, and he didn't know what it was.

He had a feeling he was going to find out pretty soon.

She didn't speak until she'd reached her apartment, unlocked the door and led him into just the kind of place he'd expected her to have. Very tasteful. Very boring.

'Before you ask, an interior decorator did the whole thing. I didn't have time to go antiquing.'

'Still pulling sixteen-hour days, Scary?'

'More or less.' She took a very nice bottle of red out of a wine rack in the ode to granite and stainless steel that served as her kitchen. 'This OK?'

'Fine, but let me, or I'm going to start to feel surplus to requirements.'

She handed him the bottle and a corkscrew. 'Trust me, Chase, you are not surplus to requirements.'

'What's going on, Millie? Besides a friendly drink?'

'I have a deal to offer.'

A deal. Of course. He wasn't even surprised and yet his blood still sang. The cork came out with a satisfying pop and he poured them both glasses. 'What kind of deal?'

'One night.'

His hand involuntarily jerked, and a blood-red drop of wine splashed onto the counter. Millie swiped it and then licked the wine off her thumb. Chase went hard. 'What do you mean, one night?' he asked in as mild a voice as he could manage. Millie didn't answer, just accepted the glass he handed her and took a sip. 'Cheers,' he said and tried not to drain his glass.

Millie drank and then lowered her glass, gazing at him straight-on. 'One night—my terms.'

Hell. 'Which are?'

'Need-to-know basis only, of course.'

Of course. 'Why are you suggesting this, Millie?'

'Because I can't get you out of my head. It's affecting my work, my life—what little there is of it. And I'm gambling that it's been the same for you.' He didn't answer, which was obviously answer enough. 'One night, Chase, that's all. To help us get each other out of our systems and move on.'

He almost asked if that was what she wanted now, but stopped himself. What was the point? It was what he wanted. It had to be.

'And if I don't agree?'

'Stay and enjoy a nice glass of wine with an old friend.'

And *that* sounded so appealing. 'And if I do agree?'

Her mouth curved. 'Need-to-know basis, remember?'

'Is this some kind of revenge?'

'Revenge?' She let out a low, husky laugh. When had Millie become such an accomplished seductress? So unbearably sensual? 'Definitely not. Consider it…returning the favour.'

He swallowed. Stared into his wine glass. Wondered why the hell he wasn't busting out as fast as he could. This was dangerous. Stupid. Insane.

And he wanted it. So badly. Just one night. One more time with Millie.

'All right, Scary. I agree.'

'Even without knowing what you're getting into?'

'I think I can handle it.'

'Funny,' she murmured. 'That's what I thought when I first met you. Boy, was I wrong.'

She set her wine glass back down on the work top and walked past him towards the living room. 'Where you going, Scary?'

She glanced over her shoulder. 'To the bedroom, of course.'

Adrenalin pumped through him. 'That's kind of quick.'

'The only part of the evening that will be.'

Good Lord. Chase closed his eyes. This was the stuff of fantasies, of his dreams, for the last three months. He followed her into the bedroom.

The shades were drawn against the night, the king-sized bed covered with a pale-blue duvet that matched the curtains and carpet. The room was as tastefully boring as the rest of the apartment, but with Millie standing in the middle of it—her hands planted on her hips; one long, lovely leg thrust out as her gaze roved over him—it felt like the most erotic chamber he'd ever entered.

He shut the door behind him and leaned against it. 'Well?'

'Take off your clothes.'

He heard the slightest tremble in her voice and knew she wasn't quite the confident seductress she'd first seemed to be. Somehow that made him glad.

'Will do,' he drawled, and tugged off his tie. Millie watched him, her gaze dark and hot as he undid the studs of his shirt and cummerbund and tossed both on the floor. He raised his eyebrows. 'Well?'

'The trousers too, hotshot.'

He slid out of his trousers and kicked them off; his boxers and socks followed. He was naked and fully aroused while Millie was still in her clothes, even her high heels.

She looked him up and down and then lifted her honest, open gaze to his. 'I missed you, Chase.'

Chase didn't say anything. She was investing this night with emotion, emotion he felt. This was so dangerous. And exciting. He couldn't have walked away even if he'd wanted to. She nodded towards the bed. 'Get on there.'

Smiling a little, he stretched out on the bed just as she once had, hands behind his head, the image of someone totally at ease. Tension still raced through him. He didn't know what Millie planned, but he knew it was something. He could tell by the set of her shoulders, that glint in her eyes, the sense of expectation that pulsed in the room.

What was she going to do to him?

In one fluid movements Millie unzipped her dress and stepped out of it.

'I see you've bought some sexy lingerie since we last saw each other,' Chase said, and had to clear his throat.

Millie smiled. She was wearing a black satin bra and matching thong, and those suspenders. Sheer black stockings encased her lovely legs. She put one foot on the bed and slowly, languorously, rolled the stocking down her calf. Chase watched, mesmerised. Then she did the same with the other leg and stood up, the stockings held in her hand, the black lace suspenders discarded.

'Is this some kind of striptease thing? Because I like it.'

'I'm so glad,' she purred, and then leaned over him. Chase was so distracted by the close-up of her high, firm breasts encased in black satin that he didn't realise what she was doing with those sheer stockings. And when he did realise, it was too late.

'You tied me up.' One hand to each bed post.

'That's right.'

Chase pulled one hand, tested the weight of the bind. She'd tied a good knot, but he could still break out pretty easily. He wasn't going to, though. He was too intrigued by what Millie intended to do.

She ran one fingertip down the length of his chest, across his hip, and then down his inner thigh. His reaction to that little touch was, in his rather exposed and vulnerable state, completely obvious.

She stood up, hands on her hips, and Chase arched his eyebrows. 'What now, Scary?'

'You'll see.' She reached behind her for something long and silky. 'Or, actually, you won't.'

She was blindfolding him. Chase remained passive as she tied the scarf around his eyes, still too curious to stop this little game. 'You didn't ask if this was OK with me, you know. You're not being very PC about this.'

'I didn't want to ask,' Millie replied. 'There's no getting out of this, Chase.'

For the first time actual unease prickled between his shoulder blades. He kept his tone light. 'What are you going to do to me, Millie?'

'Make you tell the truth.'

Chase stiffened. 'The truth?' he repeated neutrally, because suddenly this didn't seem like such a sexy little game anymore.

'Yes, the truth.' He could tell by the sound of her voice that she was walking around the bed, and he felt more exposed than ever. 'Because it's taken me this long to realise you weren't telling me the truth when you said how you didn't want me to go through all the heartache of losing someone again, blah, blah, blah. Yawn, yawn, yawn.'

He managed a smile. 'You are reducing my heartfelt sensitivity to something rather trite.'

'It wasn't trite,' Millie said, and he knew she'd come closer. 'It was a lie.'

And Chase couldn't think to respond for a moment because she'd straddled his hips, lowered herself onto his thighs. He could feel the damp heat of her and she brushed against him so he actually moaned.

'You're torturing me here, Millie.'

'That's the idea.'

She moved again, so her body brushed against his in the most agonisingly exquisite and intimate of sensations. Chase scrambled to think of something coherent.

'Why do you think I was lying?'

'Maybe,' Millie said thoughtfully, 'you didn't realise you were lying. You'd convinced yourself you didn't want to hurt me.'

She leaned forward so her breasts brushed his chest, trailed a few lingering kisses along his shoulder. Thinking anything sensible was nearly impossible.

'I didn't want to hurt you,' he managed, his voice strangled. 'I still don't.'

'No, Chase,' she said softly, and her breath fanned against

his bare skin. 'You didn't want to hurt yourself. You still don't.'

For the first time Chase considered freeing himself, ending this farce. What the hell was she talking about? Then he heard the tear of foil and felt her slowly roll a condom onto him. His breath came out in a shudder as she lowered herself onto him.

'Millie—'

'I didn't see it at first,' she said, setting a slow pace that had him arching instinctively upwards. 'How you needed to lose control as much as I did.'

Somehow he found the strength to speak. 'I think I'm seconds from losing control right now.'

'Not that kind of control.' He heard amusement in her voice and she slowed the pace, rocking her hips just a little. 'But I want to spin this out a bit longer, so bear with me.'

Chase cursed. Millie laughed softly. 'Now, now, Chase.'

'Do you know what you're doing to me?'

She rocked her hips again. 'I sort of think I do.'

'What do you want, Millie?'

'I told you—the truth.'

'I gave you the truth.'

'No. The truth, Chase, is that you aren't afraid of leaving me alone. You're afraid of *being* alone. You're afraid I wouldn't be able to hack it and I'd walk away, leave you to suffer by yourself. Break your heart.' As she spoke she'd started moving again, setting a faster and faster rhythm so her voice was soft and breathless and Chase couldn't speak at all.

He could only listen, which he knew was exactly what she wanted.

'Hurting you just like your mother hurt you by dying when you were only a boy. Like your father, by never forgiving you and disinheriting you. Like your brothers, by not caring enough even to ask what's going on in your life. You gave me all the pieces of the puzzle, Chase, but I was so wrapped up in my own pain that it took me too long to fit it all together.'

Feeling blazed through him. Too much feeling. He was on the brink of the most intense orgasm he'd thought he'd ever had even as his heart started to splinter. *Shatter.*

Because she was right.

'Millie!' he gasped, her name torn from him.

She leaned over him, freed his hands and took off his blindfold. Chase blinked back sudden tears as she cradled her face in his hands, her expression so tender and fierce and loving. 'I'm sorry for not getting it sooner. I'm sorry I waited so long.' She kissed him long and deep. 'I'm not going to leave you, Chase. I'm not going to leave you even if you're sick and scared and dying. We have something special, something amazing, and I'll fight for it for the rest of my life.'

Then she kissed him again, still moving on top of him, and with a shudder of joy he came, his arms around her, drawing her even closer to him.

He was never going to let her go.

Some time later, after more love-making and honest words, Millie lay in his arms as Chase stared up at the ceiling. His mind and body still buzzed with everything that had happened. 'You know,' he said, running his hand up and down her arm, 'that was so not the deal we made.'

'It was better,' she murmured, and snuggled closer.

And Chase had to agree. This deal was much better. In fact, it was perfect.

EPILOGUE

Four years later.

MILLIE gazed out at the tranquil aquamarine sea and gave a sigh of pure contentment. She could hear Chase in the kitchen of the villa, humming as he made dinner for the two of them.

They'd come to St Julian's to celebrate the fifth anniversary of his diagnosis, a red-letter day, because his doctor had declared him officially in remission. As of now, he had the same life expectancy as a person without CML, which was to say, who knew how long? Who knew how long anyone had?

There was just this moment. This happiness. And enjoying what they'd been given for as long as they'd been given it.

The last four years hadn't been without some fear and heartache. Right after their wedding, his symptoms had played up and his doctor had prescribed a drug that was still in clinical trials. Thankfully, it had seemed to work.

Chase had told his brothers about his condition, and several years ago they'd had a reckoning, a reunion. Millie would never forget the wonder and gratitude she'd seen in Chase's eyes when he'd embraced the brothers who had rallied around him even though he'd secretly feared they wouldn't.

'It's almost ready,' Chase called, and Millie smiled, her hand resting against her still-flat tummy.

She had something else to be happy about, something secret and precious and scary too. Something she hadn't yet told Chase about, because she hadn't even been sure how she felt about it. It had taken four years to get to this moment, this willingness to risk so much again.

She felt ready now; being with Chase had given her the strength, the courage, to try, even while knowing that there were no guarantees. Life was scary, uncertain and full of pain. But it was also full of hope—glorious, prevailing, strong.

'Sweetheart?' Chase called and, smiling, ready to tell her secret, Millie rose from the sand and went to her husband.

* * * * *

IN THE HEAT OF
THE SPOTLIGHT

BY
KATE HEWITT

To my big brother Geordie,
the real writer of Aurelie's song.
Thank you for always being my (tor)mentor. Love, K.

CHAPTER ONE

LUKE BRYANT STARED at his watch for the sixth time in the last four minutes and felt his temper, already on a steady simmer, start a low boil.

She was late. He glanced enquiringly at Jenna, his Head of PR, who made useless and apologetic flapping motions with her hands. All around him the crowd that filled Bryant's elegant crystal and marble lobby began to shift restlessly. They'd already been waiting fifteen minutes for Aurelie to make an appearance before the historic store's grand reopening and so far she was a no-show.

Luke gritted his teeth and wished, futilely, that he could wash his hands of this whole wretched thing. He'd been busy putting out corporate fires at the Los Angeles office and had left the schedule of events for today's reopening to his team here in New York. If he'd been on site, he wouldn't be here waiting for someone he didn't even want to see. What had Jenna been thinking, booking a washed-up C-list celebrity like Aurelie?

He glanced at his Head of PR again, watched as she bit her lip and made another apologetic face. Feeling not one shred of sympathy, Luke strode towards her.

'Where is she, Jenna?'

'Upstairs—'

'What is she doing?'

'Getting ready—'

Luke curbed his skyrocketing temper with some effort. 'And does she realise she's fifteen—' he checked his watch '—*sixteen* and a half minutes late for the one song she's meant to perform?'

'I think she does,' Jenna admitted.

Luke stared at her hard. He was getting annoyed with the wrong person, he knew. Jenna was ambitious and hardworking and, all right, she'd booked a complete has-been like Aurelie to boost the opening of the store, but at least she had a ream of market research to back up her choice. Jenna had been very firm about the fact that Aurelie appealed to their target group of eighteen to twenty-five-year-olds, she'd sung three chart-topping and apparently iconic songs of their generation, and was only twenty-six herself.

Apparently Aurelie still held the public's interest—the same way a train wreck did, Luke thought sourly. You just couldn't look away from the unfolding disaster.

Still, he understood the bottom line. Jenna had booked Aurelie, the advertising had gone out, and a significant number of people were here to see the former pop princess sing one of her insipid numbers before the store officially reopened. As CEO of Bryant Stores, the buck stopped with him. It always stopped with him.

'Where is she exactly?'

'Aurelie?'

As if they'd been talking about anyone else. 'Yes. Aurelie.' Even her name was ridiculous. Her real name was probably Gertrude or Millicent. Or even worse, something with an unnecessary i like Kitti or Jenni. Either way, absurd.

'She's in the staff break room—'

Luke nodded grimly and headed upstairs. Aurelie had been contracted to sing and, damn it, she was going to sing. Like a canary.

Upstairs, Bryant's women's department was silent and empty, the racks of clothes and ghostly faceless mannequins seeming to accuse him silently. Today had to be a success. Bryant Stores had been slowly and steadily declining for the last five years, along with the economy. No one wanted overpriced luxuries, which was what Bryant's had smugly specialised in for the last century. Luke had been trying to change things for years but his older brother, Aaron, had insisted on having the final say and he hadn't been interested in doing something that, in his opinion, diminished the Bryant name.

When the latest dismal reports had come in, Aaron had finally agreed to an overhaul, and Luke just prayed it wasn't too late. If it was, he knew who would be blamed.

And it *would* be his fault, he told himself grimly. He was the CEO of Bryant Stores, even if Aaron still initialled many major decisions. Luke took responsibility for what happened in his branch of Bryant Enterprises, including booking Aurelie as today's entertainment.

He knocked sharply on the door to the break room. 'Hello? Miss…Aurelie?' *Why* didn't the woman have a last name? 'We're waiting for you—' He tried the knob. The door was locked. He knocked again. No answer.

He stood motionless for a moment, the memory sweeping coldly through him of another locked door, a different kind of silence. The scalding rush of guilt.

This is your fault, Luke. You were the only one who could have saved her.

Resolutely he pushed the memories aside. He shoved his shoulder against the door and gave it one swift and accurate kick with his foot. The lock busted and the door sprang open.

Luke entered the break room and glanced around. Clothes—silly, frothy, ridiculous outfits—were scattered across the table and chairs, some on the floor. And something else was on the floor.

Aurelie.

He stood there, suspended in shock, in memory, and then, swearing again, he strode towards her. She was slumped in the corner of the room, wearing an absurdly short dress, her legs splayed out like spent matchsticks.

He crouched in front of her, felt her pulse. It seemed steady, but what did he really know about pulses? Or pop stars? He glanced at her face, which looked pale and was lightly beaded with sweat. Actually, now that he looked at her properly, she looked awful. He supposed she was pretty in a purely objective sense, with straight brownish-blonde hair and a lithe, slender figure, but her face was drawn and grey and she looked way too thin.

He touched her cheek and found her skin clammy. He reached for his cell phone to dial 911, his heart beating far too hard. She must have overdosed on something. He'd never expected to see this scenario twice in one lifetime, and the remembered panic iced in his veins.

Then her eyes fluttered open and his hand slackened on the phone. Luke felt something stir inside him at the colour of her eyes. They were slate-blue, the colour of the Atlantic on a cold, grey day, and they swirled with sorrow. She blinked blearily, struggled to sit up. Her gaze focused in on him and something cold flashed in their blue depths. 'Aren't you handsome,' she mumbled, and the relief he felt that she was okay was blotted out by a far more familiar determination.

'Right.' He hauled her up by the armpits and felt her sag helplessly against him. She'd looked thin slumped on the floor, and she felt even more fragile in his arms. Fragile and completely out of it. 'What did you take?' he demanded. She lolled her head back to blink up at him, her lips curving into a mocking smile.

'Whatever it was, it was a doozy.'

Luke scooped her up in his arms and stalked over to the bathroom. He ran a basin full of cold water and in one quick and decisive movement plunged the pop star's face into the icy bowlful.

She came up like a scalded cat, spluttering and swearing. 'What the *hell*—?'

'Sobered up a bit now, have you?'

She sluiced water from her face and turned to glare at him with narrowed eyes. 'Oh, yes, I'm sober. Who are you?'

'Luke Bryant.' He heard his voice, icy with suppressed rage. Damn her for scaring him. For making him remember. 'I'm paying you to perform, princess, so I'll give you five minutes to pull yourself together and get down there.' She folded her arms, her eyes still narrowed, her face still grey and gaunt. 'And put some make-up on,' Luke added as he turned to leave. 'You look like hell.'

Aurelie Schmidt—not many people knew about the Schmidt—wiped the last traces of water from her face and blinked hard. Stupid man. Stupid gig. Stupid her, for coming today at all. For trying to be different.

She drew in a shuddering breath and grabbed a chocolate bar from her bag. Unwrapping it in one vicious movement, she turned to stare at the clothes scattered across the impromptu dressing room. Jenna, the Bryant stooge who had acted as her handler, had been horrified by her original choice of outfit.

'But you're *Aurelie*… You have an *image*…'

An image that was five years past its sell-by date, but people still wanted to see it. They wanted to see her, although whether it was because they actually liked her songs or just because they hoped to see her screw up one more time was open to debate.

And so she'd forsaken the jeans and floaty top she'd been wanting to wear and shimmied into a spangly minidress instead. She'd just been about to do her make-up when she must have passed out. And Mr Bossy Bryant had come in and assumed the worst. Well, she could hardly blame him. She'd done the worst too many times to get annoyed when someone jumped to that rather obvious conclusion.

Clearly she was late, so she wolfed down her chocolate bar and then did the quick version of her make-up: blush, concealer, eyeliner and a bold lipstick. Her hair looked awful but at least she could turn it into a style. She pulled it up in a messy up-do and sprayed it to death. People would like seeing her a little off her game anyway. It was, she suspected, why they were here; it was why the tabloids still rabidly followed her even though she hadn't released a single in over four years. Everyone wanted to see her fail.

It had been a good twenty minutes since she was meant to perform her once-hit single *Take Me Down*, and Aurelie knew the audience would be getting restless. And Luke Bryant would be getting even more annoyed. Her lips curved in a cynical smile as she turned to leave the break room. Luke Bryant obviously had extremely low expectations of her. Well, he could just join the club.

Stepping onto a stage—even a makeshift one like this—always felt like an out-of-body experience to Aurelie. Any sense of self fell away and she simply became the song, the dance, the performance. Aurelie as the world had always known her.

The crowd in front of her blurred into one faceless mass and she reached for the mike. Her stiletto heel caught in a gap in the floor of the stage and for a second she thought she was going to pitch forward. She heard the sudden collective intake of breath, knew everyone was waiting, even hoping,

she'd fall flat on her face. She righted herself, smiled breezily and began to sing.

Usually she wasn't aware of what she was doing onstage.
She just did it. Sing, slink, shimmy, smile. It was second
nature to her now, *first* nature, because performing—being
someone else—felt far easier than being herself. And yet
right there in the middle of all that fakery she felt something
inside her still and go silent, even as she sang.

Standing on the side of the makeshift stage, away from
the audience assembled in the lobby, Luke Bryant was staring right at her, his face grim, his eyes blazing. And worse,
far worse, since he *should* be staring at her, was the realisation that she was staring back at him. And some part of
herself could not look away even as she turned back to face
the crowd.

Luke watched as Aurelie began her routine, and knew that
was what it was. She was on autopilot, but she was good
enough that it didn't matter. Her whipcord-slender body
moved with an easy, sensual grace. Her voice was clear and
true but also husky and suggestive when she wanted it to be,
like sunshine and smoke. It was a sexy voice, and she was
good at what she did. Even annoyed as he was with her, he
could acknowledge that.

And then she turned and looked at him, and any smug
sense of detachment he felt drained away. All he felt was…
need. An overwhelming physical need for her but, more than
that, a need to…to *protect* her. How ridiculous. He didn't
even like her; he *despised* her. And yet in that still, silent
second when their gazes met he felt a tug of both heart and…
well, the obvious.

Then she looked away and he let out a shuddering breath,
relieved to have that weird reaction fade away. Clearly he

was overtired and way too stressed, to be feeling like that
about someone like Aurelie. Or anyone at all.

He heard her call out to the crowd to sing along to the
chorus of the admittedly catchy tune, and watched as she
tossed her head and shouted, 'Come on, it's not that old a hit
that you can't remember!'

He felt a flicker of reluctant admiration that she could
make fun of herself. It took courage to do that. Yet remembering her slumped on the break room floor made his mouth
twist down in disapproval. Dutch courage, maybe. Or worse.

The music ended, three intense minutes of song and
dance, and Luke listened to the thunder of applause. He
heard a few catcalls too and felt himself cringe. They liked
her, but part of liking her, he knew, was making fun of her.
He had a feeling Aurelie knew that too. He watched as she
bowed with a semi-sardonic flourish, fluttered her fingers
at her fans and sashayed offstage towards him. Their gazes
clashed once more and Aurelie tipped her chin up a notch,
her eyes flashing challenge.

Luke knew he'd treated her pretty harshly upstairs, but
he wasn't about to apologise. The woman might have been
on *drugs*. Now that she had done her act he wanted her out
of here. She was way too much of a wild card to have in the
store today. She came towards him and he reached out and
curled one hand around her wrist.

He felt the fragility of her bones under his fingers, the
frantic hammering of her pulse, and wished he hadn't touched
her. Standing so close to her, he could smell her perfume, a
fresh, citrusy scent, feel the heat from her body. He couldn't
quite keep his gaze from dipping down to the smooth round-
ness of her breasts and the gentle flaring of her hips, outlined all too revealingly under the thin, stretchy material of
her skimpy dress. His gaze travelled back up her body and
he saw her looking at him with an almost weary cynicism.

He dropped her wrist, conscious that he'd just given her a very thorough once-over. 'Thank you,' he said, and heard how stiff his voice sounded.

Her mouth twisted. 'For what, exactly?'

'For singing.' He hated the lilt of innuendo in her voice.

'No problem, Bossy.'

Annoyance flared. 'Why do you think I'm bossy?'

'We-ell…' She put her hands on her hips. 'You dunked me in a sink of cold water and expected me to thank you for it.'

'You were passed out. I was doing you a favour.'

Her lips curved and her eyes glittered. Everything about her mocked him. 'See what I mean?'

'I just want you to do what you're meant to do,' Luke said tightly. The sooner this woman was out of here, the better. The store opening didn't need her. He didn't need her.

With that same mocking smile she placed one slender hand on his chest so he could see her glittery nail varnish—and she could feel the sudden, hard thud of his heart. He could feel the heat of her hand through his shirt, the gentle press of her slender fingers and, irritatingly, his libido stirred.

'And what,' she asked, her voice dropping an octave, 'am I meant to do?'

'Leave,' he snapped. He couldn't control his body's reaction, much as he wanted to, but he could—and would—control everything else.

She just laughed softly and pressed her hand more firmly against the thin cotton of his shirt, spreading her fingers wide. He remained completely still, stony-faced, and she dropped her gaze downwards. 'You sure about that?' she murmured.

Fury beat through his blood and he picked up her hand—conscious again of its slender smallness—and thrust it back at her as if it were some dead thing. 'I'll have security escort you out.'

She raised her eyebrows. 'And that will look good on today of all days.'

'What do you mean?'

'Having Aurelie escorted out by your security buffoons? The tabloids will eat it up with a spoon.' She folded her arms, a dangerous glitter in her eyes. It almost looked as if she was near tears or, more likely, triumph. 'Your big opening will be made into a mockery. Trust me, I know how it goes.'

'I have no doubt you do.' She'd been ridiculed in the press more times than he cared to count.

'Suck it up, Bossy,' she jeered softly. 'You need me.'

Luke felt his jaw bunch. And ache. He was tempted to stand his ground and tell her to leave, but rationality won out. Too much rode on this event to stand on stupid pride. 'Fine,' he said evenly. 'You can circulate and socialise for an hour, and then leave of your own accord. But if you so much as—'

'What?' She raised her eyebrows, her mouth curving into another mocking smile. 'What do you think I'm going to do?'

'That's the problem. I have absolutely no idea.'

She'd looked so coy and cat-like standing there, all innuendo and outrageous suggestion, but suddenly it was as if the life had drained out of her and she looked away, her expression veiled, blank. 'Don't worry,' she said flatly. 'I'll give everyone, even you, what they want. I always do.' And without looking back at him she walked towards the crowd.

Watching her, Luke felt a flicker of uneasy surprise. He'd assumed Aurelie was as shallow as a puddle, but in that moment when she'd looked away he'd sensed something dark and deep and even painful in her averted gaze.

He let out a long, low breath and turned in the opposite direction. He wasn't going to waste another second of his time thinking about the wretched woman.

Now that the mini-concert was over, the crowd milled around, examining the glass display cases of jewellery and make-up, the artful window dressings. Luke forced himself to focus on what lay ahead. Yet even as he moved through the crowd, smiling, nodding, talking, it seemed as if he could still feel the heat of her hand on his chest, imagined that its imprint remained in the cloth, or even on his skin.

Aurelie turned around to watch Luke Bryant walk away, wondering just what made Mr Bossy tick. He was wound tight enough to snap, that was for sure. When she'd placed her hand on his chest she'd felt how taut his muscles were, how tense. And she'd also felt the sudden thud of his heart, and knew she affected him. Aroused him.

The knowledge should have given her the usual sense of grim satisfaction, but it didn't. All she felt was tired. So very tired, and the thought of performing on a different kind of stage, playing the role of Aurelie the Pop Star for another hour or more, made her feel physically sick.

What would happen, she wondered, if she dropped the flirty, salacious act for a single afternoon, stopped being Aurelie and tried being herself instead?

She thought of the PR lady's look of horror at such a suggestion. No one wanted Aurelie the real person. They wanted the pop princess who tripped through life and made appalling tabloid-worthy mistakes. That was the only person they were interested in.

And that was the only person she was interested in being. She wasn't even sure if there was anything left underneath, inside. Taking a deep breath, she squared her shoulders and headed into the fray.

The crowd mingling in the elegant lobby of Bryant's was a mix of well-heeled and decidedly middle class. Aurelie had known Bryant's as a top-of-the-line, big-name boutique but, from a glance at the jewellery counter, she could tell the reopening was trying to hit a slightly more affordable note.

She supposed in this economy it was a necessary move and, from her quick once-over, it didn't seem that the store had sacrificed style or elegance in its pursuit of the more price-conscious shopper. Ironic, really, that both she and Bryant's were trying to reinvent themselves. She wondered if Luke would make a better job of it than she had.

For three-quarters of an hour she worked the crowd, signing autographs and fluttering her fingers and giggling and squealing as if she was having the time of her life. Which she most certainly was not. Yet even as she played the princess, she found her gaze wandering all too often to Luke Bryant. From the hard set of his jaw and the tension in his shoulders, he looked as if he wasn't having the time of his life, either. And, unlike her, he wasn't able to hide it.

He was certainly good-looking enough, with the dark brown hair, chocolate eyes and powerful body she remembered the feel of. Yet he looked so serious, so stern, his dark eyes hooded and his mouth a thin line. Did he ever laugh or even smile? He'd probably had his sense of humour surgically removed.

Then she remembered the thud of his heart under her hand and how warm his skin had felt, even through the cotton of his shirt. She remembered how he'd looked down at her, first with disapproval and then with desire. Typical, she told herself, yet something in her had responded to that hot, dark gaze, something in her she'd thought had long since died.

His gaze lifted to hers and she realised she'd been staring at him for a good thirty seconds. He stared back in that even, assessing way, as if he had the measure of her and found it decidedly lacking. Aurelie felt her heart give a strange little lurch and deliberately she let her gaze wander up and down his frame, giving him as much of a once-over as he'd given her. His mouth twisted in something like distaste and he turned away.

Aurelie stood there for a moment feeling oddly rebuffed, almost hurt. How ridiculous; all she'd been trying to do was annoy him. Besides, she'd suffered far worse insults than being dismissed. All she had to do was open a newspaper or click on one of the many celebrity gossip sites. Still, she couldn't deny the needling sense of pain, like a splinter burrowing into her heart. Why did this irritating man affect her so much, or even at all?

She heard the buzz of conversation around her and tried to focus on what someone was saying. Tried to smile, to perform, yet somehow the motions wouldn't come. She was failing herself, and in one abrupt movement she pivoted on her heel and walked out of the crowded lobby.

Luke watched Aurelie leave the lobby and felt an irritating mix of satisfaction and annoyance war within him. He didn't particularly want the woman around, yet he hadn't liked the look on her face, almost like hurt, when he'd gazed back at her. Why he cared, he had no idea. He *didn't* care. He wanted her gone.

And yet he could remember the exact blue-grey shade of her eyes, saw in that moment how they had darkened with pain. And despite every intention to stay and socialise, he found himself walking upstairs, back to the break room where he figured Aurelie had gone.

He pushed open the now-broken door without knocking, stopping suddenly when he saw Aurelie inside, in the process of pulling her dress over her head.

'Excuse me—'

'No need to be shy, boss man.' She turned around wearing nothing but a very skimpy push-up bra and thong, her hands on her hips, eyebrows raised, mouth twisted. 'Now you can have the good look you've been wanting.'

He shook his head. 'You're really unbelievable.'

'Why, that's almost a compliment.'

And Luke knew he *was* having a good look. Again. He could not, to his shame, tear his gaze away from those high, firm breasts encased in a very little bit of white satin. Furious with himself, he reached for a gauzy purple top lying on the floor and tossed it to her. 'Put something on.'

She glanced at the top and her mouth curled in a feline smile. 'If you insist.'

She didn't look any more decent in the see-through top. In fact, Luke decided, she looked worse. Or better, depending on your point of view. The diaphanous material still managed to highlight the slender curves that had been on such blatant display. She was too skinny, he told himself, yet once again he could not keep his gaze from roving over her body, taking in its taut perfection. He felt another stirring of arousal, much to his annoyance. Aurelie's mouth curved in a knowing smile.

'I came up here,' he finally bit out, 'to see if you were all right.'

She raised her eyebrows, and he sensed her sudden tension. 'And why wouldn't I be all right?'

'Because—' What could he say? *Because I saw such sadness in your eyes.* He was being ridiculous. About a completely ridiculous woman. 'You seemed troubled,' he finally answered, because he didn't dissemble or downright lie. He wouldn't, not since that moment twenty-five years ago when he'd put his heart and soul on the line and hadn't been believed.

'Troubled?' Her voice rang out, incredulous, scornful. Yet he still saw those shadows in her eyes, felt the brittleness of her confident pose, hands on hips, chin—and breasts— thrust out. She cocked her head, lashes sweeping downwards. 'Aren't you Mr Sensitive,' she murmured, her voice dropping into husky suggestion that had the hairs on the back of

Luke's neck prickling even as his libido stirred insistently. It had been far too long since he'd been in a relationship. Since he'd had sex. That had to be the only reason he was reacting to this woman at all.

She sashayed towards him, lifted her knowing gaze to his. Luke took an involuntary step backwards, and came up against the door. 'I think you're the troubled one, Mr Bossy,' she said, and with a cynical little smile she reached down to skim the length of his burgeoning erection with her fingertips. Luke felt as if he'd been jolted with electricity. He stepped back, shook his head in disgust.

'What is *wrong* with you?'

'Obviously nothing, judging by your reaction.'

'If I see a fairly attractive woman in her underwear, then yes, my body has a basic biological reaction. That's all it is.'

'Oh, so your little show of concern for my emotional state was just that?' She stepped back, and her smile was now cold, her eyes hard.

'You think I was coming on to you?' He let out a short, hard laugh. 'If anything, you're the one who's been coming on to me. I don't even like you, lady.'

She lifted her chin, her eyes still hard. 'Since when did like ever come into it?'

'It does for me.'

'How quaint.' She turned away and, reaching for a pair of jeans, pulled them on. 'Well, you can breathe a sigh of relief. I'm fine.'

And even though he knew he should leave—hell, he should never have come up here in the first place—Luke didn't move. She didn't *seem* fine.

He stood there in frustration—sexual frustration now, too—as Aurelie piled all the clothes scattered around the room into a big canvas holdall. She glanced up at him, those stormy eyes veiled by long lashes, and for a second, no more, she looked young. Vulnerable. Then she smiled—he hated that cold, cynical smile—and said, 'Still here, Bossy? Still hoping?'

'I'm here,' he said through gritted teeth, remembrance firing his fury, 'because you're a complete disaster and I can't trust you to walk out of here on your own two feet. An hour ago you were passed out on the floor. The last thing I need is some awful exposé in a trashy tabloid about how pop princess Aurelie ODed in the break room.'

She rolled her eyes. 'Oh, and here I was, starting to believe you were actually *concerned* about me. Don't worry, I told you, I'm fine.'

Luke jerked his head into the semblance of a nod. 'Then I'll say goodbye and thank you to use the back door on your way out.'

'I always do. Paparazzi, you know.' She smiled, but he saw her chin tremble, just the tiniest bit, and with stinging certainty he knew that despite her go-to-hell attitude, he'd hurt her.

And even though he knew he shouldn't care, not one iota, he knew he did. 'Goodbye,' he said, because the sooner he was rid of her, the better. She didn't answer, just stared at him with those storm cloud eyes, her chin lifted defiantly— and still trembling. Swearing aloud this time, Luke turned and walked out of the room.

CHAPTER TWO

'"BRYANT'S REOPENING HIT exactly the right note between self-deprecation and assurance,"' Jenna read from the newspaper as she came into Luke's office, kicking the door closed behind her with one high-heeled foot. She glanced at him over the top of the paper, her eyes dancing. 'It was a total hit!'

Luke gave a rather terse smile back. He didn't want to kill Jenna's buzz, but he hadn't meant the reopening to be 'self-deprecating'—whatever that was supposed to mean. A quick scan of the morning's headlines had reassured him that the opening had been well received, if not exactly how he'd envisioned, and the till receipts at the end of the day had offered more proof. It was enough, Luke hoped, to continue the relaunch of Bryant Stores across the globe—if his brother Aaron agreed.

He felt the familiar pang of frustration at still having to clear any major decisions with his brother, even though he was thirty-eight years old and had been running Bryant Stores for over a decade. He'd surely earned a bit more of Aaron's trust, but his brother never gave it. Their father had set up the running of Bryant Enterprises in his will, and it meant that Aaron could call all the shots. And that, Luke knew, was one thing Aaron loved to do.

'Getting Aurelie really worked,' Jenna said. 'All the papers mention her.'

'They usually do,' Luke answered dryly. He spun around in his chair to face the rather uninspiring view of Manhattan's midtown covered in a muggy midsummer haze. He did *not* want to think about that out-of-control pop princess, or the shaming reaction she'd stirred up in him.

'Apparently it was a stroke of genius to have her sing,' Jenna continued, her voice smug with self-satisfaction.

'Hitting the right note between self-deprecation and assurance?' Luke quoted. The newspaper had managed to ridicule Aurelie even as they lauded the opening. *Even if Aurelie is too washed up to reinvent herself, Bryant's obviously can.* Briefly he closed his eyes. How did she stand it, all the time? Or did she just not care?

'Maybe you should have her perform at all the openings,' Jenna suggested and Luke opened his eyes.

'I don't think so.'

'Why not?' Jenna persisted. 'I know she's a bit of a joke, but people still like her music. And the newspapers loved that we hired a has-been to perform… They thought it was an ironic nod to—'

'Our own former celebrity. Yes, I read the papers, Jenna. I'm just not sure that was quite the angle we were going for.' Luke turned around and gave his Head of PR a quelling look. He liked hiring young people with fresh ideas; he wanted change and innovation, unlike his brother. But he didn't want Aurelie.

Actually, the problem is, you do.

'Maybe not,' Jenna persisted, 'but it worked. And the truth is that nobody wants the old Bryant's any more. You can only coast on a reputation for so long.'

'Tell that to Aurelie,' he said, meaning to close down the conversation, but Jenna let out a sharp little laugh.

'But that's all she has. Do you know she actually wanted

to sing something new—some soppy folk ballad.' Jenna rolled her eyes, and Luke stilled.

'A *folk* ballad? She's a pop star.'

'I know, ridiculous, right? I don't know *what* she was thinking. She wanted to wear jeans, for heaven's sake, and play her *guitar*. Like we hired her for that.'

Luke didn't answer, just let the words sink in. 'What did you say to her?' he asked after a moment.

'I told her we'd hired her to be Aurelie, not Joan Baez.'

He rolled a silver-plated pen between his fingers, his gaze resting once more on the hazy skyline. 'What did she say?'

Jenna shrugged. 'Not much. We're the ones who hired her. What could she do, after all?'

Nothing, Luke supposed. Nothing except lash out at anyone who assumed she was just that, only that—Aurelie, the shallow pop princess. An uncomfortable uncertainty stole through him at the thought.

Who *was* Aurelie, really?

'That will be all, Jenna,' he said and, looking faintly miffed since he'd always encouraged a spirit of camaraderie in the office, she left. Luke sank back into his chair and rubbed his hands over his face.

He didn't want to think about Aurelie. He didn't want to wonder if there was more to her than he'd ever expected, or worry about what she must have been feeling. He didn't want to think about her at all.

Sighing, he dropped his hands to stare moodily out of the window. Jenna's suggestion was ridiculous, of course. There was absolutely no way he was hiring Aurelie to open so much as a sugar packet for him. He never wanted to see her again.

Then why can't you get her eyes out of your mind?

Her eyes. When he closed his own, he saw hers, stormy and sad and *brave*. He was being ridiculous, romantic, and about a woman whose whole lifestyle—values, actions, everything—he despised. She might have written some soppy new song, but it didn't change who she was: a washed-up, over-the-top diva.

Yet her eyes.

He let out a groan of frustration and swivelled back to face his computer. He didn't need this. The reopening of the New York flagship store might have been a success, but he still had a mountain of work to do. Bryant Enterprises had over a hundred stores across the world and Luke intended to overhaul every single one.

Without the help of Aurelie.

Aurelie bit her lip in concentration as she played the four notes again. Did it sound too melancholy? She had to get the bridge right or—

Or what?

She glanced up from the piano to stare unseeingly around the room she'd converted into a work space. Nobody wanted her music any more. She might be good for rehashing a few of her hit singles, but nobody wanted to hear soulful piano and acoustic guitar ballads. She'd got that loud and clear.

When she'd stupidly mentioned such an idea to her agent, he'd laughed. *Laughed.* 'Stick with what you're good at, babe,' he'd said. 'Not that it's all that much.'

She'd fired him. Not that it mattered. He'd been about to let her go anyway.

Sighing, she rose from the piano bench and went to the kitchen. She'd been working all morning and it was time for a coffee break. She hated indulging in self-pity; she knew there was no point. She'd made her bed and she'd spend the rest of her life lying in it. No one was going to let her change. And, really, she didn't need to change. At least not publicly. She could spend the rest of her life living quietly in Vermont. She didn't need a comeback, despite her pathetic attempt at one.

Just the memory of the Bryant's booking made her cringe. The only reason she'd accepted it was to have a kind of test run, to see how people responded to a new and different Aurelie. And it had failed at the very first gate. The Head of PR who had booked her had been appalled by her suggestion she do something different. *People are coming to see the Aurelie they know and love, not some wannabe folk singer. We only want one thing from you.*

Sighing again, she poured herself a coffee and added milk, stirring moodily. She'd given them the old Aurelie, just as that woman had wanted. She'd given it to them in spades. Briefly she thought of bossy Luke Bryant, and how she'd baited him. Even now she felt a flicker of embarrassment, even shame. All right, yes, she'd seen the desire flaring in his eyes, but instead of ignoring it she'd wound him up on purpose. She'd just been, as always, reacting. Reacting to the assumptions and sneers and suggestions. When she was in the moment it was so incredibly hard to rise above it.

The doorbell rang, a rusty croak of a sound, surprising her. She didn't get visitors. The paparazzi didn't know about this house and the townspeople left her alone. Then she remembered she'd ordered a new capo, and went to answer it.

'Hey...' The word died off to nothing as she stared at the man standing on the weathered front porch of her grandma's house. It wasn't the postman. It was Luke Bryant.

Luke watched the colour drain from Aurelie's face as she stared at him, obviously shocked. As shocked as he had been when he'd found this place, for an old farmhouse in a sleepy town in Vermont was not what he'd expected at all. He'd supposed it was a pretty good cover for someone like her, but it had only taken about ten seconds standing on her front porch to realise this wasn't a bolt-hole. It was home.

'What…' She cleared her throat, staring at him with wide, dazed eyes. 'What are you doing here?'

'Looking for you.'

'Why?' She sounded so bewildered he almost smiled. Gone was any kind of innuendo, any flirt. Gone, in fact, was so much as a remnant of the Aurelie he'd encountered back in New York. He looked at her properly for the first time, and knew he wouldn't have even recognised her if not for the colour of her eyes. He'd remembered those straight off. The woman in front of him was dressed in faded jeans and a lavender T-shirt, her silky hair tossed over one shoulder in a single braid. She wore no make-up, no jewellery. She was the essence of simplicity and, despite the slight gauntness of her face and frame, Luke thought she looked better now than he'd ever seen her in person or on an album cover.

'May I come in?'

'I…' She glanced behind her shoulder, and Luke wondered what she was hiding. Suspicion hardened inside him. All right, the house might be quaint in a countrified kind of way, and her clothes were…well, normal, but could he really doubt that this woman was still the outrageous, unstable pop star he'd met before?

Well, yes, he could.

He'd been doubting it, aggravatingly, ever since Jenna had suggested he book her for a string of openings and he'd refused. Refused point-blank even as he couldn't get her out of his mind. Those eyes. That sense of both sadness and courage. And how she must have come to Bryant's wanting to be different.

That was what had finally made him decide to talk to her. What a coup it would be to have Bryant's orchestrate a comeback for a has-been pop star that no one believed could change.

Although if he were honest—which he was determined

always to be—it wasn't the success of the store that had brought him to Vermont. It was something deeper, something instinctive. He understood all too well about wanting to change, trying to be different. He'd been trying with the store for nearly a decade. And as for himself… Well, he'd had his own obstacles to overcome. Clearly Aurelie had hers.

Which had brought him here, five weeks later, to her doorstep.

'May I come in?' he asked again, politely, and she chewed her lip, clearly reluctant.

'Fine,' she finally said, and moved aside so he could enter.

He stepped across the threshold, taking in the overflowing umbrella stand and coat rack, the framed samplers on the walls, the braided rug. Very quaint. And so not what he'd expected.

She closed the door and kept him there in the hall, her arms folded. 'How did you find me?'

'It was a challenge, I admit.' Aurelie had been off the map. No known address besides a rented-out beach house in Beverly Hills, no known contacts since her agent and manager had both been fired. Jenna had contacted her directly through her website, which had since closed down.

'Well?' Her eyes sparked.

'I'm pretty adept with a computer,' Luke answered. 'I found a mention of the sale of this house from a Julia Schmidt to you in the town property records.' She shook her head, coldly incredulous, and he tried a smile. 'Aurelie Schmidt. I wondered what your last name was.'

'Nice going, Sherlock.'

'Thank you.'

'I still don't know why you're here.'

'I'd like to talk to you.'

She arched an eyebrow, smiled unpleasantly. 'Oh? That wasn't the message you were sending me back in New York.'

'That's true. I'm sorry if I appeared rude.'

'Appeared? Well, I *appeared* like I was strung out on drugs, so what does it really matter?' She pivoted on her heel and walked down a dark, narrow hall, the faded wallpaper cluttered with photographs Luke found he longed to look at, to the kitchen.

'Appeared?' he repeated as he stood in the doorway, sunlight spilling into the room from a bay window that overlooked a tangled back garden. Aurelie had picked up a mug of coffee and took a sip. She didn't offer him any.

'I told you, it doesn't matter.'

'Actually, it does. If you have a substance abuse problem, I need to know about it now.' That was the one thing that had almost kept him from coming at all. He would not work with someone who was unstable, who might overdose. He would never put himself in that position again.

'You need to know?' she mocked. She held her coffee mug in front of her as if it was some kind of shield, or perhaps a weapon. Luke stayed by the door. He didn't want its contents thrown in his face. 'What else do you *need*, Luke Bryant?'

Her eyes flashed and he tensed. He hated innuendo, especially when he knew it held a shaming grain of truth.

'I have a proposition to put to you,' he said evenly. 'But first I need to know. Do you have a substance abuse problem, of any kind?'

'Would you believe me if I told you?'

'Yes—'

'Ri-ight.' She shook her head. 'Why are you really here?'

'I told you, I have a proposition to put to you. A business proposition.'

'It's always business, isn't it?'

Luke bit down on his irritation. Already he was regretting the insane impulse to come here. 'Enough. Either you listen to me or you don't. If you're interested in making a comeback—'

He saw her knuckles whiten around her coffee mug. 'Who said I was interested in that?'

'Why else accept the Bryant's booking?'

She raised her eyebrows. 'Boredom?'

Luke stared at her, saw the dangerous glitter in her eyes, the thin line of her mouth. The quivering chin. 'I don't think so,' he said quietly.

'Why are you interested in me making a comeback?' she challenged. 'Because you certainly weren't in New York.'

'I changed my mind.'

'Oh, really?'

'Look, I'll tell you all about it if you think we can have a civil conversation, but first just answer the question. Do you have a substance—'

'Abuse problem,' she finished wearily. 'No.'

'Have you ever?'

'No.'

'Then why were you passed out in New York?'

Her expression was blank, her voice flat. 'I hadn't eaten anything. Low blood sugar.' Luke hesitated. It hadn't seemed like just low blood sugar. She eyed him cynically. 'Clearly you believe me, just like you said you would.'

'I admit, I'm sceptical.'

'*So* honest of you.'

'I won't have anything to do with drugs.'

'That makes two of us. Amazing,' she drawled, 'we have something in common.'

He thought of the tabloids detailing her forays into rehab. The pictures of her at parties. He really should turn around and walk right out of here. Aurelie watched his face, her mouth curling into a cold smile he didn't like. 'That doesn't mean I've been a Girl Scout,' she told him. 'I never pretended I was.'

'I know that.'

'So what do you want?'

What *did* he want? The question felt loaded, the answer more complicated than he wanted it to be. 'I want you to sing. At the reopening of four of my stores.'

He felt her shock even though her expression—that cold, cynical smile—didn't change. 'Why?' she finally asked. 'You certainly didn't seem thrilled I was singing at your New York store.'

'No, I didn't,' he agreed evenly. 'Bryant Stores is important to me and I didn't particularly like the idea of endorsing a washed-up pop star as its mascot.'

'Thanks for spelling it out.'

'I've changed my mind.'

She rolled her eyes. 'Well, *that's* a relief.'

'The opening was well received—'

'Oh, yes, the papers loved the irony of a store trying to reinvent itself hiring a pop star who can't. I got that.' Bitterness spiked her words, and Luke felt a rush of something like satisfaction. She *was* trying to change.

'People still wanted to see you.'

'The most exciting part was when I almost tripped. People want to see me fail, Bryant. That's why they come.' She turned away and he gazed at her thoughtfully, saw the way the sunlight gilded the sharp angles of her profile in gold.

'I don't want to see you fail.'

'What?' She turned back to him, surprise wiping the cynicism from her face. She looked young, clear-eyed, even innocent. The truth of her revealed, and it gave him purpose. Certainty.

'I don't want to see you fail. Give yourself a second chance, Aurelie, and listen to what I have to say.'

* * *

Aurelie stared at him, wishing she hadn't revealed so much. *People want to see me fail.* Why had she told him the truth? Even if he already knew it, he hadn't known that she knew it. And, worse, that it hurt her. Yet she was pretty sure he knew now, and she hated the thought.

She hated that he was here. She couldn't act like Aurelie the go-to-hell pop princess here, in her grandma's house. Her home, the only place she'd ever been able to be herself. Be safe.

She felt a tightness in her chest, like something trying to claw its way out, finally break free. 'I want you to leave,' she said, and thankfully her voice came out flat. Strong. 'I'm not interested in anything you have to say, or any job you might have for me, so please, *please* leave.' Her voice wasn't strong then. It trembled and choked and she had to blink hard, which made her all the more furious.

Why did this man affect her like this? *So much?* In sudden, fearful moments she felt as if he saw something in her no one else did, no one else even wanted to. What a joke. There was nothing there to see. And, even if there were, he wouldn't be the one to see it. He still probably thought she did drugs.

'I will leave,' Luke said steadily. 'But please let me say something first.'

He stood in the doorway of her kitchen, so still, so sure, like a rock. A mountain. She couldn't get him out of here if she tried. Yet bizarrely—and terrifyingly—there was something steady about his presence. Something almost reassuring. Which was ridiculous because she didn't trust any men, and especially not ones who strode in and blustered and proclaimed, insisting that they were going to rescue you as if they were some stupid knight. All Luke Bryant needed was a white horse and a big sword.

Well, he *had* a big sword. She was pretty sure about that.

And she knew exactly how to knock him off his trusty steed. Men were all the same. They might say they wanted to help you or protect you, but really? They just wanted you. And Luke Bryant was no different.

'All right.' She folded her arms, gave him a cool smile. 'So tell me.'

'I'm overseeing the launch of our stores in Asia, and I'd like to hire you to perform at the reopening of each.'

'So you want me to sing *Take Me Down* at each one? Slink and shimmy and be outrageous?' The thought made her feel ill. She could not do that again. She wouldn't.

'No,' Luke said in that calm, deep voice Aurelie found bizarrely comforting. 'I don't want you to do any of those things.'

'That's what your Head of PR paid me to do.'

'And this time I'm paying you to do something else.'

She felt that creeping of suspicion, and a far more frightening flicker of hope. 'And what would that be, Mr Bossy?'

'To sing your new song. The one I heard while I was standing on your front porch.'

CHAPTER THREE

AURELIE ALMOST SWAYED, and Luke took an instinctive step towards her. Clearly he'd surprised her with that one. Well, he'd meant to. He had to do something to shock her out of that jaded superstar persona she wore like rusty armour. And the fact that he knew it was armour, no more than a mask, made him more certain.

She *was* different.

But how different? And how crazy was he, to come here and suggest they do business together? She might still possess a certain popularity, but he knew he was taking a huge risk. And he wasn't entirely sure why he was doing it.

'Well?' he asked, pushing away those irritating doubts. She had turned away from him, her arms wrapped around herself, her head slightly bowed. Luke had to fight the ridiculous and completely inappropriate impulse to put his arms around her. *That* would really go down well.

Then she lifted her head and turned to face him with an iron-hard gaze. 'You came all the way to Vermont without hearing that song, so that wasn't your original intention.'

'Actually, it was. But hearing it was a nice confirmation, I'll admit.'

She shook her head. 'How did you even know—'

'Jenna, my Head of PR, told me that you'd asked to sing a new composition.' *Some soppy folk ballad* had been her actual words, but Luke wasn't about to say that. And one glance at Aurelie's stony face told him he didn't need to.

'Somehow I don't think you came here on Jenna's recommendation,' she said flatly. 'She hated the song.'

'I'm not Jenna.'

'No,' she said, and her gaze swept over him slowly, suggestively. 'You're not.' She'd dropped her voice and it slid over him, all husky sweetness. Luke felt that prickling on the back of his neck. He hated how she affected him. Hated and needed it both at the same time, because there could be no denying the pulse of longing inside him when that husky murmur of a voice slid over him like a curtain of silk and she turned from innocent to siren. *Innocent Siren*, that had been the name of her first album.

Except there was nothing innocent about her, never had been, he was delusional to think that way—and then Luke saw she was walking towards him, her slender hips swaying, her storm cloud eyes narrowed even as a knowing smile curved those soft pink lips that looked so incredibly kissable.

'So why are you really here, Luke?' she asked softly. He felt his neurons short-circuit as, just as before, she placed one slender hand on his chest. He could feel the heat of her through the two layers of his suit, the thud of his own heart in response.

'I told you—' he began, but that was all he could get out. He could smell her perfume, that fresh, citrusy scent. And her hair tickled his lips. He definitely should have got a handle on his libido before he came here, because this woman made him *crazy*—

'I think I know why you're here,' she whispered, and then she stood up on her tiptoes and brushed her lips across his.

Sensation exploded inside him. He felt as if Catherine wheels had gone off behind his eyes, throughout his whole body. One almost-nothing kiss and he was firing up like a Roman candle.

'Don't—' he said brusquely, pulling away just a little. Not as much as he should have.

'Don't what?' she teased, her breath soft against his mouth, and then instinct and desire took over and he pulled her towards him, his mouth slanting over hers as he deepened her brush of a kiss into something primal and urgent. His arms came around her, his hands sliding down the narrow knobs of her spine to her hips where they fastened firmly as if they belonged there and he brought her against him. He claimed that little kiss, made it his.

His, not hers. Not theirs. Because in some distant part of his brain he realised she'd gone completely still, lifeless even, and all the while he was kissing her like a drowning man clinging to the last lifebelt.

With a shaming amount of effort he pushed himself away from her, let out a shuddering breath. His heart still thudded. 'What the hell was that about?'

She gazed back at him in stony-faced challenge, seeming completely unaffected by something that felt as if it had almost felled him. 'You tell me.'

'Why did you kiss me?'

'Are you trying to act like you didn't want it?'

'I—' Damn. 'No, I'm not.' Surprise rippled in her eyes like a shadow on water but she said nothing. 'I admit, I'm attracted to you. I'd rather not be. And it has nothing to do with why I came here.'

She arched her eyebrows, elegantly incredulous. 'Nothing?'

Luke expelled an exasperated breath. He didn't lie. Couldn't, ever since he'd told the truth in one of the most defining moments of his life and hadn't been believed. He'd been blamed instead, and maybe—

He pushed the thought away. 'It probably had something to do with it,' he admitted tersely. 'But I wish it didn't.'

'Really.' She sounded utterly disbelieving, and he could hardly blame her. From the first moment he'd met her his body had been reacting. Wanting. He knew it, and obviously so did she.

'Why did you kiss me?' he countered. 'Because I admit I might have taken over, but you started it and there's got to be a reason for that.'

'Does there?'

'I think,' Luke said slowly, 'there's a reason for everything you do, even if it seems completely crazy from the outside.'

She let out a little laugh, the first genuine sound of humour he'd heard from her. 'Thank you for that compliment… I think.'

'You're welcome.'

They stared at each other like two wrestlers on either side of the mat. Some kind of truce had been called, but Luke didn't know what it was. Or why he was here. His calm, no-nonsense plan to hire Aurelie for the Asia openings— to change the public's opinion of both her and the store, the ultimate reinvention—seemed like the flimsiest of pretexts after that kiss.

He'd come here because he wanted her, full stop. It really was that simple.

Aurelie stared at Luke, wondered what tack he'd try next. The honesty had surprised her. Unsettled her, because she knew he was speaking the truth and she didn't know what to do with it. She wasn't used to honesty.

Trying for something close to insouciance, she turned away from him, picked up her discarded mug of coffee and kept the kitchen counter between them.

Luke folded his arms. 'So you still haven't told me why you kissed me.'

She shrugged. 'Why not?' That kiss had started out as a way to prove he just wanted one thing and it wasn't her song. But then she'd felt the softness of his lips, his hair, and she'd forgotten she'd been trying to prove a point. She'd felt a flicker of…something. Desire? It seemed impossible. And then Luke had deepened the kiss and she'd felt herself retreat into numbness as she always did.

She took a sip of her now-cold coffee. She shouldn't have kissed him at all. She didn't want to be Aurelie here, in the only place she'd ever thought of as home. She wanted to be herself, but she didn't know how to do that with someone like Luke. Or with anyone, really. She'd been pretending for so long she wasn't sure she could stop. 'Why don't you tell me why you want to hire me for these reopenings.'

'I told you already.'

'The real reason.'

He stared at her, his dark eyes narrowed, lips thinned. He really was an attractive man, not that it mattered. Still a part of her could admire the chocolate-coloured hair, could remember how soft it had felt threaded through her fingers. How hard and toned his body had been against hers. How *warm* his eyes had seemed—

She needed to put a stop to that kind of thinking right now. 'Well? Why?'

'It's more complicated than I'd prefer it to be,' Luke said, the words seeming wrested from him. 'It makes good business sense on one level, and on another…yes.' He shrugged, spread his hands. 'Like I said before, attraction comes into it. Probably. It doesn't mean I'm going to act on it.'

'Despite the fact that you just did.'

'If you thrust your tongue into my mouth, I'll respond. I'm a man.'

Exactly. And she knew men. Still, the extent of his honesty unnerved her. He could have easily denied it. Lied. 'What are you,' she said, 'Pinocchio?'

He glanced away, his expression shuttering. 'Something like that.'

The man could not tell a lie. How fascinating, considering she told dozens. Hundreds. Her whole *life* was a lie. 'So if I asked you anything, you'd have to tell me the truth?'

'I don't like lying, if that's what you mean.'

'Don't like it, or aren't good at it?'

'Both.'

She was tempted to ask him something really revealing, embarrassing even, yet she decided not to. Any more intimacy with this man was not advisable.

'Okay, then. Tell me just what this whole Asia thing is about.'

'I'm relaunching four stores across Asia. Manila, Singapore, Hong Kong and Tokyo. I want you to sing at each opening.'

'Sing my new song.'

'That's about it.'

'That's kind of a risk, don't you think?'

He raised his eyebrows in both challenge and query. 'Is it?'

'How long were you standing on my porch?'

'Long enough.'

She had the absolutely insane impulse to ask him what he'd thought of that song. She'd been working on it for months, and it meant more to her than she ever wanted to admit—which was why she wouldn't ask. 'Why don't you want my usual Aurelie schtick?' she asked instead.

He nodded, and it felt like an affirmation. 'That's what it is, isn't it? A schtick. An act. Not who you really are.'

She didn't like the way his gaze seemed to sear right

through her. She didn't like it at all, and yet part of her was crying out yes. *Yes, it's pretend, it's not me, and you're the only person who has ever realised that.* From somewhere she dredged up the energy to roll her eyes. Laugh it off. 'Of course it's a schtick. Any famous person is just an act, Bryant. A successful one.'

'Call me Luke.' She pressed her lips together. Said nothing. He took a step towards her. 'So will you do it?'

'I can't give you an answer right now.'

'You'd better give me an answer soon, because I fly to the Philippines next week.'

She let out a low breath, shook her head. She wasn't saying no, she just felt...

'Scared?'

'What?'

'You're scared of me. Why?' She stared at him, wordless with shock, and he gave her a little toe-curling smile. 'The honesty thing? It goes both ways. I call it as I see it, Aurelie. Always. So why are you scared?'

She bristled. 'Because I don't know you. Because you practically stalked me, coming to my house here, muscling your way in—'

'I asked. Politely. And you're the one who kissed me, so—'

'Just forget it.' She turned away, hating how much he saw and didn't see at the same time. Hating how confused and needy he made her feel.

'Tell me why you're scared.'

'I'm not scared.' She was terrified.

'Are you scared of me, or of singing?' He took another step towards her, his body relaxed and so contained. He was so sure of himself, of who he was, and it made her angry. Jealous. *Scared.*

'Neither—' *Both.*

'You know you're not that great a liar, either.'

She whirled around to face him, to say something truly scathing, but unfortunately nothing came to mind. All her self-righteous indignation evaporated, and all the posturing she depended on collapsed. She had nothing. And she was so very tired of pretending, of acting as if she didn't care, of being someone else. Even if the thought of being herself—and having people see that—was utterly terrifying.

'Of course I'm a little…wary,' she snapped, unable to lose that brittle, self-protective edge. 'The press lives to ridicule me. People love to hate me. Do you think I really enjoy opening myself up to all that again and again?'

He stared at her for a moment, *saw* her, and it took all her strength to stand there and take it, not to say something stupid or suggestive, hide behind innuendo. She lifted her chin instead and returned his gaze.

'You act like you do.'

'And I told you, every famous person is an act. Aurelie the pop star isn't real.' She couldn't believe she was saying this.

'Then who,' Luke asked, 'is Aurelie Schmidt?'

Aurelie stared at him for a long, helpless moment. She had no answer to that one. She'd been famous since she was sixteen years old. 'It hardly matters. Nobody's interested in Aurelie Schmidt.'

'Maybe they would be if they got to know her.'

'Trust me, they wouldn't.'

'It's a risk you need to take.'

It was a risk too great to take. 'Don't tell me what I need.'

Luke thrust his hands into his pockets. 'Fine. Let me take you to dinner.'

Suspicion sharpened inside her. 'Why?'

'A business dinner. To discuss the details of the Asia trip.'

She started to shake her head, then stopped. Was she really

going to close this down before it had even started? Was she that much a coward? 'I haven't said yes.'

'I know.'

Slowly she let out her breath. She *was* scared. Of singing, and of him. Of how much he seemed to see. Know. And yet part of her craved it all at the same time. Desperately. 'All right.'

'Any recommendations for a good place to eat around here?'

'Not really. There's a fast food joint in the next town over—'

'Anything else?'

'Nothing closer than thirty miles.'

He said nothing, but his thoughtful gaze still unnerved her. This whole thing was a bad idea, and she should call it off right now—

'Tell you what,' Luke suggested. 'I'll cook for you.'

'What?' No man had ever cooked for her, or even offered.

'I'm not Michelin, but I make a decent steak and chips.'

'I don't have any steak.'

'Do you eat it?'

'Yes—'

'Then I'll go out and buy some. And over a meal we'll discuss Asia.'

It sounded so pleasant, so *normal*, and yet still she hesitated. Pleasant and normal were out of her realm of experience. Then she thought of what Luke was offering her—an actual *chance*—and she nodded. Grudgingly. 'Okay.'

'Good.' He turned to go. 'I'll be back in half an hour.'

Thirty minutes' respite. 'Okay,' she said again, and then he was gone.

Luke gave her nearly an hour. He thought she needed the break. Hell, he did too. He took his time choosing two thick fillets, a bag of potatoes, some salad. He thought about buying a bottle of wine, but decided against it. This was a business dinner. Strictly business, no matter how much his libido acted up or how much he remembered that mind-blowing kiss—

Hell.

He stopped right there in the drinks aisle and asked himself just what he was doing here. His brain might be insisting it was just business, but his body said otherwise. His body remembered the feel of her lips, the smoke of her voice, the emotion in her eyes. His body remembered and wanted, and that was dangerous. *Crazy.*

He straightened, forced himself to think as logically as he always did. All right, yes, he desired her. He'd admitted it. But this was still business. If Aurelie's performance at Bryant's gave her the kind of comeback he envisioned, it would create fantastic publicity for the store. It was, pure and simple, a good business move. That was why he was here.

As he resolutely turned towards the checkout, he felt a prickle of unease, even guilt. He'd told Aurelie he didn't lie, but right then he was pretty sure he was lying to himself.

By the time he made it back to the house on the end of the little town's sleepiest street it was early evening, the sun's rays just starting to mellow. The air was turning crisp, and he could see a few scarlet leaves on the maple outside the weathered clapboard house Aurelie called home.

He rang the doorbell, listened to it wheeze and then her light footsteps. She opened the door and he saw that she'd showered—squash *that* vision right now—and her hair was damp and tucked behind her ears. She'd changed into a pale green cashmere sweater and a pair of skinny jeans, and when he glanced down he saw she was wearing fuzzy pink socks. Fuchsia, actually.

He nodded towards the socks. 'Those look cosy.'

She gave him the smallest of smiles, but at least it felt real. 'My feet get cold.'

'May I come in?'

She nodded, and he sensed the lack of artifice from her. Liked it. *Who is Aurelie Schmidt?* Maybe he'd find out.

But did he really want to?

She moved aside and he came in with the bag of groceries. 'Do you mind if I make myself comfortable in your kitchen?'

She hesitated, and he could almost imagine her suggestive response. *You go ahead and make yourself comfortable anywhere, Luke.* He could practically write the script for her, because he was pretty sure now that was all it was: a script. Lines. This time she didn't give them to him; she just shrugged. 'Sure.'

He nodded and headed towards the back of the house.

Fifteen minutes later he had the steaks brushed with olive oil and in the oven, the potatoes sliced into wedges and frying on the stove, and he was tossing a salad. Aurelie perched on a stool, her fuzzy feet hooked around the rungs, and watched him.

'Do you like to cook?'

'Sometimes. I'm not a gourmet, by any means. Not like my brother Chase.'

'He's good?'

Luke shrugged. He wished he hadn't mentioned Chase, or anything to do with his family. He preferred not to dredge those dark memories up; he'd determinedly pushed them way, way down. Yet something about this woman—her fragility, perhaps—brought them swimming up again. 'He's good at most things,' he replied with a shrug. He reached for some vinaigrette. 'Do you have brothers or sisters?'

'No.' From the flat way she spoke Luke guessed she was as reluctant to talk about her family as he was to talk about his. Fine with him.

He finished tossing the salad. 'Everything should be ready in a few minutes.'

Aurelie slid off her stool to get the plates. 'It smells pretty good.'

He glanced up, smiling wryly. 'Are we actually having a civil conversation?'

'Sounds like it.' She didn't smile back, just took a deep breath, the plates held to her chest. 'Look, if you came here on some kind of mercy mission, just forget it. I don't need your pity.'

He stilled. 'I don't pity you.'

'If not pity, then what?'

A muscle bunched in his jaw. 'What are you saying?'

She lifted her chin. 'I find it hard to believe you came all the way to Vermont to ask me to sing. You hadn't even heard that song. It could have sucked. Maybe it does.'

'I admit, it was a risk.'

'So why did you come? What's the real reason?' Suspicion sharpened her voice, twisted inside him like a knife. Did she actually think he'd come here to get her into bed?

Had he?

No, damn it, this was about business. About helping the store and helping Aurelie. The ultimate reinvention. Luke laid his hands flat on the counter. 'I don't have some sexual agenda, if that's what you're thinking.'

She cocked her head. 'You're sure about that?'

He shook his head slowly. 'What kind of men have you known?'

'Lots. And they're all the same.'

'I'm different.' And he'd prove it to her. He took the plates from her, his gaze steady on her own stormy one. 'Let's eat.'

Luke dished out the meal and carried it over to the table in the alcove of the kitchen. Twilight was settling softly outside, the sky awash in violet. Used to the frantic sounds of the city, he felt the silence all around him, just like he felt Aurelie's loneliness and suspicion. 'Do you live here most of the time?' he asked.

'I do now.'

'Do you like it?'

'It'd be a pretty sad life if I didn't.'

He sat opposite her and picked up his fork and knife. 'You're not much of a one for straight answers, are you?'

She met his gaze squarely, gave a small nod of acknowledgement. 'I guess not.'

'All right. Business.' Luke forced himself to focus on the one thing he'd always focused on, and was now finding so bizarrely hard. He wanted to ask her questions about the house, her life, how she'd got to where she was. He wanted to go back in the hallway and look at the photographs on the walls, he wanted to hear her play that song, he wanted—

Business.

'It's pretty simple,' he said. 'Four engagements over a period of ten days. You sing one or two of your new songs.'

'The audience won't be expecting that.'

'I know.'

'And you're okay with that?' She raised her eyebrows. 'Because your Head of PR definitely wasn't.'

'Good thing I'm CEO of the company, then,' Luke said evenly.

'You know,' Aurelie said slowly, 'people want things to be how they expect. They want me to be what they expect. What they think I am.'

'Which is exactly why I want you to be different,' Luke countered. 'Bryant's is an institution in America and other parts of the world. So are you.'

'Now that's something I haven't been compared to before.'

'If you can change your image, then anyone can.'

'Judging by the papers, you've already changed the store's image successfully. You don't need me.'

Luke hesitated because he knew she was right, at least in part. 'I didn't like the way the press spun it,' he said after a moment.

'The whole self-deprecating thing?' she said with a twisted smile. 'Former celebrity?'

'Exactly. I want a clean sweep, home run. No backhanded compliments.'

'Maybe you should just take what you can get.'

He shook his head. 'That's not how I do business.'

She glanced away. When she spoke, her voice was low. 'What if I can't change?'

'There's only one way to find out.' Aurelie didn't say anything, but he could see her thinking about it. Wondering. Hoping, even. He decided to let her mull it over. Briskly, he continued, 'Your accommodation will be provided, and we can negotiate a new rate for the—'

'I don't care about the money.'

'I want to be fair.'

She toyed with her fork, pushing the food around on her plate. He saw she hadn't eaten much. 'This still feels like pity.'

'It isn't.'

She glanced up and he saw the ghost of a smile on her face, like a remnant of who she had once been, a whisper of who she could be, if she smiled more. If she were happy. 'And you can't tell a lie, can you?'

'I won't tell a lie.'

She eyed him narrowly. 'But it's something close to pity.'

'Sympathy, perhaps.'

'Which is just a nicer word for pity.'

'Semantics.'

'Exactly.'

His lips twitched in a smile of his own. 'Okay, look. I told you, I don't pity you. I feel—'

'Sorry for me.'

'Stop putting words in my mouth. I feel...' He let out a whoosh of exasperated breath. He didn't like talking about feelings. He never did. His mother had died when he was thirteen, his father had never got close, and his brothers didn't ask. But here he was, and she was right, he couldn't lie. Not to her. 'I know how you feel,' he said at last, and she raised her eyebrows, clearly surprised by that admission. Hell, he was surprised too.

'How so?'

'I know what it feels like to want to change.'

'You've wanted to change?'

'Hasn't everybody?'

'That's no answer.'

He shrugged. 'I've had my own obstacles to overcome.'

'Like what?'

He should never have started this. The last thing he wanted to do was rake up his own tortured memories. 'A difficult childhood.'

Her mouth pursed. 'Poor little rich boy?'

He tensed, and then forced himself to relax. 'Something like that.'

She lifted her chin, challenge sparking in her eyes. 'Well, maybe I don't want to change.'

It was such obvious bravado that Luke almost laughed. 'Then why write a different kind of song? Why ask to sing it? Why accept the Bryant's booking when you haven't performed publicly in years?'

Her mouth twisted. 'Done a little Internet stalking, have you?'

'I didn't need to look on the Internet to know that.' She shook her head, said nothing. 'Anyway,' he continued in a brisker voice, 'the point is, I've been trying to reinvent Bryant's for years and—'

'What's been stopping you?'

Luke hesitated. He didn't want to bring up Aaron and his constant quest for control. 'Change doesn't happen overnight,' he finally said. 'And Bryant's has a century-old reputation. There's been resistance.'

'There always is.'

'So see? We have something else in common.'

'You want to reinvent a store and I want to reinvent myself.'

Luke didn't answer, because there was an edge to her voice that made him think a simple agreement was not the right choice here. He waited, wondered why it mattered to him so much.

He didn't need Aurelie. He didn't need her to open a store or sing a damn song. He didn't need her at all.

Yet as she gazed at him with those rain-washed eyes he felt a tug deep inside that he couldn't begin to understand. More than lust, deeper than need. Despite having had three long-term satisfying relationships, he'd never felt this whirlpool of emotion before, as if he were being dragged under by the force of his own feelings. Never mind her being scared. He was terrified.

The smart thing to do right now would be to get out of this chair, out of this house. Walk away from Aurelie and all her crazy complications and go about his business, his *life*, the way he always had. Calm and in control, getting things done, never going too deep.

He didn't move.

Aurelie drew a deep breath, let it out slowly. 'Let me play you my song,' she finally said and, surprised and even touched, Luke nodded.

'I'd like that.'

She smiled faintly, that whisper of a promise, and wordlessly Luke followed her out of the room.

CHAPTER FOUR

AURELIE LED LUKE into the music room at the front of the house, her heart thudding, her skin turning clammy. She felt dizzy with nerves, and silently prayed that she wouldn't pass out. The last thing she needed was Luke Bryant to think she'd ODed again.

She paused in front of the piano, half-regretting her suggestion already. No, not even half—*totally*. Why was she opening herself up to this? She didn't need money. She didn't need to sing in public again. She didn't need any of this.

But she wanted it. She actually wanted to share something that was important to her, share it with this man, never mind the public, even as it scared her near witless.

'Aurelie?'

There was something about the way he said her name, so quietly, so *gently*, that made her ache deep inside. She swallowed, her face turned away from him. 'It sounds better with guitar.'

'Okay.'

She reached for her acoustic guitar, the one her grandmother had bought her just before she'd died. *Don't forget who you really are, Aurie. Don't let them turn your head.* But she had let them. She'd forgotten completely. Her fingers curled around the neck of the guitar and, unable to look at Luke—afraid to see the expression on his face—she bent her head and busied herself with tuning the instrument. Needlessly, since she'd played it that afternoon.

After a few taut minutes she knew she couldn't wait any longer. Yet she was terrified to play the song, terrified to have Luke reject it. *Her*. He'd let her down easily because, no matter what he said, she knew he did feel sorry for her. But it would still hurt.

'So has this song got some kind of long silent intro or what?'

She let out a little huff of laughter, glad he'd jolted her out of her ridiculous stage fright. 'Patience.' And taking a deep breath, she began. The first few melancholy chords seemed to flow through her, out into the room. And then she began to sing, not one of the belt-it-out numbers of her pop star days, but something low and intimate and tender. *'Winter came so early, it caught me by surprise. I stand alone till the cold wind blows the tears into my eyes.'* She hesitated for a tiny second, trying to gauge Luke's reaction, but the song seemed to take up all the space. *'I turn my face into the wind and listen to the sound. Never give your heart away. It will only bring you down.'* And then she forgot about Luke, and just sang. The song took over everything.

Yet when the last chord died away and the room seemed to bristle with silence, she felt her heart thud again and she couldn't look at him. Staring down at her guitar, she idly picked a few strings. 'It's kind of a downer of a song, isn't it?' she said with an unsteady little laugh. 'Probably not the best number to open a store with.'

'That doesn't matter.' She couldn't tell a thing from his tone, and she still couldn't look at him. 'Of course, if you had another one, maybe a *bit* more hopeful, you could sing that one too.'

Something leapt inside her, a mongrel beast of hope and fear. A dangerous animal. She looked up, saw him gazing

at her steadily, yet without any expression she could define.
'I could?'

'Yes.'

'So…' She swallowed. 'What did you think? Of the song?'

'I thought,' Luke said quietly, with obvious and utter sincerity, 'it was amazing.'

'Oh.' She looked back down at her guitar, felt tears sting
her eyes and blinked hard to keep them back. Damn it, she
was not going to cry in front of this man. Not now. Not ever.
'Well…good.' She kept her head lowered, and then she felt
Luke shift. He'd been sitting across from her, but now he
leaned forward, his knee almost nudging hers.

'I can understand why you're scared.'

Instinct kicked in. 'I never actually said I was scared.'
And then she sniffed, loudly, which basically blew her cover.

'You didn't have to.' He placed one hand on her knee,
and she gazed down at it, large, brown, strong. Comforting.
'That song is very personal.'

Which was why she felt so…*naked* right now, every protective layer peeled away. She swallowed, stared at his hand,
mesmerised by the long, lean fingers curled unconsciously
around her knee. 'It's just a song.'

'Is it?'

And then she looked up at him, and knew she was in trouble. He was gazing at her with such gentle understanding,
such tender compassion, that she felt completely exposed
and accepted at the same time. It was such a weird feeling,
such an *overwhelming* feeling, that it was almost painful.
She swallowed. 'Luke…' Her voice came out husky, and
she saw his pupils flare. Felt the very air tauten. This tender
moment was turning into something else, something Aurelie knew and understood.

This was about sex. It was always about sex. And while
part of her felt disappointed, another part flared to life.

Luke straightened, taking his hand from her knee. 'I should go. It's late.'

'You can't drive all the way back to New York tonight.'

'I'll find a place to stay.' He made to rise from his chair, and Aurelie felt panic flutter like a trapped, desperate bird inside her.

'You could stay here.'

He stared at her, expressionless, and Aurelie put away her guitar, her face averted from his narrowed gaze. Her heart was pounding again. She didn't know what she was telling him. What she wanted. All she knew was she didn't want him to go.

'I don't think that's a good idea,' Luke said after a moment and Aurelie turned to face him.

'Why not?'

He smiled wryly, but she saw how dark and shadowed his eyes looked. 'Because we're going to have a business relationship and I don't want to complicate things.'

She lifted her eyebrows, tried for insouciance. 'Why does it have to be complicated?'

'What are you asking me, Aurelie?'

She liked the way he said her name. She'd always hated it, a ridiculous name given to her by an even more ridiculous mother, but when he said it she felt different. She felt more like herself—or at least the person she thought she could be, if given a chance. 'What do you want me to be asking you?'

He laughed softly. 'Never a straight answer.'

'I'd hate to bore you.'

'I don't think you could ever bore me.' He was staring straight at her, and she could see the heat in his eyes. Felt it in herself, a flaring deep within, which was sudden and surprising because desire for a man was something she hadn't felt in a long time, if ever. Yet she felt it now, for this man. This wasn't about power or control or the barter that sex had always been to her. She simply wanted him, wanted to be with him.

'Well?' she asked, her voice no more than a breath.

Luke didn't move. Didn't speak. Aurelie saw both the doubt and desire in his eyes, and she took a step towards him so she was standing between his splayed thighs. With her fingertips she smoothed the crease that had appeared in his forehead. 'You think too much.'

His mouth curved wryly. 'I think I'm thinking with the wrong organ at the moment.'

She laughed softly. 'What's wrong with thinking with that organ on occasion?' She let her fingertips drift from his forehead to his cheek, felt the bristle of stubble on his jaw. She liked touching him. How strange. How *nice*.

Luke closed his eyes. 'I really don't think this is a good idea.'

'That's your brain talking now.'

'Yes—'

She let her thumb rest on his lips. They were soft and full and yet incredibly masculine. With his eyes closed she had the freedom to study his face, admire the strong lines of his jaw and nose, the sooty sweep of his lashes. Long lashes and full lips on such a virile man. Amazing.

'Shh,' she said softly, and then slowly, deliberately, she slid her finger into his mouth. His lips parted, and she felt the wet warmth of his tongue before he bit softly on the pad of her finger. Lust jolted like an electric pulse low in her belly, shocking her. Thrilling her. Luke opened his eyes; they blazed with heat and need. He sucked gently on her finger and she let out a shuddery little gasp.

Then he drew back, his eyes narrowing once more. 'Why are you doing this?'

She smiled. 'Why not?'

'I don't want you throwing this in my face, telling me I'm just like every other man you've met.'

'I won't.' She knew he wasn't. He was different, just like he'd said he was. And she wanted him to stay. She *needed* him to stay. 'You really do think too much,' she murmured. She stepped closer, hooked one leg around his. She hooked her other leg around so she was straddling him. Then she lowered herself, legs locked around his, onto his lap. She could feel his arousal pressing against her and she shifted closer, settling herself against him.

'That's a rather graceful move,' Luke said, the words coming out on a half-groan.

'All that dancing onstage has made me *very* flexible.'

'Aurelie…'

'I like how you say my name.'

Luke slid his hands down her back, anchored onto her hips, holding her there. 'This really isn't a good idea,' he muttered, and Aurelie pressed against him.

'Define good,' she said, and as he drew her even closer she knew she had him. She'd won, and she felt a surge of both triumph and desire. Yet amidst that welter of emotion she felt a little needle of disappointment, of hurt. Men really were all the same.

He was being seduced. Luke had realised this at least fifteen minutes ago, when Aurelie had first got that knowing glint in her eyes, and even though just about everything in him was telling him this was a bad idea, his body was saying something else entirely. His body was shouting, *Hell, yes*.

He felt as if he were two men, one who stood about five feet behind him, coldly rational, pointing out that he was doing exactly what Aurelie had accused him of doing. Coming here with a sexual agenda, with a plan to get her into bed—

Except she was the one trying to get *him* into bed.

And he wanted to go there.

Still, that cold voice pointed out, sleeping with Aurelie was a huge mistake, one that would cause countless complications for their proposed business trip to Asia, not to mention his personal life. His *sanity*.

The other man, the one curving his hands around her hips, was insisting that he wasn't sleeping with Aurelie, he was sleeping with Aurelie *Schmidt*. The woman who had sung that beautiful, heartbreaking song, who hid her heart in her eyes, whom he'd recognised from the first moment she'd looked up at him.

Yet maybe that was even worse. That woman was confusing, vulnerable, and far more desirable than any persona she put on. And whether it was the pop star or the hidden woman underneath on his lap, he knew it was still a hell of a mistake.

And one he had decided to make. Luke slid his hands up her back to cradle her face, his fingers threading through the softness of her hair. And then he kissed her, his lips brushing once, twice over hers before he let himself go deep and the coldly rational part of himself telling him to stop went silent.

Somehow they got upstairs. It was hazy in his mind, fogged as it was with lust, but Luke remembered stumbling on a creaky stair, opening a door. There was a bed, wide and rumpled. And there was Aurelie, standing in front of it, a faint smile on her face. Luke slid her sweater over her head, unbuttoned her jeans. She wriggled out of them and lay on the bed in just her bra and underwear, waiting, ready.

Except her damn chin was quivering.

Luke hesitated, the roar of his heated blood and his own aching need almost, almost winning out. 'Aurelie—'

He saw uncertainty flicker in her eyes, shadows on water, and then she reached up to grab him by the lapels of his suit; he was still completely dressed.

'It's too late for second thoughts,' she said, and as she

kissed him, a hungry, open-mouthed kiss, he had to agree that it just might be.

He kissed her back, desire for her surging over him in a tidal wave, drowning out anything but that all-consuming need, and he felt her fumble with the zip of his trousers.

'Aurelie...' He groaned her name, felt her fingers slide around him. He pushed aside the lacy scrap of her underwear, stroked the silkiness of her thigh. He slid his fingers higher, kissed her deeper, his body pulsing with need, aching with want. Yet even as his hands roamed over her, teasing and finding, a part of his brain started to buzz.

Distantly he realised she'd stopped responding. Her arms had fallen away from him and she was lying tensely beneath him, stiff and straight.

She let out a shudder that could have been a sob or a sigh, and Luke pulled back to look down at her.

Her eyes were scrunched shut, her breathing ragged, her whole body radiating tension. She looked, he thought with a savage twist of self-loathing, as if she were being tortured.

Swearing, Luke rolled off her. His body ached with unfulfilment and his mind seethed with regret. He'd *known* this was a mistake.

He raked a hand through his sweat-dampened hair, let out a shuddering breath. 'What happened?' he asked in a low voice, but Aurelie didn't answer. Silently she slid off the bed and disappeared into the bathroom. Luke heard the door shut and he threw an arm over his eyes. He didn't know what had just happened, but he was pretty sure it was his fault.

From behind the closed door he heard her moving around, a cupboard opening and closing. Seconds ticked by, then minutes. Unease crawled through him, mingling with the virulent regret and even shame he felt. He hated locked doors. Hated that damning silence, the helplessness he felt on the other side, the creeping sense that something wasn't right. Something was very, very wrong.

He got up from the bed, pulled up his trousers and buckled his belt, then headed over to the door.

'Aurelie?' No answer. His unease intensified. 'Aurelie,' he said again and opened the door.

As soon as he saw her Luke swore.

She stood in front of the sink, one arm outstretched, a fully loaded syringe in the other. Acting only on instinct, Luke knocked the syringe hard out of her hand and it went clattering to the floor.

Aurelie stilled, her face expressionless. 'Well, *that* was a waste,' she finally said, her voice a drawl, and bent to pick up the syringe.

'What the hell are you doing?'

She eyed him sardonically. 'I think the more important question is, what do you think I'm doing?'

He stared at her, confusion, fury and shame all rushing through him in a scalding river. This woman drove him *insane*.

Would you believe me if I told you I didn't? He'd said he would. 'It looks,' he said as evenly as he could, 'like you're shooting yourself up with some kind of drug.'

Her lips curved in that way he knew and hated. Mockery. Armour. 'You get a gold star,' she said as she swabbed off the syringe with a cotton pad and some rubbing alcohol. 'That's exactly what I'm doing.'

And he watched as she carefully injected the syringe into the fleshy part of her upper arm.

Luke felt his hands clench into fists at his sides. 'Why don't you tell me what's really going on here?'

She put the syringe away in a little black cosmetic bag. Luke glimpsed a few clear phials inside before she zipped it up and put it away. She gave a small, tired sigh. 'Don't worry, Bryant. It's only insulin.'

She walked past him back into the bedroom, and Luke turned around to stare at her. '*Insulin?* You have diabetes?'

'Bingo.' She reached for a fuzzy bathrobe hanging on the back of the door and put it on. Sitting on the edge of the bed, swallowed up by fleece, she looked young and vulnerable and so very alone.

'Why didn't you tell me?'

'When should I have done that? When I was passed out on the dressing room floor, or after you dunked me in the sink?'

Slowly he walked into the bedroom, sank onto a chair across from her. He raked his hands through his hair, tried to untangle his tortured, twisted thoughts. 'So when you were passed out in New York, it was because of low blood sugar?' Just like she'd said.

'I forgot to check my bloods before I went.'

'That's dangerous—'

She let out a short laugh. 'Thanks for the warning. Trust me, I know. I've been living with diabetes for almost ten years. I was keyed up about the performance and I forgot.' And then as if she realised she'd revealed too much, she folded her arms and looked away, jaw set, eyes hard.

'Why didn't you tell me earlier? In the kitchen, when I *asked*?'

'You wouldn't have believed me—'

'I said I would—'

'Oh, yes, you *said*.' Her eyes flashed malice. 'Well, maybe you're not such a Boy Scout after all, because I don't think you were telling the truth.'

'It was,' Luke said, an edge creeping into his voice, 'a little hard to believe you were passed out just from lack of food. If I'd known you had a *condition*—'

'And maybe I don't feel like explaining myself every time

something looks a little suspicious,' she snapped. 'If you were passed out, would someone assume you'd done drugs? Were a junkie?'

'No, of course not. But I'm not—'

She leaned forward, eyes glittering. 'You're not what?'

Luke stared at her, his mind still spinning. 'I'm not you,' he said at last. 'You're *Aurelie*.' The moment he said it, he knew it had been completely the wrong thing to say. To think.

She turned away from him, her jaw set. 'I am, aren't I,' she said quietly.

Luke dropped his head in his hands. 'I only meant you've been known to…to…'

'I know what I've been known to do.' Her eyes flashed, her chin trembled. He could always tell the truth of her from that chin. She was scared. And sad. Hell, so was he. *How had they got here?*

He shook his head, weary and heartsick, but also angry. 'What happened back there on the bed, Aurelie? Why did you look like…' He could barely say it. 'Like you were being tortured? Or attacked? Were you trying to prove some point?' Had she set him up, shown him to be exactly what she'd accused, just another man determined to get her into bed? 'Well, I guess you made it,' he said heavily when she didn't answer. 'Congratulations.'

Still she said nothing, just stared him down, and in that silence Luke wondered if things could have turned out any worse.

'Do you still want me to go?' she finally asked. 'To Asia?'

He let out a short, disbelieving laugh. 'Do you still *want* to go? After this?'

She raised her eyebrows, her expression so very cold. 'Why shouldn't I?'

He felt a rush of anger, cleaner than shame. She'd *played* him. Admittedly, he'd let himself be played. He'd been willing to be seduced, had turned it to his advantage. But the fact remained that she'd used him, coldly and deliberately, to prove some twisted, paranoid point. He hadn't had a sexual agenda until she'd sat in his lap.

Liar.

'Yes, you can go to Asia,' he told her wearily. Something good would come out of this unholy affair. 'I'll have my PA email you the details. You need to be in Manila on the twenty-fourth.' With that he stood up and he saw, with some gratification, that her eyes had widened.

'You're going?'

'I don't want to stay and, frankly, I don't think you want me to, either. Like I said, you made your point.'

She stared at him, still swallowed up by her bathrobe, her eyes wide and stormy. Luke felt the shame slither inside him again. 'I didn't come here intending to sleep with you,' he said. 'I swear to God I didn't.'

She said nothing and with a shake of his head he left the room.

CHAPTER FIVE

AURELIE GAZED AT her reflection for the fifth time in the hall mirror of the deluxe suite Luke had booked for her in the Mandarin Oriental in Manila's business district. She'd arrived a few hours ago and was meeting Luke in the bar in ten minutes.

And she was sick and dizzy with nerves.

She let out a deep breath and checked her reflection again. She wore just basic make-up, mostly to disguise the violet circles under her eyes since she hadn't had a decent night's sleep since Luke had walked out of her bedroom ten days ago.

She closed her eyes briefly, the memories making her even dizzier. She couldn't think about Luke without reliving that awful encounter. The condemnation and disgust in his eyes. The *confusion*. And her own impossible behaviour.

She hadn't brought him to her bed to set him up, the way Luke had so obviously thought. She'd been acting out of need and maybe even desire—at least at first. When she'd touched him she'd felt something unfurl inside her, something that had been desperately seeking light. But then it had all gone wrong, as it always did. The moment she was stretched out on that bed she'd gone numb. He'd become just a man who wanted something from her, and he'd get it, no matter what. She'd give it to him, because that was what she did.

Except he hadn't taken it, which made him different from every other man she'd known. Why did that thought scare her so much?

He obviously didn't think *she* was different. She could still see the look of disgust twisting Luke's features, the condemnation in his eyes when he'd opened the door to the bathroom. He thought she'd been doing drugs. And then those damning words, words she felt were engraved on her heart, tattooed on her forehead. Impossible to escape.

You're Aurelie.

For a little while she'd thought he believed she wasn't but now she knew the truth. He might want her to be different on stage, but he didn't think she could really change as a person.

Aurelie with a folk ballad and guitar was just another act to Luke Bryant, a successful one that would help with his stupid store openings.

And as long as she remembered that, she'd be fine. No more longing to reach or be reached. To know or be known. No more giving in to that fragile need, that fledgling desire.

This was business, strictly business, a chance for her to validate her career if not her very self. And that was fine. She'd make sure it was.

Aurelie straightened, briskly checked her reflection for the sixth time. She looked a little pale, a bit drawn, but overall okay. The lime-green shift dress struck, she hoped, the right note between fun and professional. With a deep breath, she left her suite and went downstairs to meet Luke.

The tropical heat of the Philippines had hit her the moment she'd stepped off the plane, and she felt it drape over her once more as she stepped outside like a hot, wet blanket. Luke had texted her to say he'd meet her in the patio bar and she walked through the velvety darkness looking for him, the palm trees rustling in a sultry breeze, the sounds of a vibrant and never-sleeping city carrying on the humid air.

She found him sitting on a stool by the bar, and everything inside her seemed to lurch as she looked at him. He wore a slightly rumpled suit, his tie loosened, and in the glint of the bar's dim lighting she could see the shadow of stubble on his jaw. His head was bowed and he held a half-drunk tumbler of whisky in his hand. She stared at him almost as she would a stranger, for he looked so different and yet so much the same. So *sexy*.

Then he glanced up and as he caught sight of her it was as if that sexy stranger had been replaced by a mannequin. His face went blank, his eyes veiled even as his lips curved in a meaningless smile and he crossed the patio towards her.

'Aurelie.' He kept his gaze firmly on her face, that cool, professional smile in place. He didn't offer her a hand to shake or touch her in any way. Stupidly, she felt his chilly withdrawal like a personal rejection.

No, she would not let this be personal. This was her chance at a comeback, and to hell with Luke Bryant.

'Luke.' She nodded back at him, tried to ignore the painful pounding of her heart. *This didn't hurt.*

'Would you like a drink?'

'Just sparkling water, please.'

Luke signalled to the bartender and ushered her towards a private table tucked in the corner, shaded by a palm tree.

'Trip all right?' he asked briskly. 'Your suite?'

'Everything's lovely.'

'Good.'

The bartender came with their drinks and Aurelie sipped hers gratefully. She had no idea what to say to this man. She didn't *know* this man. And she knew that shouldn't be a surprise.

'So everything is set for tomorrow,' he said, still all brisk business. 'I have a staff person on site, Lia, who will tour you around the store, get you sorted for the performance at three.'

Aurelie stared at his blank eyes and brisk smile and thought suddenly, *You're lying.* So much for honesty. This whole conversation was forced, fake. A lie.

Yet she had no idea what he really felt. Was he disgusted with her, with who he thought she was? *You're Aurelie.*

Or could she dare hope that some remnant remained of the man who had smiled at her with such compassion, such understanding, and seemed to believe she was different?

No, she didn't dare. There was no point.

'That all sounds fine,' she said, and he nodded.

'Good.' He hadn't finished his drink, but he pushed it away from him, clearly done. 'I'm afraid I have quite a lot of work to do, but I'll probably see you at the opening.'

Probably? Aurelie felt her throat go tight and took another sip of water. Somehow she managed a breezy smile. 'That sounds fine,' she said again, knowing she was being inane, but then he was too. This whole conversation was ridiculous. And a desperate part of her still craved something real.

'Fine,' Luke said, and with one more nod he rose from the chair. Aurelie rose too. She hadn't finished her water but neither was she about to sit in the bar alone. So that was it. Yet what had she really expected?

Even so, she could not keep a sense of desolation from sweeping emptily through her as Luke strode away from the bar without a backward glance.

That went well. *Not.* Luke tugged his tie from his collar and blew out his breath. He knew he didn't possess the charm of his brother Chase or Aaron's unending arrogance, but he could definitely have handled that conversation better. He'd been trying to keep it brisk and professional, but every time he looked at her he remembered how she'd felt in his arms, how much emotion and desire she'd stirred up in him, and business went right out of the window.

Maybe it wasn't actually Aurelie who was doing this to him. Maybe he was just out of practice. He hadn't had sex in a while, and he'd always been careful with his partners. A relationship came first with him, always had, because he'd never wanted to be like his father, going after everything in a skirt and ruining his mother's life in the process.

But maybe if he'd indulged in a few more flings, he wouldn't be feeling so…lost now. He'd gone over their encounter—was there really another word for it?—far too many times in his mind. Wondered when it had started to go wrong, and why. Had Aurelie been setting him up, the way he'd believed? Proving her damn point that he'd only come there to get into her bed? It seemed obvious, and yet a gut-deep instinct told him it wasn't the whole story.

He remembered the raw ache in her voice when she'd spoken to him. *I like how you say my name.* The way her fingers had trailed down his cheek, eager and hesitant at the same time, the tremble of her slender body against his. She'd felt something then. Something real.

And then she'd gone so horribly still beneath him and he'd felt as if he were…*attacking* her. He'd never felt so repulsed, so ashamed.

The best thing to do, he told himself now, the *only* thing to do, was to avoid her. Easier for both of them. He'd only suggested this meeting as a way to clear the air, draw a firm line under what had happened. And that at least had been accomplished, even if he still felt far from satisfied in any way.

As he headed back up to his suite, Luke had a feeling the next ten days were going to be a whole new kind of hell.

Aurelie stood to the side of the makeshift stage in Bryant's lobby and tried not to hyperventilate. A thousand people mingled in the soaring space, all modern chrome and glass, so different from the historic and genteel feeling of the New York store.

She'd spent the morning with Lia, touring all ten floors of the store on Ayala Avenue and then running through sound checks and getting ready. And trying not to think about what lay ahead.

What was happening *now*, with the crowd waiting for her to walk out and be Aurelie.

Fear washed coldly through her, made her dizzy. At least she'd checked her blood sugar. If she passed out now, it would simply be from nerves.

'Thirty seconds.' The guy who was doing the sound nodded towards her, and somehow Aurelie nodded back. She was miked, ready to go—and terrified.

She peeped out at the audience, saw the excited crowd, some of them clutching posters or CDs for her to sign. They were, she knew, expecting her to prance out there and sing *Take Me Down* or one of the other boppy, salacious numbers that had made her famous. They wanted her to sing and shimmy and be outrageous, and she was going to come out in her jeans, holding her guitar, and give everyone an almighty shock.

What had she been thinking, agreeing to this? What had Luke been thinking, suggesting it? It wasn't going to work. It was all going to go hideously, horribly wrong, for the store, for her, for everyone, and it was too late to do anything about it.

She closed her eyes, terror racing through her.

I can't do this. I can't change.

She wished, suddenly and desperately, that Luke were here. A totally stupid thing to want considering how cold he'd been to her last night, but just the memory of his voice, his tender, gentle look when he'd said her song was amazing gave her a little surge of both longing and courage.

'You're on.'

On wobbly, jelly-like legs she walked onto the stage. Considering she'd played sold-out concerts in the biggest arenas in the world, she should not be feeling nervous. At all. This was a tiny stage, a tiny audience. This was nothing.

And yet it was everything.

She felt the ripple of uneasy surprise go through the audience at the sight of her, felt it like a serpent slithering round the room, ready to strike. Already she was not what anybody had expected.

She sat on the stool in the centre of the stage, hooked her feet around the rungs and looked up to stare straight at Luke. He stood at the back of the lobby near the doors, but it was a small enough space she could make out his expression completely.

He looked cold, hard and completely unyielding. Their gazes met and, his mouth thinning, he looked away. Aurelie tensed, felt herself go brittle, shiny.

'Give us a song,' someone called out, impatience audible. 'Give us Aurelie!'

Well, that was easy enough. That was who she was. Drawing a deep breath, she started to play.

Luke stood in the back of the lobby waiting for Aurelie to come on, battling a disagreeable mix of anxiety and impatience. He'd been deliberately avoiding her since their drink together last night, had convinced himself that it was the best way forward. Yet, standing there alone, he felt an irritating needle of doubt prick his conscience.

Avoidance had never been his style. Avoidance meant letting someone down, and that was something he never intended to do again. He'd worked hard all his adult life to exorcise the ghosts of his past, to earn the trust and respect of those around him.

Even Aurelie's.

He didn't like the thought of her getting ready for this performance on her own. He knew this had to be pretty terrifying for her. He should have sought her out, offered her—what? Some encouragement?

He knew where that led.

No, it was better this way. It had to be. And it wasn't as if Aurelie actually needed him.

Luke heard the ripple of uneasy surprise move through the audience as she walked onto the stage. She looked vibrant and beautiful in a beaded top and jeans, her hair loose about her shoulders. Then she looked at him, her eyes so wide and clear, and a sudden, sharp longing pierced him. He looked away.

Someone called out, and Aurelie started to play. It took him a few stunned seconds to realise she wasn't singing the song he'd heard in her house back in Vermont. She was singing one of her old hits, the same boppy number she'd sung in New York, but this time to acoustic guitar. She glanced up from her guitar, gave the audience a knowing, dirty smile. A classic Aurelie look, and one Luke already hated. Everyone cheered.

Disappointment and frustration blazed through him. This wasn't what they'd agreed. Why had she changed their deal? Was it fear—or some kind of twisted revenge?

The song ended, and Luke heard the familiar mixture of catcalls and cheers. Nothing had changed. So much for the ultimate reinvention. Aurelie walked off the stage, and even though there were several local dignitaries waiting for him to escort them through the store, Luke turned and walked away from it all.

He found her in the break room she'd been using, just as before, to change. Her back was to him as she put her guitar away, and under the flowing top he could see the knobs of her spine, the bared nape of her neck as she bent her head. Desire and anger flared inside him, one giving life to the other.

'You didn't play your song.'

She turned towards him, her face completely expressionless. 'Actually, I did.'

'You know what I mean.'

'It wasn't going to work. I warned you, you know.'

'You didn't give it a chance.'

'I could tell. Honestly, Bryant, you should be thanking me. I just saved your ass.'

'You saved your own,' he retorted. 'What happened, you chickened out?'

'I prefer to think of it as being realistic.'

Frustration bit at him. 'I didn't hire you to be Aurelie all over again.'

'Oh?' She raised her eyebrows, her mouth curving in that familiar, cynical smile, innuendo heavy in her tone. 'What *did* you hire me for?'

He shook his head, the movement violent. 'Don't.'

'Don't what?'

'Don't,' Luke ground out, 'make this about sex.'

'Everything's about sex.'

'For you, maybe.'

'Oh, and not for you? Not for the saintly Luke Bryant who said he had a business proposition for me and two hours later was in my bed?'

Luke felt his fists clench. 'You wanted me there.' At least at the start.

'I've never denied it. You're the one swimming down that river.'

His nails bit into his palms. This woman made him feel so *much*. 'I'm not denying anything. I never have.' He let out a long, low breath, forced himself to unclench his fists.

To think—and react—calmly. 'Look, we obviously need to talk. I have to go out there again, see people—'

'Do your schtick?' She gave him the ghost of a smile, and Luke smiled back.

'Yeah. I guess everyone has one.' For one bittersweet moment he felt they were in agreement, they understood each other. Then Aurelie looked away, her expression veiled once more, and Luke felt the familiar weary frustration rush through him. 'But we are going to talk,' he told her. 'There are things I have to say.' She just shrugged, and with a sigh Luke turned towards the door.

Aurelie let out a shuddering breath as she heard the door close behind him. She put her hands up to her face, felt her whole body tremble. *Why* had she done that? Acted like Aurelie, not just to a faceless audience, but to *him*?

She'd been reacting again, she knew, to the rejection. It didn't take a rocket scientist to figure that out. Nobody would let her change, so she wouldn't. It was, she knew, a pretty pathetic way of trying to stay in control.

And clearly it wasn't working because she didn't feel remotely in control. She felt as if she were teetering on the edge of an abyss, about to fall, and she didn't know what waited darkly beneath her.

Maybe this whole thing had been a mistake. Trying to change. Wanting to be different. The audiences weren't going to accept it. *Her*. And, no matter how he fussed and fumed, neither was Luke.

Drawing another deep breath, Aurelie reached for her bag. She'd fix her make-up, and then she'd go out and mingle. Smile and chat. She'd get through this day and then she'd tell Luke she was going home. She was done.

* * *

Four hours later the opening was over and Aurelie was back in her suite at the Mandarin, exhausted and heartsore. She'd managed to avoid Luke for the entire afternoon, although she'd been aware of him. Even as she chatted and smiled and laughed, nodded sympathetically when people told her they didn't really like the guitar or the jeans, she'd been watching him. *Feeling* him.

He looked so serious when he talked to people. He frowned too much. He stood stiffly, almost to attention. Yet, despite all of it, Aurelie knew he was being himself. Being real.

Something she was too afraid to be.

She'd been resigned to giving up the rest of the tour and going back to Vermont. Staying safe. Being a coward. Yet four hours later Aurelie resisted the thought of slinking away like a scolded child. Never mind what Luke thought, what anyone in the audience thought or even wanted. She needed to do this for herself.

Yet the realisation filled her only with an endless ache of exhaustion. She didn't think she had the strength to go on acting as if she didn't care when she did, so very much.

Wearily she kicked off her heels and stripped the clothes from her body. She needed a stingingly hot shower to wipe away all the traces of today. She knew Luke had said he wanted to talk to her, but the last time she'd seen him he'd been in deep discussion with several official-looking types. He'd probably forgotten all about her and the things he supposedly needed to say.

Fifteen minutes later, just as she'd slipped into a T-shirt and worn yoga pants, a knock sounded on the door. Aurelie sucked in a deep breath and ran her fingers through her hair, still damp from her shower. A peep through the eyehole confirmed her suspicions. Luke hadn't forgotten about her after all.

She opened the door and something inside her tugged hard at the sight of him, his hair a little mussed, his suit a little rumpled. He looked tired.

'Long day?' she asked and he nodded tersely.

'You could say that. May I come in?'

He always asked, she thought. Always asked her permission. Strangely, stupidly, it touched her. 'Okay.'

She stepped aside and Luke came into the sitting area of the suite. She saw his glance flick to the bedroom, visible through an open door, the wide bed piled high with silken pillows.

Then he turned back to face her with a grim, iron-hard resolution. 'We need to talk.'

With a shrug she spread her hands wide and moved to sit on the sofa, as though she were actually relaxed. 'Then talk.'

He let out a long, low breath. 'I'm sorry about the way things happened back in Vermont. I didn't want it to be like that between us.'

He looked so intent, so sincere, that mockery felt like her only defence. '*Us*, Bryant?'

'Don't call me Bryant. My name is Luke and, considering we almost slept together, I think you can manage my first name.'

She tensed. 'Almost being the key word. That doesn't give you some kind of right—'

'I'm not talking about rights, just common civility.' He sat across from her, his hands on his thighs, his face still grim. 'I'm being honest here, Aurelie—'

'Sorry,' she drawled, 'that doesn't score any Brownie points. I already know you can't be anything else.'

'Just stop it,' he bit out. 'Stop it with the snappy one-liners and the bored tone and world-weary cynicism—'

'My, that's *quite* a list—'

'*Stop.*' He leaned forward, his face twisting with frustration or maybe even anger. 'Stop being so damn fake.'

She stilled. Said nothing, because suddenly she had nothing to say. She'd defaulted to her Aurelie persona, to the bored indifference she used as a shield, but Luke saw through it all. He stared at her now, those dark eyes blazing, burning right through her. She swallowed and looked down at her lap. 'What do you want from me?' she asked in a low voice.

'I want to know what *you* want from *me*.'

She looked up, surprise rendering her speechless once more. Her throat dry, she forced herself to shrug. 'I don't want anything from you.'

'Why did you want to sleep with me?'

She tensed, tried desperately for that insouciant armour. 'Why not?'

'Well, obviously not because you were enjoying it.'

She lifted her chin. 'How do you know I wasn't enjoying it?'

'I don't know what your experience with men has been, but most of us can tell when a woman is or isn't enjoying sex.' Luke's mouth quirked upwards even as his eyes blazed. 'Generally when a woman enjoys sex, she responds. She kisses you and makes rather nice noises. She wraps her legs around you and begs you not to stop. She doesn't lie there like a wax effigy.'

Aurelie could feel herself blushing. Her whole body felt hot. 'Maybe I thought I would enjoy it,' she threw back at him. 'Maybe you were a disappointment.'

'I have no doubt I was,' Luke returned, his tone mild. 'I confess I was a little impatient. I haven't had sex in quite a while.'

That made two of them. Aurelie swallowed. 'I don't know why we're having this conversation.'

'Because if we're going to work together for the next nine

days, I need to—' He stopped suddenly, shook his head. 'No, that's not the truth. This isn't about forging some adequate working relationship.'

Aurelie eyed him uneasily. 'What is it about, then?'

'It's about,' Luke said quietly, 'the fact that I can't stop thinking about you, or wondering how it all went so terribly wrong in the course of a single evening.'

She had no sharp retort or bantering comeback to *that*. She had no words at all. She made herself smile even though she felt, bizarrely, near tears. 'You are *so* honest.'

'Then be honest back,' Luke answered. 'Did you sleep with me to prove a point? To show me I was like all the other men you've ever known?'

'No.' It came out as no more than a whisper. Lying no longer felt like an option, not in the face of his own hard honesty. 'It was because I wanted to. Because I didn't want you to go and I…I liked being with you.' Her voice came out so low she felt the thrum of it in her chest. She stared down at her lap, wondered why anyone ever chose to be honest. It felt like peeling back your skin.

'Then what happened?' Luke asked, and his voice was low too, a gentle growl, a lion's purr.

She shrugged, her gaze still on her lap. 'Look, I've never enjoyed sex, okay? So don't worry, it wasn't an insult to your manhood or something.' She'd tried for lightness even now, and failed miserably. Luke had fallen silent, and after a few taut moments she risked a glance upwards. He was gazing at her narrowly, a crease between his eyes, as if she was a problem he had to solve.

'Never?' he finally said, and he sounded so quiet and sad that Aurelie had to blink hard.

'I wasn't abused or raped or something, if you're thinking along those lines.'

'But something happened.' It was a statement, and one

she could not deny. Yes, something had happened. Her innocence had been stripped away in the course of a single evening. And she'd allowed it. But since that night she'd never
again thought of sex as something to be enjoyed. It was just
a tool, and sometimes a weapon, to get what you wanted,
or even needed.

'It doesn't matter,' she snapped. 'I don't even know why
we're talking about this. Business relationship only, remember?'

'I remember.'

'So.' She straightened, gave him an expectant this-is-your-
cue-to-leave look. He ignored it.

'Aurelie.' She wished he hadn't said her name. He said it
the way he always said it, deliberately, an affirmation, and it
made her ache inside. Stupid, because it was just her name.
A name she hated and yet—

When Luke said it, she didn't feel like Aurelie the pop
star. She felt like Aurelie the girl who'd grown up wanting
only to be loved.

'What?' she demanded, too harshly, because he'd stripped
away all her armour and anger was her last defence.

He shook his head. 'I'm sorry.'

She stared at him wordlessly, dread rolling through her,
making her sick. He was letting her down. Of course. The
concert hadn't worked and he didn't want her Aurelie act,
so he was going to tell her to go home. It was over. So much
for trying to change.

Four hours ago she'd told herself she wanted that but now
she felt the sting of tears. Another failure.

'Well,' she forced herself to say, even to smile, 'we tried,
didn't we? Never mind. I knew it was a long shot.' And she
shrugged as if it were no big deal, even managed a wobbly
laugh.

Luke frowned, said nothing for a long, taut moment. 'What do you think I'm talking about?' he finally asked.

She eyed him uncertainly. 'The concerts, right? I mean… the audience didn't really go for it today—'

'They would have if you'd done what you were supposed to, and sung your song.' He spoke without rancour, but she still prickled.

'They would have gone for it even less.'

'Yet you weren't willing to risk that. I'm sorry for that too. I should have spoken to you before you went onstage. I was trying to keep my distance because—' He stopped, blew out a weary breath. 'Because it seemed simpler. Easier. But I think I just made it harder for you. I'm sorry I let you down.' She didn't answer. This conversation had gone way outside her comfort zone. She had no comebacks, no words at all. 'But I wasn't apologising for the concerts,' Luke continued quietly. 'I'm not cancelling them. I still think you can turn this around.'

'You do?' She felt a stirring of hope, like a baby's first breath, infinitesimally small and yet sustaining life.

'Yes. But I don't want to talk about that.' He gazed straight at her then, and she saw the hard blaze of his eyes, golden glints amid the deep brown. 'I want to talk about us.'

'*Us*—' The word ended on a breath. She had no others.

'Yes, us. I'm still attracted to you.' Aurelie felt her heart lurch with some nameless emotion, although whether it was fear or hope or something else entirely she couldn't say.

'So it is about sex.'

Luke said nothing for a moment. He gazed out of the window, the sky turning dark, twinkling with the myriad lights of the city. 'Do you know how many women I've slept with?' he finally asked.

'I'm not sure how I would have come by that information—'

'Three.' He glanced back at her with a rueful smile, his eyes still dark. 'Three, four if I include our rather mangled attempt.'

'Right.' She had no idea what to make of that.

'I've had three relationships. *Relationships.* They all lasted months or even years. And the women involved were the only women I've ever had sex with.'

'So you really are a Boy Scout.' She felt incredibly jaded, with way too much bad experience behind her.

'No, I just…I've just always taken sex seriously. It's meant something to me. Emotionally.'

'Except with me.'

Luke was silent for so long Aurelie wondered if he'd heard her. She sought for something to say, something light and wry to show him she didn't care, it didn't matter, but it was too late for that. He'd already seen and heard too much.

'It did mean something,' he finally said, his voice so low she almost didn't hear him. 'From the moment I saw you slumped on the floor from what I thought—assumed—was an overdose. You opened your eyes and I…I felt something.'

'Felt something?' she managed, still trying for wryness. 'What, annoyance?'

'No.' He glanced up at her, and she saw the honesty blazing in his eyes. 'I don't know what it was. Is. But I can't pretend I don't feel something—for you. For the you hiding underneath the pop star persona, the you who wrote that song.'

She swallowed. 'But you didn't even hear that song until—'

'I saw it in your eyes.'

She looked away. 'I never took you for a romantic.'

'I didn't, either.'

Aurelie could feel her heart beating so hard it hurt. She felt dizzy and weirdly high, as if she were floating somewhere up near the ceiling. And she felt scared. Really scared, because she didn't know what Luke was trying to tell her.

She licked her lips, found a voice. 'So what…what are you saying exactly?'

'I don't even know.' He raked a hand through his hair, let out a weary laugh. 'Part of me thinks we should keep this strictly professional, get through the next nine days, and never see each other again.'

'That would probably be the smartest move,' she agreed, trying to keep her voice light even as her mouth dried and her heart hammered and she *hoped*. Yet for what?

'I think it would be,' Luke agreed. 'But here's the thing. I don't want to.'

'So what do you want?' Aurelie whispered.

He stared at her for a long moment, and she saw the conflict in his eyes. Felt it. He didn't want to want her, but he did. 'I want to start over,' he said at last. 'I want to forget about what happened—or didn't happen—between us. I want to get to know you properly.'

'Are you sure about that?' she joked, but her voice wavered and it fell flat.

'I'm not sure about anything,' he admitted with a wry shake of his head. 'I'm not even sure why I'm saying this.'

'Ouch. Too much honesty, maybe.'

'Maybe.' His gaze rested on her. 'But I want a second chance. With you. I want you to have a second chance with me.'

A second chance. Not professionally, but personally. So much more dangerous. And so much more desirable. A chance to be real. Aurelie closed her eyes. She didn't know what to feel, and yet at the same time she felt so much. Too much.

'The question is,' Luke asked steadily, 'is that what you want?'

She opened her eyes. Stared. His hair was still mussed, his suit still rumpled. He had shadows under his eyes and he badly needed to shave. He looked wonderful.

'Why?' she finally whispered.

'Why what?'

'Why do you want a second chance—with me?'

His mouth twisted. 'Is it so hard to believe?'

'You don't even know me.'

'I know enough to know I want to know more.'

She felt a tear, a terrible, treacherous tear, tremble on her lash. 'I would have thought,' she said in a low voice, 'that what you know would make you not want to know more.'

'Oh, Aurelie,' Luke said quietly, 'I think I know what's an act and what's real.'

'How can you know that?' She felt that tear slide coldly down her cheek. 'I don't even know that.'

'Maybe that's where I come in.'

She prickled instinctively, reached for her rusty armour. 'You think you can help me? *Save* me?'

He stilled, went silent for so long Aurelie blinked hard and looked up at him. 'No,' he said with a quiet bleakness she didn't understand. 'I know I can't save anyone.' He smiled, but it still seemed sad. 'But I can think you're worth saving. Worth knowing.'

She swallowed, sniffed. 'So what now?'

'You answer my question.' Words thickened in her throat. She didn't speak. 'Do you want to try again?' Luke asked. His gaze remained steady on her, and she found she could not look away. 'Do you want a second chance, with me?'

She couldn't speak, not with all the words thick in her throat, tangling on her tongue. Words she was desperate not to say. *Yes, but the thought terrifies me. What if you find out more about me and you hate me? What if you hurt me?*

What if it doesn't work and I feel emptier and more alone than ever? What if I can't change?

'Aurelie,' Luke said, and it wasn't a question. It sounded like an affirmation. *I know who you are.*

Except he didn't.

He was still gazing at her, still waiting. Aurelie swallowed again, tried to dislodge some of those words. She only came up with one.

'Yes,' she said.

CHAPTER SIX

LUKE STARED AT Aurelie's pale face, her eyes so wide and blue, that one tear tracking a silvery path down her cheek.

Hell.

He'd come up here to talk to her, to tell her what he'd started out saying, which was that he was sorry for what had happened but they'd keep this whole thing professional and try to avoid each other because clearly that was the safest, sanest thing to do.

Except he'd said something else instead, something totally dangerous and insane. *I know enough to know I want to know more.* No, he didn't. He didn't want to know one more thing about this impossible woman. He wanted to walk away and forget he'd ever met her.

Except that honesty thing? It got him every time. Because he knew, even as he stared at that silver tear-track on her cheek, that he'd been speaking the truth.

He felt something for her. He *did* want to get to know her, even though there could be no doubting she was fragile, damaged, *dangerous*. The possibility of hurting her was all too real—and terrifying.

'Luke?' She said his name with a soft hesitancy that he'd never heard before. She felt vulnerable, he knew. Well, hell, *he* felt vulnerable. And he didn't like it. He raked his hands through his hair, tried to find something to say.

Aurelie rose from the sofa and grabbed a tissue, her back to him as she wiped her eyes, as if even now she could hide her tears.

'Look,' she said, her back still to him, 'maybe this is a mistake.'

Luke straightened, dropped his hands. 'Why do you say that?'

She turned around. 'Because of the look on your face.'

'What—'

'You're looking like you seriously regret this whole thing.'

'I wouldn't say *seriously*.' He'd meant to joke, but she just stared at him hard. He sighed. 'Aurelie, look. This is new territory for me. I'm stumbling through the dark here.'

'You and me both.'

'Have you ever been in a serious relationship before?'

Her eyes widened, maybe with fear. 'Is that what this is?'

'No.' He spoke quickly, instinctively, and she gave him a wobbly smile. They were both scared here, both inching into this…whatever *this* was. 'One day at a time, right?' He smiled back. 'I just wondered.'

She turned away again, her hair falling in front of her face. 'You're asking because of the sex thing, right? Because I didn't enjoy it.'

'That among other things.' *The sex thing.* Yeah, that was something else they'd have to deal with. Something had happened to her, he just didn't know what. And he didn't know if he even wanted to know. His three relationships, he realised, had not prepared him for this. They'd been safe, measured, considered things, and even though he'd had a deep affection for each of the women he'd shared a part of his life with, he hadn't felt *this*.

This tangle of uncertainty and exhilaration, this terror that he could hurt her, that he might fail. What had he got himself into?

'I've been in one relationship,' she said quietly, her face still turned away from him. 'Just one. But it lasted over three years.'

'It did?' He shouldn't be surprised. He might not have seen a mention of such a relationship in the press, but he'd known from her song that she'd had her heart broken. The thought filled him with something that felt almost like jealousy.

She kept her face averted. 'I'd rather not talk about it.'

'All right.' He drew a breath, felt his way through the words. 'But if we're going to…to try this, then we need to be honest with each other.'

She let out a short laugh. 'Well, that's obviously not a problem for you.'

'Actually it is. I might be honest but that doesn't mean I wear my heart on my sleeve. No one in my family talks about emotional stuff.' And he didn't even like admitting *that*. There was a reason for his family's distance, their silence and secrets. A reason locked deep inside him.

Aurelie hunched her shoulders, folded her arms. 'Well, I'm never honest. I don't even know if I can be. I've been on my guard for so long I don't know how to let it down.' She stared at him with wide eyes. 'I honestly don't know.'

'Well, see,' Luke said lightly, 'you were being honest right there.'

She let out a shaky laugh, the sound trembling on the air. Luke felt an ache deep inside. He didn't know everything she'd been through, but he knew it had to have been a lot. And he wanted, on a deep, gut and even heart level, to make it better. To have her trust him. He wanted to redeem her, yes, maybe even save her, and save himself in the process. This time he could make it right.

'Give us a chance, Aurelie.'

'How?'

How to begin? 'We don't have to be in Singapore until the day after tomorrow. Give me tomorrow.'

She eyed him warily. 'One day?'

'One day. One date. It's a start.' For both of them.

'And then?'

'We'll see. We'll take one day at a time and see how we go.' He had a feeling one day at a time was all they could handle. He didn't know what he was asking, what he wanted. This was new territory for both of them.

'One day,' she repeated, as if she liked the sound of it. 'One date.' Luke nodded, felt his heart lift. 'Okay,' she said, and smiled.

Aurelie stood in the lobby of the hotel and tried not to fidget. Luke had told her he'd meet here at nine for their day out. Their *date*.

When had she last had a date?

She couldn't remember, although it wasn't for lack of men. There had, she knew, been far too many men in her life. But she hadn't dated them. The whole concept of a date made her feel like a giddy girl, young, innocent, full of hope.

Ha.

She was none of those things. She might only be twenty-six, but she'd lived enough for three lifetimes. And as for innocent, *hopeful*…Luke Bryant might stir something inside her she'd long thought destroyed, but he couldn't change her and she didn't think she could change herself.

And when Luke discovered that… Swallowing, she forced the fluttery panic down. There was no point thinking about the future. Luke was giving her one date. One day. And by the end of it he'd probably have had enough.

'Ready?'

She whirled around, saw Luke smiling at her. He wore a dark green polo shirt and khaki shorts, and she realised it was the first time she'd seen him in casual clothes. The shirt hugged the lean, sculpted muscles of his chest and shoulders, and the shorts rested low on his trim hips. Her gaze travelled down his tanned, muscular legs to the pair of worn trainers and then back up again to his face, where a surprising grin quirked his mouth.

'Finished?'

She had, Aurelie realised with some mortification, been checking him out. And not in a deliberate, outrageous, Aurelie-like way. No, this had been instinctive, helpless, yearning admiration. Somehow she managed to smile, nod.

'Yeah, I'm done.'

'And do I pass?'

'You'll do.'

He chuckled and placed one hand on the small of her back. She felt the warm, sure press of his palm against her skin and the answering shivers of sensation that rippled out through her body from that little touch.

'So where are we going?' she asked as they left the hotel. A luxury sedan with tinted windows and a driver at the wheel waited for them at the kerb. Luke opened the door and ushered her into the sumptuous leather interior.

'Camiguin.'

'Cami-what?'

He smiled and slid in next to her, his thigh brushing hers. Aurelie didn't know why she was suddenly hyper-aware of his movements, his body. She'd already been naked with this man; he surely shouldn't have this effect on her.

And yet, somehow, he did.

'Camiguin,' Luke repeated. 'A small island province in the Bohol Sea.'

'So we're not taking this car there, I assume?'

'No, we're taking this to the airport, and then a private

plane to Mambajao, the capital city. And then we'll hire a Jeep.'

'Planes, trains and automobiles.'

'It shouldn't take more than two hours, overall.'

'A private jet is pretty classy.'

Luke gave her the glimmer of a smile. 'I can be a pretty classy guy.'

She felt a ripple of something like pleasure at the light remark, the curve of his mouth. She'd spent so much of her time trying to push Luke away and protect herself. It felt amazingly liberating not to do it. To banter without the barbs, to relax into a—

A what? A *relationship*? She didn't do relationships. Luke might go for them, but they didn't work for her. She turned to stare out of the window, told herself this was *one date*. It was nothing. By this time tomorrow they'd probably have decided they'd *both* had enough.

The private jet was waiting for them on the tarmac at Manila's International Airport. Aurelie had taken private jets before, back in her heyday, but she hadn't been on one in over four years and it felt strange. She stood in the main cabin, glancing around at the leather sofas, the champagne chilling on ice, and felt something cold steal inside her.

Luke paused in the doorway, his gaze on her face. 'What is it?'

She glanced up at him, bemused that he would sense her mood so quickly and easily. She wasn't even sure what she was feeling. 'Nothing. Everything's very nice.'

'That's a scathing indictment if I ever heard one.' His gaze moved slowly over her, assessing, understanding. His forehead creased and he nodded. 'I guess you've taken a few of these in your time.'

She shrugged. 'One or two.'

'Does it bring back memories?'

Did it? 'No, just a feeling.'

'Not a very nice one.'

She opened her mouth to deny it, then said nothing. This honesty thing was *tough*. 'Maybe,' she finally allowed, and Luke smiled faintly, as if he knew how difficult she found this kind of talking. Sharing. All of it awkward, awful, painful.

'How have you flown under the radar for so long?'

'By holing up in Vermont.'

'And no one there gives you away?'

'They're a close-mouthed bunch. And they're loyal to my grandmother.' Too late she realised she'd said more than she meant to. Funny how that happened. You started being a little honest and then other things began to slip out. Soon she wouldn't be able to control it.

'Your grandmother? Was Julia Schmidt your grandmother, then?'

'No.' She moved over to sit on the sofa, rubbing her arms in the chilled air of the plane's interior. 'Are we going to get going?'

Luke sat across from her. 'As soon as we're cleared for take-off.' He didn't speak for a moment, just studied her, and Aurelie looked away from his gaze. She heard the plane's engines thrum to life with a feeling of relief. 'Champagne?' he asked, and she nodded, glad he wasn't going to ask any more questions.

It wasn't until he'd handed her a glass and raised his own in a toast that he finally spoke again. 'You know, this second chance thing?' She eyed him warily. 'It doesn't work if you're going to guard everything you say.'

'I wasn't,' she protested, and Luke just arched an eyebrow. She took a sip of champagne, glad for the distraction. 'I told you I'm not good at this.' He said nothing and, goaded, she said a bit sharply, 'It's not like you've been baring your soul.'

'Haven't I?' he asked quietly. He looked away then, and Aurelie felt a strange twisting inside as she thought of his words last night. Words which made a shivery thrill run all the way through her. *I know enough to know I want to know more.*

Did she want to be known?

She took a sip of champagne, the bubbles seeming to fizz all the way through her. Maybe she did. At least for one day. One date. That was safe enough, surely.

'All right.' She set her champagne glass on the coffee table between them. 'What do you want to know?'

Luke turned back to her, bemused. 'You look like you're facing the firing squad.'

'It feels that way, a little bit.'

'I suppose you've always had to be careful about what you say.'

'I haven't always been careful enough.' He acknowledged the point with a nod. There had been several tell-all exposés in various tabloids, all with too much truth in them. Aurelie felt herself start to prickle. 'So what do you want to know?'

'What do you want to tell me?'

She gave a soft laugh. 'Not much.'

'There must be something. Some small, innocuous bit of information that you don't mind imparting.'

She smiled, felt the tension inside her ease, at least a little bit. 'Well…I like bubblegum ice cream.'

'*Bubblegum?*' His jaw dropped theatrically. 'You have got to be kidding me.'

'It's delicious.'

'It's way too sweet—'

She leaned forward. 'And pink and sugary and with little bits of gum in the ice cream. Yum.'

'Whoa.' He held up a hand. 'TMI.'

A bubble of laughter erupted from her, surprising them

both. He smiled, a real smile, lightening his stern features in a way that made her feel suddenly breathless. His dark eyes glinted gold. She shook her head slowly. 'I didn't think you had a sense of humour, you know.'

'It's a shy creature. It only appears on rare occasions.'

'So it does.' She gazed at him thoughtfully. 'What's your favourite flavour of ice cream?'

'Not bubblegum.'

'We've established that.'

'Probably vanilla.'

'Vanilla?' She rolled her eyes. 'Could you be more boring?'

His mouth twitched. 'Probably not.'

'What's there to like about vanilla?'

'It never lets you down. Other flavours can be so disappointing. Not enough mint in the mint chocolate chip, too many nuts in Rocky Road.'

'I have been seriously disappointed, on occasion, with the lack of cookie dough in cookie dough ice cream.'

'Exactly.' He nodded his approval. 'But vanilla? Never a disappointment. Completely trustworthy.'

Like you are? She almost said the words. And meant them. No snide mockery, just truth. Too much truth. She wasn't ready for that.

'Well.' She shifted in her seat, gave him a breezy smile. 'Now we've broken the ice.'

'Or the ice cream.'

'That was a seriously weak joke.'

'I told you, my sense of humour only appears on rare occasions. Anyway—' he glanced at her as he took a sip of champagne '—can you eat bubblegum ice cream? Or does that send your glucose levels through the roof?'

'Everything in moderation.'

He nodded towards the handbag at her feet. 'I should have asked before, but did you bring everything you need?'

She nodded. 'I have a little kit for testing my blood. It travels easily.'

'When were you diagnosed?'

'When I was seventeen.' She swallowed, remembering those awful early days. At the time she'd just been moving from one event to another, dazed, incredulous, hopeful and yet still afraid.

Too late she realised Luke was watching her face, and she knew he could see the emotions in her eyes. Emotions she'd meant to hide. 'Anyway,' she said, apropos of nothing.

'How did it happen?'

'The usual symptoms. Weight loss, excessive thirst, dizzy spells.'

His eyes narrowed, and she could almost see his mind working. Understanding. 'And the tabloids claimed you had anorexia. A drinking problem. A drug overdose.'

She lifted one shoulder in a shrug. 'That's what they like to do. And in any case I haven't been a saint.' She lifted her chin a notch, tried to smile again, but her heart was thudding hard.

Luke gazed at her steadily. 'Who has?'

'You seem to have been a regular Boy Scout.'

'No, not a Boy Scout.' He rubbed his jaw, a movement that Aurelie couldn't help but notice was inherently sexy. Although, perhaps the sexiest thing about Luke Bryant was how unaware he seemed of his own attractiveness. He moved with unconscious grace, and her gaze was helplessly drawn to the shrug of his broad shoulders, the reassuring squareness of his jaw. Everything about him solid and strong. *Safe*.

'Why haven't you ever talked about your diabetes publicly? Issued a statement?'

She leaned her head back against the seat, suddenly tired. 'It's quite a boring disease.'

'*Boring?*'

'Much more interesting to let them wonder. So my agent told me.'

'Your agent sucked.'

She let out a surprised laugh. 'Yeah, he wasn't that great. I fired him a couple of years ago.'

'You could have said something since then.'

She opened her eyes. 'Maybe I didn't want to.'

'Why?'

'Because telling the truth and having no one believe you is worse than not telling the truth and having people assume the worst. But I guess you wouldn't understand that,' she finished lightly, 'what with this compulsion to honesty that you have.'

Luke didn't say anything for a moment, yet Aurelie felt him tense, saw something dark flash in his eyes before he angled his head away from her. Had she inadvertently touched on something painful with her offhand remark? 'I understand,' he said finally, his voice low, and she almost asked him what he meant. She didn't, though, because they'd surely had enough honesty for one day.

By the time they arrived in Camiguin Aurelie had started feeling relaxed again. Luke had steered the conversation back to lighter subjects, moving from ice cream flavours to movie preferences and whether she supported the Mets or the Yankees.

'Mets all the way,' he'd assured her solemnly, but she saw a glint in his eyes that made her smile.

They disembarked the plane at the tiny airport and took an island taxi—basically, a rusted-out Jeep—into Mambajao. The capital of Camiguin was no more than a small town of rickety buildings with wooden verandas and tin roofs, the narrow streets bustling with bicycles and fruit vendors and raggedy children darting in and out of everything. It was so different from Aurelie's usual experience of travelling, when she kept to limos and high class hotels and never stepped outside of a severely controlled environment. She loved this. Craved the feeling of possibility and even hope wandering around the dusty streets gave her.

'What are we doing first?' she asked Luke, and he smiled and took her elbow, steering her away from a man on a bike pulling a cartload of pineapples.

'I thought we could pick up some lunch in the market, and then we'll take it out to the falls for a picnic.'

'The falls?'

'The Tuwasan Falls. They're pretty spectacular.'

'You've been there before?'

'I stopped over here the last time I came to Manila.'

She felt a completely unreasonable prickling of jealousy. Had he taken one of his serious *relationships* to this falls? Was this his go-to place for a romantic date in the tropics?

'Alone,' Luke said quietly, yet with a hint of humour in his voice that made her blush. Again. She'd never blushed so much with a man, had never had a reason to. She was Aurelie, she was worldly-wise and weary, beyond shame or embarrassment.

But that act was falling away, flaking off like old paint. What would be left when it was gone? Something good, or even anything at all? She still wasn't sure of the answer.

'Come on,' Luke said, and he guided her to a market stall overflowing with local produce and fish. 'Anything look good?'

Aurelie surveyed the jumbled piles of fruits and vegetables, the pots of noodles and trays of spring rolls.

'Crispy *pata*?' Luke suggested. 'It's deep fried pig's leg.'

She winced. 'I don't think I'm feeling quite that adventurous.'

'It's quite tasty.'

'You've had it before?'

'I like to try new things.'

She pointed to a tray of round yellowish fruit that looked a bit like potatoes. 'What's that?'

'*Lanzones.*'

'Have you had those?'

'Yes, but you have to be careful. If they're not ripe, they taste horribly sour. If they are, incredibly sweet. You just have to take your chances.' He picked up a fruit, testing its ripeness with his thumb. 'Try it.' The fruit seller quickly peeled the *lanzone* with a knife and handed her a piece. Warily, she bit into it and then, without thinking, spat the piece out into her hand. 'Yuck!'

'Bitter, huh?'

'You don't sound surprised.'

He shrugged, and she hit him in the shoulder. 'You did that on purpose!'

'Try this one.'

'Why should I trust you?' she demanded even as she took the second peeled *lanzone*.

'Because even *lanzones* deserve a second chance.'

Something in his quiet, serious tone made her mouth dry and her heart beat hard. She took a bite, and her mouth filled with the intense sweetness of the fruit. Her eyes widened. 'Wow.'

'See?' He sounded so satisfied, so smug, that Aurelie rolled her eyes.

'Thank you very much for that life lesson. Message received. Everything deserves a second chance.'

'Not everything.' After handing the vendor some coins,

he'd placed his hand on the small of her back and was guiding her to the next stall. 'Just me and the fruit.'

He acted, Aurelie thought, as if he were the only one who'd made a mistake. Who needed a second chance. Yet when she thought of her behaviour at their first meeting—and even their second—she felt as if *she* was the one who needed to change. Who wanted to prove she was different. Not Luke.

She glanced at him, her gaze taking in his stern profile, the hard line of his mouth, the latent strength of his body. What was he trying to prove?

He'd put several *lanzones* into a straw basket he'd bought from another vendor, and they added mango, spring rolls and some local sausage and cold noodles to their purchases. The sun was hot overhead even though the air felt swampy, and Luke bought two bottles of water and some sun hats as well.

'Now to the falls,' he said, and Aurelie followed him to a tin-roofed garage where he conferred with a young man who couldn't be more than sixteen before leading her around to the back where a battered-looking Jeep awaited.

'Your carriage, madam.'

She eyed it dubiously. 'I don't particularly relish breaking down in the middle of the jungle.'

'Don't worry, we're not taking this into the jungle.'

'Where, then?'

'A car park about five kilometres from here. Then we walk.'

'Walk? In the jungle?'

'It's worth it.'

'It'd better be.'

Luke stowed their provisions in the bag, handed her a sun hat, and then swung into the driver's seat. Aurelie could not keep her gaze from resting on his strong, browned forearms, the confident way he manoeuvred the rusty vehicle through the crowded streets of Mambajao and then out onto the open road, no more than a bumpy, rutted track.

The breeze was a balmy caress on her skin, the sun a benediction. In the distance the lush mountains—active volcanoes, Luke had told her—were dark, verdant humps against a hazy sky. Aurelie leaned her head back against the seat and closed her eyes.

When had she last felt this relaxed, this *happy*?

It was too long ago to remember. Smiling, she let her thoughts drift as the sunlight washed over her.

'We're here.'

She opened her eyes and saw that Luke had pulled into a rectangle of gravel and dirt that was, apparently, a car park. Their Jeep was the only car.

She rubbed her eyes. 'I must have dozed.'

'Just a little.' There was something intimate about the way he said it, and Aurelie imagined him watching her sleep. Had she rested her head on his shoulder? Had she *drooled*? More blushing.

'So where is here exactly?'

'Well, nowhere, really.' Luke slid out of the Jeep and reached for their basket. 'But we can follow a path through the jungle to the Tuwasan Falls. It's about a mile.'

'A mile in the jungle?' She glanced down at her leather sandals dubiously. 'You should have told me we were enacting *Survivor*.'

He made a face. 'Sorry. But it's mostly wooden walkways, so I think you'll be okay.'

'If you say so.'

She followed him away from the car park and onto exactly what he'd said—a wooden walkway on stilts over the dense jungle floor. Within just a few metres of going down the walkway she felt the air close around her, hot, humid and dense. Birds chirped and cicadas chirruped—at least she thought they were cicadas—and she could feel the jungle like a living, breathing entity all around her. A bright green lizard scampered across the walkway, and in the distance some animal—Aurelie had no idea what—gave a lonely, mournful cry.

'Wow.' She stopped, her hands resting on the cane railings, her heart thumping. 'This is…intense.'

Luke glanced back at her. 'You okay?'

'Yes, I guess I just thought, you know, first date, maybe a movie?'

He smiled wryly. 'I know you think I'm boring, but Jeez. A movie? I think I can do better than that.'

'I don't think you're boring.'

'You think I'm the human equivalent of vanilla ice cream.'

She gazed at him, the railings slick under her palms. Her heart was still thumping. 'I do,' she admitted quietly, and it felt like the most honest thing she'd ever said. 'Completely trustworthy.'

Luke's eyes darkened and the moment spun out between them, a thread of silence that bound them together, and tighter still. 'Don't speak too soon,' he finally said, and turned away from her to walk further down the path.

'You mean you're not?'

'I mean you don't trust me yet, and why should you? It's something I have to earn.'

Despite the damp heat all around them her mouth felt dry. She swallowed. 'And you want to earn it?'

He glanced back at her, and his eyes were darker than ever. 'Yes.'

Her mind spun with this revelation. She wanted to tell him that he'd already earned it, that she trusted him now, but somehow the words wouldn't come.

They didn't talk for a little while after that, because the

wooden walkway became decidedly rickety, and then it stopped altogether at the bank of a rushing stream.

Aurelie raised her eyebrows. 'What now, Tarzan?'

'We cross it.'

'Did I mention my leather sandals?'

'You might have.'

'And?'

'I didn't think you were the type to care about shoes.'

She wasn't. 'No, but I'm the type to care about getting my big toe eaten by a giant barracuda.'

He laughed then, a great big rumbling laugh that had a silly grin spreading wide across her face. She liked the sound of his laughter. 'I don't think there are any giant barracudas.'

'No?'

'Only medium-sized ones.'

She pursed her lips, hands firmly planted on her hips. 'Is that your sense of humour appearing on this rare occasion?'

'Oops, it darted away again.' He stepped onto a flattish rock in the stream, the water flowing all around him, and stretched out his hand. 'Come here.'

Cautiously she reached out and put her hand in his. His clasp was dry, warm and firm, and with his other hand on her arm he helped her onto the rock. Their hips bumped. Heat flared.

'This is cosy,' she murmured and he gave a tiny smile.

'That's the idea. Next rock.'

He stepped backwards onto another rock, sure and agile, and Aurelie followed him. She could hear the water rushing past them, felt the warm spray of it against her ankles. In the middle of the stream she looked down and saw a bright blue fish darting very near her toes. She slipped and Luke slid an arm around her waist, balanced her. Easily.

'The secret is not to look down.'

'Now you tell me.'

Another rock, and then another, and then they were on the other side. Luke smiled at her rather smugly, and Aurelie shook her head.

'This is all a big lesson, isn't it? How to Trust 101.'

'Is it working?'

'A little,' she admitted. 'What if I'd fallen?'

'But you didn't.'

'But what if I had? What if you'd slipped?'

'Me? Slip?' He shook his head, then gazed at her, his head tilted to one side. 'Do you think it would have ruined everything?'

Her lips curved. She liked being with this man. 'Not everything. But after the *lanzone*...'

'It was delicious.'

'The second one.'

'Exactly.'

He hadn't let go of her hand, and now he led her alongside the stream, the ground soft and loamy beneath them. Aurelie found she quite liked the feel of his fingers threaded through hers. They walked along the bank, winding their way up through the dense foliage, until Luke stopped suddenly.

'Close your eyes.'

More trust. 'Okay.' She closed her eyes and felt Luke tug on her hand. She took a step. Another.

'Open them,' he said softly, and she did. And gasped in wonder.

CHAPTER SEVEN

'Wow.'

'Definitely worth it, huh?'

She turned from the stunning view of the falls to Luke's rather smug smile. 'I wouldn't say definitely. I think my sandals are ruined.'

'Leather dries.'

'It is amazing,' she admitted and his smile widened. Not so smug, she decided. More like…satisfied. *Happy.*

'Let's find a place for a picnic.' He tugged on her hand again and they picked their way along the rocks until they found a large flat one, warm from the sun and perfect for a picnic.

Aurelie stretched out on top of it as Luke unpacked their lunch, her gaze on the waterfall once more. It truly was a spectacular sight, a crystalline fountain flowing from the fern-covered rocks, falling in a sparkling stream to a tranquil pool fifty feet or more below.

She turned to watch Luke peel a *lanzone* with a knife. He glanced up, smiling, a decidedly wicked glint in his eyes. 'Care to try another?'

'I don't know if I dare.'

'This one's sweet, I promise.' And with that wicked glint still in his eyes he fed her a chunk of the sweet, moist fruit, his fingers brushing her lips as she ate it. The barest touch

of his fingers against her mouth sent little pulses of awareness firing through her, flaring deep down. *Desire.* It seemed
amazing that she could feel it. Want it—and him. She'd never
wanted anyone before, not like that. Not since Pete.

'Tasty,' she managed, and swiped at the droplets of juice
on her lips. Her heart rate was skittering all over the place,
and all from that simple touch and the feelings and thoughts
it had triggered, a maelstrom swirling through her.

'You know,' she said as Luke arranged the rest of their
picnic items onto two paper plates, 'I don't really know anything about you.'

'What do you want to know?'

'Something. Anything. Where did you grow up?'

'New York City and Long Island.'

'The Hamptons?' He nodded, and she hugged her knees to
her chest. 'I guess you grew up pretty privileged, huh? Bryant Enterprises and all that?' She didn't know much about
the Bryant family, but she knew they were rich. Featured
in the society pages rather than the trashy tabloids like her.
'And you have a brother, you mentioned?'

'Two.'

'Are you close?'

'No.' Luke spoke mildly enough, but Aurelie sensed a dark
current of emotion swirling underneath the words, a tension
and repressiveness. She was getting to know this man, and
now she wanted to understand him.

'Why aren't you?'

He lifted one shoulder in a shrug. 'The short answer? Because Aaron's an ass and Chase checked out a long time ago.'

'Those are rather nice alliterations, but what does that
really mean?'

Luke sighed and sat back, his arms braced on the rock
behind him. 'It means my older brother, Aaron, loves to be
the boss. I can't really blame him, because my father encour-

aged it, told him he was going to be CEO of Bryant Enterprises when he was older, and he needed to be responsible, authoritative, et cetera. Let's just say Aaron got the message.'

Aurelie observed the tightening of Luke's mouth, his eyes narrowed as he gazed out at the falls, the sunlight catching the spray and causing it to glitter.

'And Chase?'

'Chase is my younger brother. He was always a rebel, got in trouble loads of times, expelled from boarding school, the whole bit. My father disinherited him when he was in college.'

'Ouch.'

'I don't know if Chase even cared. He made his own fortune as an architect and he hardly ever gets in touch.'

Aurelie hugged her knees. 'That's sad.'

'Is it?' He glanced at her, eyebrows raised. 'Maybe he's better off. When I do see him, he always seems happy. Joking around.'

'Maybe that's his schtick.'

'Maybe.'

'And what about you?' Aurelie asked quietly, because that was what she really wanted to know. 'Where did you fit into that picture?' Luke hesitated, and she knew she was getting closer to understanding. 'Or didn't you?'

'I suppose I was the classic middle child.'

'Which is?'

'Caught between two larger personalities. As we got older we all drifted apart and that seemed easier.'

'It doesn't sound like a very comfortable place.'

'No, I don't suppose it was.' Luke turned to her with a faint smile, although Aurelie could still sense that dark emotion swirling underneath. 'I don't miss my childhood, at any rate. I was shy, awkward, and I even had a stammer.' He spoke lightly, but it didn't matter. Aurelie knew it hurt. 'My

father didn't have much time for me, to tell you the truth.'
He glanced away. 'He didn't have time for me at all.'

'Sounds a bit like my childhood,' Aurelie answered quietly.

Luke turned back to her, his gaze sharp now, eyes narrowed in concern. 'Oh? How so?'

She swallowed past the ache that had started in her throat, an ache of sympathy and remembrance. She'd never told anyone about her childhood. In the world of celebrity, it held a touch too much pathos to be interesting. 'Well, my mother didn't have much time for me. And my father wasn't in the picture.'

'Who raised you?' That thoughtful crease appeared between his brows. 'Your grandmother?'

'I wish. I only stayed a summer with her, when I was eleven, but it was the happiest time of my life.'

'Then where did you grow up?'

'Nowhere. Everywhere. My mom never stayed in the same place for more than a few months, sometimes a few weeks. She'd get a job in a local diner or something, enrol me in school and find a deadbeat boyfriend. When he started stealing her money or knocking her around, she'd move on, dragging me with her.'

'That's terrible,' Luke said quietly, and Aurelie shrugged.

'I got over it.'

'Julia Schmidt,' he said after a moment. 'Your mother. You bought the house from her, didn't you?'

She nodded. 'When my grandmother died she left it to my mom. I was only seventeen, and I think she hoped it would help my mom settle down.'

'But?'

Aurelie sighed. 'My mom didn't want to settle down. So I bought the house from her for far more than it was worth. I was famous by then, so I had the money.'

'And you finally had a home.'

She blinked hard, amazed at how quickly and easily he understood her. How in this moment it felt good and right and safe, rather than scary.

'It must have been a huge loss when your grandmother died,' he said after a moment, and she nodded.

'I still miss her.'

'And your mother?'

A shrug. 'Around. Who knows? She used to appear every so often asking for money, but now that I'm not in the spotlight any more—at least not for any good reason—she's disappeared.' She sighed and stretched out her legs. 'She'll surface one day, I'm sure.'

'So you really are alone.'

So alone. Although she didn't feel alone right now. She wanted to tell him that, confess just a little of the happiness in her heart that he'd helped to create, but fear held her back. Rejection was still a distinct and awful possibility. There was still so much Luke didn't know.

'What about your parents? Are they around?'

He shook his head. 'Both dead.'

'I'm sorry.' Aurelie gazed at him, saw how he'd carefully schooled his features into a completely neutral mask. 'How did they die?'

'My father of a heart attack when I'd just finished college.' A pause, a telling hesitation. 'My mother developed breast cancer when I was thirteen.'

'I'm sorry. That's terrible.'

He jerked his head in a semblance of a nod, his face still so very neutral. He was holding something back, Aurelie suspected, some pain that he didn't want to share with her. She decided not to press.

'So you're alone too,' she said quietly and after a taut moment of silence Luke reached for her hand.

'Not right now,' he said, and as Aurelie's heart turned right over he tugged her to her feet. 'Let's swim.'

'Swim?' Aurelie eyed the deep, tranquil pool below the falls with a dubious wariness. 'What about the giant barracudas?'

'You mean the medium-sized ones? They're friendly.'

'I didn't bring a swimsuit.'

'I'm sure we can improvise.' She hesitated and Luke added quietly, 'Unless you don't want to.'

Was this another trust exercise? she wondered. She was so used to men seeing her as an object. A trophy. She'd encouraged it, after all. And yet she knew Luke was different, knew he saw her differently.

'Okay,' she said. 'Let's do it.'

Luke led her down a narrow path to the pool. Aurelie tilted her head up to watch the waterfall cascade down the rock, churning foam that emptied into a surprisingly placid pool.

'Good thing you're not shy any more,' she said as Luke tugged his shirt over his head. Then her mouth dried, for the sight of his bare chest was glorious enough to start her heart thumping. His shoulders were broad, his chest powerful and browned and perfectly taut. Washboard abs, trim hips. She was gaping like a fool, and realised it when Luke gave her a knowing grin and dropped his shorts.

He wore boxers, and Aurelie could not draw her gaze away from his powerful thighs. As for what was hidden beneath the boxers…

'Look at me like that much longer and I'm going to embarrass myself,' Luke said, a thread of humour in his voice although she caught the ragged note of desire too. And it thrilled her.

She wasn't sure how it could feel so different from before, when she'd wielded his desire for her like a weapon. Now it felt like a joy. She glanced up and smiled right into his eyes.

'I don't think that would necessarily be a bad thing.'

He nodded towards her pale pink sundress. 'Your turn.'

He'd already seen her naked. He'd seen her in her skimpy Aurelie underwear several times. Yet this felt different too, more honest, more bare. She slid the straps from her shoulders and shrugged out of the dress.

'Sorry. I'm wearing boring underwear.' Just a plain cotton bra and boy shorts. Really, incredibly modest. Yet she felt nearly naked, and her body responded to Luke's heated gaze, an answering heat flaring within her, stirring up all sorts of wants. As well as just a tiny little needle of fear. No, not fear, but uncertainty. Memory.

Luke smiled and turned towards the pool. 'Last one in,' he called, and dived neatly into the water below. Aurelie watched him surface, sluicing the water from his face, clearly enjoying himself. He glanced up at her. 'Is a rotten egg,' he finished solemnly and she laughed. Still didn't move.

'Are you chicken?'

'I prefer the word cautious.' She hadn't swum in anything but a lap pool in years.

'Didn't you swim in a lake or watering hole that summer you spent in Vermont?' Luke called up to her. 'This is no different. In fact, it's nicer because the bottom is sand and rock rather than squishy mud.'

She stared at him, amazed at how much he guessed. Knew. She had swum in a lake in Vermont, a muddy-bottomed pond that she'd spent hours in.

'Come on,' Luke called. 'I'm right here. I promise you can scramble onto my shoulders if a medium-sized barracuda happens by.'

More trust. Funny, how trusting in these silly little things made her start to unbend to the notion of trusting him with the bigger things. Like the truth. No, she'd been honest enough about her past for one afternoon. But this she could do.

Taking a deep breath, she took a running jump into the pool. The water closed over her head and for a moment she remained below the surface, treading water and enjoying the complete stillness and silence until she felt Luke's hands close around her shoulders and he hauled her upwards.

'What—'

'You want to scare me to death?' he demanded, but she saw that telltale glint in his dark eyes. 'I thought you were drowning.'

'I can swim, you know.'

'Maybe one of those barracudas had got you.'

She laughed, but the sound trembled and died on her lips as she saw Luke's eyes darken, his pupils dilate, and she felt the pulse of desire in herself. He still held her by the shoulders, and she was close enough to see the droplets of water clinging to his skin, the enticing curve of his mouth, a mouth that she knew was soft and warm and delicious.

Then Luke let her go, easing away from her, and struck out towards the falls. 'Come see this,' he called over his shoulder, and Aurelie felt a flicker of disappointment. Had she wanted him to kiss her?

Yes, she had.

How novel. How exciting. How disappointing that he hadn't.

With a little shake of her head, she swam over to join him at the waterfall.

'There's a little cave behind the falls,' Luke explained. 'Just swim underneath the waterfall and you'll come up right into it.'

'Okay.'

Luke dived down first and Aurelie followed him, surfacing a few seconds later into a shallow fern-covered overhang, the waterfall a sparkling crystalline curtain hiding them from the world. Luke hauled himself up onto a ledge and extended a hand to her.

They sat side by side in silence for a moment, and to Aurelie it seemed completely relaxed, completely wonderful. She'd never felt so much in accord with another human being before, and she knew she wanted to tell him. Forget the fear. Screw rejection. This was too incredible, too important.

She turned to him with a smile. 'It's amazing. This whole day has been amazing.'

Luke touched her cheek, no more than a brush of his fingers. 'It has been for me too.' His gaze was tender and yet intent on hers, the curve of his mouth so close—

'Luke—' She wasn't sure what she was going to say. *Kiss me,* maybe, because she wanted him to. Desperately. But he didn't. Didn't even let her finish, just slipped off the ledge and swam underneath the falls once more.

With a little sigh Aurelie followed him.

They swam a bit more in the shallows of the pool, splashing, teasing and laughing and finally they got out and returned to the sun-warmed rock to dry.

Aurelie sat there, her arms braced behind her, her legs stretched out, wearing only her underwear. And felt completely natural, no Aurelie artifice or armour. She was, she knew, being herself; she'd been herself for nearly the whole day. There *was* something there, underneath all the posing, and she'd needed Luke to show her.

'So if your mother was dragging you around in pursuit of her deadbeats, how did you actually become famous?' Luke asked after they'd sat in a comfortable silence for a little while.

'At a karaoke night at a bar in Kansas, if you can believe it,' Aurelie answered.

'You sang karaoke?'

'We both did. It was a mother-daughter thing.'

'Ah.'

'What do you mean, *ah*?' she asked, because he sounded as if she'd just said something significant.

'Well, your mother isn't famous, is she?'

'No—'

'I'll bet she wasn't pleased that her teenage daughter—how old were you, sixteen?'

'Fifteen,' Aurelie said softly. 'It was a month before my sixteenth birthday.'

'Young and gorgeous,' Luke stated, 'and about to be famous. And your mother wasn't any of those things.'

Strange, she'd never thought of it that way. She'd never considered that her mother might have been jealous of her. Yet now, looking back on that fateful, life-altering night, she remembered how quiet her mother had been. Of course, Pete had done all the talking, made his promises, told Aurelie she was going to be a star. She swallowed, willing the memories away. It had begun right there, she knew, the destruction of herself. The building up of Aurelie.

'It's hard to remember, isn't it,' Luke said quietly. 'I'm sorry.'

She shook her head, her throat tight. 'In some ways it was the happiest—well, I felt the happiest then than I had in such a long time. But if I'd known, if anyone could have told me—'

'Told you what?'

She swallowed. Here was the honesty that hurt. 'That I'd lose my soul. That I'd sell it, because I didn't even know what I was giving away.'

Luke frowned. 'I suppose fame will do that to you.'

'It wasn't fame. It was—' She stopped because she didn't want to tell him, didn't even know how. 'It was awful,' she finished quietly.

He was silent for a long moment. '"Never give your heart

away,"' he quoted her song softly. 'Is that what happened, Aurelie? Someone broke your heart?'

She swallowed. 'Yes.'

He nodded, sorrowfully understanding. 'Three years is a long time. It must have hurt when it was over.'

She let out a sudden, hard laugh because Luke had completely the wrong idea and she didn't want to have to correct him. 'It felt like forever,' she agreed after a moment. 'But my heart didn't break when it was over, Luke. It broke when it began.'

CHAPTER EIGHT

IT BROKE WHEN it began.

Aurelie had said the words with such flat finality, such aching sorrow, that Luke knew she meant them. He just didn't know what they meant.

'I don't understand,' he said quietly, but she shook her head.

'I don't want to talk about it. I don't want to ruin this perfect day by bringing all that up. And it has been perfect, Luke. Everything.' She gazed at him with those wide rain-washed eyes and Luke felt everything in him twist and yearn.

He'd wanted to kiss her so many times today. When she'd planted her hands on her hips and given him an impish look, when she'd tossed him a teasing glance, when he'd held her in the water and longed to pull her close, their wet limbs sliding over each other, twining around.

Hell, he'd been in a permanent state of arousal, it seemed, for half the day. Yet he'd kept his distance, and he would now, because this wasn't about desire.

It was about trust.

He'd meant what he said about earning it. He'd let her down before, but he wouldn't again. He had, despite his instinct which insisted there was so much more, taken her at face value. Aurelie the go-to-hell pop star. And he'd allowed her to seduce him, allowed himself to give in to his own need because the desire had been so strong. Only when he had seen the pain on her face, written on her heart, and known he'd shown her he was just like all the others, had he been able to stop. Yet he feared the damage had been done.

It broke when it began.

What did she mean? Had some bastard abused her? The sudden strong urge to kill such a man with his bare hands surprised him. Aurelie aroused all sorts of feelings in him, feelings he hadn't had in a long time. He had, he saw now, been skimming through life, never going too deep, using work as an excuse because this—this emotion, this intensity—was frightening. Reminded him of how much you could lose, how much risk and pain was involved in any real relationship.

Not pain for him—he didn't care about that—but pain for her. He didn't want to hurt her, and he was so afraid that he might.

How did your parents die?

For a second, no more, he'd wanted to tell her the truth. Yet honesty only went so far, and that secret was buried so deep inside him he didn't think he could let it out if he tried. He tried not to think about it, yet being with this woman brought his own secrets swimming upwards to the light, just like hers.

They were *both* being real.

'It has been perfect,' he agreed. 'But it's getting late and we've got a mile trek through the jungle as well as a ride in the Jeep and a plane to catch.'

'Back to reality,' Aurelie said, making a face, and Luke reached for her hand.

'Maybe reality won't be so bad,' he said quietly. This new reality, with the two of them in it together. *One day at a time.* Yet what would tomorrow hold?

They walked back to the Jeep in companionable silence,

the jungle lush and vibrant all around them. As they emerged into the sunlight a brilliant blue morpho butterfly fluttered close to Aurelie's face and briefly alighted on her hair. She laughed aloud, and Luke smiled to see her joy. Then suddenly, impulsively perhaps, she leaned over and brushed her lips against his.

He stilled under that little kiss, felt a flare of heat inside, the instant arousal, yet something more. Something precious, because he knew that little kiss hadn't been calculated. It had been an expression of her heart.

'What was that for?' he asked, and she shrugged, smiling.

'Just because I wanted to.' She paused, bit her lip. 'Do you mind?'

Mind? 'No,' Luke said. 'I don't mind at all.'

'Good.'

And that, he knew, was a very good start.

By the time they got on the plane Aurelie was feeling sleepy. She curled up in a corner of one of the leather sofas, and when Luke came and sat down right beside her it felt amazingly natural to rest her head on his shoulder. Luke curved his arm around her, drew her closer so her cheek rested against his chest, and with a kind of wonderful incredulity Aurelie realised that felt natural too. It felt right. She snuggled closer, and by the time the plane took off her eyes were drifting shut.

They got back to the hotel after dark, and Luke walked her all the way to the door of her suite. Aurelie turned to him, felt her heart throw itself against her ribs. Should she ask him to come in? Did she want him to? Part of her did, desperately, and another part still felt that old fear.

She took out her keycard, hesitated and turned to Luke. 'Well.' She swallowed, smiled. Sort of.

Luke smiled back and cupped her cheek. The feel of his warm palm against her skin was both reassuring and exciting. Yet even so Aurelie felt herself tensing. She wanted this, she did, and yet…

'Goodnight, Aurelie.' Luke dropped his hand and turned to walk back down the corridor. Aurelie stared at him in disbelief, a little disappointment.

'You mean you aren't…you aren't going to kiss me?'

Luke glanced back, eyes glinting. 'No.'

'But—'

'You didn't want me to.'

'I did,' she said, but she knew she didn't sound that convincing.

'Maybe,' Luke suggested quietly, 'you didn't know what you wanted. And until you do, completely, I'm not going to touch you.'

Aurelie stared at him, her mind spinning. 'Why not?'

'I think the better question is, why would I?' She had no answer to that one. With one last smile Luke walked down the hallway and left her there, half-wishing he'd kissed her and half-glad he hadn't.

The next morning dawned hot and bright and Aurelie lay in bed, her mind tumbling over the events of yesterday—including Luke's non-kiss—and then suddenly freezing on the realisation of what today was.

Today they travelled to Singapore, and she was giving another concert for the store opening tonight. Swallowing hard, she drew her knees up to her chest and hugged them tight. Somehow she didn't think her fans in Singapore wanted to hear her new song any more than the ones in the Philippines had. Which left her…where?

She avoided the question as she got dressed and ate breakfast, meeting Luke down in the lobby at nine, as they'd agreed earlier. They were taking his private jet to Singapore, and from there going on to the Fullerton Bay Hotel on Marina Bay. They'd check in and go directly to Bryant's.

By the time she'd boarded Luke's jet Aurelie could no longer ignore the fluttering nerves that were threatening to take her over. She glanced at Luke sitting across from her, a sheaf of papers on his lap, his thumb and forefinger bracing his temple. He looked so serious and stern, and yet a lock of unruly dark hair had fallen across his forehead and Aurelie longed to brush it away, to savour its softness under her fingers. She'd been wanting to touch him more and more. Luke was awakening a desire in her she hadn't thought she possessed, and all by *not* touching her.

Yet what would happen when he did?

He glanced up as if aware of her gaze, smiled ruefully. 'You're nervous.'

For a stunned second she thought he'd guessed the nature of her thoughts, then realised with some relief that he was talking about the concert. 'Yes, I am.'

'You'll be fine.'

'You don't know that.'

'True.' He stretched his legs in front of him and put the papers back in a leather case. 'What did you do when you had all those big concerts? To warm up, I mean, and get rid of stage fright?'

Aurelie shrugged. 'Honestly, I don't know. I didn't really have stage fright.'

Luke arched an eyebrow. 'Never? Not even when you played to ten thousand people in Madison Square Garden?'

She laughed, but the sound trembled. 'No, because it was all an act. It wasn't really me, and so I didn't…I didn't really care.'

'And now it's you, and you care,' he finished softly, and she nodded, stared at her hands. Luke covered her hand with his own, twined his fingers through hers. He didn't say anything, didn't offer false promises about how they'd all love her, and she was glad. Silence could be honest too.

Yet her nervousness came back as they landed in Singapore and took a limo to the hotel. Aurelie barely registered the sumptuous suite with its view of the bay from one balcony and the city skyline from the other. All she could think about was how in just a few hours she would walk onto that stage and bare her soul.

Why had she written the damn song, anyway? And why had she ever played it for Luke?

'It doesn't matter what they think, you know,' Luke said. She turned and saw him standing in the doorway of her suite. 'It doesn't mean anything if they don't like it.'

'Doesn't it?'

'No. What matters is what you think of it. How you think of yourself.'

How she thought of herself? She couldn't answer that one. Being herself still felt so new, so strange. She still wasn't sure she even knew who she was.

'We'd better get going,' she said, and slipped past him out into the corridor.

Luke stayed with her as they toured the store, five floors on Orchard Road, and showed her the new café, the glittering beauty hall, the department for crafts and clothing all supplied by local artisans, clearly his brain child.

'Don't you have important people to see?' she asked, half-joking, as he escorted her to the dressing room where she was to get ready. Already people were milling about the marble lobby, waiting for the official opening.

'I'll check in with a few people now, and come back before you go on.'

Aurelie swallowed. Luke had done a good job of distracting her with the tour, but the fear—the *terror*—was now coming back in full force.

'Okay,' she said, still trying for insouciance and failing miserably. He put his hands, strong and comforting, on her shoulders and smiled down at her.

'Forget about the crowd,' he said quietly. 'Forget about me. Sing your song for yourself, Aurelie. You need that.'

Somehow, despite the tears now stinging her eyes, she dredged up a smile. 'I knew this was pity,' she joked, and he pressed his lips to her forehead.

'You can do it. I know you can.'

And then he was gone, and Aurelie sagged against the door, completely spent from that small encounter.

By the time Luke returned half an hour later she was ready—or at least as ready as she'd ever be. She wore a sundress this time, in a soft, cloud-coloured lavender, and cowboy boots. Her hair fell tousled to her shoulders, and she carried her guitar.

Luke smiled. 'You look fantastic.'

She smiled back, wobbly and watery. 'I feel like complete crap.'

'You can do it,' he said, and this time it wasn't an encouragement, it was a statement. He believed in her. More, perhaps, than she believed in herself.

A few minutes later she was miked and ready to go, and then she was on. She heard the hiss of indrawn breath as she walked onstage. Another surprised, perhaps even outraged, audience. She sat on the stool, stared into the faceless crowd. Swallowed. Her heart hammered so hard it hurt, and she felt a blind panic overwhelm her like a fog. She couldn't do this.

Then she felt Luke's presence on the side of the stage, just a few feet away. Strange, impossible even, to feel someone when he didn't move or speak, yet she did. He felt warm, and his warmth melted away the fog. She glanced sideways, saw his steady gaze, his smile. She took a breath. Blinked. And started to play.

Distantly she heard the rippled murmur of confusion as she began to play a song they didn't recognise. Her song. But then the song took over and she knew it didn't matter what anyone in the audience thought. Luke had been right; she wasn't doing this for them. She wasn't doing it just for herself, either.

She was doing it for him. Because he was the one person who had believed in her, more than she'd been able to believe in herself. Already he'd given her back her soul; he'd shown her how to reclaim it. She played the song for him, for her, for *them*.

And when it was over and the last note faded away, you could have heard a pin drop on the marble floor of the lobby. You could have heard the tiniest sigh, because no one did anything. No one clapped.

They didn't, Aurelie knew numbly, know *what* to do with her. How to react.

Then, from the side of the stage, she heard the sound of someone clapping. Loudly. *Luke.* And the sound of his clapping was like the trigger to an avalanche, and suddenly everyone was clapping. Aurelie sat there, her guitar held loosely in one hand, blinking in the bright lights and smiling like crazy. And crying too, at least she was as she walked offstage and straight into Luke's arms.

He enveloped her in a tight hug, his lips against her hair. 'You did it. I knew you could.'

She tried to speak, but there was too much emotion lodged in a hot lump in her throat, too many tears in her eyes. So she did what she wanted to do, what she needed to do. She kissed him.

This wasn't a tentative brush of her lips against his. She kissed him with all the passion and hope, the gratitude and joy that she felt. She dropped her guitar and wrapped her arms around him, and Luke took her kiss and made it his own, kissing her back with all he felt too.

It was, Aurelie thought dazedly, the most wonderful kiss.

The rest of the evening passed in a happy blur. Luke kept her by his side, introducing her to various officials and dignitaries, and for once in her life Aurelie didn't feel like the pop star performing for another sceptical crowd. No, with Luke next to her, she simply felt like herself. A woman whose hand was being held by a handsome and amazing man.

She was, Aurelie thought distantly, halfway to falling in love with him. It didn't seem possible after such a short time, and yet she felt the truth of it inside her, like a flame that had ignited to life. She never wanted it to go out.

And yet what *did* she want? The memory of that passionate kiss by the side of the stage had seared itself into her senses, but she still felt her insides jangle with nerves at the thought of what else could happen. What she wanted to happen…and yet was afraid of, both at the same time.

Despite her wonder and worry about what might happen later, she still enjoyed every minute of the evening spent by Luke's side. A dinner for the VIP guests had been arranged in the conservatory on top of the store, with the lights of Singapore stretched out in a twinkling map on three sides, and the bay with its bobbing yachts and sailing boats on the other. A silver sickle moon hung above them, and she felt the warm pressure of Luke's hand on the small of her back.

'Are you having a good time?'

'Very.' She turned to smile at him. 'You've done an amazing job with all these openings. I've heard a lot of great things about the new design of the store.'

'I've heard a lot of great things about your new song.'

She let out a little laugh. 'If you hadn't started clapping, I'm not sure anyone would have.'

'They would have. They just needed a little nudge.'

'Maybe next time you should hold up cue cards. Flash "Clap" in big letters as soon as I finish.'

'Next time they'll know. There were a lot of media people out there in the audience tonight. Word will get around.'

She drew a deep breath and let it out rather shakily. 'That's a scary thought.'

'Is it?'

'I don't know what the response will be.'

'Does it matter?'

She stared at him, surprised, until she realised it *didn't* matter. She hadn't written or performed the song to impress people or even make them change their minds about her. She didn't even want a comeback. She wanted…this.

Acceptance and understanding of who she was, not by a faceless crowd or the world at large, but by Luke—and by herself. And somehow he'd known that even before she had.

'Come on,' he said, 'I have some people I want you to meet.' And with his hand still on her back he guided her through the room.

Luke watched Aurelie chat and laugh with the CEO of the Orchard Bank of Singapore and felt something inside him swell. He loved her like this, natural and friendly and free. He loved *her*.

The thought, sliding so easily into his mind, made him still even as he attempted to keep involved in the conversation. He was trying to negotiate a new deal with a local clothes retailer to design exclusively for Bryant's. It would be an important agreement, and he couldn't afford to insult the CEO across from him.

And yet…he loved her? After just a few short days? When he still couldn't really say he knew her, not the way he'd known the three women with whom he'd had significant relationships. They'd dated for years, had known each other's peeves and preferences, had run their relationship like a well-oiled machine. And yet now he felt he could barely remember their faces. Had he loved them? Not like this, maybe not at all. He'd been emotionally engaged, certainly, although it hadn't hurt that much when they'd mutually agreed to end it.

But this? Her? It felt completely different. Completely overwhelming and intoxicating and scary. Was that love? Did he want it, if it was?

Did he have a choice?

And could she love him, when there were things he hadn't told her? Failures and weaknesses he hadn't breathed a word about? His insides clenched at the thought. She'd been slowly and deliberately baring herself—her soul, her secrets—while he'd kept his firmly locked away.

Could love exist with that kind of imbalance?

'Mr Bryant?'

Too late Luke realised he hadn't heard a word the man in front of him had said. He swallowed, tried to smile.

'I'm sorry?'

Several hours later Luke found Aurelie laughing with the wife of a foreign diplomat and placed a proprietorial hand on the small of her back. He liked being able to touch her in this small way, even if the ways he really wanted to touch her—had been dreaming of touching her—were still off-limits. He'd told her he wouldn't touch her until she wanted him to, until she was certain, and he knew she wasn't yet. He saw the shadows in her eyes even when she was smiling.

'I'm sorry to steal Aurelie away from you,' he told the woman, 'but we have a full day tomorrow and she needs her rest.' He smiled to take any sting from the words, and the woman nodded graciously. 'Been having a nice time?' he asked Aurelie as they headed down to the limo he had waiting.

'Amazing, actually. I thought it would be completely boring, but it wasn't.'

'That's refreshingly honest.'

She laughed, the sound unrestrained, natural. 'Sorry, I didn't mean to be insulting. It's just I've gone to so many parties and receptions and things and it's always been so exhausting.'

'Another performance.'

'Exactly. But it wasn't tonight. I was just able to be myself.' She shook her head slowly. 'I never thought that playing my song would give me anything but a kind of vindication that I could be something other than a pop star, but it has. It's made me feel like I can be myself…anywhere. With anyone.' She paused before adding softly, 'With you.'

She gazed up at him with those wide stormy-sea eyes and Luke felt that insistent flare of lust. He wanted her so badly. His palms itched with the need to slide down the satiny skin of her shoulders, fasten on her hips. Draw her to him and taste her sweetness.

She must have seen something of that in his face because her tongue darted out to moisten her lips and she took a hesitant step closer to him. 'Luke—'

He didn't know what he might have done then, if he would have taken her in his arms just as he'd imagined and wanted, but then the doors pinged open and a crowd of guests moved aside to let them pass. Luke let out a shaky breath and led Aurelie towards the limo.

They didn't speak in the intimate darkness of the car, but he felt the tension coiling between and around them. Felt her thigh press against his own when the limo turned a curve, and the length of his leg felt as if it had been dusted with a shower of sparks. He heard, as if amplified, every draw and sigh of her breath, the thud of his own heart.

He hadn't felt this overwhelmed by desire since he'd been

about eighteen. He let out another audible, shaky breath and stared blindly out of the window.

They remained silent as the limo pulled in front of the hotel, and then in the lift up to their separate suites on the same floor. Luke took out his keycard; it was slick in his hand. His mouth had dried but he forced himself to speak. To sound as if he were thinking of anything other than hauling Aurelie into his arms and losing himself deep inside her.

'So. Another big day tomorrow.'

'Is it? What's the schedule exactly?'

Was he imagining that she sounded just a little breathless? Her cheeks were flushed, her eyes bright. She tucked a strand of hair behind her ear, and Luke's gaze was irresistibly drawn to the movement, the curve of her ear and the elegant line of her neck.

He swallowed. 'We fly to Hong Kong, spend a day touring the city with some officials and then have the opening on the following day, along with a reception. Then two days' rest and on to Tokyo.'

'Right.' She glanced away, and the lift doors swooshed open. Luke walked down the corridor, conscious, so conscious, of Aurelie by his side. The whisper of her dress against her bare legs, the citrusy scent of her, the way each breath she took made her chest rise and fall.

She stopped in front of the door to her suite, and he stopped too. She waited, her hand on the door, her eyes wide. Expectant. But he'd promised himself—and her—that he wouldn't touch her until she asked. Until no uncertainty remained.

Standing there, he knew that time had not yet come. Unfortunately for him.

'Goodnight, Aurelie.' He cupped her cheek, just as he had the night before, because despite all his promises he couldn't resist touching her, just a little. Aurelie closed her eyes. Waited. It would be so easy to brush his lips against hers, to deepen the kiss he knew she wanted. But it was too soon, and he'd still seen the shadows in her eyes.

With a supreme act of will he dropped his hand from her face. He smiled—at least he thought he did—and walked down the hall towards his own lonely suite of rooms.

Aurelie stepped inside her empty suite and leaned against the door, her eyes closed.

Damn.

Why hadn't he kissed her? He'd wanted to, she knew that. She'd wanted him to, had willed him to close that small space between them, but instead he'd pulled away.

Maybe you didn't know what you wanted. And until you do, completely, I'm not going to touch you.

His words from yesterday reverberated through her, made her think. Wonder. Was he waiting for her to take the lead? To say she had no more uncertainty, no more fear?

Did she?

No. She was still afraid. She'd been telling Luke the truth when she said she'd never enjoyed sex. If she'd been totally honest, she would have told him she dreaded it. Hated it, and yet used it because at least then she had some control.

And now? She wanted sex—sex with Luke—to be something different. Something more. And that terrified her more than another bout of unenjoyable coupling.

She opened her eyes, paced the room, her mind racing. She wanted this. She wanted Luke. And, just like with her song, with the trust, with the intimacy, she knew she needed to push past the fear. For her sake as much as Luke's.

So…what did that mean, exactly? Right here, right now? She ran her now-damp palms down the sides of her dress.

Brushed her teeth and hair, applied a little perfume. And then before she could overthink it and start to get really nervous, she went in search of Luke.

CHAPTER NINE

LUKE YANKED OPEN his laptop and stared at the spreadsheet he'd left up on the screen. Work was as good an antidote as any to sexual frustration. He didn't have any better ideas, at any rate.

Sighing, he raked his hands through his hair, loosened his tie and stared hard at the screen.

Five minutes later a knock sounded on the door of his suite.

Luke tensed. He wasn't expecting anyone, and his staff would call or text him before disturbing him in his private quarters. So would anyone from the hotel. Another knock, soft, timid. He knew who it was.

'Hello, Aurelie.' He stood in front of the doorway, drinking her in even though he'd seen her just a few minutes ago. Her hair looked even more tousled, her lips soft and full. She'd sunk her teeth into the lower one and he could see the faint bite marks.

'May I come in?'

It reminded him, poignantly, of when he'd first come to her house in Vermont. How he'd asked, how she'd been so reluctant to let him in.

As reluctant as he was now, because he knew how weak he was when it came to this woman. 'All right.' He stepped aside, felt her dress whisper across him as she passed by.

'Do you need something?' he asked as he closed the door. He heard how formal and stiff he sounded, and he could tell she did too.

Her mouth quirked upwards and she took a deep breath. 'Yes. You.'

God help him. Her direct look, eyes wide, lips parted, had pure lust racing right through him. He clenched his fists, unclenched them. Breathed deep. 'I don't think this is a good idea, Aurelie.'

'Funny, I think you've said that before.'

'I know. And it wasn't a good idea then, either.' Hurt flashed across her face and she glanced away. 'It's too soon,' Luke said quietly. 'This is too important to rush things.'

She took a step towards him. 'Maybe it's too important to hold back.'

He shook his head. 'I don't think you're ready.'

'Shouldn't I be the judge of that?'

'Yes, but—' He hesitated. Wondered just why he was fighting this so much. Then he remembered the look on her face when he'd rolled off her before, as if she'd been cast in stone. He'd felt…he'd felt almost like a rapist. Sighing, he raked a hand through his hair and sank onto the sofa. 'Why don't you sit down?'

Gingerly she sat across from him. He thought of how he'd first met her, the cold cynicism in her eyes, the outrageous smile, the constant innuendo. She was so different now, so real and beautiful and vulnerable. He was so afraid of hurting her. Of failing her.

It was a fear, he acknowledged bleakly, that had dogged him for most of his life. Twenty-five years, to be precise, since he'd battered helpless fists against a locked door, begged his mother to let him in. Tried to save her…and failed.

This is your fault, Luke.

He blinked, forced the memory away. He hardly ever

thought of it now, had schooled himself not to. Yet Aurelie's fragile vulnerability brought it all rushing back, made him agonisingly aware of his own responsibility—and weakness.

'It's not as if I'm a virgin,' she said, clearly trying to sound light and playful and not quite achieving it. 'Even if you're acting as if I am.'

'In some ways you are,' Luke answered bluntly. 'If you've never enjoyed sex—'

'I'm what? An enjoyment virgin?' Her eyebrows rose, and he saw a faint remnant of the old mockery there.

'An emotional one, perhaps.'

She sighed. 'Semantics again.'

'I don't know what sex has been to you in the past, but it's not anything I want it to be with me.'

A blush touched her cheeks. 'I know that. I want it to be different.'

'How?'

She swallowed. 'Maybe you should tell me what it's been to you in the past.'

Now he swallowed. Looked away. He was so not used to these kinds of conversations. Honesty and emotional nakedness were two totally different things. 'Well, I suppose it's been an expression of affection.' *Coward.* 'Of…of love.'

They stared at each other, the silence taut with unspoken words, feelings too new and fragile to articulate. 'Did you love the women you've been with before?' Aurelie asked in a low voice.

'I suppose I thought I did. But honestly, I'm not sure.' He raked a hand through his hair. 'It didn't feel like this.'

This. Whatever was between them, whatever they were building. Luke didn't know how strong it was, whether a single breath would knock it all down.

'That's what I want,' Aurelie finally managed, her voice no more than a husky whisper. 'I know we've only known each other a short while and I'm not saying—' She cleared her throat. 'I'm not trying to, you know, jump the gun.'

His mouth twisted wryly. 'Aren't you?'

'Well, not the emotional gun. Physically, maybe.'

He shook his head slowly. 'They go together, Aurelie. That's the only kind of sex I want with you.'

He saw the fear flash in her eyes but she didn't look away. 'That's what I want, Luke. That's what I want with you.'

And he wanted to believe her. Yet still he hesitated; they'd only known each other, really, for a handful of days. Intense days, yes, amazing days. But still just days.

'Please,' she whispered, her voice low and smoky, and he felt his resistance start to crumble. Not that there had really been much to begin with. He was honest enough—hell, yes, he had to be—to know that any resistance he'd given had been token, merely a show. He wanted this too.

'Anything that happens between us,' he said, his tone turning almost severe, 'happens at a pace I control.'

She stilled for just a second, then gave him a small smile. 'Yes, boss.'

'And if I think it isn't…it isn't working, then we stop. *I* stop. Got that?'

'Got it.'

Hell. He hadn't exactly set the mood, had he? Yet he wanted her to know he wasn't going to rush things, take advantage. In this crucial moment, he wanted her to trust him. He wanted to trust himself.

He swallowed, felt her gaze, wide-eyed and expectant, on him. He could not think of a single thing to say.

A tiny smile hovered around Aurelie's mouth and her eyes lightened with mischief. 'So what now?'

'Hell if I know.'

And then she laughed, a joyous bubble of sound, and he

laughed too, and he felt them both relax. Maybe it would be okay after all. Maybe it would even be wonderful.

He stood up, held his hand out to her. She took it instantly, instinctively, trusting him already. 'Come on.'

He led her to the bedroom in the back of the suite, two walls of windows overlooking the inky surface of Marina Bay. Aurelie only had eyes for the bed. It was big, wide and piled with pillows in different shades of blue silk. She turned to him and licked her lips, a question in her eyes.

'Let's just relax.' He kicked off his shoes, took off his tie and stretched out on the bed. Aurelie sat on its edge and took off her boots. Gingerly she scooted up next to him, lay her head back on the pillows. Luke laughed softly. 'You look like you're on an examining table.'

'I feel a bit like that too.'

'We're not rushing this, you know.'

'I almost wish you would.'

'Oh?' He arched an eyebrow. 'You think you'd enjoy that?'

Now she laughed, the soft sound trembling on the air. 'Probably not.'

Gently he traced the winged arches of her eyebrows, the curve of her cheek. Her eyes fluttered closed and he let himself explore the graceful contours of her face with his fingertips: the straight line of her nose, the fullness of her lips. 'Tell me,' he asked after a moment, 'what your favourite room is in your house in Vermont.'

'What?' Her eyes opened and she stared at him in surprise. Luke smiled and gently closed them again with his fingertips.

'Your favourite room,' he repeated and continued to stroke her face with whisper-light touches. He felt her relax, just a little.

'The kitchen, I suppose. I always remember my grandmother there.'

'She liked to bake?'

'Yes—'

'And you helped her that summer?'

Her eyes opened again, clear with astonishment. 'Yes—' Gently he nudged them closed once more. She relaxed back into the pillows again. 'I always liked helping her with things,' she said after a moment. 'I suppose because she always liked me to help.'

'You must miss her,' Luke said quietly, and she gave a little nod.

'You must miss your mother,' she said, her voice hardly more than a whisper, and for a second his fingers stilled on her face. He hadn't expected her to say *that*. She opened her eyes, gave him a small smile. 'This honesty thing? You told me it went both ways.'

'Yes.' But he really didn't want to talk about his mother.

'Do you miss her?'

'Yes.' He swallowed, felt his throat thicken. 'Every day.' Gently he traced the outline of her parted lips with his fingers and then slowly, deliberately, dropped his finger to her chin. Rested it there for a moment. 'You know, the first time I met you I knew the truth of you from your chin.'

'My chin?'

'It quivers when you're upset.'

She laughed softly. 'No one's ever told me that before.'

'Maybe no one's ever noticed.' He lowered his head and pressed a kiss to the point of her chin. He felt her still, hold her breath. *Wait.* He lifted his head and smiled. 'I like it.'

'I'm glad.'

He touched her chin once more with his fingertip, and then trailed it slowly down the curve of her neck, rested it in the sweet little hollow of her throat. Stroked. He heard her breath hitch and she shifted on the bed. Luke felt the impatient stirring of his own desire. He'd told her they'd go slowly, and he meant it. Even if it was a rather painful process for him. 'Your skin is so soft. I thought that the first time I met you too.'

'You didn't.'

'I did. I was attracted to you from the moment you opened your eyes. Why do you think I was so ticked off?'

She let out a shuddery little laugh as he continued to stroke that little hollow. 'Because I was passed out and running late, I thought.'

'That was just my cover.' He let his finger trace a gentle line from the hollow of her throat down to the vee between her breasts. And he rested it there, the sides of her breasts softly brushing his finger, and waited.

Her cheeks were faintly flushed now, and her eyes had fluttered closed. He heard her breath rise and fall with a slight shudder and he felt a deep surge of satisfaction. She wanted this. She wanted him. He trailed his finger back up to that hollow, and she opened her eyes.

'This is going to take forever.'

He laughed softly. 'Not forever, I hope. That would kill me.' He let his finger trail back down, brushed the soft sides of her breasts this time, and felt her shiver. 'But long enough.' He pressed his lips to the hollow of her throat and then he slid his palm down to cup the soft fullness of her breast. She tensed for a second and then relaxed into the caress with a soft sigh.

Luke felt a powerful surge of protectiveness. He wanted to do this right. But it was killing him to go so slowly, to take the time he knew she needed. He flicked his thumb over the peak of her nipple and heard her indrawn breath, then another sigh. He smiled and moved his hand lower, onto the taut muscles of her tummy.

She opened her eyes, gazed up at him. 'You're being incredibly patient.'

'It's worth it.'

'You don't know that.'

'I know.' He slid his hand lower, down to her bare knee, and rested it there. Watched her eyes widen in expectation, maybe alarm. He stroked the back of her knee, down to the slender bones of her ankle, and then back up again. A little further up, so his fingers brushed the tender, silky skin of her inner thigh and then down again to the safety of that knee.

She let out a little laugh. 'You're torturing me.'

'Am I?' With his other hand he touched her cheek, the fullness of her lower lip, her chin, the hollow of her throat. Saw her eyes go hazy and dark with desire. She reached her hands up and tangled them in his hair, drew him closer.

'Kiss me,' she commanded, her voice husky, and Luke obliged.

He brushed his lips across her once, twice, and then went deep, tasting her as she tasted him. His hand tightened instinctively on her knee, slid upwards. She parted her legs and he felt her hands go to the buttons of his shirt.

'Too many clothes,' she mumbled against his mouth, and in a couple of quick shrugs—and a few buttons popping—he was free of his shirt, the garment tossed to the floor.

'How about your dress?'

She swallowed, nodded, and he slid the skinny straps from her shoulders. One quick, sinuous tug on the zip on the back and she shimmied out of the dress, kicking it away from her ankles.

Luke gazed at her. He'd seen her in her underwear before, of course, but he still loved to look at her. He let his gaze travel back up to her face, those wide, stormy eyes. 'Okay?' he asked quietly, and she nodded.

Still he waited. She nodded towards his trousers. 'Maybe you should deal with those.'

'Maybe you should.'

She arched her eyebrows, then smiled and nodded. Luke bit down on a groan as her fingers brushed his arousal. She fumbled a bit with the belt and zip, which made it all the more of an exquisite torture. Then she slid his trousers off his hips, and he kicked them the rest of the way. All they were wearing was their underwear, and it felt like way too much clothing to him. He smoothed his hand from her shoulder to her hip, revelling in the feel of her satiny skin. She shivered under his touch and he moved his hand upwards again, cupped her breast and smiled as she arched into his hand.

He kissed her again, deeply, and felt her respond, her arms coming around him, one leg twining with his. He moved his hand lower, across her tummy to the juncture of her thighs. Waited there, feeling her warmth, until she parted her legs and he slipped his fingers inside her underwear, felt her tense and then will herself to relax, arching her hips upwards as his fingers explored and teased her.

He felt his control slipping a notch as her own hand skimmed his erection and their tongues tangled, heard her breathing hitch—or was it his? He was so, so ready for this, and she *felt* ready—

He pressed another kiss to her throat, willed his heart to stop racing. 'Okay?' he muttered against her neck, and felt her nod. He slid her underwear off, kicked off his own boxer shorts. And then he was poised between her thighs, aching with need for her, their bodies pressed slickly together, all of him anticipating and straining towards this—

He looked down and saw she'd gone still, actually *rigid*, with her eyes scrunched tightly shut.

Damn.

It took all, absolutely all of Luke's self-control to stop. He took a deep, shuddering breath and rolled off her onto his back. Stared at the ceiling and felt his heart wrench inside him when he heard Aurelie let out a tiny hiccup of a sob. *What had gone wrong?* And how had he let this happen—again?

'I'm sorry,' she finally whispered into the silence.

'No. Don't be.' He was still staring at the ceiling, still feeling that scalding rush of shame and guilt. He was also feeling incredibly, painfully aroused. 'Let me just take a shower,' he muttered and, rolling off the bed, he headed towards the bathroom.

Aurelie lay on the bed and listened to Luke turn on the shower. She blinked hard and tried not to cry. *What had gone wrong?*

She honestly didn't know. One second she'd been lost in Luke's little touches, aching for his deeper caress—and the next? She'd felt the heavy weight on top of her and his breath in her ear and suddenly, painfully been reminded of the first time with Pete.

Let me...

She blinked hard again, forced the memories back. She did not want to think of them now, to bring them into this moment, this bed.

Drawing a deep breath, she reached for her scattered clothes. She didn't even remember Luke unclasping her bra, but he must have done. It was lying on the floor. She dressed quickly, furtively, afraid Luke would come out of the bathroom—and then what? Was he angry? Frustrated, no doubt, in more ways than one. And knowing Luke—which she did now, she realised—he'd want answers. Answers she didn't want to give, because she knew they wouldn't reflect well on herself.

Sighing, she sat back down on the bed and waited.

A few minutes later Luke emerged from the bathroom, a towel around his hips. Aurelie swallowed dryly at the sight of his chest, broad, browned and shimmering with droplets of water. Just a few minutes ago she'd had the power to touch it at her leisure, had felt that hard, muscular body pressed against hers. Just the memory caused a pulse of desire low in her belly. *How* had it all gone wrong? Could memories really have that much power?

Luke reached for a T-shirt and dropped his towel, oblivious to his own nakedness. Aurelie was not. She swallowed again, felt her heart start to thud. He slipped on a pair of boxers and then sat on the edge of the bed. She tensed, waited.

He smiled wryly, his eyes dark, his hair damp and spiky. She wanted to comb it with her fingers, to feel its damp softness. She folded her hands together in her lap.

'I guess you realise we need to talk.' She nodded, and Luke sighed. 'I'm sorry for the way things happened.'

'Don't be.' It hurt to squeeze those two words out, for her throat had got absurdly tight. 'It's not your fault.'

'It's not yours, either.' She didn't answer, and Luke reached over and placed his hand over her tightly clasped ones, his thumb stroking her fingers. 'Tell me what happened to you, Aurelie.'

'Nothing happened.' She shook her head, impatient with the way he was making her a victim. She'd never wanted pity. She'd made all her choices willingly. She *had*.

'Why, then,' Luke asked evenly, 'did you freeze up at a rather crucial point? Everything was going well, wasn't it?'

She let out a little choked sound, half-laugh, half-sob. 'Very well.'

'And then?'

'I don't know. I just—' She moistened her lips, forced herself to continue. 'I just froze up, like you said. To be honest, you're the only one who's ever noticed.'

'Then you haven't had very considerate lovers.'

'No.'

Luke sighed and squeezed her hand. 'I appreciate that I

may not have earned enough of your trust to tell me what happened to you, because something did. Some experience has made you fear sex and, until I know what it is, I can't help you. And,' he added, a wry note entering his voice, 'I can't make love to you, which is a shame.'

Aurelie lifted her gaze to his. 'We could try again—'

'No.' Luke spoke with such flat finality that she recoiled. 'I don't think you realise,' he added more quietly, 'how it makes me feel to see you beneath me, looking like you're bracing yourself for some kind of torture.'

She blinked, felt the hot wetness of tears behind her lids. She hadn't thought of that. She'd only thought of herself, and how disappointing she must be to him. 'I'm sorry,' she whispered.

'I don't want your apologies. I just want your honesty. But I can wait.'

She sniffed. Loudly. 'So what now?'

'How about we go to sleep?'

Hope stirred inside her, a tiny, fragile bud emerging amidst the mire of desolation. 'Here? Together?'

'That's the idea.' And then, gently, perhaps even lovingly, he pulled her into his arms so her cheek rested against that wonderfully hard chest. She felt the reassuring thud of his heart and closed her eyes. 'I'm a patient man, Aurelie.'

She smiled against his chest, even though the tears still felt all too close. 'That's good to know.'

Yet as she snuggled against him beneath the covers, his arms securely around her, she wondered if she was the impatient one. She'd changed and grown so much over the last few days, but she wanted more. She wanted to be different in *every* way, and especially in this one. Yet with this—this crucial intimacy—she didn't know how to change, or even if she could.

CHAPTER TEN

MORNING SUNLIGHT SPILLED across the bed, created pools of warmth amidst the nest of covers. Aurelie rose on one elbow and stared down at the sleeping form of the man she loved.

Yes, loved. She'd been skirting around that obvious truth for days now, because it was too scary and even impossible to grasp. How could she love a man she'd known for such a short time? And why would she, when she knew what happened when you gave your heart away? You lost not just the heart you'd freely given, but your soul as well. Your very self.

She knew Luke was different. She knew it bone-deep, *soul*-deep, and yet that knowledge didn't stay the tattoo of fear beating through her blood. The memory of how absolutely wrecked she'd been when Pete had finally ended it, and how she'd realised she had nothing, *was* nothing but a shell, remained with her. Infected her with doubt.

She didn't doubt that Luke was different; she feared that she wasn't. Even now a sly, insidious voice mocked that she hadn't changed at all, not in the way that mattered most. She'd give herself to him, body and heart and soul, and he would take it and use it and there would be nothing left. She'd be nothing.

And yet, despite that consuming fear, she still felt that baby's breath of hope, and Luke's steady presence, his arms cradling her all night long, had fanned it into something strong and good.

She wanted to take a chance again. With Luke, and with herself.

He opened his eyes.

'Good morning.' His voice was low and husky, and its warmth flooded through her. She smiled.

'Good morning.'

He shifted so she was cradled once more by his arm, and she rested her head on his shoulder, breathed in the warm, woodsy scent of him. Idly he ran a few strands of hair through his fingers. 'Sleep well?'

'Better than I can ever remember.'

He pulled her just a little bit closer, that primal part of him clearly satisfied. 'Good.'

Aurelie took a breath. And another, because this was hard. *So* hard, and as she took another breath she knew she was already starting to hyperventilate. She let it out slowly, a long, breathy sigh, and Luke's hand stilled on her hair. He was waiting.

'I want to tell you some things,' she began, and deliberately he began stroking her hair again, his fingers sifting through the strands.

'Okay.'

'I think I'm ready to…to do that.' He didn't answer, just kept stroking, and Aurelie closed her eyes. 'Not that it's that big a story. I mean, if you're expecting me to tell you something horrible to explain…well, to explain my behaviour, it wasn't like that.'

'You don't need to make any judgements, Aurelie. I won't.'

She felt her eyes scrunch shut, as if she could block out the truth she was about to tell. 'You might.'

'No.'

'I told you I haven't been a Girl Scout. Some of those tabloid stories—a lot of them—are true.' She spoke almost defiantly now, daring him to be shocked. Disgusted.

'I know that,' Luke answered steadily. He was so steady, even when she was doing her best to push him away and pull him closer both at the same time.

'I have to go back to the beginning.'

'I told you I am a patient man.'

'I know.' And now all there was left to do was begin. At the beginning. 'You remember I told you I was discovered at that karaoke night in Kansas?'

'Yes.'

'The man who discovered me was named Pete.'

'Pete Myers,' Luke clarified, and Aurelie realised that he'd heard of him, of *course* he'd heard of him. Pete was famous. He'd managed several major bands, had judged a couple of TV talent shows. He was practically a household name.

'Right,' she said, and continued. 'Well, Pete was amazing back then. He came up to me, told me he could make me a star. He took my mom and me to dinner, told us his whole plan. How I'd become Aurelie.'

'So he was the one behind your image.' Luke spoke tonelessly, but Aurelie still felt the censure. She stiffened.

'I went along with it. Innocent siren, those were his words.'

'You were only fifteen.'

'Almost sixteen. And I thought it all sounded incredibly cool.' She sighed, hating that already she was having to explain, to justify. Luke's arm tightened around her.

'I'm sorry. Continue.'

'Those first few months were a whirlwind. Pete took us all over, to LA, New York, Nashville. I met with agents and songwriters and publicity people and, before I knew what was happening, I was recording and releasing a single, and it was huge. I felt like I was at the centre of a storm.'

'What about your mother?'

'She disappeared a couple of months after Pete discovered me. I think she realised people didn't really want her around, that she was just getting in the way. When she left, Pete offered to have me stay with him. I was still a minor, and he had to make some kind of legal guardian arrangement with my grandmother—' She stopped then, because her throat had become so tight. That had been the last time she'd seen her grandmother alive. She'd given her the guitar, begged her to stay the same. And she hadn't.

'Anyway,' she continued, trying desperately for briskness, 'Pete was great about it all. He gave me my own floor in his house, treated me like—' the word stuck in her throat '—a daughter. At least, he felt like a father to me. The dad I'd never had. He gave me a lot of good advice in the early days, how not to take any of the criticism to heart, how to stay sane amidst all the craziness. He even remembered my birthday—he got me a cake for my seventeenth.'

'A paragon,' Luke said flatly, and she squirmed in his arms to face him.

'I told you not to make judgements.'

'I'm not. I'm just wondering where this is going.'

'I'll tell you.' She took another breath, let it out slowly. 'I'd been living with Pete for a little over a year. He'd seen me through some tough times—my grandmother dying, being diagnosed with diabetes. He was the one who found me, you know. I'd passed out in the bathroom, and he took me to ER. Stayed with me the whole time, made sure I got the proper treatment and counselling once I was diagnosed.' She felt Luke's tension; his shoulder was iron-hard under her cheek. 'I'm telling you all this just to…to explain the relationship. How close we were.'

'I get it.' His tone was even, expressionless, and yet Aurelie sensed the darkness underneath. And she hadn't really told him anything yet.

'So fast forward to my eighteenth birthday. He took me out to dinner at The Ivy, told me how happy he was that I'd made it, how much he cared about me.' She paused, tried to choose her words carefully. She needed the right ones. 'I look back on that as one of the happiest nights of my life.' Before it had all changed.

She fell silent, the only sound in the bedroom the draw and sigh of their breathing. 'And then?' Luke asked eventually. 'What happened?'

'Pete took me home. I went to bed. I was just changing into my pyjamas when he…he came into the room.' He hadn't, she remembered now, asked to come in. Not like Luke. She still remembered that ripple of shocked confusion at seeing Pete standing in the doorway. Staring at her.

'And?' Luke asked very quietly. Aurelie realised she'd stopped speaking. She was just remembering, and she hated it.

'He told me he loved me. He'd always loved me, and then he…he kissed me.'

'Not,' Luke said quietly, 'like a dad.'

'No. Not like a dad.' She still remembered the shocking feel of his mouth on hers, wet and insistent. The way his hands had roved over her body, with a kind of tentative urgency. He'd been crying a little bit, and he kept begging her. *Let me,* he had whispered over and over again, and she had.

'What did you do?' Luke asked. He was still stroking her hair, still holding her. Aurelie blinked back the memories.

'I let him.'

'Let him?'

'He kept saying that. *Let me.* And I did, because…well, because I didn't want to lose him. He was the most important person in my life at that point, the only person in my life. And, looking back, I can see how I got it wrong. He never wanted to be my dad. I was the one who wanted that.'

Luke's hands had stilled. 'So he…he kissed you?'

'We had sex,' Aurelie said flatly. 'That night. It was, if you can believe it, my first time. That whole innocent siren thing? It was pretty much true.'

Luke swallowed, said nothing. 'I didn't enjoy it,' she continued. She felt weirdly emotionless now, as if none of it mattered. 'I hated it. It felt…well, it felt gross, to be honest. But I knew it was what he wanted and so I made myself want it too.'

'And what happened then? After?'

She shrugged. 'We started dating.'

Dating?

'A relationship. Whatever. I was already living with him, so—'

'Are you telling me,' Luke asked, and his voice shook slightly, 'that Pete Myers was your serious relationship? The one that lasted three years?'

'Yes—'

'God, Aurelie.' He sank back onto the pillows and when she risked a look at his face she saw he looked shocked. Winded, as if she'd just punched him. Maybe she had.

'I thought you kind of knew where this was going.'

'Well, when you started talking about Myers, I figured he'd…he'd taken advantage of you somehow. But you'd said you weren't abused or raped—'

'I wasn't.' She stared at him in surprise. 'I told you, he asked.' *Let me.* 'And I said yes.'

Luke stared at her. He still looked dazed. 'You remember when we talked about semantics?'

'Yes—'

'Yeah. That.'

She shook her head. 'I wasn't a victim. If I'd told him to leave, he would have.'

'You think so?'

'I know it. Luke, you weren't there. You didn't see how... how pathetic he looked. I felt sorry for him.' Almost.

'Yeah, I'm sure he could look pathetic when he wanted to. He's also one of the richest, most powerful men in the music world, Aurelie. You don't think he might have been taking advantage of you?'

'Maybe,' she allowed, 'but I allowed it to happen.'

'For three years.'

'It was a *relationship*.' She didn't like the tone Luke took, as if she'd been used. Abused. A victim.

'A secret relationship. I've never seen this mentioned in the press.'

'Pete didn't want the tabloids to trash us. He was being protective—'

'Very thoughtful of him.'

'Don't,' she said furiously. 'Don't make this about me being used by him. I was *not* a victim.'

Luke just gazed at her. 'Go on,' he finally said quietly. 'Tell me what happened.'

'When?'

'How did it end?'

'He ended it. He said it wasn't working, that I was too clingy.'

'Too clingy.'

'Yes. And I was, I can see that now. The fame had started to get to me, and I felt like Pete was the only person who knew who I really was. My mom was still out of the picture, my grandma was dead, and I'd never stayed in one place long enough to get to know anyone.'

'So,' Luke said slowly, 'he was all you had.'

'It felt that way. But he started losing interest and my

music started slipping, the media noticed, and when he finally ended it—' She took a breath, plunged. 'I went off the deep end.'

'You weren't,' Luke said, and she almost heard a sad smile in his voice, 'a Girl Scout.'

'No. I pretty much did what the press said I did. I drank, I did drugs, I partied hard and slept around, and my career tanked.' She swallowed, sniffed. 'So there you have it.'

Luke said nothing, and Aurelie felt condemnation in his silence. She'd done so many things she wasn't proud of, the first one being that she'd given in to Pete that first night. That she'd been so clingy and needy and starved of love, she'd taken what she could get. And then when he'd decided he didn't want her any more, she'd spun out of control because she'd felt so horribly empty.

And she was so afraid of that happening again.

'Which part of all that,' Luke finally asked, 'did you not want to tell me?'

She let out a wobbly laugh, surprised by the question. 'All of it.'

'But which part in particular?' He shifted so he was facing her, his gaze intent, his eyes blazing. 'The part at the end? About how you went off the deep end? How you partied and slept around and lost yourself?'

She squirmed under that gaze, those pointed, knowing questions. 'Yes, basically.' *Lost yourself.* That was exactly what had happened, yet even now she couldn't admit as much to Luke. Admit that she was afraid of it happening again, and worse this time. She'd finally found herself again, thanks to Luke. But what if she lost herself once more because she couldn't handle being in a relationship? Being hurt?

What if he grew tired of her like Pete had, like the whole *world* had?

'And what about sex?' he asked quietly. 'Enjoying it? Why do you think you don't?'

She swallowed, wished he didn't have to be quite so blunt. 'I suppose because of my experience with Pete. I was never attracted to him, and being with him like that for so long… it just killed that part of me.'

'And when I'm with you? And you freeze? Why do you think that is?'

'I don't know.' She felt herself getting angry again. She hated him asking so many terrible questions, stripping her so horribly bare. 'I suppose I remember that first time. It was awful, okay?' Tears sprang to her eyes and she turned her face away from him. *'Awful.* I couldn't breathe. He was so heavy. And it…hurt.' She gasped the last word out, tears pooling in her eyes. If she blinked they would fall, and she couldn't have that. If she let those first tears out, too many more would follow, and she was afraid she would never stop crying.

'What about with other men?' Luke asked quietly.

Aurelie sniffed, her face still averted, her voice clogged with all those mortifying tears. 'They were all pretty much the same. They only wanted one thing from me, and I knew that. I was a trophy. I got it, and I used it because—' She stopped, and Luke finished for her, his voice so soft and sad.

'Because it was better than being used.'

She said nothing. Words were beyond her. She wished she'd never told him, desperately wished she hadn't opened up this Pandora's box of tawdry memories. 'Don't judge me,' she finally whispered, a plea, and Luke shook his head.

'I'm not judging you. Not at all.'

He sounded so weary, so resigned, that Aurelie felt her spirits plummet, and they were already pretty low. He was disgusted by her. Of course he was. How could he not be, after all the things she'd told him? She'd known this would happen. She'd been expecting it. She slipped away from him, rolled out of bed and hunted for her dress.

'I should go back to my room.'

'Why?'

'We're going to Hong Kong today, right? I need to shower and get dressed.' She didn't look at him as she slipped her dress on, tugged on her boots. Her hair was a disaster, but all she needed to do was walk down the hall.

'We're not finished here, Aurelie.'

'I'm finished.'

'You're scared.'

Hell, yes. She glanced up at him, hands on her hips. 'Oh, you think so? Of what?'

'A lot of things, I suspect.'

Luke sounded so calm, so relaxed, and here she was feeling like a butterfly pinned to a board. Unable to protect or hide herself, just out there for his relentless examination. 'Well, I'm not scared,' she snapped. 'But I don't particularly like talking about all that, and since we have a full day I'd like to get on with it. That all right by you?' She spoke in a sneering drawl, the kind of voice she'd used so many times before. The kind of voice she hadn't used with Luke since they'd started on their second chance.

Well, so much for that.

'It's all right by me,' he said quietly and, without another word, Aurelie whirled around and stalked out of his bedroom.

Luke lay on the bed and stared at the ceiling, too dazed to do anything but try and process what Aurelie had told him. *Pete Myers.* A man who had to have been at least fifty when he'd first started with Aurelie. A man who had abused her affection, used her body and her trust. And Aurelie didn't see it that way.

She saw it as a *relationship.* Hell, no.

Sighing, he ran his hands through his hair, pressed his fists into his eyes. He had no idea what to do. He was still so afraid of failing her. Failing her like he had last night, when he'd gone about it completely wrong. He'd been trying to ease Aurelie into love-making gently, sweetly, but he'd been the one in control. Hell, he'd told her that before they even started. *Anything that happens between us, happens at a pace I control... Got that?*

He winced at the memory. He'd thought it would help her, to know they would go slowly, but now he saw how it must have accomplished the opposite. He'd been just another man controlling her, using her body. Luke swore aloud.

He saw now that Aurelie needed to feel in control. To *be* in control. That was, he suspected, why she insisted on believing Pete hadn't taken advantage of her, that it had been a willing, committed relationship—because then it was something she could control.

And last night, in an utterly misguided attempt to help her, he'd quite literally taken all the control away from her. Groaning aloud, Luke dropped his fists from his eyes and stared at the ceiling once more. It was time, he knew, for a third chance. Time to earn her trust once more.

By the time he'd showered and dressed, eaten and answered emails, he was near to running late. He'd knocked on the door of Aurelie's room but there had been no answer and he felt a flicker of foreboding. Was she trying to avoid him? Well, that could only last so long.

His mouth firming into a determined line, he headed downstairs.

Aurelie was waiting in the lobby, dressed in a mint-green shift dress, her hair tucked behind her ears, her arms folded. She was fidgeting and she didn't meet his gaze as he came towards her. Clearly now was not the time to have some kind

of emotional discussion, and maybe he needed the time—
the break—too.

'All ready?' he asked lightly, and she nodded tensely, her
gaze fixed somewhere around his shoulder.

They didn't speak in the limo on the way to the airport, or
as they boarded the jet that would take them to Hong Kong.
Luke pulled out some papers, thinking to work, but then he
decided he wasn't that patient after all.

'Aurelie.' She turned towards him, still not meeting his
eyes. 'You're doing a pretty good job of avoiding me even
though I'm right here.'

She lowered her head so her hair fell forward in front of
her face. 'I don't know what to say to you.'

'Maybe you could tell me what you're thinking.'

'That.'

He sighed and slipped his papers back into a manila folder.
'What else?'

She shook her head, bit her lip. Luke just waited. 'I'm
thinking I wish I hadn't told you everything I did this morning.'

'Why not?'

'Because…' she lifted her gaze to his, and he saw the
storm in her eyes '…because you think of me differently
now, and I can't stand that—'

'I wouldn't say differently.'

'What, then?'

'More sympathetically—'

She shook her head, the movement violent. 'I don't want
your pity.'

'It's not pity to be able to understand you—'

'I am not some kind of psychological *specimen*—'

'I never said you were.' Luke felt his temper start to fray.
He would *never* say the right thing. 'Aurelie, you're going

to tank us right here and now if you keep fighting me like this. I'm just trying to make this *work*.'

She hunched her shoulders, her chin tucked low. 'Maybe it can't.'

'Is that what you want?' he asked evenly, and she didn't answer for a moment. Fear lurched inside him. Already he couldn't stand the thought of losing her.

'No,' she finally said, her voice so low he had to strain to hear her. She sighed and rested her head against the seat, her eyes closed. 'Look, I know I'm making a mess of this. But I told you in the beginning that I don't know how to let my guard down—'

'You've already let your guard down. Now you're just desperately trying to assemble it again.'

She let out a soft huff of laughter and lifted her wry, slate-blue gaze to his. 'That's not working, is it?'

'No. And I don't want it to work.' He didn't know what the future held, and he still felt that old fear, but he did know he wanted to keep trying. He hoped she did too.

She glanced away. 'I don't, either.' She nibbled her lip, and he thought about reaching out to touch her. Comfort her. He stayed where he was. The physical aspect of their relationship would be dealt with later. He hoped. 'I'm scared,' she said softly, still not looking at him. 'I'm so scared of losing myself again. Of losing control, of not being able to change.'

'Every relationship contains an element of loss of control, but that doesn't mean you have to lose yourself completely. A relationship should make you better, stronger. More of yourself rather than less.' He smiled wryly. 'Or so all the chat shows and women's magazines tell me.'

She arched her eyebrows. 'You watch chat shows and read women's magazines?'

'All the time.'

She laughed, and he smiled. Miraculously, it felt okay again. 'Sorry,' she said softly, and he shook his head.

'This isn't about sorry.'

'What is it about, then?'

'Trust. You're still learning to trust me. I'm still trying to earn it.'

'You have earned it, Luke.'

He didn't feel as if he had. He'd let her down too many times already. *You're always letting people down. The people that matter most.*

That sly inner voice mocked him, reminded him of his failures. The locked door, his mother's silence. His own. He was still living in the long shadow of that moment, and he hated it. So much of Aurelie's life had been defined by one man's selfish actions. Had his life been similarly defined? Destroyed?

Could he rebuild it again, now, with her?

'We land in an hour,' he said, trying to smile, and felt his heart lift and lighten when Aurelie smiled back.

Aurelie had never been to Hong Kong before, and even though she'd seen photos she wasn't prepared for the sheer scale of the city, the skyscrapers clustered so close together, right to the edge of Victoria Harbour, piercing the sky.

She still felt raw from the conversation with Luke on the plane. This honesty was a killer. And when she caught him looking at her with a kind of sorrowful compassion, she froze inside. Part of her ached for the understanding he offered, and yet another part scrambled away in self-protection. Did she really want to be understood, all the dark parts of herself brought to glaring light?

He knew the worst, at least in broad strokes. He knew that she'd gone into a relationship—an awful, unhealthy relationship—out of pathetic loneliness and fear, and he understood, if not in the tawdry particulars, how she'd reacted when it had ended. The many, many bad choices she'd made.

And he's still here.

The voice that whispered inside her wasn't sly or cynical for once. It was the still, small voice of hope, of truth. *He's still here.*

She'd told him he'd earned her trust, but she wasn't acting as if he had. She wasn't, Aurelie knew, acting as if she trusted him at all.

Could she act that way? Deliberately, a decision? Was change not so much a wishing or a hoped-for thing, but a choice? An act of will?

'You ready?' Luke called back to her and, nodding, Aurelie stepped from the plane.

The day passed in an exhausting blur of meetings with various important people, touring the city. As if from a distance, Aurelie took in the Peak, the Jade Market, the Giant Buddha. She chatted and smiled and laughed and listened, yet all the while she felt as if she were somewhere else, thinking something else.

Can I do this? Can I act differently with Luke, even when every part of me struggles to protect myself?

After a lengthy dinner with many speeches and toasts, they boarded a yacht for a pleasure cruise in the harbour. Aurelie watched Luke circulate through the guests, and realised with a pang that he looked more relaxed than when she'd seen him in New York or Manila. He looked happy.

Acting differently was a *choice*. An act of will. It had to be. Deliberately she walked across the deck to join him. He stopped his conversation to smile at her briefly, then resumed describing his plan to incorporate more local artists and artisans in the Hong Kong store. He spoke with authority, with a kind of restrained pride, that made Aurelie's heart swell.

She loved this man. She was terrified, but she loved him.

A few minutes later they'd been left alone, and Luke placed his hand on the small of her back as he guided her to the railing. 'Look.'

She looked towards the shore, and saw that the skyscrapers were shimmering with lights.

'It's the Symphony of Lights. It comes on every night at eight o'clock.'

'Amazing.' And it was amazing, to be standing here with this wonderful man, the air warm and sultry, the sky lighting up all around them. She turned to smile at him, felt the smile all the way through her soul. And Luke must have felt it too, must have seen it, because he drew her softly towards him and brushed his lips against hers. A promise. A promise Aurelie intended to keep.

They rode home from the party in a limo, their thighs brushing, the silence between them both comfortable and expectant. Aurelie followed Luke into the lift, up to the top floor where they had separate suites. She stopped at his door, and he looked at her, eyebrows raised.

Aurelie felt her heart beat hard, her mouth dry. She lifted her chin. 'I want to come in.'

Luke rested his keycard in the palm of his hand, gazed at her seriously. She stared steadily back. *This was a choice.* 'We don't have to rush things, Aurelie.'

'I'm not rushing things.'

He gazed evenly at her, assessing, understanding. Then he nodded. 'All right. But I have one condition.' He unlocked the door and opened it, and Aurelie followed him in, her heart thudding even harder now.

'And that is?' she asked when he hadn't said anything, just shed his jacket and loosened his tie.

Luke turned to her, his eyes glinting, everything about him sexy and rumpled and gorgeous. 'My condition,' he said, taking off his tie, 'is that we do this on your terms.'

CHAPTER ELEVEN

'WE...WHAT?' AURELIE blinked. '*My* terms?'

Luke nodded, his eyes still glinting, his mouth curving in a smile even though she could sense how serious he was. 'Yes. Your terms. I've been thinking a lot about what happened before and I realise I handled everything wrong—'

'Everything, Luke? I think that might be a slight exaggeration.'

'Slight,' he agreed wryly. 'But I was the one in control, wasn't I? I told you that from the beginning. I said I'd set the pace, and I'd call it off if I didn't think it was working.'

Warily she nodded, folded her arms. She wasn't sure where he was going with this. 'Your terms.'

'Yes, and they weren't the right ones.'

'Why not?'

'From what you've told me, and from what I know about you, control is kind of a big thing.'

She prickled, resisting any kind of analysis. 'You think?'

'I do.'

She let out a slow breath, forced herself to relax even though every instinct had her reaching for armour, for the defence of mockery. 'Well, who doesn't want to be in control, really?'

'No one, I suppose,' Luke agreed quietly, 'and especially not someone who had no choice about where to live or when to move or what school to go to. Or even, really, how famous she wanted to be.'

She felt that first, sudden sting of tears and shook her head. 'Don't.'

'Why not?'

'Because I can't stand being pitied, I told you that—'

'I know, and that's a kind of keeping control, isn't it? You keep insisting that everything was your choice because if it wasn't you're a victim and you can't stand that thought.'

No, she couldn't, and even though she'd never articulated it to herself, Luke had. Luke understood her—far too well. She managed a very shaky smile. 'These are so not my terms.'

'I know, Aurelie. I'm breaking my own rules here, but I need to say this.' He took a step closer to her. 'As soon as the clothes start coming off, you can call all the shots.'

She let out a wobbly laugh. 'Promise?'

'Cross my heart.' He took another step towards her, reached for her hands. 'What you had with Pete Myers was *not* a relationship.'

Her hands tensed underneath his. 'It felt like one.'

'No, it didn't. You have nothing to compare it with, so trust me on this, okay?'

Trust. It always came down to trust. She blinked, swallowed. Willed herself to keep her hands in his, not to pull away. For once. 'So what was it, then?'

'Abuse.'

'*No.*' Now she did pull her hands away from his. She turned away from him, wrapping her arms around herself as if she were cold. She was cold, but on the inside.

'How old was he when he first kissed you?'

'Why does the age difference even matter? Plenty of people—'

'Fifty?'

'Forty-nine,' she snapped. 'That doesn't *matter.*'

'It doesn't always matter,' Luke agreed quietly. 'But in this case, when you were young, impressionable, utterly dependent on him—he must have known you thought of him like a father, Aurelie. And he knew you had no one else in the world. He took advantage of you—'

'That doesn't make it *abuse.*'

'I won't argue about semantics. What I'm trying to say is you can't judge any other relationship by what happened with that man. It wasn't healthy or right. Whether you acknowledge it or not, he took all the control away from you, even if you think you let him. Your responses weren't normal because the situation wasn't normal or fair. At all.'

She didn't answer because she had no words. She realised, belatedly, she was shivering. Uncontrollably. She hated everything Luke was saying. She hated it because she knew, in a deep and dark part of herself, that he was right.

And she couldn't stand that thought. Couldn't bear to think so much of her life had been wasted, *used.* She'd been such a pathetic victim.

'I'm sorry,' Luke said softly. 'I'm sorry for what happened to you.'

She didn't answer. Words wouldn't come. She blinked hard and turned around. 'So my terms, right?'

Luke hesitated, his gaze sweeping over her. 'Do you really think this is a good—'

'My terms, you said—' she cut across him, her voice hard '—didn't you? So why are you still trying to take control?'

He stilled. 'I'm not.'

'No?' She took a step towards him, amazed at how angry she felt. Not at Luke, not at herself for once. Yet she still felt it, that hot tide washing over her, obliterating any rational thought. 'All right, then. Here are my terms. Strip.'

He blinked. 'Strip?'

She nodded, her jaw bunched. 'Strip, Luke.'

For a second he looked as if he was going to object. Refuse. Aurelie put her hands on her hips, her eyebrows raised in angry challenge. She could hear her breathing coming hard and fast.

'Okay,' he said quietly, and began to unbutton his shirt.

Aurelie felt a little shiver of disbelief. He was actually obeying her. *She was in control.* She watched, her eyes wide, as he finished unbuttoning his shirt, shrugging out of the expensive cotton. She loved his chest. Loved the hard planes, the way that broad expanse narrowed to those slim hips.

'Your belt,' she snapped. 'Your trousers.'

His gaze steady on her, he undid his belt. Took off his trousers.

'Socks?' he asked, eyebrows raised, and she felt an almost hysterical laugh well up inside her. She nodded. Luke took off his socks. He only wore a pair of navy silk boxers. He waited, and so did she, because hell if she knew what she wanted now.

'Go lie down on the bed,' she said, and heard the waver in her voice. She wasn't sure about this any more. She'd started out angry and strong but now she just felt confused. Sad too, and dangerously close to tears.

She followed Luke into the bedroom and watched as he sat on the edge of the bed, swung his legs over. Lay down and waited, hands behind his head.

She let out a trembling laugh. 'You look a lot more relaxed than I would.'

'I am relaxed.'

'Really?' She sat on the edge of the bed.

'What do you want, Aurelie?' Luke asked quietly, and she knew, she knew that whatever she said she wanted, he would find a way to make it happen. He'd put himself completely in her hands, and she understood that that was what trust was.

Luke trusted her.

And she wanted to trust him.

'I want,' she said, her voice shaking, 'you to hold me. Just hold me.'

And he did, pulling her gently into his arms. She curved her body around his, craving his solid warmth. And as he stroked her hair she did the one thing she'd never, ever wanted to do.

She cried.

Sobbed, really, ugly, harsh sounds that clawed their way out of her chest and tore at her throat. She wrapped her arms around Luke and he held on tight as she sobbed out all the loneliness and pain and confusion she'd ever felt.

Just when she thought she might get a handle on it, she felt new sobs coming up from deep within her and after fifteen minutes or an hour—she had no idea which—she finally managed to wipe her blotchy face and laugh shakily.

'I'm a complete mess.'

'You're beautiful.'

She laughed again, the sound even shakier. 'You cannot mean that.'

'Don't you know by now I never lie?'

She tilted her head to look up at him and saw the truth shining in his eyes. 'How,' she whispered, 'did I ever deserve someone like you?'

'I could ask the same thing.'

She shook her head. 'I don't see how.'

'You're selling yourself short, Aurelie. You often do, you know.' Tenderly he wiped the damp strands of her hair away from her face, tucked them behind her ears. 'You make me laugh. You challenge and thrill me. You stun me with your talent and your courage. Of course I could ask the same question.'

She shook her head, still incredulous, and tenderly Luke

kissed her eyelids, her nose, and then her mouth. 'I do ask it,' he whispered against her lips and, without even thinking about it, just needing to, Aurelie kissed him back. Softly, yet with intent. With promise.

Luke hesitated, just for a second, but long enough so she whispered, 'My terms.'

His hands stilled on her shoulders. 'Which are?' he asked softly.

'I want to kiss you. And you've got to kiss me back.'

'Those are terms I can live with.' She felt him smile against her mouth and then she kissed him again, deeper this time, exploring him in a way she never had before, because she hadn't dared or dreamed of it.

Now she had the time, the desire and most of all the control to kiss him at leisure. In depth. She rolled him onto his back and propped herself up on her elbow, kissing every part of him that she wanted to: his lips, his eyes, the curve of his neck, the line of his jaw. His ear, his shoulder, the taut skin of his chest. She heard him groan softly and she felt a thrill of—no, not power. This wasn't even about power. It was about pleasure and trust and love.

His response made her own need flare deeper, and she kissed his mouth again, deeply, rolling on top of him. Luke placed his hands on her hips to steady her and as Aurelie pressed against him she felt that need flare again, white-hot, burning so brightly she couldn't think for a moment.

'Touch me,' she whispered. 'Touch me back.'

'Where?' Luke whispered, and she felt another thrill of pleasure just at the question.

She took his hand and slid it up along her side, placed it on her breast and closed her eyes. 'There.' And when Luke took that touch and made it his own, his fingers stroking her softness, she let out a shudder. 'And here.' She took his other hand and placed it on her tummy, dared to slide it lower, and another shudder ripped through her as his hands slid under her dress, edged her underwear aside. 'Yes…' She pressed against him as his fingers moved deeper, pleasure shooting like sparks through her whole body. There was a freedom in this, and a wonder. She felt a kind of amazed joy, that she could feel so good, that a man could make her feel so good. That Luke could.

'I want to take off my clothes,' she managed.

'With or without my help?'

She heard a smile in Luke's voice and smiled back. 'With.'

He tugged the zip down her back and she shrugged her shoulders so the dress slid off her. Luke managed the rest, and her bra and panties too. She was naked, and with one swift tug of his boxers he was naked too.

'There.' She spoke on a sigh of satisfaction and Luke smiled as he stretched out next to her.

'Now what would you like?'

She laughed, because it felt so amazing to be asked. 'Hmm…let me think.' She touched his cheek, his jaw, the smooth hardness of his chest. Slid her hand lower to the dip of his waist, and then slowly, wonderingly, wrapped her fingers around the length of his erection. 'More of the same, really,' she whispered, and on a groan Luke kissed her.

They didn't say much of anything any more; she didn't need to give instructions and he didn't need to ask permission. This was what sex was supposed to be, she thought hazily. *Making love.* Moving in silent and loving synchronicity, hands and mouths and bodies, all of it as one together.

And when he finally slid inside her, filling her right up, she felt a sense of completion and wholeness she'd never felt before. Never even known you could have.

Gently, still moving inside her, he wiped the tears that had sprung unbidden to her eyes, kissed her damp eyelids. Aurelie let out a wobbly laugh.

'I'm just so *happy*,' she choked, and Luke kissed her mouth.

'I know,' he said. 'I am too.'

Sunlight streamed through the bedroom windows, touched Aurelie's sleeping form with gold. Smiling, Luke rolled over on his side, smoothed her skin from her shoulder to hip with his hand. He loved the feel of her. Loved the taste of her too, the look of her, and most definitely the sound of her. He loved her, full stop.

It didn't scare him, now that he knew who she was. And who she wasn't. No, it thrilled him and made him incredibly thankful at the same time, because he was pretty sure she loved him too. He'd earned her trust. He'd won her love. He felt a sense of completion and wholeness that came not just from last night, but from finally, wondrously coming full circle after a lifetime of feeling only failure and regret. He'd made this right. He'd made *them* right.

Aurelie's eyes fluttered open and, still hazy with sleep, she smiled. Reached for him with such simple ease that Luke's heart sang. Who would ever have thought that it could be so easy between them? That it would be so wonderful?

'Good morning,' he murmured, and kissed her. She kissed him back.

A little—or perhaps a long—while later, they showered and dressed and ate breakfast out on the terrace overlooking Victoria Harbour.

'Look at this.' He'd been scanning the headlines on his tablet computer and now he handed it to Aurelie. She glanced at the article, her eyebrows rising at the headline: *Aurelie Returns, Better than Ever.*

'That was quick.'

He smiled. 'I knew they'd like the song.'

'That's just one article. There will be others.'

'Does that bother you?'

She handed back the tablet, a furrow between her eyes. 'It doesn't bother me, not the way it used to, when I felt defined by what people wrote or said about me.' She let out a slow breath, and he knew this kind of emotional intimacy was still new for her, still hard. 'It doesn't bother me because I have someone in my life who knows who I really am.' She offered him a tentative smile. 'I never had that before.'

Luke reached for her hand. 'I'm glad you have it now.'

'But I don't want a comeback. I don't want to be famous again.'

'You don't?'

She shook her head. 'Singing in public again was more for me than the audience. I wanted to…to vindicate myself, I suppose. But I don't want to be Aurelie again, not in any incarnation. I've had enough of fame to last several lifetimes.'

He twined his fingers with hers. 'And what if these concerts catapult you back into the spotlight?'

'The spotlight will move off me in a few weeks or months or maybe even days, when I refuse to give them what they want. More concerts, more tabloid-worthy moments. I'm done with all that.'

'You're sure?'

'Yes.' She glanced up at him, worry shadowing her eyes, darkening them to slate. 'Do you mind?'

'Mind? Why would I mind?'

She shrugged. 'I don't know. The fame thing, it's kind of big.'

'To be honest, I'd have a harder time following you around on a concert circuit, but I'd do it if that's what you wanted.'

'And what about what you want?'

'I've got everything I want.' He smiled and squeezed her hand. 'You sing this afternoon, and then we have two days until Tokyo. Let's go away somewhere, just the two of us.'

Her eyes widened, her mouth curving in anticipation. 'Where?'

'I'll surprise you.'

He chose an incredibly exclusive resort on a tiny island off the coast of Hong Kong, the kind of place reporters or paparazzi could never find. The kind of place where he could pamper Aurelie all he wanted and they could revel in each other, in long, lazy days on the beach and long, loving nights in their bed, or the hot tub, or even on the beach again. Everywhere.

The night before they were to leave for Tokyo they lay in bed, the sliding glass doors open to the beach, the ocean breeze rustling the gauzy curtains. Moonlight slid over the rumpled covers, their twined legs. Aurelie was silent, one slender hand resting on his bare chest, over the steady thud of his heart.

Luke brushed his lips against her hair. 'What are you thinking?' he asked quietly, because he sensed something from her that was thoughtful, maybe even sad.

'Just how I don't want this to end. I don't want to go back to real life.'

'I'm not sure I know what real life is any more.' He paused, thinking to say more, then decided not to. He hadn't told her he loved her yet, and she hadn't said it, either. He wasn't afraid of saying those three little words, but he wondered how Aurelie felt about hearing them. This was all still so new, and maybe even fragile. There would be time enough later to figure out how this—*them*—was going to work.

On the plane to Tokyo he reluctantly refocused on work. He hadn't given Bryant's or business a single thought in forty-eight hours, which had to be a record for him. Now he checked his phone and groaned inwardly at the twenty-two texts he'd been sent. Most of them, fortunately, concerned minor matters, but one was a tersely worded command from his brother Aaron.

Wait for me in Tokyo.

Irritation rippled through him. Was his brother actually going to fly all the way to Tokyo to boss him around? No doubt he'd seen some of the press about Aurelie and the openings and wanted to throw his weight around, as he always did.

'What's wrong?' Aurelie asked quietly, and Luke glanced up. Over the last few days they'd become amazingly attuned to one another. Aurelie knew him as well as he knew her.

Not quite.

The thought slid slyly into his mind. She might have completely unburdened herself, but in many ways—crucial ways—he was still buttoned up as tight as ever. He still had secrets, and ones he had no desire or intention to share. She had enough to deal with; she didn't need his remembered pain. He slid his phone into his jacket pocket, glanced away. 'Just work stuff.'

Twenty minutes later they landed in Tokyo.

They took a limo to The Peninsula, the luxury hotel Luke's PA had booked overlooking the Imperial Palace Gardens. The air was crisper than in any of their other destinations, a hint of autumn on the breeze that ruffled the leaves of the trees lining the street.

'I cancelled your hotel suite,' he told her as they checked in. Fortunately there was no message from Aaron, and Luke half-hoped his brother had decided to abandon the trip. He turned to Aurelie. 'I hope you don't mind.'

She smiled, eyebrows raised. 'Why would I mind?'

'You might want a bit of privacy.'

'I think a two thousand square metre suite should provide enough of that,' she answered with a little laugh.

The bellhop led them to the penthouse suite, showed them

all of its rooms and wraparound terrace. When they were alone Luke pulled her into his arms, kissed his way down her throat. He loved the feel of her, the sense of rightness she gave him. 'As much as I'd like to finish what I've started,' he murmured against her skin, 'you have a concert to get to.'

'I know,' she agreed on a sigh of disappointment.

He straightened, bringing her with him so he could look into those slate-blue eyes he loved. 'Are you nervous?'

'No, which is amazing considering how terrified I was a few days ago.'

'You've changed.'

'Thanks to you.' She smiled. 'I know I'm not going to get glowing reviews all around. Someone will hate it, and they'll make sure to let me know.' Her mouth twisted wryly. 'But it doesn't matter. It really doesn't.'

'I'm glad,' Luke said, and with one more kiss because he just couldn't resist he smoothed her hair and dress and they went to get ready for the opening.

Two hours later Luke was standing by the side of the stage watching as Aurelie miked up to go on. She wore a flowing dress of pale green silk with a gauzy overlay, her hair pulled up in a loose chignon. She looked effortlessly beautiful, wonderfully natural. His heart swelled with love.

'What the hell,' a voice snapped out from behind him, 'is she doing here?'

Luke turned around to stare into the furious face of his brother Aaron.

CHAPTER TWELVE

'HELLO, AARON,' LUKE said evenly. 'I think I could ask you the same question.'

Aaron just shook his head. 'What are you talking about?'

'What the hell,' Luke asked mildly, 'are you doing here?'

'Saving your ass. Didn't you get my text?'

'Last time I checked, it didn't need saving.' Aaron opened his mouth but Luke forestalled him with one up-flung hand. 'Be quiet. She's about to start.'

Eyes narrowed, Aaron closed his mouth. Aurelie started to sing, and Luke listened to her smoky voice float through the crowd, hushing even the tiniest whisper. Everyone was entranced, including him.

But not Aaron. The second her voice died away Aaron grabbed his arm. Luke shook it off.

'She goes, Luke.'

Luke turned around. 'What do you mean, she goes?'

'She goes. Now. The last thing Bryant's needs is someone with her reputation linked to it—'

Luke eyed him coldly. 'Aurelie has done wonders for Bryant's image, Aaron.'

Just then she came off the stage, her widened gaze taking in the two of them.

Luke knew he didn't want his brother talking to Aurelie. Aaron had the tact of a tank when it came to getting his own way. 'Just give us a minute please, Aurelie,' he told her, and he heard the suppressed anger in his voice. So did she. She tensed, her eyes going wide before she nodded and, still holding her guitar, walked past them to her dressing room.

'Let's take this somewhere private,' Luke said coolly. 'The *really* last thing Bryant's needs is two of the Bryant brothers coming to blows in front of a thousand guests.'

'Coming to blows?' Aaron arched an eyebrow. 'All over a woman, Luke? Didn't you learn anything from our father?'

'Aurelie is nothing like our father's mistresses,' Luke snapped. Not trusting himself to say another word, he turned on his heel and went upstairs to one of the corporate offices. Aaron followed him, closing the door behind him and leaning against it with his arms folded.

'I appreciate she's probably pretty good in the sack, but she goes, Luke.'

Luke didn't think then. He just swung. His fist connected with his brother's jaw and white-hot pain radiated from his knuckles. Aaron doubled over, righting himself with one hand on the desk, the other massaging his already swelling jaw.

'Damn it, Luke. What the hell has gotten into you?'

'I should have done that years ago,' Luke said grimly. He cradled his throbbing hand. It had felt amazingly good to hit his brother. 'You stay out of this, Aaron. Stay out of my personal life and stay out of the store.'

'The store? The store is part of—'

'Bryant Enterprises. Yeah, I get that. I also get that you've got to have your sticky fingerprints on every part of this empire, even though there's plenty for both of us, and Chase too, if he'd wanted it.'

'Chase,' Aaron answered, 'was disinherited.'

'You could have given it back to him. You knew Dad was just acting out of anger.'

'I wasn't about to go against our dead father's wishes.'

'Oh, give it up.' Luke turned away, suddenly tired. 'Like you've ever cared about that.'

Aaron was silent for a moment. 'You have no idea,' he finally said, his voice flat and strange. Luke turned around.

'No?'

'No. And the fact remains that you might be CEO of Bryant Stores but I'm still your boss, and I say she goes.'

Impatience flared through him at his brother's autocratic tone. 'Have you read the papers? Have you seen the positive press—'

'Yes, and along with the positive press they're raking up every bit of tabloid trash that woman has generated. Do you *know* how many photos there are of her—'

'Stop.' Luke held up a hand. 'Stop, because I don't want to hear it and if we continue this conversation I'll punch you again.'

'This time I'll be ready for it,' Aaron snapped. 'I don't care if you're screwing her, Luke, but she can't—'

'Shut. Up.' Luke's voice was low, deadly in a way neither of them had ever heard before. 'Don't say one more word about Aurelie, Aaron. Not one word.' Aaron remained silent, his mouth thinned, his eyes narrowed. Luke let out a low breath. 'Bryant Stores is under my authority. I've been trying to prove to you for over fifteen years that I'm perfectly capable of managing it myself, but you always step in. You've never trusted me.'

'I don't trust anyone.'

Surprise rippled through Luke; he hadn't expected Aaron to say that, to admit so much.

'Why not?'

Aaron lifted one shoulder in an impatient shrug. 'Does it matter?'

'It matters to me. Do you know how hard I've worked—'

'Oh, yes, I know. You've worked hard for everything in your life, Luke, always waiting for that damn pat on your head. You didn't get it from Dad and you won't get it from me.'

Rage coursed through him. 'That's a hell of a thing to say.'

'It's true, though, isn't it?' Aaron stared at him in challenge. 'You've always been working for other people's approval. Trying to prove yourself, and you never will.'

Luke stared at his brother, realisation trickling coldly through him. He didn't like the way Aaron had put it, but he recognised that his brother's words held a shaming grain of truth. He'd been trying to prove himself for so long, to earn people's trust as if that would somehow make up for that one moment when he'd lost his father's.

'I'll stop now, then,' he said evenly. 'You either step off Bryant's or I do.'

Aaron raised his eyebrows. 'Are you threatening to quit?'

'It's not a threat.'

'Do you know what that kind of publicity could do—'

'Yes.'

'You've worked for Bryant's your whole adult life. You really want to just leave that behind?'

Luke knew his brother was testing him, looking for weaknesses. He wouldn't find any. He'd never felt so sure about anything in his life. 'I'll leave it behind if I have to keep answering to you. I'm done proving myself, Aaron. To you or to anyone.'

Aaron's mouth curved in a humourless smile. 'Well, look at you. All right. I'll think about it.'

Luke shook his head. 'Forget it. I resign.'

'You don't need to overreact—'

'No. But I need to stop working for you. In any capacity. Don't worry, Aaron. I'm sure you'll find someone else to be your stooge.' Luke turned away and he heard Aaron's exasperated sigh.

'It's that woman, isn't it? She's changed you.'

'Yes, she's changed me. But not in the way you think. She's *believed* in me, trusted me, and that's something you've never done. And I don't want that pat on the head, Aaron. I'm done. I'm done trying to earn it from you or anyone.'

With one last hard look at his brother, determination now surging through him, Luke left the office.

Aurelie clutched a flute of champagne and eyed the circulating crowd nervously. She still didn't see Luke or the man she knew must be his brother Aaron. He'd looked just like him, except a little taller and broader, a lot angrier.

She took a sip of champagne, forced herself to swallow. When she'd walked offstage she'd felt the tension between the two men and she'd had a horrible, plunging feeling they'd been arguing about her. No doubt Aaron wasn't pleased about her part in the reopening galas. And as for Luke?

What did he feel?

She realised she didn't know the answer to that question. The last few days had been wonderful, but had they been real? You could probably fall in love with anyone in this kind of situation, out of time and reality. And she knew she must be different from the women Luke had known, those three serious relationships he'd had. Maybe the novelty had worn off. Maybe Aaron had made him realise that she wasn't really a long-term proposition.

'I should congratulate you.' She froze, then slowly turned to face the unsmiling gaze of Aaron Bryant. His assessing look swept her from her head to her toes and clearly found her lacking. 'You've managed to ensnare my brother, at least for the moment.'

It was so much what Aurelie had been thinking, what

she'd feared, that she struggled to form any kind of reply. 'I haven't ensnared anyone,' she finally answered, her voice thankfully even.

'No? It's true love, then, is it?' He sounded so mocking, so disbelieving, that Aurelie stiffened. Didn't say anything, because she wasn't about to give this man any ammunition.

And she didn't even know if Luke loved her. He hadn't said those three important words yet, but then neither had she.

Aaron shook his head. 'Be kind to him when you're finished, at least. He deserves that much.'

Surprise flashed through her. She hadn't expected Aaron to care about Luke's feelings. 'I have no intention of finishing with him.'

'No? Then perhaps he'll wise up and finish with you.' With one last dismissive glance, he turned away.

Aurelie stood there, her fingers clenched around the fragile stem of her flute of champagne, the cold fingers of fear creeping along her spine. She knew Aaron had been trying to get to her, to wind her up or put her down or both. It didn't matter what he had said.

What mattered was her response. It all felt so *familiar*, this encroaching panic, the ensuing clinginess. The terror that Luke would leave her, that she'd be lost without him. She'd lose herself.

She'd changed in so many ways, so many wonderful ways, thanks to Luke. But she hadn't, it seemed, changed in the way that mattered most.

She was going to lose herself again. She felt it, in the hollowness that reverberated through her, a sudden, sweeping emptiness at the thought that Luke might leave her. Maybe she couldn't do relationships after all. Maybe this was what would always happen with her.

Somehow she circulated through the crowd, smiled, nodded, said things, although she wasn't sure what they were. She looked for Luke and caught a glimpse of him across the crowded room.

He was deep in discussion, a frown settled between his brows. Aurelie stared at him for a taut moment and then, without thinking, she turned on her heel and made it to the safety of her dressing room.

She kept her mind blank as she threw her belongings into a bag and grabbed her coat. Her plane left for New York tomorrow, but she could go standby. Hell, she could hire a private jet if she wanted to. And what she wanted in that moment was to escape. To flee to a safe place where she could untangle her impossible thoughts, her encroaching fears, and figure out if there was anything left.

She slipped out of the store, hailed a cab to take her back to the hotel. She was still operating on autopilot, reacting as she always had before, and while part of her knew she should stop, wait, *think*, the rest of her just buzzed and shrieked, *Get out. Get away and save yourself...if there's anything left to save.*

She'd packed her suitcases and was just slipping on her coat when she heard the door to the suite open. Luke stood there, looking tired and rumpled, the keycard held loosely in his hand.

'Someone told me you'd left early—' He stopped, his gaze taking in her packed cases, her coat. He stilled, and the silence stretched on for several seconds. 'What are you doing, Aurelie?'

She swallowed. 'I thought I'd leave a little early.'

'A little early,' Luke repeated neutrally. He came into the room, tossing the keycard on a side table. 'Were you going to inform me of that fact, or were you hoping to slip out while I was still at the opening?'

'I...' She trailed off, licked her lips. 'I don't know.'

He stared at her, his face expressionless, eyes veiled. 'What happened? Did Aaron talk to you?'

'Yes, but that doesn't really matter.'

'Doesn't it?'

'No. I just…I need some space, Luke. Some time. I'm not sure…' Her voice cracked and she took a breath, tried again. 'I'm not sure I can do this.'

'This,' he repeated. 'We never did decide what *this* was.'

Was, not is. So maybe her worst fears were realised, and he was leaving her. Not that it mattered either way. This was her problem, not Luke's.

'And you don't think you could have told me any of this?' he asked, his voice still so very even. 'You don't think you could have shared any of this with me before you tried to bust out of here?'

'I'm telling you now—'

'Only because I came back early!' His voice rose in a roar of anger and hurt that had Aurelie blinking, stepping back. 'Damn it, Aurelie, I trusted you. And I thought you trusted me.'

'This isn't about trust—'

'No? What's it about, then?'

'It's my problem, Luke. Not yours.'

'That's a rather neat way of putting it, considering it feels like my problem now.'

'I'm sorry.' Her throat ached with the effort of holding back tears. 'I just…I can't risk myself again. I can't open myself up to—'

'To being mistreated and abused like that scumbag Myers did to you?'

She felt hot tears crowd her eyes. 'I suppose. Yes.'

Luke let out a hard laugh, the kind of sound she'd never heard from him before. 'And you say this isn't about trust.'

'It isn't,' she insisted. 'This is about what's going on in my own head—'

'You want to know what's going on in my head?' Luke cut her off and Aurelie stilled. Nodded.

'Okay,' she said cautiously.

'I've had a few revelations today. Starting with the fact that I've resigned from Bryant Stores.'

'Resigned—'

'My brother told me I was always trying to prove myself to people, trying to earn their trust. And he was right. I was certainly trying to earn it with you.'

'I know you were, Luke. And you did earn it—'

'Obviously I didn't, if you're trying to sneak away now.' Luke shook his head, his gaze veiled and averted so Aurelie had no idea what he was thinking. 'But this goes back before you. Way back.' He let out a slow breath. 'I told you my mother died of breast cancer, but she didn't.'

'She didn't?' Aurelie repeated uncertainly.

'She killed herself.' Aurelie blinked. Luke stared at her grimly, his gaze unfocused, remembering. 'I was the only one home. I'd come back from boarding school, Chase and Aaron were still at sports camps. My father was on a business trip.'

'What happened?' Aurelie whispered.

'She was hysterical at first. She'd just found out about another of my father's mistresses. He always had some bimbo on the side, which is why I've been a bit more discerning with my own relationships. I saw what it did to my mother. Anyway—' he shrugged, as if shaking something off '—she sat me down in the living room, told me she loved me. I'd always been the closest to her, really. And then she said she was sorry but she couldn't go on, dwindling down towards death while my father flaunted his affairs.' Luke paused, and Aurelie could see how he was gripped by the force of such a terrible memory. 'I didn't realise what she meant at first. Then it hit me—she was actually going to kill herself. She'd gone upstairs, and I ran after her, but the door was locked.' He shook his head. 'I tried to reason with her. I pleaded, I shouted, I even cried. But all I got was silence.'

'Oh, Luke.' Tears stung her eyes as she imagined such a terrible, desperate scene.

'I tried to break the door open, but I couldn't. I *couldn't*.' His voice broke, and Aurelie felt something in her break too.

'I believe you,' she whispered.

'In the end I called 911 but it was too late. She'd slipped into a coma by the time the medics arrived, and she died later that night, from a drug overdose. Anti-depressants.'

Oh, God. So much made sense to her now. She blinked, swiped at her eyes. 'I'm so sorry.'

'So am I. I'm sorry I've let that whole awful episode define and cripple me for so many years. My father blamed me, you see, and so I blamed myself. He said I could have saved her, that I was the only one, that I should have done something. For so long I believed him. I told myself I didn't, but inside? Where it counts? I did. I spent years trying to earn back his trust and respect. His love. And he died without ever giving it to me.' Luke drew a deep breath, met her gaze with a stony one of his own. 'I should have told you this before. I thought it didn't matter, that I'd put it all behind me, but I've been doing the same thing with you, haven't I? I even told you I was. I was trying to earn your trust. I was trying to save you and I can't.'

'I don't want you to save me,' Aurelie whispered.

'Then what do you want, Aurelie? Because I'm done with trying to prove myself. You're either in or you're out. You either love me or you don't.'

Love. She swallowed, her mouth dry, her heart pounding like crazy. 'Luke—'

'I love you. Do you love me?'

Yes. She wanted to say it, felt it buoy up inside her, the pressure building and building, but no words came out. She was still so afraid. Afraid of losing herself, giving up control—

'I see,' Luke said quietly.

'It's not that simple,' she whispered.

Luke stared at her for a long moment. He looked so unyielding, yet a bleak sorrow flickered in the dark depths of his eyes. 'Actually,' he said, 'it is.'

Without another word, he turned and walked out of the room.

The flight back to New York was a blur, as was the drive up to Vermont. Aurelie arrived back at her grandma's house twenty-four hours after she'd left Tokyo. Left Luke, and her heart with him.

She dropped her bags by the door and walked through the rooms like a sleepwalker. She'd only been gone a little less than two weeks, yet it felt like forever. She'd lived a lifetime in the space of ten days. Lived and died.

For she was back exactly where she'd started, where she'd been stuck for years. Alone, hopeless, unable to change.

Just the memory of the hard, blazing look on Luke's face as he asked her if she loved him made her cringe and want to cry. She'd been too much of a coward to admit the truth, to take that leap.

She'd failed him, and failed herself. Fear rather than trust—*love*—had guided her actions.

In her more rational moments she convinced herself that it really was better this way, that Luke would be better off with someone more like him. Someone steady and balanced, who didn't drag a lifetime of emotional baggage behind her.

Yet in the middle of the night when her bed felt far too

empty, when she stared at her guitar or piano and couldn't summon the will to play, when every colour seemed to have been leached from the landscape of her life, she thought differently. She thought she might do anything to get him back, to have the chance to tell him that she loved him and was willing to take that risk, that he didn't have to earn anything because she'd give it all to him, gladly. So gladly.

Two weeks after she'd returned someone rang her doorbell, which was surprising in itself because she received pretty much zero visitors. She opened it, her heart lurching when she saw the familiar figure standing on her front porch.

'Luke—'

'Sorry. I know I must be a disappointment.'

The man in front of her wasn't Luke, but he looked a lot like him. His eyes and hair were a little lighter, but he had the same tall, powerful frame, the same wry smile.

'I'm Chase,' he said, and held out his hand. 'Chase Bryant.'

'You like to cook,' Aurelie said dumbly, because she was so surprised and that was the only thing she could remember. No, there was something else. *Chase checked out.*

'I do make a mean curry.' He raised his eyebrows. 'Luke's been talking about me, huh?'

'A little bit.'

'May I come in?'

He sounded so much like Luke that her eyes stung. Wordlessly Aurelie nodded and led him through the front hall to the kitchen. 'Do you want something to drink? A coffee or tea?'

'I'm good. I know you're wondering why I'm here.'

'I'm wondering how you even know who I am.'

Chase smiled wryly. 'That part's not so hard. The fame thing's a bitch though, I'm sure.'

She raked a hand through her hair. 'Oh. Right.'

'I saw Luke back in New York. He's not looking so good.'

That probably shouldn't have lifted her spirits, but it did. 'No?'

'No. In fact, he looks like crap and I told him so.' Chase paused. 'He told me about you.'

Aurelie stiffened. 'What exactly did he tell you?'

'Not much. And not willingly. I've gone pretty emo since I've become engaged, but Luke's still working on getting in touch with his feelings.'

She laughed, surprising herself because she hadn't laughed for so long. Since Luke. 'So what did he tell you?'

'That it didn't work out.'

'It didn't.'

'Yeah, I kind of figured that one out.' Chase took a step towards her. 'The thing is,' he said, and now he sounded serious, 'I'm in love with this amazing woman, Millie. And I almost completely blew it because I was afraid. You know the whole relationship/love/commitment thing is kind of big.'

'Yeah.' She took a deep breath, let it out slowly. 'It is, isn't it?'

Chase smiled at her gently. 'What exactly are you afraid of, Aurelie?'

'Everything,' she whispered and blinked hard.

'Are you afraid Luke will leave you? Hurt you? Because that was my thing. But maybe yours is something else.'

She glanced down. 'I don't think he'll mean to.'

'But you still think he will?'

She looked up, her eyes filled with tears. 'I'm just so afraid that I can't change.'

Chase tilted his head, regarded her quietly. 'How do you want to change?'

She sniffed. Loudly. 'I was in a relationship before and when it ended I…I was wrecked. Completely wrecked. I spun out of control and I can't stand the thought of that happening again, of losing myself again—'

Chase laughed softly, a gentle sound without any malice. 'Sweetheart, we're all afraid of that. That's what happens when you love someone, when you give everything. If Millie ever left me I'd be lost, completely lost.'

'Then how—'

'Because,' Chase said simply, 'life with her is worth any possible risk. But I'll admit, it took me a while to realise that. And maybe,' he added quietly, 'it will be different this time with you. Knowing Luke, I'm pretty sure it will.'

She sniffed again. Nodded. Because she knew Luke, and he was nothing, *nothing* like Pete Myers. And she was nothing like the way she'd been with Pete. With Luke she was different, new, *changed*.

She *had* changed. Why hadn't she believed it in the critical moment? Why had she blanked and backed away, defaulting to her old self?

She glanced sadly at Chase. 'I think it might be too late.'

He shook his head. 'I was just with Luke. Trust me, it's not too late.'

Two days later Aurelie stood in front of the renovated warehouse that housed Luke's new enterprise. Chase had told her that after resigning from Bryant's Luke had formed his own charitable foundation. She'd been surprised, and also pleased for Luke. He had never seemed like he actually enjoyed working for Bryant's.

And now she was here in lower Manhattan, terrified. Trying to change.

Taking a deep breath she opened the warehouse's heavy steel door and stepped into the building. The space was basically just one cavernous room, with folding chairs and stepladders and sheets of plastic all over the place. A young, officious-looking woman bustled towards her.

'May I help?'

'I'm looking for Luke Bryant—'

The woman's eyes widened in recognition. 'Are you—'

'Yes. Do you know where I can find Luke?'

Her eyes still wide, the woman nodded and gestured towards a door in a corner of the warehouse. Taking another deep breath Aurelie headed towards it.

Luke's back was to her as she opened the door. He was scanning some blueprints. 'Is that lunch?' he asked without looking up.

'Sorry, I don't have any sandwiches.'

Luke glanced up, everything about him stilling, blanking as he gazed at her. Aurelie tried to smile. 'Hi.'

'Hi.'

She couldn't tell a thing from his tone. 'I like the name,' she said, pointing to a sign on the door. *The Morpho Foundation*. 'Reminds me of a really great date I went on, when this butterfly landed in my hair and I kissed a man and it felt like the first real kiss I'd ever had.'

A muscle flickered in Luke's jaw and he dropped his gaze. 'Morpho is the Greek word for change, and this foundation's all about change.'

She swallowed. 'Change is good.'

He glanced up at her, and she saw that something had softened in his face. 'But yeah, it's about the butterfly too.' He paused, and one corner of his mouth quirked the tiniest bit upwards. 'And the kiss.'

It was more than enough of an opening. 'I miss you, Luke. I'm sorry I messed up so badly. I panicked and I acted on that panic instead of trusting you like I should have.'

He shook his head slowly, and Aurelie's heart free-fell towards her toes. 'I messed up too. I should have told you what was going on in my mind. The stuff about my mother. I just hadn't put it all together until that moment.'

'And I was so wrapped up in my own pain and past that I didn't think about yours.' She managed a smile. 'I thought you had it all together.'

'So did I.'

'I'm sorry about your mom,' Aurelie said quietly. 'I can't imagine how hard that must have been.'

'It wasn't easy.'

'I like the idea behind your foundation.' She'd read online that the foundation would be supporting children of parents in crisis. Like a mom with cancer.

'You gave me the idea, actually.'

'Me?'

'I thought about how alone you were, at such a young age. If you'd had one stable adult in your life things might have turned out differently for you.'

She nodded slowly. 'They might have.'

'Anyway—' Luke shrugged '—there's a lot of work to do before this thing is even off the ground.'

'Still, I'm glad you're doing it.' They both lapsed into silence then, and Aurelie's heart started thudding. Again. She'd thought they were getting there, working towards one another, but Luke still looked terribly remote. He didn't move towards her even though she desperately wanted him to. She wanted him to take her in his arms and kiss her, tell her it was all going to work out.

She wanted him to do all the work.

And suddenly she got it. This wasn't about Luke having to prove himself or earn anything from her. She gave it all freely, because she knew this man, and she loved and trusted him so much.

'I'm sorry for walking out on you in Tokyo,' she said. Luke didn't answer. 'You thought I didn't trust you and I can see how you would think that. How it looked that way. But the truth is I didn't trust myself. I was protecting myself, because I was so afraid of feeling like I did before. Out of control. Lost.'

'You'd only feel that way if I left you, if I let you down.'

'No. I never thought you'd let me down. I just…I saw you looking tense and angry with Aaron, and I knew he was probably telling you to forget me—'

'And you thought I'd listen?'

'No. But just the possibility had me panicking, and that scared me. I felt out of control already, and I didn't want that. But the thing I've finally realised—at least I'm starting to—is that love *requires* a loss of control. A giving of trust. And I was fighting against that because it still scared me.'

Luke was silent for a long moment. 'And now?' he finally asked.

'I'm still scared,' Aurelie admitted. 'I wish I wasn't, but I am. This is all terrifying for me, and I'll probably panic again. But I know I'm miserable without you, and I want to make this work. I want to be with you…if you still want to be with me.' Luke didn't say anything, and so she kept speaking, the words tumbling from her mouth, her heart. 'I know I'll mess up again, and I'll probably even hurt you. We'll hurt each other but I won't run away and I'll keep trying to change. It's a process.' She pointed to the foundation's sign. 'A metamorphosis takes a little time, you know.'

'I know. You're not the only one who needs to change.'

She swallowed, made herself say the hardest and most vulnerable words of all. The most changing. 'I love you, Luke.'

He didn't speak and Aurelie felt dizzy with nerves. Maybe she needed to check her blood sugar. 'Say something,' she managed, 'or you might have to dunk me in the sink a second time.'

Luke didn't say anything, though. He just crossed the room in two long strides and pulled her into his arms before he finally spoke. 'I love you too,' he said. 'So much. I'm sorry I ever walked away from you.'

'I'm not,' Aurelie answered, 'even though these last few weeks have been hell. I needed to be the one to walk *to* you for once.'

'Well, now neither of us is going anywhere,' Luke muttered against her throat, and then he was kissing her and Aurelie felt dizzier than ever. Dizzy with joy.

* * * * *

HIS BRAND
OF PASSION

BY
KATE HEWITT

To Zoe,
thanks for your inspiration and friendship,
love, K.

CHAPTER ONE

HE WAS CHECKING his *phone.*

Zoe Parker twitched with irritation as she watched the groom's best man thumb a few buttons on his smart phone. Discreetly, at least, but *honestly.* Her sister Millie and her husband-to-be Chase were saying their vows, and Aaron Bryant was texting.

He was unbelievable. He was also a complete jerk. A sexy jerk, unfortunately; tall, broad and exuding authority out of every pore. He also exuded a smug arrogance that made Zoe want to kick him in the shin. Or maybe a little higher. If she could have, she would have reached across the train of her sister's elegant cream wedding dress and snatched the mobile out of his fingers. Long, lean fingers with nicely square-cut nails, but who was noticing? She certainly wasn't.

She turned back to the minister, determinedly giving him her full attention. Maybe Aaron the Ass would pick up a few pointers. Honestly, the man was a gazillionaire and was a regularly attender at Manhattan's most elite social functions— did he really need a brush-up course on basic etiquette? Based on his behaviour since he'd strode into the rehearsal forty-five minutes late last night, clearly impatient and bored before he'd so much as said hello, Zoe was thinking yes.

She glanced at Millie, who thankfully had not noticed the phone. She looked beautiful, radiant in a way Zoe had never seen before, her eyes shining, her cheeks flushed. Everything about her was happy.

Zoe smothered the very tiny pang of something almost like envy. She wasn't looking for Mr Right. She'd gone for too many Mr Wrongs to think he existed, or to want to find him if he did. Although admittedly Millie's almost-husband was pretty close. Chase Bryant was charming, genuinely nice and *very* attractive.

Just like his brother.

Instinctively Zoe slid her gaze back to Aaron. He was still on the phone. Forget charming or nice but, yes, he was most definitely attractive. A faint frown creased his forehead and his lips thinned. He had nice lips, even pursed as they were in obvious irritation. They were full, sculpted, yet completely masculine too. In fact, everything about this irritating man was incredibly masculine, from the breadth of his shoulders to the near-black of his eyes and hair to the long, lean curve of his back and thigh…

'By the power vested in me, I now pronounce you husband and wife.'

Zoe yanked her gaze upwards from her rather leisurely perusal of Aaron Bryant's butt in time to see Millie and Chase kiss—and Aaron slide his phone back into the side pocket of his suit blazer.

Ass.

The congregation broke into spontaneous and joyous applause and Millie linked arms with Chase as she turned to leave the church. Aaron followed and, as maid of honour, Zoe had to accompany him up the aisle. She slid her arm through his, realising it was the first time she'd actually touched him since he'd breezed in too late to the rehearsal to practise going through the recessional together.

Now she was annoyingly conscious of the strength of his arm linked in hers, his powerful shoulder inches from her cheek—and her fingers inches from his pocket. With the phone.

Zoe didn't think too much about what she was doing. On the pretext of adjusting her bridesmaid's dress, she slid her arm more securely in Aaron's and her fingers slipped into his pocket and curled round the phone.

Chase's other brother Luke and his fiancée Aurelie fell in step behind them and they processed out onto the church steps and the summer sunshine of Fifth Avenue. Aaron pulled away from her without so much as a glance, and in one fluid movement Zoe took the phone from his pocket and hid it in the folds of her dress.

Not that it mattered. To all intents and purposes, according to Aaron she'd ceased to exist. He was gazing at his brother as if he were a puzzle he didn't understand and absent-mindedly patting his pocket. His phoneless pocket.

Zoe took the opportunity to tuck the phone among the blossoms of her bouquet. A little judicious tugging of ribbon and lace, and you wouldn't even know it was there.

Not that Zoe even knew what she was going to do with Aaron Bryant's phone. She just wanted to see his face when he realised he didn't have it.

Apparently that moment wasn't going to be now, because someone approached him and he dropped his hand from his pocket and turned to talk to whatever schmoozy bigwig wanted to hear about Bryant Enterprises, blah, blah, blah. This was *so* not her crowd.

It was Millie's crowd, though, and it was certainly Chase's. Millie was marrying into the Bryant family, a trio of brothers who regularly made the tabloids and gossip pages. Aaron certainly did; when Zoe flicked through the mags during the slow periods at the coffee shop, she almost always saw a picture of him with some bodacious blonde. Judging from the way he'd dismissed her upon introduction last night with one swiftly eloquent head-to-toe perusal, skinny brunettes were not his type.

'Zoe, the photographer wants some shots of the wedding party.' Amanda, Zoe's mother, elegant if a little fraught in pale blue silk, hurried up to her. 'And I think Millie's train needs adjusting, darling. That's your job, you know.'

'Yes, Mum, I know.' This was the second time she'd been Millie's maid of honour. She might not be as organised as her sister—well, not even remotely—but she could handle her duties. She'd certainly given Millie a great hen party, at any rate.

Smiling at the memory of her uptight sister singing karaoke in the East Village, Zoe headed towards the wedding party assembled on the steps of the church. The photographer wanted them to walk two blocks to Central Park, and Chase looked like he'd rather relax with a beer.

'Come on, Chase,' Zoe said as she came to stand next to him. 'You'll be glad of the photos a couple of months from now. You and Millie can invite me over and have a slideshow.'

Chase's mouth quirked in a smile. 'I'm not sure who that would torture more.'

Zoe laughed softly and went to adjust Millie's aforementioned train. 'Has Mum sent you over here to fuss?' Millie guessed, and Zoe smiled.

'I never fuss.'

'That's true, I suppose,' Millie said teasingly and they started walking towards Central Park. 'You don't know the meaning of the word.'

An hour later the photos were over and Zoe was circulating through the opulent ballroom of The Plaza Hotel, a glass of champagne in hand. She'd been keeping an eye out for Aaron, because she still wanted to see his face when he realised he didn't have his phone. During the photos she'd taken the opportunity to remove the phone from her bouquet and put it in her clutch bag. The little luminous screen had glowed accusingly at her; there were eleven missed calls and eight new texts. Clearly Aaron was a *very* important person. Was it a scorned lover begging him back, or some boring business? Either way, he could surely do without it for an hour or so.

It was easy enough to keep track of him in the crowded ballroom; he was a good two inches taller than any other man there, and even without the height his sense of authority and power had every female eye turning towards him longingly—and Zoe was pretty sure he knew it. He walked with the arrogant ease of someone who had never needed to look far for a date—or a willing bed partner.

Zoe's mouth twisted downwards. She really disliked this man, and they hadn't even had a conversation yet. But they surely would; they were seated next to each other at the wedding party's table. Although, come to think of it, Aaron seemed perfectly capable of ignoring someone seated next to him. He'd texted during a wedding ceremony, after all.

Smiling, she patted her bag. She looked forward to seeing the expression on his face when he realised he didn't have his phone—and she did.

Aaron Bryant surveyed the crowd with edgy impatience. How long would he have to stay? It was his brother's wedding, he knew, and he was best man—two compelling reasons to stay till the bitter end. On the other hand, he had a potential disaster brewing with some of his European investments and he knew he needed to keep close tabs on all the interested parties if Bryant Enterprises was going to weather this crisis. Automatically he slid his hand into his pocket where he kept his phone, only to remember with a flash of annoyance and a tiny needling of alarm that it was gone. He'd had it during the wedding, and he was never one to leave his phone anywhere. So where had it gone? A pickpocket on the way to Central Park? It was possible, he supposed, and very frustrating.

People had started moving towards the tables, and with a resigned sigh Aaron decided he'd stay at least through dinner. His phone, thankfully, was backed up on his computer, and he could access everything he needed at the office. It was password-protected, so he didn't need to worry about information leaks, and as soon as he got to the office he could put a trace on it. Still, he didn't like being without it. He was never without his phone, and too much was brewing for him not to be in touch with his clients for very long.

He approached the wedding-party table, steeling himself for an interminable hour or two. Millie and Chase were wrapped up in their own world, which he couldn't really fault, and his relationship with his brother Luke's fiancée Aurelie was, at best, awkward.

A few months ago he'd tried to intimidate her into leaving Luke, and it hadn't worked. He'd been trying to protect Luke and, if he were honest, Bryant Enterprises. Aurelie was a washed-up pop star whom the tabloids ridiculed on a daily basis, not someone Aaron had wanted associated with his family. Admittedly, she'd staged something of a comeback in the last year, but relations with both Luke and his fiancée were still rather strained.

He slid into his seat and offered both Luke and Aurelie a tight-lipped smile. He couldn't manage much more; his mind was buzzing with the stress of work and the half-dozen crises that were poised to explode into true chaos. A woman came to sit next to him and Aaron glanced at her without interest.

Zoe Parker, Millie's sister and maid of honour. He hadn't spoken to her last night or this morning, but he supposed he'd have to make some conversation over the meal. She was pretty enough, with wide grey eyes and long, dark hair, although her skinny, sinewy figure wasn't generally his preference. She glanced at him now, her lips curving in a strangely knowing smile.

'How are things, Aaron? You don't mind if I call you Aaron?'

'Of course not.' He forced a small smile back. 'We're practically family, after all.'

'Practically family,' she repeated thoughtfully. 'That's right.' She flicked her long, almost-black hair over her shoulders and gave him another smile. Flirtatious? No—knowing. Like she knew something about him, some secret.

Absurd.

Dismissing her, Aaron turned to the walnut and blue-cheese salad artfully arranged on the plate in front of him. He'd just taken his first bite when he heard a familiar buzz—an incoming text or voicemail. Instinctively he reached into his pocket, only to silently curse. It couldn't be his phone that was buzzing. He heard the sound again, and saw it was coming from Zoe's lacy little clutch bag that she'd left by the side of her plate.

He nodded towards it. 'I think your phone is ringing.'

She glanced at him, eyebrows raised. 'I didn't bring my phone.'

Aaron stared at her, completely nonplussed. 'Well,' he said, turning back to his salad, 'something's buzzing in your bag.'

'That sounds like an interesting euphemism.' Aaron didn't reply, although he felt a surprising little kick of something. Not lust, precisely; interest, perhaps, but no more than a flicker. 'Anyway,' she continued, her tone breezy, 'that's not *my* phone.'

There was something about the way she said it, so knowingly, so provocatively, that Aaron turned towards her sharply, suspicion hardening inside him. She smiled with saccharine sweetness, her eyes glinting with mischief.

'Whose phone is it, then?' Aaron asked pleasantly, or at least he hoped he sounded pleasant. This woman was starting to seriously annoy him.

Zoe wasn't able to reply for someone had tapped their fork against their wine glass and, with a round of cheers, Millie and Chase bowed to popular demand and kissed. Aaron turned back to his salad, determined to ignore her.

The phone buzzed again. Zoe made a tsking noise and reached for her bag. '*Someone* gets a lot of messages,' she said and, opening the little clutch, she took out his mobile.

The expression on Aaron Bryant's face was, Zoe decided, priceless. His mouth had dropped open and he stared slack-jawed at the sight of his phone in her hand. She glanced at the screen, saw there were now fourteen texts and nine voice-mails, and with a shake of her head she slipped it back into her bag.

She glanced back at Aaron and saw he'd recovered his composure. His eyes were narrowed to black slits, his mouth compressed into a very hard line. He looked as if he were carved from marble, hewn from granite—hard and unyielding and, yes, maybe even a little scary. But beautiful too, like a darkly terrifying angel.

Zoe felt her heart give a little tremor and she reached for her bread roll as if she hadn't a care in the world. 'Where,' Aaron asked in a low voice that thrummed through his chest and through Zoe, 'did you get that phone?'

She swallowed a piece of roll and smiled. 'Where do you think I got it?'

His eyes blazed dark fire as he glared at her. 'From my pocket.'

'Bingo.'

He shook his head slowly. 'So you're a thief.'

She tilted her head to one side as if considering his statement, although her heart was beating hard and adrenalin pumped through her. 'That's a bit harsh.'

'You *stole* my phone.'

'I prefer to think of it as borrowing.'

'Borrowing.'

She leaned forward, anger replacing any alarm she'd felt. 'Yes, *borrowing* it—for the duration of my sister and your brother's wedding reception. Because, no matter how much of a bigwig business tycoon you might be, Aaron Bryant, you don't text during a wedding ceremony. And I don't want you ruining this day for Millie and Chase.'

He stared at her, colour washing his high cheekbones, his eyes glittering darkly. He was furious, utterly furious, and Zoe felt a little frisson of—fear? Maybe, but something else too. Something like excitement. Smiling, she patted her bag with the still-buzzing phone. Good Lord, he received a lot of calls. 'You can have it back after Millie and Chase leave for their honeymoon.'

Aaron's expression turned thunderous and he leaned forward, every taut line of his body radiating tightly leashed anger. 'I'll have it back now.'

'I don't think so.'

She saw him reach for the bag and quickly she grabbed it and put it in her lap. Aaron arched an incredulous eyebrow.

'You think that's going to stop me?' he murmured, and it sounded almost seductive. Zoe felt a sudden, prickling awareness raise goosebumps all over her body. Before she could make any answer, Aaron slid his hand under the table. Zoe stiffened as she felt his hand slide along her thigh. The man was audacious, she had to give him that. Audacious and fearless.

She felt his fingers slide along her inner thigh, his palm warm through the thin silk of her dress. To her own annoyance and shame she could not keep a very basic and overwhelming desire from flooding through her, turning her insides warm and liquid. She shifted in her seat, and just as Aaron's hand reached the bag in her lap she slid the phone out of it.

'Give me that phone, Zoe.' His hand was clenched in her lap and, even though seduction had to be the last thing on his mind, Zoe could still feel her body's pulsing awareness of him. All he'd done was touch her leg. She had to get a grip and remember this was about the phone. Nothing else.

She raised her hand above the table, the phone still clutched in it, and slowly shook her head. 'No.'

Aaron's lips thinned. 'I could take it from you by force.'

She had no doubt he could. 'That would cause a scene.'

'You think I care?'

No, Zoe realised, she didn't think he did. Considering his behaviour so far, she didn't think he cared at all. She imagined him prying the phone from her hand. It would be like taking candy from a baby. She was no match for his strength, and she couldn't stand the thought of enduring Aaron's mocking triumph for the rest of the evening.

Impulsively, her gaze locked on Aaron's, she slid the phone down the front of her dress. He stared back at her and something flared in his eyes that made the awareness inside her pulse harder.

'That looks a little…strange,' he remarked, and Zoe glanced down to see her cleavage obscured by a bulky object in the middle of the dress. It did, indeed, look a bit strange.

'Easily fixed,' she replied breezily, and with a bit of pushing and pulling of the strapless dress she managed to get the phone to lie flat under the shelf of her breasts. Still a little strange, but not too bad. And totally impossible for Aaron to access.

He sat back in his chair, shook his head slowly. 'You really are a piece of work.'

'I'll take that as a compliment.'

'It wasn't meant as one.'

'Even so.'

He chuckled softly, the sound hard and without humour,

and leaned forward again. 'You think,' he murmured, his voice stealing right inside her, 'I can't get that phone out of your dress?'

Zoe glanced at him, tried for haughty amusement. 'Not easily.'

'You have no idea what I'm capable of.'

'Actually, based on your behaviour so far, I think I have a fairly good idea of the level of boorishness you're willing to sink to,' she replied. 'But even you, I believe, would draw the line at mauling the maid of honour in the middle of a wedding reception.'

Aaron stared at her for a few seconds, his gaze flicking over her face, seeming to assess her. His face had turned blank, expressionless, which made Zoe uneasy. She couldn't read him at all. Then he shrugged and turned back to his meal. 'Fine,' he said, and he sounded completely bored, utterly dismissive. 'Give it back to me in a couple of hours.'

Zoe sat there, the phone hot and a little sweaty against her chest, and felt weirdly deflated. She'd enjoyed sparring with him, she realised. It had been invigorating and, yes, a tiny bit flirtatious. But, based on the way Aaron was now focused completely on his salad, she was now the furthest thing from his thoughts. Well, she thought with a sigh, wriggling a little to make herself a bit more comfortable with a phone inside her dress, at least she'd taught him a lesson.

Aaron knew about patience. It was a lesson he'd learned from childhood, when his father would summon him to his study only to make him wait standing by the door for an hour or more, while he concluded some trivial piece of business.

It was a lesson he'd needed, for it had taken patience to rebuild Bryant Enterprises from the ground up when his father had left it to him fifteen years ago, utterly bankrupt.

It was a lesson he would use now, for he knew it was only

a matter of time before he found an opportunity to corner Zoe and get his phone back.

He had to admire her bravado and tenacity, even if the whole exercise annoyed the hell out of him. She was different from most women he knew, utterly uninterested in impressing him. In fact, she seemed to want the opposite: to aggravate him. Well, it was working.

An hour into the festivities Zoe excused herself from the table. Aaron watched her head to the ladies' room with narrowed eyes. He waited a few seconds before he excused himself and followed her out of the ballroom.

The ladies' room was one of those ridiculously feminine boudoirs, complete with spindly little chairs and embroidered tissue boxes. Aaron slipped inside and put a finger to his lips when an elderly matron applying some garishly bright coral lipstick stared at him in shock.

'I want to surprise my girlfriend,' he whispered, and then mimed getting down on one knee as if in a marriage proposal. The woman's face suffused with colour to match her mouth and she bobbed her head in understanding before hurrying outside.

He was alone with Zoe.

He heard the toilet flush and stepped back so she couldn't see him as she came out of the stall. He watched as she moved to the sink and washed her hands, humming under her breath. He took the opportunity to admire her figure, skinny though it was. She had some nice curves, highlighted by how they were encased in tight pink silk. A very nice bottom, as a matter of fact, and long, lean legs. He didn't usually pay attention to the backside of a woman, but standing behind Zoe he found his gaze riveted—and his body responding in the most elemental way.

Then she looked up, and her eyes widened as she caught

sight of him in the mirror just a few feet behind her, lurking like a dark shadow.

'Hello, Zoe.'

She turned around slowly, drying her hands. 'This *is* the ladies' room, you know,' she remarked, and to her credit she sounded as light and wry as ever.

'I know.'

'What are you doing here?'

He took a step towards her and was gratified to see her eyes widen a little more. She *should* be afraid of him. Or, if not afraid, then at least a little wary. 'What do you think I'm doing here? I want my phone.'

She crossed her arms over her chest. 'Sorry, Bryant. You'll have to wait until the reception is over.'

'I don't think so.'

Her lips parted and he saw something flare in her eyes. Fear? No, it was excitement. He felt it himself, a surprising little pulse of anticipation. She was so not his type, and yet in that moment he knew he was quite looking forward to putting his hand down her dress.

'And how,' she asked, her voice turning husky, 'do you think you're going to get it back?'

'Quite easily.' He took another step towards her, so she was pressed against the sink, her head angled up towards him. She didn't move, didn't even try to escape him. Was she wondering if he'd dare do it? Or did she want him to? As much as he did, perhaps.

His gaze fastened on hers, and something pulsed and blazed between them. Aaron felt it, felt the very air seem to tauten around them, crackle with the sudden, electric energy they had created. Slowly, deliberately, he reached out and slid a few fingers down the bodice of her dress. Her skin was silky and warm, the sides of her breasts brushing his fingers. Zoe gasped aloud. Aaron smiled even as desire arrowed through him. 'Quite a tight fit.'

'Quite,' she managed.

With the tip of his fingers he could just touch his phone, but there was no way he could actually get it. Not without unzipping the dress completely…which was a possibility. Anything felt possible right now.

'You are outrageous,' Zoe gasped, and Aaron chuckled softly.

'I'm not the one who started this, sweetheart.'

'Yes, you did. When you texted—'

He was stroking the sides of her breasts with his fingers in an attempt to reach the phone and Aaron knew that neither of them was immune. He saw Zoe's pupils dilate with desire and felt himself harden even more.

He slid his hand lower.

'You're not going to get it,' Zoe said breathlessly, and Aaron arched an eyebrow.

'One way or another, I'll get it.'

'I don't think so,' she answered, her tone mocking his perfectly. He almost laughed. His fingertip brushed the phone and then, to his annoyance, the damn thing slid lower so it was resting against her stomach. There was no way he could get it now.

Unless…

'Don't you dare,' Zoe whispered and Aaron smiled.

'I think this whole encounter is about daring, don't you?' He removed his hand from her dress, allowing his fingers to stroke her soft, small breasts on the way up. Zoe stared at him, pupils still dilated, lips parted, her breath coming in little pants.

'You wouldn't.'

'Want to bet?'

And, with his gaze still hard on hers, he put his hand up under her skirt.

Zoe stood rigid, unable to believe Aaron Bryant had just put his hand up her dress. And he'd already put it down her dress. Her whole body felt as if it were on fire from those few, calculated little touches. She was hopeless. Hopelessly attracted to this arrogant ass of a man.

So much so that she didn't even move as his hand slid up her thigh, his fingers warm and seeking on her bare flesh. His gaze was riveted on hers, and she knew, no matter how angry or determined he was, he felt something for her. She could feel the attraction between them, heavy and thick. His hand slid higher, smoothing along her hip before he finally found the phone with his fingers and tugged it down. And she hadn't resisted at all, not even the tiniest bit.

'I can't believe you,' she whispered and he smiled.

'Believe it.' He slid his hand lower to the juncture of her thighs, the phone in his palm. Zoe's breath came out in a devastated rush as he pressed his hand against her, the phone still in it, cool against her heated and tender flesh. Sensation sizzled straight through her and she sagged against the counter.

'You are incredible.'

'Why, thank you.' He pressed again and she closed her eyes, feeling utterly exposed and shameless, yet helpless to prevent it.

'It wasn't a compliment,' she managed, and he laughed softly.

'Considering the response I'm coaxing from you, I rather think it was.'

Zoe opened her eyes, forced herself to straighten. 'What I really meant is that you're incorrigible.'

'True.' His hand was still between her legs, teasing her, tormenting her. It took all her effort to remain still, not to allow her body to invite his deeper caresses. 'But then so are you.'

He stared at her for a long moment, and then with one last press of his hand he stepped away. 'Thanks for my phone,' he said, and then he was gone.

Aaron stalked from the bathroom, his whole body blazing with unfulfilled desire. He had not expected that to happen, for that skinny, seriously annoying woman to awaken in him such a fierce need. Well, she had, and it was going to be incredibly difficult to focus on work as he needed to.

Swearing under his breath, he found a private alcove in the ballroom and checked his messages and texts. Just as he'd thought, the European market was imploding and his investors were panicking. He spent thirty minutes doing damage control and then he slid his phone back into his pocket.

He stared into space for a few minutes, felt the familiar cold wash of fear sweep through him. He hated these close calls. Hated feeling, as he'd felt for fifteen years, like Bryant Enterprises was about to slip out of his grasp even as it remained the chain that bound and choked him.

How much had those few hours without his phone cost him? It was impossible to measure, yet Aaron knew there was a cost. There always had been, always would be. And with a sudden, cold certainty, he also knew who was going to pay this time.

He strode back into the reception and saw that things were starting to wind down. Chase and Millie were coming out in their going-away clothes for a week's honeymoon on St Julian's, the Bryants' private island in the Caribbean. Zoe stood behind her sister, smiling, although Aaron thought she looked rather wistful, maybe even sad. She hardly seemed like the type to want a ring on her finger, but who knew? Most women wanted one. Wanted the ridiculous fairy tale, the impossible dream.

He waited until Chase and Millie had left and the other

guests were starting to trickle away. He said goodbye to Luke and Aurelie, managing a few minutes' stilted conversation, before he went in search of Zoe.

She was standing by their table, picking some bits of confetti out of her bouquet. Her hair streamed over her shoulders in a dark ribbon, her body lithe and slender, and Aaron remembered just how silky and warm her skin had felt, how her body had helplessly yielded to his.

He strode towards her. She glanced up at him, and he felt her tense, her eyes dark with shadows. 'What do you want now?'

'You,' he said flatly, and her jaw dropped.

'What—?'

'I have a limo waiting outside.'

She stared at him in disbelief and Aaron wondered in a detached sort of way if she'd refuse. He'd felt her response earlier, the heat and the strength of it. He was pretty sure she'd felt his own. If she refused, she had more scruples—or at least more self-control—than he'd credited her with.

Wordlessly Zoe tossed her bouquet back on the table. 'Let's go,' she said and, with a smile of triumph curling his mouth, Aaron led her out of the ballroom.

CHAPTER TWO

SHE DIDN'T DO stuff like this—one-night stands, flings with strangers. It was crazy. *She* was crazy, Zoe thought as she followed Aaron outside into the warm summer air and then straight into the luxurious leather interior of the limo that was waiting by the kerb, just as he'd said.

What on earth had made her agree? She didn't even like him. But she was incredibly, irresistibly attracted to him. And, Zoe realised with a sudden flash of insight, the fact that she didn't like him made this whole encounter emotionally safe. Aaron Bryant was no danger to her already battle-worn heart. Even if this whole scenario was way outside her comfort zone.

'Where are we going?' she asked as the limo pulled away from the Plaza.

'My apartment.'

She nodded, felt a little frisson of something close to fear. This was so not her. She might give off that reckless, devil-may-care attitude, but in her relationships she'd been depressingly, boringly conservative. And she'd got hurt time and time again as a result.

Maybe this *was* the way to go.

'Nervous?' Aaron asked, the word mocking, and Zoe just shrugged.

'Going home with a strange man to his apartment is a little

out of the usual for me, no matter what you might think. But, considering how well-known you are, I think I'm pretty safe.'

Aaron stretched his arms out along the seat, his fingers just brushing her shoulder. Zoe resisted the urge to shiver under that thoughtless touch. 'How do you reckon that?' he asked.

'I don't think,' Zoe said, 'you want any bad publicity.'

He frowned, his eyes narrowing, before his wonderfully mobile mouth suddenly curved into a surprising smile. 'Are you actually threatening me?'

'Not at all. Just stating facts. And in any case, like you said earlier, we're practically family. It's hard to believe you're related to Chase, but since you are I'll assume you're not a complete psycho.'

'Thanks very much for that vote of confidence,' Aaron said dryly. He turned to gaze out of the window. 'Why is it hard to believe I'm related to Chase?'

Zoe shrugged. 'Mainly because he's actually nice.'

'I see.' He didn't seem at all offended, more amused. Zoe glanced out of the window at the cars and taxis streaming by in a blur. 'So where is your apartment, exactly?'

'We're here.'

'Here' was a luxury high-rise on West End Avenue, and Aaron's apartment was, unsurprisingly, the penthouse. The lift doors opened right into the living area, and Zoe stepped into a temple of modern design with floor-to-ceiling windows on three sides overlooking the city and the Hudson River.

'Nice,' she remarked, taking in the black leather sofas, the chrome-and-glass coffee table, the modern sculpture, and the white faux fur rug. A granite-and-marble kitchen opened onto a dining area with an ebony table that seated twelve. Everything was spotless, empty, barren. The place, Zoe decided, had no soul. Just like the man.

She walked to the window overlooking the Hudson, the inky-black river glimmering with lights. She felt Aaron approach from behind her, and then she shivered as he moved her hair and brushed his lips across the bared nape of her neck.

His hands fastened on her hips and then slid slowly upwards over the silk of her dress to cup her breasts. Zoe shivered again and then, with effort, stepped away.

'I don't know what impression you've formed of me, but I like a little conversation along with the sex.' She spoke lightly, even though she felt a tremble deep inside. She'd had plenty of boyfriends, but she'd never done this before, and never with a man like Aaron. Powerful. Overwhelming. A little...frightening.

'Conversation?' Aaron repeated, sounding completely nonplussed. 'What do you want to talk about? The latest film? The weather?'

'I think you could do better than that,' she answered tartly. 'And, actually, what I'd really like to talk about is food.'

Aaron arched one dark eyebrow, unsmiling. 'Food.'

'I'm hungry. Starving, actually. I never eat at parties.'

He simply stared and Zoe almost laughed. At least she felt a little easing of the tension coiling tighter and tighter inside her. She doubted Aaron was used to women who did anything more than nibble at the occasional lettuce leaf and take their clothes off on his command. She was determined to be different.

'I don't have any food,' he said after a moment, his gaze still hard and assessing on her. 'I always order in or eat out.'

'Perfect,' Zoe replied breezily. 'We can order in.'

He still looked nonplussed, frankly incredulous. 'What do you want to order?'

'A California roll.'

'*Sushi?*'

'If by sushi you mean the non-raw fish kind, then yes.'

She was inexplicably gratified to see his mouth curve in the tiniest of smiles.

'If we're going to order sushi, we'll do it properly,' he said and slid his phone out of his pocket.

Zoe smiled. 'At last you're putting your phone to good use.'

This woman drove him crazy. In far too many ways. His palms itched to touch her, yet here she was insisting they order *sushi,* as if they were some couple about to have a quiet night in. He'd almost asked her if she wanted to rent a DVD while they were at it, but then he decided not to risk it. She might take him seriously.

The women he knew—and, more importantly, the women he went to bed with—didn't behave the way Zoe Parker did, which begged the question why he'd brought her back here in the first place.

He was used to women going along exactly with what he wanted. What he commanded. Hell, everyone did. He didn't allow for anything else.

And yet here he was, ordering her damn food. Still, he *was* hungry. He hadn't eaten much at the reception either, and he was willing to go along with Zoe's crazy ideas—to a point. Eventually and inevitably she would have to understand and accept who was calling the shots.

He slid his phone back into his pocket. 'The food should be here in about fifteen minutes.'

A flirty, cat-like smile played around her mouth. 'So what should we talk about for fifteen minutes?' she asked, and he could tell from her tone that she was laughing at him, that she knew the thought of making conversation for that long exasperated and annoyed him.

He didn't want to *talk.*

'I have no idea,' he said shortly, and her smile widened.

'Oh, I've got plenty of ideas, don't worry.' She walked over to the sofa and stretched out, her legs long and slim in front of her, her arms along the back. 'Let's see… We could talk about why you live in such an awful apartment.'

'Awful apartment?' he repeated in disbelief and she smiled breezily.

'I've been in morgues with more warmth. Or we could talk about how you don't get along with anyone in your family, or why you're so obsessive about work.' She batted her eyelashes. 'Are you compensating for something else, do you think?'

'Or,' he growled, 'we could both shut up and get on with what we came here for.'

'Now, that's a come-on I haven't heard before. Really charming. Makes me want to strip naked right now.'

Fury pulsed through him. He'd never met a woman who dished it out so much before. Most women wanted to impress him. He took a step towards her. 'A few hours ago you were practically melting in a puddle at my feet. I don't think I have much to worry about there, sweetheart.'

Her eyes flashed silver. 'Honestly, you are the most arrogant ass of a man I have ever met. I'm amazed there's enough room in this apartment for you, me and your ego.'

He stared at her, disbelief making his mind go blank. No one talked to him like this. *No one.* Zoe's mouth curled into a saccharine smile.

'I suppose no one has dared to tell you that before?' She didn't wait for an answer. 'I think Millie and Chase will be happy together, don't you?' Her eyes danced as she posed the question oh, so innocently and Aaron gritted his teeth. As if he wanted to talk about weddings, marriages and happy endings. He didn't want any of it, at least not for himself.

'I suppose so,' he said in a bored voice. 'I haven't really given it much thought.'

'What a surprise.'

'Why do you want to talk to me, anyway?' he asked. He

hated the way she made him feel as if he'd lost control, and he was determined to get it back—however he could. 'You obviously don't like me, or anything about me. So what's there to chat about, really, Zoe?' He spread his hands wide, his eyebrows raised in challenge. For a moment she didn't answer and he felt a surge of triumph. *Gotcha.*

'Well,' she finally said, her mouth curving upwards once more, 'I always live in hope. No one's irredeemable, surely? Not even you.'

'What a compliment.'

'It wasn't meant to be one,' she answered, and he knew she was intentionally parroting what he'd said to her earlier. She eyed him mischievously. 'But take it as one, if you like.'

'I'm not interested in anything you say,' Aaron snapped. 'Compliments or otherwise. I think we've talked enough.'

'We're still waiting for the sushi,' Zoe reminded him and Aaron nearly cursed.

He shouldn't have ordered the damn sushi. He shouldn't have gone for any of this, he realised. The moment Zoe had slipped out of his arms and stopped playing by his rules he should have shown her the door. So why hadn't he?

Because he wanted her too much. And because not having her felt like losing. They'd been locked in a battle from the moment she'd taken his phone, and Aaron knew only one way of assuring sweet, sweet victory.

'I think we can make good use of the time while we wait,' he said, his voice deepening to a purr, and with a savage satisfaction he saw awareness—and perhaps alarm—flare in her eyes.

'I'm sure we could.' She crossed her legs. 'So were any of those messages on your phone actually important?'

'Critical,' Aaron informed her silkily. He loosened the knot of his ascot and saw how her gaze was drawn to the movement. 'Absolutely crucial.'

She pursed her lips. 'Oh, dear.'

'Considering all the inconvenience you put me to, I think you owe me.'

She raised her eyebrows. 'Owe you?'

'Definitely.' He shed his tie and unbuttoned the top few buttons of his shirt. 'And I can think of several ways you can pay me back.'

'Oh, I'm sure you could.' Her eyes narrowed as if she wanted to argue, but he saw the rapid rise and fall of her chest and knew she was affected. As affected as he was… Hell, he'd been in a painful state of arousal since she'd first slid into his limo.

The intercom buzzed, and the tension that had been coiling and tautening between them was, for the moment, broken. Aaron strode towards the door and buzzed the delivery man up, conscious of Zoe; she'd risen from the sofa and was wandering around the living room, glancing at a few of the paintings on the walls, her body like a lithe shadow as she moved through the darkened room.

She turned and joined him at the door, and he breathed in the scent of her, some soap or shampoo that smelled like vanilla. The ends of her hair brushed his shoulder. 'So what kind of sushi did you order, anyway?'

'The real kind.' Not that he had any interest in eating anything. The doorbell rang and he dealt with the delivery man before turning back to her. 'And you have to try some before I give you your California roll.'

'Oh, do I?' Her eyes glinted and she looked intrigued, maybe even a little confused. Hell, he was. Why was he playing this game? Why didn't he toss her the food, tell her to eat and then take her to bed? Even if that did have a touch of the Neanderthal about it, it was still more his style. Yet some part of him actually enjoyed their sparring. It invigorated him, at least and, even if taking her to bed would be the simpler and more expedient option, he wasn't quite ready to let go of all the rest.

He grabbed some plates and glasses and a bottle of wine from the kitchen and took it all over to the living area. After a second's pause he put it all on the coffee table and stretched out on the rug. Everything felt awkward, unfamiliar. He didn't do this. He didn't socialise with the women he slept with, he didn't *romance* them.

Zoe sat down next to him, a willing pupil. 'So what am I going to try first?'

'We'll start gently. Futomaki.'

'Which is?'

'Cucumber, bamboo shoots and tuna.'

She wrinkled her nose. 'Okay.'

Aaron handed her a roll and took one himself. Then he opened the wine and poured them both glasses. 'Cheers.'

'Cheers.' She took a sip of wine and a small bite of the sushi roll.

'Well?'

'It's okay. I can taste the tuna, though.'

He laughed, the sound strangely rusty. 'You don't like fish?'

'Not particularly.'

'Well, I admire your willingness to try.' He bit into his own roll, surprised and discomfited at how he was almost—almost—enjoying himself. Relaxing, even, which was ridiculous. He didn't do either—enjoyment or relaxation. He worked. He strove. Sometimes he slept.

'I admire your willingness to try too,' Zoe said, and Aaron glanced at her sharply.

'What do you mean?'

'I sense this is outside of your comfort zone,' she said, a

hint of laughter in her voice. 'I imagine the women you take to bed go directly there, do not pass go, do not collect two hundred dollars.' She arched an eyebrow. 'They don't sit on your rug, drinking wine and eating sushi.'

He stilled, feeling weirdly, terribly exposed and even angry. 'No, they don't.'

'Sorry not to fall in step with your plans.' She didn't sound remotely sorry.

'I can be flexible on occasion.'

'How encouraging.'

'Try this one.' He handed her another sushi roll. Zoe stared at it in distaste.

'What is this?'

'Narezushi. Gutted fish in vinegar, pickled for at least six months.'

'You've got to be kidding me.'

'I don't make jokes.'

'Ever?'

He considered. 'Pretty much.'

She put the roll aside, shaking her head, her lips pursed and her eyes glinting. 'Why, Aaron, I almost feel sorry for you.'

'Don't,' he said roughly, the word a warning.

'Don't what?'

'Don't even think about feeling sorry for me.' No one did. No one should. He had everything he'd ever wanted, everything anyone wanted. He didn't need Zoe Parker's pity.

She laughed softly. 'Touched a sore spot, did I?'

He saw now that with the wine and the food she was getting over-confident. Presumptuous. Thinking that this meant something, that they were creating some kind of intimate situation here. It was time to start calling the shots, Aaron decided. And to let Zoe know the only kind of *intimate* he was interested in.

* * *

She was annoying him, Zoe knew. Making him angry. Shame, because for a little while there things had almost seemed pleasant. Aaron had almost seemed…normal.

And she liked baiting him. She needed to do it, because the intensity of her attraction—and her emotion—scared her. She didn't do intense, not anymore. Teasing him defused that, at least a little.

Except now the very air felt thick with tension, with desire. She saw his dark eyes flare darker and he set his plate and glass aside as Zoe braced herself, knowing the pleasant little interlude was over. Aaron Bryant was ready to get down to business.

She met his gaze, determined to stay insouciant, never to let him know how much he affected her. How much power he had over her. 'Party over?'

'I wouldn't say that.' He reached out one powerful hand and closed it around her wrist, pulling her slowly and inexorably towards him. Zoe didn't resist. She couldn't; already she felt that heavy languor steal through her veins, take over her brain. She was just way too attracted to this man. 'I'd say it's just beginning.'

Aaron pulled her onto his sprawled thighs, his hands on her hips so she was straddling him. She felt the press of his erection against the juncture of her own thighs and pleasure bolted straight through her. It took all her will-power not to press back, not to admit with her body how much she wanted him. She needed to keep some kind of pride. Some kind of defence.

'A different kind of party,' Aaron murmured and slid his hands up along her hips and waist to cup her breasts only briefly and then frame her face. He brought her forward to brush his lips against hers, and distantly Zoe realised this was the first time they'd kissed.

It started gently but within seconds it flamed into something else entirely—something deep, primal and urgent. His tongue slid inside the warmth of her mouth and his hips rocked against hers—and so much for her pride, because she rocked back helplessly, her body taking over, already desperately seeking release.

His hands slid back down to her waist, and then to her thighs, and he edged the dress over her bottom so it was rucked about her waist. She was bare below except for a skimpy thong. He slid his fingers along the silky length of her thigh to the heat of her. 'No phones here,' he murmured, and Zoe would have laughed except he was kissing her again. His fingers were working deft magic, and all she could think about was how much she wanted this.

In one easy movement Aaron rolled her onto her back so she was splayed out on the fur rug, her dress still around her waist. Aaron lay poised over her, his cheeks faintly flushed, his eyes gleaming with desire, his breath a little ragged. He looked beautiful, dark and powerful and he stole Zoe's breath away.

He tugged down the zip of her dress and in just a few seconds it was gone, tossed to the side of the room. Zoe stared up at him, wearing only a strapless bra and matching thong, wondering what Aaron Bryant would do with her now. Willing him to do just about anything.

'I'm amazed you managed to fit a phone in here at all,' he said, and ran his hand between her breasts, along her stomach, then dipping once more between her thighs. Zoe arched helplessly against his hand, and Aaron slid her panties off her. The bra followed soon after.

She lay there, naked and supine on the rug, every sense spinning into aching awareness. She supposed, distantly, that she should feel bare, exposed, nervous, but she felt none of that. All she felt was a glorious anticipation, an unbearable readiness. Aaron bent his head to her and his hands, lips and tongue seemed to be everywhere at once, teasing, tasting, tormenting her.

She tangled her hands in his hair, surprised by its softness, for everything else about him was so hard: eyes, mouth, body, attitude. *Heart.* But his hair was soft and she ran her fingers through it, glorying in it even as she arched and writhed beneath him, as his mouth and hands brought her to the brink of that pleasurable precipice again and again.

And then, with a quick rustle of foil, he slid on a condom and drove inside her in one single stroke. He lay suspended above her, braced on his forearms, his body fully inside hers. For one breathless moment he gazed down at her, his eyes blazing dark fire, and Zoe felt something in her lurch, shift. She saw need and something deeper flare in Aaron's eyes, and for a second this seemed like more than sex.

Then he started to move and she wrapped her legs around his waist to bring him even closer. The moment became one of raw, primal passion, and then one of endless pleasure.

When it was over Aaron rolled onto his back and Zoe lay there, spent and breathless, her mind spinning for a few glorious minutes before she returned to earth with a dull thud. The party was over, she knew, and she didn't relish being dismissed now that she'd served her purpose. She was pretty sure that was how Aaron treated his women, at least his one-night stands, of which she was most assuredly one. Surreptitiously she rolled over and reached for her discarded underwear, only to have Aaron stay her arm.

'Where do you think you're going?'

'I need to get going,' Zoe answered, keeping her voice light. 'Not that the sushi wasn't delicious.'

Aaron let out a low rumble of laughter, surprising her. For a man who didn't joke, he'd still managed to laugh twice this evening, a thought which absurdly pleased her. What did she care if he laughed?

'Not so fast,' he said and pulled her towards him. Her body instinctively slid around his, her soft places finding his hard ones, so they fit like two pieces of a puzzle. 'We need to find my bed.'

She felt a thrill at his gruffly spoken words, a ridiculous, huge thrill. He wanted her to stay? She hesitated, knowing the better, safer thing to do would be to leave. She knew herself, knew her weaknesses. Sex was sex to a man like Aaron, but to her it was something else. No matter what her head dictated, she couldn't keep her heart from always insisting this was the one, this was love. And already she sensed that she would fall harder and longer for a man like Aaron than any of the other men she'd known. Feeling anything but basic, primal lust for Aaron Bryant bordered on the utterly insane.

'Well, actually....' she began, and that was as far as she got. Aaron was smoothing his hands over her bottom, as if he were touching a rare silk, then his fingers slid between her legs and she gave up the battle she hadn't really been fighting. 'You have a bed?' she managed, and with a throaty chuckle—his third laugh—he scooped her up in his arms and carried her to his bedroom and his wonderful, king-sized bed.

Hours later Zoe lay in that bed with dawn's first pale fingers streaking across the city sky and watched Aaron sleep. She was exhausted, totally sated, and as she looked at him she felt a little dart of sorrow arrow inside her. She didn't regret this night; it had been too amazing for that. But as she looked at his face softened with sleep, his lashes feathering his cheeks and his softly sculpted lips slightly parted, she wished things could be different. That Aaron was a different kind of man.

Don't, she warned herself. *Don't do it again. Don't insist you're in love with a complete ass.* She'd only done that about four times before. Millie always teased her about the emotional toe-rags she dated, and Zoe usually laughed it off. After all, it was true. But that didn't make it hurt less.

Silently she slipped from the bed and went in search of her clothes. The last of the moonlight spilled into the living room, bathing the chrome and glass with a pearly sheen even as the horizon pinkened with the promise of a new day. Zoe dressed quickly and, with one last bittersweet glance towards the bedroom, she left.

Three weeks later Zoe had done her best to forget that incredible night with Aaron Bryant, although she couldn't keep herself from surreptitiously scanning the headlines of the tabloids and gossip magazines for a glimpse of his name. She saw a photograph of him at a movie premier with a gorgeous B-list actress and felt something inside her tighten, twist. Surely not jealousy? she asked herself. It would be incredibly, criminally stupid to be jealous. Aaron Bryant meant nothing to her, and she obviously meant nothing to him. Their one night, fantastic as it had been, was over.

Resolutely she went to work at The Daisy Café, a funky, independent coffee shop in Greenwich Village where she worked part-time as a barista. She went to the community centre where she worked afternoons as an art therapist, and tried to keep away from the tabloids.

One afternoon in early September she was working at the café when the smell of the coffee beans nearly made her lose her breakfast.

'I must be coming down with something,' she told Violet, her co-worker, a young woman of nineteen who had multiple piercings and hair dyed like her name. 'The smell of coffee is making me sick.'

Violet raised her eyebrows. 'If I don't know better, I'd

think you were pregnant.' Zoe just stared at her, all the blood draining from her face, and Violet pursed her lips. 'Uh-oh.'

As soon as her shift ended Zoe bought a pregnancy test, telling herself she was being ridiculous. Aaron had used protection, after all. She probably just had some kind of stomach flu, but just to be safe…

She took the test in the tiny bathroom of her studio apartment, sitting on the edge of the tub while she watched two pink lines blaze across the little screen.

Pregnant.

She sat there, the test in hand, utterly in shock and completely numb. Yet as that blankness wore off she probed the emotion underneath like a sore tooth or a fresh scar and realised, to her surprise, it wasn't dismay or fear that she felt. It was almost…excitement. Happiness.

She shook her head, incredulous at her own emotions. A *baby*. The baby of a man she barely knew, didn't even like. And yet…a baby. A child, her child, already nestled inside her, starting to grow. She pressed one hand against her still-flat tummy in a kind of dazed incredulity.

She wanted this baby. Despite all the challenges and difficulties of being a single mother on a small salary, she wanted to have this child. She was thirty-one years old, and a happy-ever-after wasn't likely to be in her future. This was her chance to be a mother, a chance to find her own kind of happiness. And, even though the baby was no more than the size of a bean, it was *there*. And she wanted to nurture that tiny life, that part of her.

Over the next few days she wished she had someone to talk to, but none of her friends were remotely interested in pregnancy or babies, and ever since Millie had lost her husband and young daughter three years ago Zoe hadn't felt like she could burden her with her problems—and certainly not this. Children were still a no-go area for Millie.

There was, Zoe knew, at least one person she needed to talk to. Aaron, no matter how hands-off he intended to be—and, frankly, she hoped that was considerable—still needed to know he was going to be a father. Zoe didn't relish that conversation, but it didn't appear to be one she was going to have any time soon, for every time she called Bryant Enterprises and asked for Aaron she was put off by a prissy-sounding secretary.

She left message after message with her name and number, but a week went by of her calling every day and he never phoned back. Annoyed, she considered not telling him at all, but she knew she could never keep such a devastating secret. And, in any case, that kind of lie of omission would likely come back and bite her. Which left one other option, she decided grimly.

It didn't take too much effort to get Aaron's mobile number from Chase on a rather flimsy pretext of needing sponsors for a charity event she was supposed to be coordinating for the community centre, but when she tried his mobile he didn't answer that either. Jerk.

Ten days after she'd first taken the test Zoe resorted to a text message, which seemed appropriate, considering how a phone had figured in their first encounter.

Grimly she typed in the four words she'd decided would convey her situation to her baby's father:

I'm pregnant, you ass.

CHAPTER THREE

AARON STARED AT the text message in disbelief. He knew who it was from, even though the number wasn't one he recognised. Rather unusually, he'd only slept with one woman in the last month and, more significantly, he knew only one woman who would text him such a provocative message.

Zoe.

Pregnant?

Impossible. He'd used protection every time. Aaron stared at the text message, his eyes narrowing. He hadn't thought Zoe Parker a grasping gold-digger, but he supposed anything was possible. He'd certainly known women to reach for flimsy pretexts in an attempt to ensnare him.

In any case, this was something he could nip in the bud very easily. Frowning, he tossed his phone aside and turned to his laptop. It shouldn't be too difficult to find out where Zoe worked and lived.

Late that morning Aaron was standing in front of The Daisy Café, patrons spilling out into the September sunshine, holding their vente lattes and chai teas. Aaron could see Zoe behind the curved counter, working the espresso machine. Her hair was back in a neat ponytail, and she wore a tight black T-shirt that reminded him rather uncomfortably of what she'd looked and felt like underneath.

Pushing that unhelpful thought away with an impatient

sigh, he headed inside. Heads turned as soon as he entered. At six feet four with the shoulders of a linebacker, Aaron often caught stares. Some people recognised him, and a woman he didn't know started to shimmy towards him, a calculating hope in her eyes. Aaron headed for the counter.

'Zoe.'

She looked up, her grey eyes widening as she took in his presence in the little café. Then her mouth twisted in a sardonic smile and she put her hands on her hips.

'Well, well, you finally got my message.'

'Finally?'

'I've only been trying to call you for a week.'

Aaron just shrugged. As far as he was concerned their one night had ended at dawn, when she'd snuck out of bed before he could show her the door. He didn't do repeats.

'Is there somewhere private where we can talk?' he asked and she lifted her chin.

'I'm working.'

Aaron folded his arms. 'You've been trying to get in touch with me, and now I'm here. What more do you want?'

She glared at him, clearly unwilling to relinquish her anger at his ignoring her messages for the last week. Then she nodded, her jaw set stubbornly. The woman was impossible, yet some contrary part of him admired her spirit. 'Fine.'

She turned to the other woman behind the counter, a twenty-something woman with purple hair and too many piercings, and said a few words. Then she stalked out of the shop, leaving Aaron, irritatingly, with no choice but to follow her.

'Well?' she said once they were out in the street, hands on her hips, pedestrians streaming by in an indifferent blur.

'I'm not about to conduct this conversation in the middle of a city street,' Aaron answered tautly. 'And I'd imagine you don't want to either.'

The fight seemed to leave her then and she sagged a little bit, looking, Aaron thought, suddenly very tired. 'No, I don't. But I have to get back to work.'

'As do I.' Every minute spent arguing with this woman was costing him in far too many ways. He simply wanted it dealt with and done. 'My limo is waiting. Let's at least conduct this conversation in the privacy of my car.'

With a shrug Zoe followed him to the sleek car idling by the kerb. Aaron jerked open the door and ushered her in, sliding in across from her. He pressed the intercom for the driver.

'Drive around the block a couple of times, please, Brian.'

'Very good, sir.'

He took a deep breath and stared hard at Zoe. 'Look, let's cut to the chase, Zoe. The baby isn't mine.'

She stared at him for at least thirty seconds, her gaze sweeping over him slowly, as if taking the measure of him—and finding it decidedly lacking. Not that he cared one iota about her opinion of him. Then she let out one short huff of laughter and looked away. 'You know, I had a feeling you'd go that route.'

'Of course I would,' Aaron snapped. 'I used protection.'

'Well, Super Stud, we're in the lucky two percent when that protection fails.'

'That's impossible.'

'Statistically, no. Two percent does not equal impossible, genius.'

He closed his eyes for a second, willing himself not to lose his temper. He needed to stay in control of this conversation. 'Very unlikely, then.'

'I agree with you there.' She gave a rather grim smile. She didn't seem very pleased about this turn of events, Aaron realised. And she looked pale and drawn.

'So what do you want?' he asked, gazing at her levelly.

'From you? Nothing. If you want to deny being this baby's

father, that's fine with me. I was only telling you as a courtesy anyway.' She met his gaze, grey eyes blazing, arms folded. Aaron felt a surge of alarm—as well as another tiny dart of admiration at her strength and courage.

'So you intend to keep this baby.'

Her gaze never wavered from his but he saw shadows in her eyes, like ripples in water. 'Yes.'

'I could demand a paternity test, you know.'

'Go right ahead. I looked into it, anyway. I can have one done at nine weeks.' Her mouth curved in a humourless smile. 'Then you'll finally be able to put your mind at ease.'

Her utter certainty shook him. Was she bluffing, or did she really believe this baby was his? *Could* it be his? The thought was terrifying. And surely—*surely*—impossible? 'How do you even know this baby is mine?' he asked in a low voice.

She pressed her lips together and glanced away. 'Contrary to the impression you've obviously formed of me, I don't sleep around. You're the only candidate, hot shot.'

He felt shock bolt through him as he acknowledged for the first time that she was actually pregnant with his baby. His *child.* He let out a long, slow breath, then lifted his grim gaze to hers. 'All right, then. How much do I have to pay you to have an abortion?'

Zoe blinked and sat back as if he'd struck her. She felt literally winded by his callous cruelty. The sweet passion she'd felt in his arms felt like a distant memory, absurd in light of their relationship—or lack of it—now.

'You really are a first-class jerk,' she said slowly. 'You couldn't pay me anything. I want to have this baby.'

His mouth tightened. 'Your life is hardly set up for a baby, Zoe.'

She bristled even as she recognised the stinging truth of his words. 'What do you know about my life?'

'You work in a coffee shop.'

'So?'

'You live in a fifth-floor walk-up in a bad neighbourhood.'

'It's a fine neighbourhood,' she snapped. 'And plenty of people who aren't millionaires living in mansions have babies.'

Aaron folded his arms. 'Why do you even want this baby?'

'Why don't you?' Zoe flung back. Aaron didn't answer, although she saw how he glanced away, as if he didn't want to answer the question.

'Well?' she demanded. 'I'm not asking you for anything, you know. I'll sign whatever piece of paper you want promising never to ask you for money or help, or even acknowledge you as the father. You don't have to be on the birth certificate. You're free, Aaron.' She flung her arms wide, the gesture mocking. 'Breathe a sigh of relief, because you don't have to have a single thing to do with this baby. I'd rather you didn't. But I'm keeping it.'

Aaron turned to gaze at her once more, his face utterly without expression. 'Twenty thousand dollars,' he said in a low voice.

Zoe's lips parted but no sound came out. 'Twenty thousand dollars,' she repeated tonelessly.

'Fifty thousand,' Aaron answered. 'More money than you've ever had in your life, I'm sure.'

'To have an abortion?' she clarified. He blinked, set his jaw even as his gaze flicked away once more. Even he wasn't willing to put it into such stark words. She stared at him for a long moment, wondering if he actually thought she might consider his offer for so much as a single second. 'You're serious,' she said, and with obvious effort he glanced at her again.

'I'm just trying to be reasonable.'

'You call this reasonable?'

Aaron's jaw tightened and for a second, no more, he looked almost panicked. 'I—I can't be a father.'

She let out a harsh, ragged laugh. 'Guess what? I'm not asking you to.'

'Zoe, think about it.'

She shook her head, nausea roiling inside her. It would serve him right if she were sick all over his precious car. 'Go to hell,' she finally said, her voice raw and, with the limo stopped at a traffic light, she got out.

Zoe walked down Christopher Street with her legs shaking. She felt physically ill, worse than any morning sickness she'd experienced so far. She thought of Aaron's unyielding expression as he'd offered her more money than she'd ever had before to get rid of their child.

Helplessly she turned aside and retched onto the sidewalk pavement. People hurried by, oblivious. Zoe didn't think she'd ever felt more wretched and alone. She'd dated plenty of commitment-phobic jerks in her time, but never someone as deliberately cold and cruel as Aaron Bryant. And he was her baby's father.

She straightened, took a deep breath and wiped her eyes. 'I hope, kid,' she muttered, 'that you favour my side of the family.'

By the time she returned to the café she thought she'd got herself more or less under control, although she obviously didn't fool Violet. The other woman raised her eyebrows as Zoe came in, handing a coffee to a customer.

'So that didn't go well,' she said as Zoe came behind the counter and reached for her apron. She just shrugged in response.

'Let me guess,' Violet said after they'd dealt with the latest trickle of customers and the café was mostly empty. 'That was the father.' Zoe nodded. Violet waited a few seconds. 'And?'

Another shrug. 'He's not thrilled.'

'We're talking serious understatement here, right?'

'Maybe.' Zoe took a breath and tried to banish the sight

of Aaron's cold, autocratic expression as he'd offered her
fifty thousand dollars. 'To be fair, it had to have been a huge
shock.'

'To you, too.'

'Yes, but even so—' She stopped and shook her head. Why
on earth was she defending Aaron to Violet, or to anyone?
Why did she insist on believing the best about guys who didn't
deserve it? And Aaron Bryant most definitely didn't deserve
it. He was a cold-hearted bastard and she wouldn't give him
one iota of her compassion or understanding.

And yet he was her baby's father. They were linked, funda-
mentally and forever, no matter what his actions. That counted
for something, whether she wanted it to or not. She let out a
long, slow breath and turned to Violet. 'Anyway, it doesn't
matter. He's not going to be involved.'

Violet frowned. 'You're going to raise this kid on your
own?'

Zoe heard the scepticism in her friend's voice and bit her
lip. She thought of Aaron's scathing indictment: *your life is
hardly set up for a baby.* No, it wasn't. She lived on a shoe-
string budget and her savings were virtually nil. Her apartment wasn't suitable for a baby, no matter what she'd told
Aaron. She knew she could ask for help from her parents, or
Millie and Chase, but the thought of their disappointment and
censure—no matter if it was unspoken—made her cringe.
Millie was the one who had got married, had a real job and
lived an exemplary life. Zoe was the screw-up.

'Hey, Zo.' Violet put a hand on her shoulder. 'You know
I'll help you, right? And so will lots of people, I'm sure. You
can do this.'

Zoe blinked back sudden tears. Pregnancy hormones were
clearly making her stupidly emotional. And while she appre-
ciated Violet's offer, she wondered how much help a broke

part-time college student could really give her…compared to how much she needed.

Two days later the morning sickness really hit and Zoe went from feeling a little nauseous to barely being able to get out of bed. She dragged herself to work and back again, and the rest of the time she curled up on her sofa and nibbled dry crackers, feeling utterly miserable. She thought about calling Millie, just to have someone to share this with. She knew she'd have to tell her sister as well as her parents some time, but for the moment she couldn't bring herself to admit her dire state of affairs. *I'm pregnant by your brother-in-law and he has no interest in this baby. He offered me fifty thousand dollars to get rid of it.* It was all just too, too awful.

And then one day it all changed. She went to the ladies' during a break at the café and there was blood in her underwear. Zoe stared at that single rusty streak in disbelief. Could she actually be having a miscarriage? After all she'd endured already, to have it end before it had even begun?

Tears pricked her eyes and her heart lurched. She realised in that moment just how much she wanted this child, despite the awful nausea and Aaron's horrible rejection.

'You look like you've seen a ghost,' Violet said when she came back into the café. 'What's going on?'

Numbly Zoe told her. 'You should see a doctor,' Violet said firmly.

'Can they even do anything at this stage?'

'I don't know, but do you want to take that chance? And it might give you some peace of mind.' She paused and added somberly, 'Either way.'

Duly Zoe picked an obstetrician from the internet—she had no friends who could recommend one—and made an appointment for that afternoon.

The OB, Dr Stephens, was a brisk grey-haired woman with a practical but friendly manner. 'Bleeding in early pregnancy can be perfectly normal,' she told her. 'But it also can indicate miscarriage. There's really no telling at this point. If you experience more bleeding, with any accompanying cramping, then you should come back.'

Zoe nodded dully. 'And is there anything I can do?'

'Nature generally takes its course at this point,' Dr Stephens told her gently. 'But of course staying off your feet and resting as much as possible couldn't hurt.'

Of course. Yet both of those were virtually impossible with her work.

As she walked back to her apartment, Zoe felt even worse. Going to the doctor hadn't reassured her; it had only made her aware of all the uncertainties, the impossibilities. She was only seven weeks' pregnant and already it was so unbearably hard…and lonely.

She sniffed, then took a deep breath. 'Pull yourself together,' she told herself as she unlocked the door to her building and kicked aside the drift of takeaway menus that always littered the floor. 'You can do this. You're strong. You've survived a lot.'

She thought of Tim and how devastated she'd felt then. Nothing, obviously, compared to what Millie had been going through at the same time, with the loss of her husband and daughter. Yet the aching loneliness of his betrayal and her inability to tell anyone reminded her of how she'd endured it; she'd got through, got stronger.

She could do this.

She headed up the five narrow flights of stairs to her tiny shoebox of an apartment; each step felt like a burden. How would she manage these stairs when she was nine months' pregnant? Or with a pram? And what would she do for childcare, for *money*?

Oh, God, what she was doing? She reached the top of the stairs and pressed the heels of her hands to her eyes, willing the tears to recede. She'd never cried so much in her life before.

'Zoe.'

She dropped her hands, shock icing through her, freezing her to the floor. Aaron stood in front of her door.

She looked terrible, Aaron thought. Her face was pale and gaunt, her hair stringy. And, even more alarmingly, she seemed near to tears, which he'd never seen before. He'd thought of her as strong, invincible, yet now she looked like she needed protecting. He felt a surge of concern, an unfamiliar emotion, and he took a step towards her.

'Are you all right?'

'Clearly not,' she answered tautly. 'But why do you care?' Without another word she pushed past him and unlocked the door to her apartment.

Aaron stood there, feeling weirdly and horribly uncertain. He hated doubt, hated how it crept inside him and poisoned everything he believed and knew. He hated feeling it now, and with it another rush of guilt for the way he'd acted. Of course Zoe didn't want to see or talk to him. He'd asked her—he'd offered to pay her—to get rid of their child. It had been an impulse born of desperation, but there was no going back from it. No forgetting, and perhaps no forgiving.

He'd realised that as soon as he'd seen the look of horror and shock on her face and knew he was its cause. He'd known what he'd done was unforgivable and he'd felt a sudden, cringing shame. Was he going to let his own fear control him that much? Was he going to be that weak, that cruel?

Now he stood in the doorway of Zoe's apartment and watched as she shrugged off her coat. She tossed it onto a chair and it slithered onto the floor. Her shoulders slumped.

'May I come in?'

'Why?' She straightened, tension radiating through her lithe body.

'I want to talk to you.'

'If you're going to try to strong arm me into—'

'I'm not.' Aaron cut her off. 'That was—that was a bad idea.'

She laughed dryly, the sound without humour. 'Quite a confession, coming from you.'

'May I come in?'

She shrugged wearily and turned to face him. 'Fine.'

Aaron stepped into the apartment, blinking in the gloom until Zoe switched on a light. The place was tiny, just one rectangle of a room with a bed, a sofa, a dresser and a tiny kitchen in the corner.

'I'm sure,' Zoe said dryly, 'it horrifies you to realise people live like this.'

He glanced at her, saw her eyes sparking with some of her old fire, a sardonic smile on her lips. '"Horrifies" might be too strong a word.'

'This is actually quite a nice apartment,' she informed him. 'According to some of my friends. At least I don't have to share.'

He stepped over some pyjamas that had been left on the floor and returned her coat to the chair. 'I can't imagine sharing a place this size.'

She watched him for a moment, her face without expression. 'What do you want, Aaron?' She spoke flatly, the fire gone.

'I want to discuss our child.'

'*My* child,' she corrected. 'I think you gave up any paternal rights when you offered me that money.'

Anger flared but he forced it down. 'I told you, that was a bad idea.'

'Oh, *well,* then,' she drawled. 'Never mind.'

All right, fine. Maybe he deserved this. He most assuredly did, but that didn't make accepting it any more pleasant. 'Look, I'm sorry, Zoe. I acted on impulse.'

'Some impulse.'

'I wasn't prepared to be a father.'

'I wasn't asking you to be a father,' she shot back. 'I was simply informing you that you'd unknowingly donated some DNA. You don't have to be involved in this baby's life. Frankly, I don't want you to be involved in this baby's life. I think he or she can do without a dad like you.'

Aaron blinked, her words wounding him far more than they should have. They *hurt.* 'Probably,' he said in a low voice, when he trusted himself to speak. 'I'll probably be a pretty lousy dad.' He certainly didn't have any good experience to draw from. He took a breath, let it out slowly. 'But I still want to be involved.'

Her jaw slackened and she stared at him with wide, dark eyes. *'What?'*

'I want to be involved, Zoe. I regret my earlier…suggestion. I told you, you caught me by surprise.'

'Remind me never to do that again, then.'

'I said,' Aaron said, hearing the edge enter his voice, 'I'm sorry.'

'And sometimes, Aaron, it's just not that easy. I can't forget. And I'm still not sure I want you involved.'

'I could—' He stopped, knowing a threat wasn't the right choice now.

'You could what?' she filled in. 'Take me to court? Sue for custody? With your money you'd probably win, too.'

Aaron said, his teeth gritted, 'I'd just like to have a civil conversation.'

Her shoulders sagged then and she sank onto the sofa, her head in her hands. He resisted the entirely ridiculous and inappropriate impulse to touch her, offer her some kind of comfort. He wouldn't even know how. 'Look, it's probably all irrelevant anyway.'

'Irrelevant? What do you mean?'

She glanced up at him, and with a jolt of alarm he saw the sheen of tears in her eyes. 'I had some bleeding,' she said dully. 'I might be having a miscarriage.'

Considering his earlier stance, Aaron knew he should be feeling relieved. But he didn't. He felt…alarmed. Worried. Maybe even sad.

'I'm sorry,' he said and Zoe's mouth twisted.

'Are you?'

'Yes, Zoe, I actually am. Can you just—please stop with the little barbed comments? For a little while, at least?'

She glanced down again. 'I'm sorry.'

'Have you been to the doctor?'

'Yes.'

'What did he say?'

'*She* said there wasn't much I could do right now. Nature will take its course.'

'That's not much of an answer.' Frustration fired through him. He'd never been the kind of person just to let things happen. From the moment he'd discovered Bryant Enterprises was virtually bankrupt, he'd been striving to bring it back from the brink. Even though several financial advisors had told him to just let it go, he'd refused. He'd worked endlessly to put his family's firm in the black and he'd work just as hard now. He didn't give up. He didn't *fail*.

'There must be something you can do,' he said, keeping his tone reasonable. 'Stay off your feet, rest.'

She shrugged. 'My life isn't like yours, you know. I can't just become a lady of leisure.'

He stared at her, thinking of her on her feet all day at the café, then tramping up five flights of stairs every night to this awful apartment. 'Actually,' he said slowly, the idea just starting to take shape, 'You could.'

Her brow wrinkled and she shook her head. 'What do you mean?'

Aaron, decisive now that a solution had presented itself, said, 'You could come and live with me.'

CHAPTER FOUR

Zoe stared at Aaron, his words, his offer, seeming to echo through the apartment.

'You're joking,' she finally said, and he shook his head, the movement brisk and decisive.

'I told you, I don't joke.'

She shook her head, everything in her rejecting what he'd suggested. 'Aaron, we barely know each other.'

'We're going to have a baby.'

She hated the thrill that coursed through her at his words, at that treacherous 'we'. 'A baby you don't want.' His dark brows came together in a frown but he said nothing and Zoe sighed. 'I'd drive you crazy.'

'Probably, but I work long hours.'

'So I'd drive myself crazy, wandering around your awful apartment all day long by myself.'

His incredulous gaze swept around her tiny studio. '*My* awful apartment?'

'All that cold chrome and steel. It's heartless.'

'So the reason you're objecting to this arrangement is my choice of decor?'

'No, of course not.' Zoe folded her arms, hating how he'd already got her on the defensive. Hating how a part of her, a terrible, treacherous part, actually already wanted to say yes. How stupid was that, when they obviously had no future? When staying with him would surely make her crazy, stubborn heart start thinking and hoping for things that were impossible? Things she shouldn't even really want? 'It's just not…practical.'

'This—' Aaron said, sweeping an arm around her apartment '—is not practical.'

Zoe bit her lip. 'It probably won't make a difference, anyway. I mean…what will be, will be.'

He shook his head. 'That's never been my philosophy in life.'

'No, I didn't think so.'

'Zoe.' He took a step towards her, his voice lowering in a way that made her want to shiver. 'Admittedly, there is a chance a bit of bed rest won't make any difference. But what if it did? Would you deny our baby that chance?'

Our baby. She bit her lip harder so it hurt. 'You're blackmailing me.'

'I'm just showing you reason.'

'It's not very fair.'

'Why don't you want to come live with me, have a few weeks' holiday?' He sounded exasperated now, as if he'd expected her to fall in with his plans far more quickly than this. 'You can have your own bedroom.'

'Given.'

'And we don't— We don't even have to talk to each other, if you don't want to.'

Zoe stilled. He sounded so oddly vulnerable then, so unlike the autocratic man she'd told herself she should despise. 'I think I could handle talking to you.' She relented, if only a little.

Aaron lifted an eyebrow. 'So what's the problem?'

So much for vulnerability. 'Why are you doing this? Offering this? Because it's about one hundred and eighty degrees from what you were suggesting a week ago.'

'I know that.' He pressed his lips together, colour slashing his cheekbones. 'I've had time to think, and I've…re-evaluated my position on the matter.'

'You've re-evaluated your position,' Zoe repeated. 'This isn't a board meeting, Aaron.'

'Will you come or not?'

She hesitated. Told herself this was a bad idea…for her. But it was a good idea for the baby. It was giving her baby— their baby—a chance. 'I could just go to Millie and Chase's,' she said. 'Or my parents'.'

'You could.'

But she didn't want to. Didn't want to admit to them how desperate and alone she was. How she'd messed up…again. And she knew, no matter what she'd said to Aaron about emotional blackmail, she couldn't deny her baby this chance. Working on her feet all day and living in a fifth-floor walk-up was not advisable with a threatened miscarriage. She got that. She felt the fear, the guilt. She closed her eyes, then opened them again. Nodded. 'Okay. I'll come. For a few days, though. Maybe a week.' She said this as much for herself, because Aaron didn't respond to her addendum.

He slid his phone out of his pocket and issued a few terse instructions. Then he glanced at her, his gaze taking in the tiny apartment. 'You can pack whatever you need. My car will be here in five minutes.'

'Five *minutes*?'

A look of impatience crossed his features. 'I have to get back to work. And the sooner this situation is resolved, the better.' He turned away, scrolling through his messages as Zoe stood there, her mind whirling. *This situation.* That was what she was to him, she realised, what her—their—baby was. A situation. A problem he intended to solve as quickly and expediently as possible.

Swallowing, she turned and began to gather her things.

Sure enough, they were speeding uptown in his limo a matter of minutes later, Zoe's lone suitcase stowed in the back along with her house plant and one of her paintings. Aaron had eyed them askance and Zoe had said rather defiantly that she would not live in his morgue of an apartment without some colour.

'You can call the café where you work and give notice,' Aaron said, his gaze still on the little luminous screen of his phone.

'Give notice? It's only a leave of absence.'

He shrugged. 'Whatever. Either way I'll cover the rent on your apartment, so you don't have to worry about money.'

Zoe sat back against the seat, a new and different kind of nausea roiling through her. It might as well be her notice, she realised. Molly, the owner of the café, would have to hire a new barista while she was gone, and it wasn't as if Zoe was so valuable she'd dismiss that person when she was ready to return. Besides, when *would* she be ready to return? The future stretched in front of her, alarmingly unknown.

'I don't want to just sit around all day,' she said abruptly and Aaron glanced up from his phone.

'Even if that's best for the baby?'

'Enough with the emotional blackmail,' she snapped. 'I work afternoons as an art therapist, sitting down, very low-energy. I'm keeping that up.'

Aaron glanced at her in consideration before turning back to his phone. 'Fine. I'll arrange a car to drive you there and return you to my apartment.'

'Thank you,' she said stiffly, although she wasn't even sure what she was thanking him for. This *situation* felt uncomfortably like a prison sentence. She'd be let out for a few hours, but then swiftly returned to her cell.

Yet she'd agreed. She'd willingly put herself in Aaron's

hands and, as the limo pulled up to the high rise she hadn't seen since that fateful night, she wondered why she had.

They didn't speak as they rode the lift up to the penthouse and the doors opened directly onto Aaron's apartment. Zoe walked through the cold, modern rooms and felt a prickling of discomfort lodge between her shoulder blades.

'This brings back memories,' she said lightly, because not saying it felt ridiculous, like refusing to acknowledge the elephant lumbering alongside them.

'New memories will take the place of those,' Aaron answered without emotion. 'Let me show you your bedroom.'

It was right across from his, and just as sumptuous, with a king-sized bed, a huge plasma-screen TV and an en suite bathroom with a sunken marble tub and walk-in shower. Zoe imagined soaking in that tub and felt some of her reservations start to crumble. It would be heavenly to relax for a little while, to have a break from all the worry and fear.

'Thank you,' she said, turning to Aaron. He stood in the doorway, dark and unsmiling. 'This really is very kind of you,' she continued awkwardly. 'I'm sorry if I haven't seemed gracious.'

'It's a difficult situation. And I haven't exactly handled myself with aplomb either.' He set her suitcase down. 'Why don't you unpack? I need to return to work but I should be back around dinner time. Order whatever you like. There are menus in the kitchen, and you can just charge it to my name.'

'Okay. Thanks.'

Then with a nod of farewell he was gone, and Zoe was left alone in the huge, barren apartment, her mind spinning as she wondered just what she'd got herself into.

She unpacked her few things as Aaron had suggested and then, because she was so tired and the tub looked so heavenly, she ran a huge, steaming bath and sank into the decadent bubbles with a blissful sigh.

Soaking in the tub she was reminded, suddenly and piercingly, of the night she'd spent with Aaron. After that first time on the rug he'd taken her to the bed, and then to the shower, soaped her everywhere, and then driven himself inside her while she had wrapped her legs around his waist…

Zoe closed her eyes as the memories assailed her and fresh, ridiculous desire coursed through her. She didn't want to remember the overwhelming passion of that night. It could only confuse what was between them now, which was essentially a business partnership. At least, that was how Aaron seemed determined to conduct it, and Zoe told herself it was sensible. She didn't want to get mired in feelings she had no business having for Aaron Bryant. No matter how great a lover he was, no matter how sweet his few and surprising moments of kindness, he was still, and always would be, an arrogant and autocratic jerk.

It felt weirdly disloyal to think that now, especially considering she was soaking in his bath tub as his guest for the foreseeable future. Yet Zoe knew she had to remind herself because, knowing her track record, if she didn't she just might start to fall in love with him—and that would be really, phenomenally stupid.

Aaron couldn't concentrate on his work, which was an irritating first. He was used to being able to focus completely on business; nothing else in his life even came a close second. Yet now, as he scanned the latest reports on the stock market in Asia, he found his mind drifting to Zoe. Wondering what she was doing. Was she watching TV? Taking a bath?

Instantly his body hardened as images flashed through his mind of Zoe in his tub with nothing but a few strategically placed bubbles popping slowly and revealing the soft, tantalising skin underneath—skin he'd touched, kissed, remembered the satiny feel of.

With effort he stopped that vivid montage from reeling through his head. Unhelpful; he didn't want to think about Zoe as anything other than…what? His brain scrambled to compartmentalise her. He liked things tidy, in his control, yet nothing about this situation—about Zoe—felt that way. It had been messy and uncontrollable from the moment he'd met her, when she'd taken his phone and he'd responded by putting his hand up her skirt.

Sighing, Aaron raked a hand through his hair and tried to focus on the report in front of him. His mind had been spinning ever since that confrontation with Zoe in his limo. The look on her face when he'd made his cold-blooded offer. He cringed in shame at the memory, even as the aftershocks of surprise and even fear rippled through him. A baby. A father.

He'd never wanted to be a father. Never wanted to be that important to somebody—that critical. The opportunity to make a mistake, to *fail,* was too huge. And he knew first-hand the lasting damage a father could have on his son.

Yet over the last week he'd realised that, if Zoe was going to have this baby, if he was going to be a father whether he liked it or not, then he needed to be in that child's life. Being completely absent was surely one way to guarantee what he didn't want: to hurt an innocent child's life through his own faults and weaknesses.

Aaron glanced at the clock. It was nearly six, which was still several hours before he usually left the office, and then just to work more at home. Yet today he found himself closing his laptop, packing up his attaché case and heading outside into the still-warm September evening.

The apartment was quiet when he entered, alarmingly so. Had she left? Decided she didn't want to do this after all? And why did that thought alarm him so damn much?

Taking a deep breath, Aaron set down his case and

shrugged off his jacket. He hated feeling this uncertain. This…worried.

'Hey.'

He turned to see Zoe coming out of the kitchen dressed in a T-shirt and yoga pants, her hair tousled and damp around her shoulders. She smiled, tucking her hair behind her ears. 'I had the most decadent afternoon. I probably should feel guilty.'

Decadent? His mind was leaping to possibilities and images he had no business thinking of. 'You came here to rest,' he said, intentionally noncommittal and even gruff. But Zoe didn't seem to notice and walked closer to him instead, so he caught the vanilla scent of her hair as she waggled her fingers in front of him.

'I spent two hours in the tub. My fingers still look like prunes.'

Aaron took a step away. 'I'm sure you'll recover.'

'I ordered Chinese for dinner. I know it's completely stereotypical for a pregnancy craving, but I really wanted some pork lo mein.'

'Your body must be craving MSG.'

She raised her eyebrows, a teasing smile curling her lush mouth. 'Wait a minute, did you actually make a joke?'

'A poor one, since the local Chinese place I order from doesn't even use MSG.' He took another step away from her, needing the distance. 'I think I'll go shower and change.' Wrong thing to say, he realised immediately. It made it sound as if they were going to have a cosy night in, eating Chinese food and watching TV. How ridiculous. How *impossible*.

This whole situation was incredibly awkward, Aaron thought as he escaped to the shower. He'd offered his apartment to Zoe on impulse, because when he saw a problem and he wanted to deal with it immediately. He hadn't considered how uncomfortably intimate it would be, sharing his living space, seeing her freshly showered and talking about Chinese food…

The whole thing was absurd. And messy. The sooner Zoe had a clean bill of health and could go back to her own life…

Except when would that be? he thought suddenly, his hands stilling in the process of scrubbing his hair. If the pregnancy continued to term, his life would always intersect with Zoe's in a most critical way. He needed to develop a plan. A strategy for the future. Except he had no idea what that could be.

First things first, he decided as he stepped out of the shower and wrapped a towel around his waist. He'd get through the next few weeks of uncertainty— Hell, first he had to get through this evening. Then he could think about what the long-term future for this unexpected family of theirs would be.

Zoe set out plates and glasses with no idea of what to expect. Would Aaron be joining her for dinner? Were they actually going to sit down and have a meal together, like some bizarre, instant happy family?

Despite her decadent afternoon, she felt exhausted. Maintaining a cheerfully insouciant facade—for she knew that was all it was—with Aaron was emotionally and physically draining. But it was also armour, a way to protect herself. To show him she wasn't bothered by this unusual living arrangement, that she wasn't remembering how he'd taken her right on that rug, with the lights of the city streaming over them. How for a moment, when he'd been inside her, she'd looked into his eyes and felt far more emotion than she ever wanted to feel… Even as she craved that connection once more.

Thankfully the intercom buzzed, calling a halt to that unhelpful line of thinking. By the time Aaron came out of his bedroom she was opening the steaming cartons of fragrant Chinese food, inhaling the blissful aroma of pork lo mein.

'You look like you've just died and gone to heaven.'

'It feels like it,' she admitted, and couldn't resist eating a forkful of noodles right from the carton. 'And normally I don't even like Chinese food.'

Aaron let out a rusty laugh. 'Those pregnancy hormones must be something.'

'I guess so.' She swallowed and smiled. 'What do you like? We have the lo mein, General Tsao's chicken, moo shoo pork…'

The slight smile that had softened Aaron's features disappeared and he reached for a plate. 'I'll just have a bit of everything. And I'll eat in my study. I have work to do.'

Zoe felt the words like a rejection—and one she wasn't prepared to accept. 'You've been working all day,' she said mildly. 'And, not to sound like a nagging wife, but I'm not going to last if I have to stay in this morgue of an apartment by myself twenty-four-seven.'

Aaron frowned more in perplexity than irritation. 'What are you suggesting?'

'I think we can manage to eat dinner together,' Zoe said lightly. 'And, in any case, I want to talk to you about your decor.'

The look of patent disbelief on his face was both funny and satisfying, Zoe decided. 'My decor? Are you serious?'

'Completely.' She took her plate over to the sofa and sat down cross-legged, slurping another forkful of noodles before she resumed. 'I want to get some more things from my apartment.' His eyes widened and she held up one placatory hand. 'Don't freak, this isn't a permanent measure. But I like my things. They're *colourful*.'

'I wasn't freaking,' Aaron answered as he sat across from her, his own plate balanced in his lap.

'An eye flare is freaking for you,' Zoe tossed back. 'You are the master of control.'

'Now that's a compliment.'

'In your world, maybe.' She realised she was enjoying this banter, and the smile that twitched Aaron's lips made her heart sing. 'Anyway, back to the decor thing. I need to get some things from my apartment.'

'I can have someone take care of that.'

'I'd like to do it myself. God only knows what one of your minions would pick out.'

Aaron raised his eyebrows. 'My minions?'

'I need to go through it and see what I can bring back here. Not too much, just a few more paintings and things.'

She watched him process this, wondered how alarming it was for him to have her moving more of her stuff in. And, while it made sense, Zoe knew she was pushing just a little. She didn't really want to examine why.

'Fine,' Aaron said after a moment. 'I'll arrange a car and driver. But I don't want you to exert yourself. No lifting things.'

'Yes, sir.' She smiled, his concern warming her heart— even if it shouldn't. He was just dealing with the situation. She was the one painting rainbows.

Three days later Zoe sat at a table in the East Village's community centre art-room, watching as Robert, a very self-contained boy of six, surveyed the materials she'd set out.

'What do you feel like doing today, Robert?' she asked gently. 'Crayons, markers, paints?' Robert had been coming to the centre for nearly a month, ever since his dad had walked out without any warning and hadn't been in touch since. He had barely spoken, had never touched the art materials, yet his mother kept bringing him in the hope that something would ease the pain he held so tightly inside.

'Maybe you could try a mandala today,' Zoe suggested, taking one of the simple designs of curved shapes that children often found soothing to colour. She placed it in front of him and Robert stared down at it silently for a few seconds before he finally selected a crayon and began to carefully colour in the shapes.

Zoe watched him, occasionally making some encouraging observation, when about halfway through Robert thrust his crayon away and reached for a black marker. She watched him in silence as he vehemently scribbled black marker all over the paper, obscuring the careful design. When the page was nearly all black, ripped in some parts from the force of his scribbling, he put the marker back in the jar and sat back, seemingly satisfied.

Zoe rested a hand on his shoulder. 'Sometimes we feel like that, don't we?' she said quietly. In truth she could relate to Robert's deliberate destruction. There was your life, all carefully set out in pleasing shapes, and something happened that cancelled it all out, scribbled over your careful planning.

Robert had felt like that when his father had upped and left. And Zoe felt like that now, pregnant and alone. Despite the friendliness of that first evening, Aaron seemed determined to avoid her whenever possible. Zoe had tried to draw him out, but the emotional effort exhausted her. She didn't want to have to try so hard. She wanted something to be easy, she acknowledged ruefully. But there was nothing easy about Aaron Bryant.

That morning she'd taken a few more things from her apartment, pangs of both worry and regret assailing her as she had looked around the space she'd made her own, now empty and forlorn. A few weeks ago she'd had a home, a life, had been in control of her own destiny. Now she felt as if she were spinning in a void of unknowing and uncertainty.

Kind of like Robert felt now. She reached for a large piece of paper and the finger paints. 'Maybe,' she suggested, 'you'd like to do something messy?' The little boy was almost unbearably neat. 'Mess is okay here, you know. Everything washes off.'

He hesitated and she opened the paint pots, waited with a smile. A second later he carefully dipped one finger in the yellow paint and drew a single, cautious line on the paper, like a ray of sunlight. Zoe murmured something encouraging.

It was a start to unlocking the little boy's pain, to freeing those tightly held parts of himself. And she needed to start, too. She wasn't going to drift through the next few weeks like some desperate ghost. That had never been her style, even if men tended to bring out clinginess in her. She wouldn't be clingy with Aaron; she'd be in control. She'd claim her life back, even if it wasn't on the terms she really wanted.

She spent the rest of the afternoon arranging some of her things in Aaron's apartment, nerves battling with determination. She ordered Indian—she was methodically working through the takeaways—and set the table for two. Aaron made it home for dinner most evenings, and he almost seemed to enjoy the chatter she kept up resolutely, even if he sometimes seemed bewildered by the whole concept: dinner. Conversation. Company.

The lift doors swooshed open and Zoe turned. 'Hey there,' she said brightly and watched as Aaron's gaze moved around the apartment, taking in the plants lining the window sill and the two paintings she'd put on the walls, replacing some of the soulless modern atrocities he'd had hanging there. One canvas had been six feet of blank white with a single black splodge in the corner. Ridiculous.

'I see you've made yourself at home,' he said neutrally and Zoe gave him a teasing smile.

'I warned you, didn't I? At least this place has some colour.'

He stopped in front of an oil painting of a jar of lilacs on a kitchen table. The paint had been used liberally, creating, Zoe hoped, a messy yet welcoming feel.

'This is rather good, I suppose,' he said, sounding a bit grudging, and he turned to Zoe. 'Who's the artist?'

'Oh…no one famous.' She felt herself blush.

Aaron arched an eyebrow. 'Well, I didn't think it was Van Gogh. Is it a friend of yours?'

'Umm… It's mine, actually.' Both of the paintings were, and she suddenly realised how arrogant it might seem to hang her own art on his walls. She hadn't thought of that at the time; she just liked to be reminded of what she'd done, what she was capable of.

'I thought you were an art therapist, not an artist,' Aaron said, his brow furrowed, and Zoe shrugged.

'One's a profession, one's a hobby.'

'Did you ever want to be a professional artist?'

She shrugged. 'I don't really have what it takes. In any case, I like helping people.' She saw him frowning at her, as if she were a puzzle he didn't understand.

'I should work tonight,' he said abruptly, and Zoe's heart sank. Another night in front of the TV alone.

'Don't you get tired of working? It's practically all you do.'

'It's necessary.'

'Is it?' She kept her voice teasing. 'Will the company fall apart if you're not at the helm every second of the day, fingers twitching on your phone?'

Aaron's mouth tightened. 'It might,' he answered, and Zoe realised he was serious. Good grief, talk about a God complex.

'What happens when you get sick? Or go on vacation?'

'I don't.'

She shook her head. 'You're heading for a heart attack by the time you're forty.'

'Considering that's next year, I hope not.' He gave her the

ghost of a smile. 'But thanks for the concern.' He took his plate, clearly ready to bury himself in his office. Again. Zoe took a breath and plunged.

'Aaron…how is a baby going to fit into your life, when it's like this?'

He stilled, slowly turned around. 'Surely we don't need to talk about that now?'

'Don't we? I know everything is still uncertain, but we need to think about the future. How it's going to work.'

'It will work,' he said tautly, and she shook her head.

'A baby isn't an item on your agenda, Aaron. It's a life commitment—'

'A week or so ago you didn't even want me involved,' he said shortly. 'Now you're talking about life commitments?'

Stung, she drew back. 'You're the one who said you wanted to be involved. I'm just trying to figure out how it will work.'

'It will work,' he repeated, and Zoe knew that was all he had: sheer determination and bull-headed arrogance.

'Why did you change your mind?' she blurted, because now she needed to know. 'Less than two weeks ago you would have paid me a large amount of money to have an abortion.'

'Are you ever going to let that go?'

'It's kind of a big one.'

'I know that.' He raked a hand through his hair and Zoe could see the lines of fatigue drawn from nose to mouth.

'What made you want this baby?' she asked quietly.

Aaron didn't answer for a long moment. Zoe couldn't tell a thing from his face, his eyes so dark and fathomless, the lines of his cheek and jaw harsh and strong in the dim light.

'I wouldn't have chosen this,' he said slowly. 'It's hardly an ideal situation for anyone. But I could see that you were determined to keep this baby, and if a child of mine was going to enter the world…' He paused, his gaze distant. 'Then I wanted to be involved.'

Zoe said nothing. She felt an almost crushing sense of disappointment, which was ridiculous. What had she expected? That Aaron had had some miraculous epiphany, realised he actually wanted to be a father, a family? No, of course not. Nothing in his behaviour in the few days had indicated anything but that he was making the best of a difficult situation.

'So,' she finally said. 'You'd still prefer me to have an abortion?'

'I didn't say that,' Aaron said, irritation edging his voice. 'If I did, I would have offered that instead of having you come live with me.'

'I don't understand you,' Zoe said quietly and Aaron shrugged.

'I'm not asking you to.'

The rebuff was brutal, even though it shouldn't even have surprised her. Of course he wasn't asking for such a thing. This domestic arrangement had nothing to do with their relationship or what little of it there was, Zoe reminded herself. That was clear from how rarely she'd seen Aaron since she'd come here, how much effort she'd had to put in to getting him to so much as sit with her for a meal.

'Maybe I should just go,' she said, and felt her throat thicken with humiliating tears. 'I haven't had any bleeding since that first time, and I can't lie around all day.'

'You're not lying around all day,' Aaron pointed out, an edge to his voice. 'You're working every afternoon.'

'You don't really want me here,' she forced herself to say. 'Do you?'

Another long, taut silence, and then Aaron finally spoke, the words dragged from him with obvious reluctance. 'Yes,' he said. 'I do.'

She tried for flippancy. 'You have a funny way of showing it.'

'I know I do.' He rubbed a hand over his face. 'Look, Zoe,

I'm not good with emotions or feelings or even talking about…
anything. I admit that. But I don't want you to go. I like having you here, knowing you're safe and cared for.' He paused
and she saw a surprising vulnerability creep across his face,
soften those stern features if only for a moment. 'Maybe the
best solution is to make this…more permanent.'

'More permanent?' she repeated in disbelief. 'How?'

He took a breath, let it out. 'You stay here, with me, for
the duration of your pregnancy.'

CHAPTER FIVE

ZOE DIDN'T SPEAK for a few seconds; she was still processing what Aaron had just said. *You stay here, with me, for the duration of your pregnancy.* Finally she said the first, the only, word she could.

'No.'

'Why not?'

'Because…' Her mind grasped at reasons he would understand, that she could admit to. *It's impossible. Dangerous. I might fall in love with you.* 'I just can't.'

'Can't?' he repeated. 'Or won't?'

'Both.'

'Why not?' He sounded so reasonable, so unruffled, and she felt as if she were falling apart. Aaron's suggestion, so calmly made, had rocked her to the core.

'Why should I?' she countered, knowing she sounded childish.

'It's not practical for you to live in some walk-up studio alone—climbing all those stairs.'

'I'll get a ground-floor apartment,' Zoe said numbly.

'Never mind that. What if something happened to you? Who would even know? As far as I can tell, you've lived a very independent, isolated existence.'

'I like being independent,' she snapped. She'd ignore the

'isolated' bit. 'Anyway, what about you? I think that's the pot calling the kettle black.'

'I don't deny it,' Aaron answered evenly. 'But I'm not pregnant.'

'Being pregnant doesn't mean being ill,' Zoe flung at him and his silence was eloquent. 'You don't want me here,' she said, daring him to deny it. *I like having you here.* She forced the memory of his reluctant confession away. Not helpful now, when she was trying to be strong.

'I just said I did,' Aaron answered, his voice taut.

'Just because you want to manage me.'

'Do the reasons really matter?' *Yes.* She swallowed, said nothing. Aaron sighed impatiently. 'Why are you so against it? It seems like an obvious and easy solution to me. You've already got your stuff here.' He swept one arm out towards her paintings, the wilting ficus plant. 'You still have your life. I've arranged a car for you to go to your little art sessions.'

'My little art sessions,' Zoe repeated numbly and Aaron sighed again.

'You know what I mean.'

'I know exactly what you mean. And that's the problem, Aaron. That's the prison.'

His mouth turned down and his eyes flashed darkly. 'What are you talking about?'

'You're the prison,' she said hopelessly, because she knew it sounded melodramatic and he wouldn't understand anyway.

He didn't. 'That's nonsense.'

'It's not. You have no idea what it's like living here with someone who barely wants to talk to you.'

'That's not true.'

'Who escapes at the first opportunity.'

'I do not.'

'And hides behind work.'

'I'm not *hiding*!' he thundered, the sound of his voice

seeming to echo through the room and making Zoe fall silent. He let out an exasperated breath and raked a hand through his hair. 'Just what do you want from me, Zoe? Because I don't think it's something I have to give.'

'That's a great way to open a conversation.'

'I was trying to close it down,' Aaron snapped and Zoe shook her head.

'There's no point, is there?'

'Point to what?'

He looked so exasperated, so impatient, impervious and *blank*, and she knew he didn't get it at all. What was there even to get? What was she trying to prove here—that he didn't like her, wasn't interested in her other than as the mother of his unwanted child? *Obviously.*

'I don't know,' she whispered, all her fight and spunk gone in an instant, leaving only a weary despair. 'I don't know anything. I don't know why you want me here, what the future will look like, how you'll fit a baby into your life, never mind—' She stopped suddenly. *Never mind me.* Except he wasn't trying to fit her into his life—something else that was obvious.

Aaron didn't speak for a long moment. His irritation had gone, and he looked as weary as Zoe felt. 'Tell me what will make this work.'

She knew he meant it this time, knew this was how he operated. Life was simply a matter of function and success. But at least he was trying, at least he was waiting for her answer. She needed to try, too.

'I need more from you,' she said, and almost could have laughed at Aaron's involuntary recoil. 'I'm not asking for you to hold my hand or tuck me in bed.' She should not have mentioned bed. Or holding. Or even hands. Because everything made her think of how he'd felt on top of her, inside her. Touching her, loving her—except, stupid Zoe, because what had happened between them had had absolutely *nothing* to do with love.

'We need to figure out some kind of working relationship,' she clarified. 'If we're going to be involved in this together, as parents-to-be, never mind actual *parents*—'

'Let's cross that bridge when we come to it,' Aaron cut her off and Zoe nodded. One step at a time. One *minute* at a time.

'But even now, Aaron. I can't tiptoe around you. It'll drive me crazy.'

'I wasn't aware you were doing any tiptoeing,' he said dryly, and she let out a brief laugh of acknowledgement.

'All I'm asking for—and I know it might seem impossible, considering who we are—but can we try to get along? Be friends of a sort?'

He stared at her for a long moment, long enough for Zoe to feel like what she'd asked was impossible…at least for Aaron. And maybe it was for her, too. Contrary person that she was, half of her wanted to fall in love with him and the other half wanted to hate him. Typical.

'I hardly think it's impossible,' he said at last, and she couldn't tell a thing from his tone.

'That means,' Zoe explained, 'we have conversations. We eat dinner together—willingly. We ask about each other's day.'

'We paint each other's nails?'

She smothered a smile. 'That's the second joke you've made.'

'You must be having an influence on me.'

'Well, then?' she asked quietly. 'Could you do that? Could you try?'

Aaron let out a sigh. 'And if I do, will that be enough? Will you stay here willingly, for your pregnancy, and not complain or fight me every step of the way?'

'I'll try,' she said and his mouth quirked in a small smile, lightening his features and making her realise how rarely he smiled. How much she wanted him to.

'Then we'll both try,' he said, and held out his hand. 'Deal?'

She took his hand and let it enfold hers, felt the warmth and strength of it all the way through her. 'Deal,' she answered back.

How the hell was this supposed to work? Aaron stared moodily at the screen of his laptop as he mentally reviewed last night's conversation with Zoe. So he was just supposed to ask about her day? Eat at the same time? Instinctively Aaron knew Zoe wanted more than that. She wanted…what? A companion? A friend?

And Aaron didn't know how to be a friend. He didn't *have* any friends. He had employees, colleagues, acquaintances, siblings. None of them were friends. He'd been too private, too focused on work, too afraid of showing his weaknesses.

So how was he supposed to be a friend to Zoe?

He exhaled in an impatient sigh, resenting everything about this situation. Yet what could he have done instead? Installed Zoe in a separate apartment, he supposed, with staff. Instinctively he recoiled against such an idea, knowing she would hate it. He didn't like it much, either. She made him anxious, angry and impatient, yet he'd meant what he said. He liked having her around. He liked the sound of her laugh, the bright art on the walls, the feeling that he wasn't alone.

Good Lord. What was happening to him? And how did he make it stop?

He was still pondering the whole problem in his car on the way back to the apartment, the windows open to the warm, early-autumn air. His unseeing gaze suddenly focused on a shop sign and he pressed the button for the intercom.

'Stop the car, please.'

Fifteen minutes later he was entering the penthouse, bag

in hand. Zoe lay on the sofa, a magazine sliding from her loosened fingers, clearly asleep.

He watched her for a moment, saw how her dark lashes feathered her cheeks, her lush lips parted softly on a sigh. Her hair was tousled and spread across the sofa pillows, dark and lustrous. She looked like something out of a fairy tale, he thought suddenly, like a princess who would be wakened by a kiss.

And he wanted to be the prince that kissed her.

Not that he would. He didn't even move. Getting physically involved with Zoe at this point was dangerous. Physically dangerous, considering the state of her pregnancy, and emotionally dangerous, as well. Not for him—hell, he barely had emotions. But for her... He didn't want to complicate their situation any more than necessary. Even if right now it seemed like the most appealing thing to do.

Zoe's eyes fluttered open then and she blinked sleepily. 'I must have fallen asleep.'

Aaron felt a smile tug at this mouth, his heart inexplicably lightening. 'Clearly.'

'Sorry.'

'That's what you're here for. To rest.'

'Yes, but...' She struggled up to a seated position. 'I had dinner warming. I ordered Thai this time. I felt like sticky rice.'

'All these cravings.'

'I know. Crazy.'

He walked to the kitchen and peered in the oven where several foil cartons were warming. 'I'll dish it out,' he offered and was rewarded with a cautious smile.

Maybe this wouldn't be so bad, he thought as he ladled rice and vegetables onto two plates. Maybe Zoe just wanted a little conversation, a little company. Maybe he could handle that.

He came back with the plates and handed one to Zoe. She

took it with a murmured thanks, her feet tucked up under her, her cheeks flushed. She looked pretty, he thought. Rosy and even blooming. Wasn't that what you said about pregnant women? Like flowers.

'What did you get up to today?' he asked after a few minutes of silence. He was conscious of how awkward he felt, making small talk. He didn't do chit-chat. He gave orders, he listened to reports, he got things done. He shifted in his seat and ate another forkful of rice.

'Not much,' Zoe answered with a sigh. 'I went for a short walk, I read a book, I planned my lesson for tomorrow and then I fell asleep.'

'You're bored,' Aaron said, and he could hardly blame her.

'Out of my mind.' She smiled ruefully. 'I like being busy. I know it might not be reasonable to work on my feet at the café all day, but I need something more to do.'

As always Aaron went for solutions. 'Could you take on more hours with the art therapy?'

She shook her head. 'There's so little funding for it already. I'd love to do it full-time, but budgets are being slashed left and right.'

'What is art therapy, exactly?'

Her eyes glinted mischievously. 'My little art sessions? Technically it's the therapeutic use of art-making.'

'Which is?'

'Using art as a form of communication and healing for a variety of situations. I work with children who have usually experienced some kind of difficulty—whether it's a death, divorce or some trauma in their family.'

'And they just...draw pictures?'

'I know it probably sounds like a waste of time to you.'

'Don't put words in my mouth,' Aaron answered, although frankly it did. How could scribbling on some paper be of any help to anyone, child or adult?

'Sometimes,' Zoe said quietly, 'it's easier to express your-self through art than through words, especially for a child.'

'I suppose,' he allowed, and she gave him a small smile, as if she knew how sceptical he was. She probably did. 'You should try it. You seem to have enough trouble expressing your emotions.'

He tensed, then strove to stay light. 'Are you actually an-alysing me?'

'I wouldn't dare.' She spoke as lightly as he had, but he knew she was serious and he prickled with discomfort. 'Why is it so hard for you, Aaron? Why did you tell me you weren't good at speaking about feelings—or anything?' She cocked her head, sympathy in her studious gaze. 'Were you not en-couraged to do so as a child?'

'Is that what the textbooks say?'

She shrugged. 'It's usually a fairly good guess.'

He really didn't want to talk about himself. He never did. Yet he also knew he'd hurt Zoe if he tried to brush her off now; even that realisation surprised him. Since when did he consider anyone's feelings at all? 'I guess I wasn't,' he said after a moment, as if it were no matter. And really, it wasn't. 'We weren't ever a close family.'

'Why not?'

'I don't really know. My father was busy—elsewhere.' With his mistresses, but Aaron didn't want to reveal that much.

'And your mother?'

'Stop the interrogation, Zoe.' He heard an edge to his voice. 'I'm not one of your patients.'

Her eyes darkened but she smiled in rueful acknowledge-ment. 'Sorry. Habit, I guess.'

'I don't need therapy,' Aaron said, trying to make a joke of it even though he still felt on edge. 'And certainly not art therapy. I can't even draw stick figures.'

'That doesn't matter.' She shook her head and smiled, although he suspected it took some effort. 'I suppose I'll never make a convert of you.'

'Do you want to?'

'It would be nice if you respected what I did,' she answered, eyebrows raised, and Aaron grimaced.

'I'm afraid I'm too much of a literalist. I like firm results—tangible, quantifiable proof.'

'Life doesn't always work that way.'

He shook his head. 'Mine does.'

She stared at him, her head cocked to one side, her gaze sweeping slowly, thoughtfully over him in a way Aaron didn't like. 'And you don't feel like you're missing out on something, living like that?'

'No, I don't. I get results. Quantifiable success.'

'And healing isn't quantifiable,' Zoe surmised. 'Is it? Or happiness?'

'No, they aren't.'

She stared at him again and he felt everything inside him tense, resisting the very nature of this conversation, this *intimacy.*

'Are you happy, Aaron?'

Damn it, he did not want her to ask questions like that. He most certainly didn't want to answer them. 'What's happy?' he said, dismissive, gruff, and she smiled wryly.

'That's not an answer.'

He wasn't going to give her one. 'Are *you* happy?' he threw back, and she drew her knees to her chest, her hair brushing the tops of them, her eyes dark and soft.

'I don't know. Everything is so uncertain now. But, in general, yes. I think I've been happy. I've lived my life happily...for the most part.'

He had the strangest sensation that she was holding something back…just as he was. And he felt a stirring of uneasy guilt that she wasn't happy now, and it was his fault.

'Let me get dessert,' he said, mostly because he'd had enough of this conversation.

'Dessert?'

'I bought something. I figured you were going for the typical pregnancy cravings, so…' Quickly he went to the freezer where he'd put the bag from earlier and withdrew a pint of chocolate-chip ice cream. 'Have you had a craving for this?'

The look on her face was almost comical, Aaron thought. She looked torn, caught between regret and a smile, and he knew immediately this wasn't something she wanted.

'Don't tell me I'll have to eat this all by myself,' he said, and she gave in to the smile, whimsical and bittersweet as it was.

'I'm afraid I'm lactose intolerant. But it was a lovely thought.'

'Ah.' Lactose intolerant; right. He put the ice cream back in the freezer. 'So maybe a nice sorbet?' he suggested. He felt like a fool and a failure, which he knew was ridiculous. It was just ice-cream—and yet he'd tried. And it hadn't worked. Failure.

'Sorbet would be perfect,' Zoe said quietly, and then she was there behind him, one hand resting lightly on his shoulder. 'Thank you, Aaron,' she said softly, and for some ridiculous reason his throat tightened. He didn't answer.

It wasn't much, Zoe knew, and yet it touched her all too deeply. The hesitant confidences, the thoughtful touches… He was trying. Not very well, admittedly, but his attempts at engaging her emotionally made Zoe's heart soften and yearn. She could fall in love with this man, more than any of the men she'd convinced herself she cared for. She had a horrible feeling this could be the real deal.

And she didn't want it. She couldn't. Aaron might be try-ing, but that was all it was. Paltry attempts that she wanted to make into so much more. In the end the result would be the same: he'd break her heart. He'd crush it and he wouldn't care—or perhaps even notice.

A few days after Aaron's ice cream attempt, he came home a bit early, surprising her, and she tried to ignore the little bolt of pleasure she felt at simply seeing him walk through the door, his suit jacket hooked over one finger.

'You're home a bit early.'

'I have an invitation to a new museum opening in SoHo tomorrow night,' Aaron said. 'And I wondered if you wanted to come.'

'Oh.' She felt an unexpected burst of pleasure at the thought of a proper outing—almost a date. 'I'd love to.' She bit her lip, frowning. 'Is it fancy? I don't really have…'

'You can get something tomorrow. I'll leave you my credit card.'

Zoe arched an eyebrow, deliberately teasing him. 'You're not worried I'll go on a bender and max out your card?'

'I'm protected against such possibilities,' Aaron answered, without even a shred of humour. Zoe suppressed a sigh. Just when she thought they were getting somewhere—reaching some kind of understanding, some kind of sympathy—she felt as if she'd fallen backwards on her behind. Aaron had only offered her his credit card knowing that if she ran off with it he'd be covered. Of course.

'Well, that's a relief,' she said lightly.

'Of course, if you'd rather not shop I can have my assis-tant buy you something,' Aaron offered. He'd loosened his tie and stood at the kitchen counter, drinking a beer. If some-one could look in the window and see this scene, Zoe thought suddenly, it would seem so amazingly, achingly normal. A man and a woman chatting about their day, sharing the occasional smile or even a laugh.

Too bad the reality was so different—so much *less*. And she wanted more. Absurd, hopeless, but she could not keep herself from feeling it, craving it.

'Why don't you have your assistant pick something, then?' she said, and with effort kept her voice casual. 'I don't really like shopping.' That much was true, but she also needed to keep some kind of distance. Picking out a dress herself, knowing she'd care too much and want to please Aaron, was dangerous. If she acted like she didn't care what she wore, then maybe she wouldn't. Maybe her foolish, contrary heart would stop insisting it cared about Aaron when her head told her what an idiotic thing that would be to do.

'Fine,' he answered with a shrug. 'I'll have her pick it out and deliver it. The opening is at eight.'

When the box came the next afternoon, clearly from an exclusive and expensive boutique, Zoe couldn't keep a tremor of anticipation from going through her. She might not particularly enjoy shopping, but what woman didn't enjoy receiving new clothes? Even if they had been picked out by an indifferent secretary.

The dress wasn't indifferent, though. The dress, Zoe saw as she lifted it from the folds of tissue paper with a hushed breath, was utterly gorgeous. It was made of a silvery-grey silk that shimmered in the light, with a halter neck and a fitted bodice, before flaring out gently around the ankles.

She stripped off her jeans and T-shirt and slid the dress on, twirled around it and felt like a princess.

What would Aaron think?

Not important, she told herself. Not important at all. She was just going to enjoy herself tonight, enjoy being out and about and feeling pretty rather than something close to what the cat dragged in. And she wouldn't think about Aaron at all.

She slid the dress on a hanger and, with a smile still lingering on her lips, headed for the bath.

Several hours later she was dressed and ready. And Aaron hadn't even returned. He'd texted to say he'd be back to pick her up at a quarter to eight, but it was almost the hour and she'd had no word from him.

Sighing, Zoe stared at her reflection. At least she looked better than she had in days. She'd put her hair up in a chignon and even put on a little make-up: eye-liner to make her eyes look bigger and darker and some light blusher and lipstick.

In the box underneath the dress she'd found a pair of diamanté-encrusted stilettos, perfect to go with the dress, and amazingly in her size. She gave a twirl in front of the mirror just as she heard the lift doors ping open and Aaron come into the apartment.

Taking a deep breath, she stepped out into the hallway.

His gaze narrowed in on her right away, but he didn't say anything. Zoe held her breath, waiting—for what? A compliment? A single word of praise? Surely even Aaron could manage that much.

He tugged at his tie and gave one brusque nod. 'It fits.'

It fits? That was all? Disappointment made Zoe's throat tighten and she swallowed, made herself smile. 'Yes, it does. Your assistant must have known my size.'

Aaron didn't answer for a moment, his long, lean fingers working the silken knot of his tie. 'My assistant didn't buy it,' he finally said, sounding both gruff and reluctant.

Zoe blinked. 'She didn't?'

'No.' The knot unravelled and he slid his tie off, causing Zoe's gaze to be hopelessly drawn to the lean, brown column of his throat, the pulse she could just see flickering there as he undid the top buttons of his shirt.

'Who did, then?'

'I did,' Aaron admitted. 'I picked it out myself.'

Pleasure flooded through her in a warm rush and a silly smile spread over her face. 'You did? Why?'

'Because,' he answered, starting towards his bedroom, 'I didn't want the gossip flying, as it would if my assistant started shopping for a woman's dress. It's not my usual behaviour, and I hardly want to explain our situation just yet.'

Disappointment replaced that rush of pleasure. Of course he had a reason like that. Had she actually hoped, actually *thought* for a moment that he'd picked the dress out himself because he wanted to? What kind of fantasy land was she living in?

'Very astute of you,' she called to him, for he'd disappeared into his bedroom. 'But when do you plan on coming clean with our arrangement?' Whatever their *arrangement* actually was.

'When things are a bit more final,' Aaron answered back flatly. 'I'm just going to change. The limo's waiting downstairs.'

Zoe paced the living room while he dressed. All her anticipation about the evening, her pleasure in the dress and the shoes, seemed to have leaked right out of her, leaving her flat. And not just flat, but anxious—for what on earth did Aaron mean, when things were a bit more *final*? The decisions she'd made in moving in here felt all too final. What more was Aaron thinking of? She didn't even want to ask. She didn't want to know.

And, instead of the excitement and fragile happiness she'd been feeling at the prospect of an evening with Aaron, all she felt now was disappointment and an inexplicable, nauseating dread.

CHAPTER SIX

AARON CHANGED INTO his tuxedo with jerky movements, his body still irritatingly affected by the sight of Zoe in that dress. He'd known it was right for her as soon as he'd seen it in a shop window, imagining how the silvery fabric would bring out the shimmer in her eyes.

He'd felt a fool blundering into that shop. The sales assistant had positively cooed over him, imagining he was buying a dress for someone special.

And then when he'd actually seen Zoe in it, seen how the colour made her eyes sparkle with the brilliance of diamonds; how the silky material clung to her slender curves, the top barely covering the breasts that looked even more full and more lush than when he'd touched them, kissed them and held them in his hands...

He cursed aloud. The last thing he needed was to go into this evening in a constant and painful state of arousal. Yet he couldn't deny that since he'd been spending more time with Zoe that had been his sad state of affairs. Just sitting next to her on the sofa, or watching her slurp her ridiculous lo mein noodles, or stretch so her worn T-shirt outlined her breasts all too clearly...

Aaron cursed again.

Over the last week his mind had spun in crazy circles, thoughts darting like a rat in a maze, looking for solutions.

Always looking for solutions. Ever since that first lightning strike of guilt that had felled him after he'd offered her money, he'd been trying to figure out how this could work, what he should do. He always wanted, needed something to do—a plan, an answer. And unfortunately, in this case, he didn't have one. Yet.

Having Zoe live with him had felt like the right decision; he wanted her safe, under his watch, in his control. And, damn it, yes, he did like having her here, even if she didn't believe him and he couldn't quite believe it himself.

But what about the future? When the baby was born? They'd be a family, of sorts. A *family*. The idea was alien, impossible. His own fractured family, with parents long dead and brothers he barely talked to, was hardly an example he wanted to follow. He didn't want to be the kind of dad who breezed in and out of his child's life, gone more often than not.

Yet he didn't know what kind of father he could be, what kind of man he could be. What kind of husband.

He'd been moving carefully, reluctantly, yet with a surprising surge of anticipation towards what seemed like the obvious decision, the most permanent arrangement for him and Zoe. It had come to him in stages: first asking Zoe to stay for a few weeks, then for her entire pregnancy. And now...?

His mouth curved grimly. It wasn't ideal, of course, even if it had some rather obvious and salient benefits. But it was the solution that had presented itself, that seemed the most reasonable—and yet outrageous. Impossible, even.

By the time he emerged from the bedroom Zoe was looking a bit pale and strained, the obvious pleasure which had lit her eyes damped down completely—his effect on her, no doubt. He should have said something else, something about how beautiful she'd looked, yet the words had stuck in his throat, sharp and painful. Grimly Aaron jerked his head towards the door.

'Let's go. The car's waiting.'

'I know, you said that already,' she answered back tartly, and Aaron didn't respond. Bickering like an old couple already, he thought sourly, without so much as a shred of humour.

Neither of them spoke in the limo on the way down to SoHo. Zoe stared determinedly out of the window, and the passing streetlights highlighted the sweep of her cheek, the angle of her jaw. Aaron watched her out of the corner of his eye—was conscious of every breath she drew, the way her breasts rose and fell, the tiny sigh of exhalation. He turned away and stared out the other window.

'So what kind of art are we going to go and see?' she finally asked, after the tense silence had gone on for several minutes.

'I don't know. Something modern.'

'Why are you going, then?' Zoe asked. She sounded petulant, even childish. This evening was going downhill fast.

'Several of my clients will be there.'

'Clients? What is it you do, exactly?'

'I'm the CEO of Bryant Enterprises.'

'I know that. But what does that mean?'

It means I live on a knife-edge; I wake up at night in a cold sweat; I devote my entire life to a job I never really wanted. The sudden virulence of his thoughts shocked him. Swallowing, he turned back to the window. 'I manage the company's assets, which are varied. But my main personal responsibility is our hedge fund.'

'That's what Millie does—hedge funds. Although I'm not even sure what they are.'

'Essentially an investment fund with a wider range of trading activities than other funds.'

'Still not sure what you're talking about,' Zoe said airily, and Aaron almost smiled. He actually liked that she didn't get it. He didn't really want to explain it, or even talk about it.

'Hedge-fund managers usually invest some of their own money,' he told her. 'And the funds are not sold to the public or retail investors.'

'So you're managing your own money, as well as someone else's?'

'Essentially.'

She turned to face him, her expression strangely serious and intent in the darkness of the car. 'Do you like it?' she asked. 'Do you enjoy what you do?'

Aaron stared back at her, words lodging in his throat, choking him. 'I make money,' he finally said.

'So?'

'It's what I do,' he answered, and made his tone dismissive, even curt. 'It's what I've always done, what my family has always done.' There were no other choices.

Zoe felt her spirits lift as soon as they entered the gallery. It was all soaring space and clean angles, huge, messy canvases hanging on the otherwise stark walls. Women in elegant dresses and men in tuxedoes circulated the space amidst black-tied waiters with trays of champagne and fussy-looking hors d'oeuvres.

'I know you're not keen on modern art,' Aaron murmured as they came through the door, and Zoe arched an eyebrow.

'Who said I didn't like modern art?'

'You did say my apartment was awful,' Aaron reminded her. 'And it's rather modern.'

'True, but there are different kinds of modern. My paintings are modern, in their own way. These—' she gestured to the bright canvases on the walls '—are colourful, lively. I like them,' she stated firmly and Aaron gave the nearest painting his consideration.

'I'm not sure what it's supposed to be.'

Zoe studied it, as well. 'From a distance it looks like some kind of festival,' she said slowly. She couldn't point to any distinct figures or shapes, yet she got the sense of it—of people with arms outstretched or raised, of firelight and dancing, of joy and celebration.

Aaron nodded slowly. 'Yes…I suppose,' he said, and Zoe laughed at how dubious he sounded.

'Not a fan?' she teased. 'And with all that modern art in your apartment!'

'I never said I liked it. I certainly didn't choose it.'

'Why have it if you don't like it?'

He shrugged. 'An interior decorator chose it all, for effect and re-sale value. I spend very little time there as it is.'

'And yet I spend a lot of time there,' Zoe replied tartly. 'Maybe I should redecorate.' She saw the expression on Aaron's face freeze and she rolled her eyes. 'Chill, Aaron. I was joking. I'll stick with my few paintings and my plant. That's enough for you, clearly.'

'You can redecorate if you want,' he said stiffly. 'Since you'll be living there for at least seven months.'

At least. Because what happened after the baby was born? Zoe pushed the thought away. 'I want to study the painting,' she said, and moved closer.

Funnily enough, the closer she got to the painting the less of a sense of it she had. The festive feeling melted into blobs and streaks of oil paint, nothing more. After inspecting a few more paintings in the gallery, she realised this was the artist's intended effect: the paintings were meant to be viewed from a distance, rather than up close.

Kind of like her and Aaron. From a distance, they looked okay. Like a couple. She'd seen a few women shoot her speculative and even envious looks, and part of her had wanted to laugh, even while another part of couldn't help but preen.

Yes, I'm with him, the most handsome and enigmatic man in the room.

Except she wasn't with him, not really. Not at all.

She watched him covertly from across the room, talking to a few of his clients. He looked intent and serious and still so unbearably attractive, with his dark hair and eyes, his stern mouth, his broad shoulders. He was devastating in a tuxedo.

As if he sensed her looking at him, he glanced up and his steely gaze locked with hers for a moment, his expression utterly unreadable, and then he looked away. Zoe felt herself deflate. What had she been hoping for—a smile? A wink? Neither, unfortunately, were Aaron's style, and yet her stupid heart kept insisting on hoping.

By half past ten her feet were killing her—as gorgeous as the stilettos were, comfort was clearly not their concern—and she was nearly swaying with exhaustion.

Aaron approached her, one hand sliding firmly under her elbow. 'You look like you're about to fall over.'

'I feel like it too,' Zoe admitted with a small smile that ended on a tired sigh.

'Let me take you home.'

Home. She thought of that stark penthouse apartment where she'd already spent so many lonely days and nights. Was that home now? Would it ever be home?

Still, it was rather nice to have Aaron acting a little protective of her as he guided her from the gallery to his waiting car.

'How does your driver never get a parking ticket?' she asked as she slid inside. 'He's always double-parked.'

'He's very good,' Aaron answered. 'And he's not double-parked for long—I text him right before I need him to arrive.'

'A good use for your phone,' she said rather sleepily, for in the warm interior of the car, the leather so soft and luxurious, she felt as if she could almost fall right asleep.

'Come here,' Aaron said almost roughly, and he put his

arm around her shoulders, pulling her to him. She nestled against him instinctively, her head on his shoulder, her body snuggled against his muscular side. It felt so good to be held; to breathe in the warm, musky male scent of him; to feel the solid strength of his arm around her, drawing her close, protecting and even cherishing her.

'Thank you,' she murmured, her eyes drifting closed. 'For taking me to the gallery. I enjoyed it.'

'Did you?' Aaron sounded as gruff as always, but underneath Zoe thought she heard a thread of amusement, maybe even tenderness. Or was she just being fanciful—again? Probably. 'The last twenty minutes you looked like you were in agony.'

'These shoes hurt,' she admitted and wiggled them off, stretching her toes with a sigh of bliss.

'Ah. Sorry about that.'

'Did you pick the shoes out too?'

'The shop assistant suggested them to me.'

'Well, I love them, no matter how much they pinch.'

'I didn't mean to make your feet hurt.' She felt Aaron's hand slide down her calf and then his strong fingers were kneading the aching muscles of her feet and Zoe couldn't keep from letting out a groan of sheer pleasure. Aaron chuckled softly. 'Feels good?'

'Heaven.' She nestled closer and neither of them spoke as Aaron massaged her feet. Zoe fell into a doze, happier than she'd been in a long while.

She didn't know how long it had been when Aaron was gently nudging her awake. 'We're here,' he said quietly. 'Can you make it upstairs?'

'Yes, of course.' She straightened, embarrassed now at how she'd been cuddling into him. 'I can hardly have you carry me into your building.'

'I could,' he said, and she found herself smiling.

'I'm sure you're strong enough. But, if you thought having your assistant buy a dress would bring on the gossip, sweeping me into your building Rhett Butler style would be much worse.'

'That doesn't matter,' he said abruptly and she wished she hadn't said anything—wished she'd let that surprising tenderness they'd found inside the limo stretch on. Now she just slipped her feet into the pinching heels.

The crisp night air was enough to wake her up completely, and by the time they reached the lift Zoe was conscious of something palpable between them, something confused and yet electric, caught between the intimacy of their moments in the car and the tension that always seemed to spring up between them.

She was achingly aware too of the last time she'd been in a formal dress and Aaron had worn formal clothes. They'd rode the lift up in silence just like they were doing now, and she'd walked into his apartment and stared out at the night sky while he kissed her neck…

Was he remembering that night? Was he feeling it, wanting it like she was? Or was that just her hopeless fantasy?

She cleared her throat, the sound as loud as a gunshot in the confined space of the lift. The doors swooshed open and Zoe stepped into the penthouse, wanting to escape the confines of the lift and the expectations and memories that left her breathless and desperate with need.

The stiletto heel of her shoe caught in the gap between the lift and the floor, and she pitched forward with a sudden, indrawn gasp. Then Aaron's arms were around her, righting her, hauling her to safety against his chest.

She stared up at him, dazed, even more breathless than before, and he looked back down at her without any expression at all lighting his dark eyes.

'That was a close one,' he said, and he didn't let her go.

Zoe could feel one hand on her bare shoulder, the other seeming to burn right through the thin silk of the dress, on the small of her back. She felt the press of his body against hers, the strength of his thigh and chest, and then, amazingly—yes, wonderfully—the insistent press of his arousal.

Her lips parted and her breath came out in a soft, expectant rush; still she didn't move and neither did he. She felt his hand pressing into her back, urging her forward, and as her hips bumped against him his awareness flared white-hot, consuming her.

She knew they couldn't have sex. She didn't want to endanger her pregnancy, and she knew Aaron wouldn't take that risk either. Yet the need between them was palpable, overwhelming. Aaron's hand slid from her shoulder along her bare arm, the touch of his fingers seeming to dust her with sparks. He dipped his head lower and Zoe's own fell back, her lips parted and waiting for his kiss, every nerve inside her buzzing and humming.

'Zoe…' Her name was the softest of sighs and she felt his thumb brush her lower lip. She let out a tiny sound of want, halfway between a mewl and a moan.

With a shuddering breath, Aaron stepped away. 'You should go to bed.'

She felt as if he'd doused her with ice-water but somehow Zoe managed to nod, disappointment, a little relief and a terrible, aching unfulfillment all warring within her. 'Yes, I should.'

Aaron turned away, raking his hands through his hair before yanking off his tie. Zoe watched him, knowing he had to be as sexually frustrated as she was. She didn't want the evening to end here. She didn't want to go to bed alone. She swallowed, her throat dry, her heart beating hard.

'Aaron…'

'What?' His back was still to her, every taut line of his beautiful body radiating tension.

She shouldn't want this. Definitely shouldn't ask for it. Yet something—some great, deep need that had opened up inside her—compelled her to continue, to say aloud what she so desperately craved. 'Would you…sleep with me tonight? I mean just sleep. In the same bed.'

Aaron stilled, said nothing. Zoe felt herself flush, her insides seeming to hollow out. Then he slowly turned around; in the moonlit darkness she couldn't make out his expression. Not that she would have been able to, anyway.

'What for?'

What for? Did she really have to spell it out? Apparently. 'For company. And closeness. And because…' She swallowed, her voice dropping to a ragged whisper. 'I'm lonely.'

He stared at her for a long moment. 'I always sleep alone.'

'You slept with me that night—that other night.' She licked her lips, her mouth so dry she felt as if she'd swallowed dust. She hated that she was trying to argue him into it.

'That was—an aberration.'

Small concession as that was, it gratified her. With her, he was different. He could be different. 'And so? Tonight can be an aberration, too.'

He shook his head slowly. 'Everything between us has been an aberration, Zoe.'

That didn't sound good, even as she recognised it for truth. Nothing between them had been normal, not even this. 'So what are you saying?' Her voice was small when she wanted it to be strident. 'Is that a no?'

'I…' He shook his head. 'I don't know what it is. I'm not—I'm not good at this.'

'Good at what?'

He gestured between the two of them with one impatient hand. *'This.'*

Everything, she supposed. Conversation. Closeness. A relationship. All the things she wanted, even if she knew she shouldn't. He glared at her, yet underneath the anger in his eyes she saw fear, and it made her heart contract.

'I'm not so good at it, either,' she said quietly.

He let out a huff of disbelieving laughter. 'Really.'

'Really.' She took a deep breath. 'What scares you more, Aaron—that you don't know how or that you want to?'

'*Want* to?'

'Do you want to?' She stepped closer, gazing at him with all the honesty, hope and fear she felt. The words spilled out of her, needing to be spoken even though it might be the stupidest and most dangerous thing she'd ever said or done. 'Do you want something between us? I'm not saying I even know what it is.' She laid one hand on his arm and felt the muscles jump underneath her light touch. 'I'm not pushing for some—some kind of a relationship.'

'A relationship,' Aaron repeated tonelessly.

'But I feel something for you. And I think you feel something for me.' Zoe held her breath. Had she just ruined everything? Pushed too hard…again? Yet already she felt more for Aaron than she'd ever expected to, and it felt *real*. Not like the times before, when she'd forced a relationship because she'd been so desperate to prove she was lovable, that she wouldn't be rejected like before, and then of course she had been.

Except maybe she was still living in that fantasy world, because Aaron didn't say anything. He just stared at her, the darkness in his eyes and the grim set of his mouth making Zoe pretty sure he did not like having this conversation.

'I don't know what I feel,' he finally said, and Zoe felt incredulous hope unfurl inside her, start to bloom. It wasn't much of an admission, yet for a man like Aaron she knew it was huge. This was startling—and scary. It was new territory for him—and he was admitting it.

'That's okay,' she said, and squeezed his arm.

Aaron shook his head. 'I can't give you the things you want, Zoe.'

'How do you know what I want?'

'I could guess.'

'So what are you saying you can't give me?' She tried to stay light, but her heart was pounding. Already this conversation was out of both of their depths.

'I'm jumping ahead,' he said with another impatient shake of his head. 'This wasn't how I wanted to go about it.'

Now she really felt lost at sea, flailing with incomprehension. 'Go about what?'

Aaron took a deep breath and let it out in a shuddering, resolute sigh. 'Asking you to marry me.'

CHAPTER SEVEN

THE WORDS SEEMED to reverberate in the room between them, and vaguely Zoe realised this was the third time he'd shocked her with a suggestion—and this was the most shocking at all.

'You're joking,' she said, feebly, for of course he wasn't. Aaron didn't joke, and in any case the look on his face said enough. He looked like a man resolutely facing execution, which was not exactly the appearance one hoped for during a marriage proposal.

'You don't have to answer now,' he said steadily. 'Obviously, you need to think about it. But I've been considering what the best option is going forward—for us and for this child.'

'And you think it's *marriage*?'

His face hardened into implacable lines. 'Yes.'

Zoe shook her head, everything in her a jumble of mismatched feelings. She could not begin to sort out how she felt. 'But Aaron…'

'Like I said, you don't have to answer now. I probably shouldn't have brought it up, but it's been on my mind. Sleep on it.'

Protestations tumbled from her lips, her mind still whirling. 'But we don't even know if this pregnancy is truly viable yet.'

Aaron nodded, his gaze steady on her. He didn't seem remotely ruffled. 'And we don't have to get married tomorrow. We have time. Time to think.'

'You seem to have made up your mind,' Zoe observed numbly.

'Yes, but I realise it might be different for you.'

'Different?' Curiosity flared within her. 'How?'

He lifted one shoulder in a shrug. 'It's different for women.'

'That's a stereotype if I've ever heard one.'

He raised his eyebrows, a faint, sardonic smile curling his mouth. 'Are we really going to argue about this now?'

'You brought it up,' Zoe retorted, then closed her eyes and shook her head. 'I'm sorry. I'm shocked. I feel like you jumped a mile ahead of me.' To think a few moments ago she'd been nervous she was pushing too hard when all she'd said was she felt something for him. He'd responded with a marriage proposal.

But not with a declaration of love. Now she was clearly the one jumping ahead because obviously, *obviously,* Aaron was only talking about some kind of bizarre business arrangement.

'I'm sorry for springing it on you at this unfortunate hour,' he said tiredly. 'We can talk about it in the morning, when we're both a bit more rested.'

'That sounds like a good idea,' Zoe said shakily, and on leaden legs she headed for her bedroom. Aaron stopped her with a word.

'Wait.' She turned around, expectant, wary. 'I thought you were sleeping with me.' His eyes were dark, fathomless, intense. Zoe felt her heart beat hard.

'But I thought—' She stopped, for he simply held out his hand and after a second's uncertain pause she took it.

Lying in bed with him, with his arms tucked securely around her middle, his chin resting on her shoulder, should have felt strange. New, at least. Yet as she fit her body against him and felt his tension slowly start to ease Zoe knew it only felt right. Like coming home, which was ridiculous, yet she could not keep herself from feeling it. From wanting this and even more.

If she and Aaron married, every night could be like this. Unless, of course, he'd meant some kind of temporary marriage…until their child was a certain age? Or maybe just a cold-blooded business arrangement, which certainly seemed his style, to give their child the security of his name? Not a real marriage—a marriage that involved sharing and commitment and love, the kind of marriage she still wanted and had been searching for, even if she wasn't quite sure she believed in it anymore.

She had no answers, yet the fact that she was even asking the questions made her realise she was seriously considering Aaron's proposal. She hadn't said no out of hand. She hadn't even thought it…which was a terrifying thought in itself.

Some time near dawn she must have drifted into an uneasy doze, for when she awoke Aaron wasn't in the bed and she could hear the shower running. She sat up, pushing tangles of hair from her eyes as she heard the shower turn off. Aaron came into the room with only a towel slung low on his hips.

'Good morning.' He gave her a rather brusque nod before reaching for his clothes. The towel dropped, and Zoe's mouth dried as she took in Aaron's naked body; his back was to her, so she could observe and admire the taut, muscular lines of his back and thighs. He was perfectly proportioned and unaccountably built.

'Did you sleep well?' he asked, no more than solicitous, and Zoe yanked her gaze away from her perusal of his butt.

'Not really. Did you?'

He turned around, now clad in boxers, and gave her a surprisingly wry smile. She loved his smiles, rare as they were. They transformed his face, his whole self. They made her realise there was more to this man than taciturn author-ity. 'Actually, I did. Better than I have in ages. I suffer from insomnia.'

She smiled back. 'Maybe you should try sleeping with someone more often.'

His gaze blazed briefly into hers before he turned away. 'Maybe I will.'

Zoe slid out of the bed and went for her own shower. By the time she emerged Aaron was in the kitchen, dressed in a business suit and slicing strawberries for their breakfast.

Zoe hesitated in the doorway of her bedroom as she watched him, his movement so precise, a faint frown of con-centration settled between his brows. He did everything so seriously, as if it was a hugely important matter, even cut-ting up some fruit. She realised then that he never would have asked her to marry him lightly.

He must have thought about every angle, every possibil-ity. He'd had every answer. She walked forward with a smile on her face and Aaron turned.

'Hungry?'

'Yes. I'm always hungry in the mornings. And eating helps the nausea.' She slid onto a stool by the breakfast bar and plucked a strawberry from the bowl. 'You're usually at work by now.'

'I need to leave in a few minutes, but I thought we should talk.'

She nodded, eyeing the lines of strain from nose to mouth that never seemed to leave him. 'You work too hard, you know.'

'Not hard enough.' He spoke matter-of-factly, and Zoe stared at him incredulously.

'How can it not be hard enough? You're a millionaire, Aaron. Or is it a billionaire?' She shook her head. 'What more do you want?'

His mouth thinned as he put the rest of the sliced fruit in the bowl. 'It's not important.'

'Not important? If I'm going to marry you, don't you think I should know the answers to these questions?'

He glanced up, his gaze hooded, blazing and swift. 'So are you going to marry me?'

The breath bottled in her lungs and she held his gaze, shaking her head slowly. 'I don't know.'

'But you're thinking about it.'

'Yes,' she admitted. 'How can I not?'

'You could have dismissed it out of hand.'

Zoe felt a blush heat her cheeks. Yes, she could have—should have, probably. What sane woman even thought about marrying a man she barely knew? Wasn't always sure she liked? And when she was, unfortunately, quite positive that he didn't love her?

And yet… They shared something. She'd felt it last night, when she'd told him as much and seen the confusion in his eyes. She'd felt it when she'd lain in his arms and known there was absolutely no other place she would rather be. She felt it now…even as her brain was screaming at her to stop, not to leap into a relationship—a *marriage*—that would surely hurt her in the end.

Yet still she considered it. *Hoped.*

Typical Zoe, her sister would say, leaping ahead to a fairy-tale ending after the first date. Except this time Aaron had beaten her to it.

Except she didn't think he was envisioning fairy tales.

'I could have dismissed it,' she answered, willing her blush to fade. 'Perhaps I should. After all, this is the twenty-first century. Most people wouldn't bat an eyelid at a child with unmarried parents.'

'No,' Aaron agreed tonelessly. 'They probably wouldn't.'

'So why do you think it's a good idea?' Zoe dared to ask. 'You have to admit, it's a pretty big leap.'

'Marriage is always a pretty big leap.'

He had a pat answer for everything, but he wasn't really telling her much. Telling her the truth. 'But most people who get married have dated. Known each other.' She swallowed, forced herself to continue. 'Love each other.'

Aaron's expression didn't change. The man was like a stone, Zoe thought. 'Most people,' he agreed.

'What are you, Switzerland?' She rolled her eyes. 'Stop being so damn neutral. This isn't some negotiation.'

'Yes,' he answered. 'It is.'

Zoe leaned forward. 'Tell me the real reason, Aaron, why you want to marry me.' She saw Aaron still and his face go even blanker, if that were possible. She knew she shouldn't have said that. Shouldn't have made it about her, because it so obviously, painfully, wasn't. 'I mean,' she clarified quietly, 'Why you think marriage is the right choice in our—situation.' Now she was talking like him. Situations and solutions. So unemotional, so heartless.

Aaron didn't answer for a long moment; he seemed to be considering his words carefully. 'Because anything else is just making the best of things.'

'Isn't that what we're doing? What we should be doing?'

He shook his head. 'What's the alternative, really, Zoe? Coming to some awkward custody arrangement, where I'll get to see our child every other weekend, maybe a Wednesday evening?'

'That sounds like an ideal situation for you,' Zoe couldn't keep from replying. 'An ideal *solution*. You get to be a dad, but it doesn't impinge on your lifestyle. Your work.'

He gazed at her, giving nothing away. 'You think that's what I want?'

'It's certainly what you have seemed to want,' Zoe answered evenly. 'You've never acted like you're thrilled about this, Aaron, or like you're dying to change nappies.'

He didn't reply, just turned to pour coffee into a thick ceramic mug. 'You're off coffee, aren't you?' he asked her, his back to her, and stupidly it touched her that he'd noticed.

'I'll have tea.'

He reached for tea bags, still not answering her accusations, for that was what it felt like—like she'd lobbed a few grenades right into the kitchen. And yet she knew it was true; Aaron had never acted like he was happy about this. About her. And she wanted him to be.

'Just because I didn't choose something doesn't mean I won't do what's right,' he finally said, handing her a mug of tea. 'Trust me on that.' There was something so grim about his tone that Zoe felt as if he must be speaking from experience, although she had no idea what it could be.

'I don't want you to marry me because you think it's right,' she said, stung by the implication. 'I don't want anyone to marry me for that reason. I want to marry—'

'For love,' he finished flatly. 'I figured.'

She let out a short laugh. 'Don't sound so disgusted.'

'I'm not disgusted. Resigned, perhaps.'

'To what?'

'To the fact that you would resist because of this. Because I don't love you.'

Ouch. She blinked, willing herself not to react. Not to feel the hurt that still rushed through her like water through a burst dam. Of *course* he didn't love her. It would have been ridiculous and frankly unbelievable if he had said he had. Wasn't she glad he could be honest, at least?

She stirred her tea, staring down into its fragrant depths. 'And it doesn't bother you? The whole love thing, or lack of it?' she asked, her gaze still fixed firmly on her tea.

'No.'

Of course he didn't offer any more explanations. Getting personal information from this man was like getting blood from a stone. 'Why not?'

A shrug, a sip of coffee. 'It's not something I've ever counted on.'

'*Love?* But you must have some love in your life, Aaron. I mean, if not a woman, then your family. Your brothers.' He stared at her without expression and, exasperated, Zoe continued, 'All right—your mother, then.'

'My mother lived her life in a state of intense depression and died when I was fifteen.' He took a sip of coffee and glanced away. 'Besides, Luke was her favourite.'

It was more personal information than he'd ever offered before, and she had a feeling he regretted revealing it. 'I'm sorry,' she said quietly. 'I didn't know.'

'Why should you?'

'Is that why—why you're not interested in a loving relationship now?'

'This is not a discussion I'm interested in having,' he answered flatly. 'Next you'll be getting out the crayons and asking me to draw a picture of my feelings. Don't psychoanalyse me, Zoe, and don't hope that somehow I'll change. I suggested marriage, but I won't pretend I love you, or that I'll ever love you.'

'Ever?' she repeated, trying to make light of it rather than burst into tears, which was what at least part of her felt like doing. 'What, are you incapable?'

'Perhaps.'

'You don't even want to give it a chance?'

'No.'

No hope, then. She swallowed, nausea roiling inside her that had nothing to do with morning sickness. 'So what kind of marriage are you talking about, then?'

'A partnership. Maybe even a friendship.'

'*Maybe?*'

'I don't really do friendship. But I can try.'

'You don't *do friendship*?'

He shrugged. 'I don't have friends. I never have.'

She blinked, shocked by his admission even though part of her wasn't really surprised. 'What a lonely life you've led, Aaron.'

'You're only lonely if you feel lonely.'

'And have you felt lonely?'

He stared at her without blinking for a long moment. 'I don't know,' he finally said, and she knew it was a confession, more of one than he'd wanted to make.

'So what do you envision this marriage looking like? On, you know, a daily basis?'

He shrugged. 'I have no idea. Something the way it looks now, I suppose.'

With him working sixteen-hour days and her wandering around the apartment when she wasn't at work. Except, of course, it would be different, because she would have a child. And a life; she wouldn't be in this awful limbo, waiting for something to happen.

Except, Zoe thought with cringing insight, she would be. She would be in an even worse, endless limbo, waiting for him to love her. Even if he'd just told her he wouldn't, ever; Zoe knew that herself. Knew she would keep wishing for it, trying to make it happen, and living on the thin vapour of hope until she had nothing left.

Was that what she wanted with her life? Could she even survive it?

'Obviously,' Aaron said dryly, 'That doesn't sound very appealing to you.'

Zoe forced a smile. 'Did my face give it away?'

'Pretty much. You looked horrified. Still do.'

She let out a weary sigh. 'Love is kind of a big thing, Aaron, to give up forever.'

'I know that. And I understand that a marriage between us will involve a sacrifice on your part.'

'And yours too, I imagine.' He might live a lonely life, but he still was a player, enjoyed affairs, flings. Although he hadn't actually *said* he would give those up…or if this partnership would be in name only and not in the bedroom.

'It's not the same for me,' he answered with a shrug. 'I'm not giving up on a dream.'

Zoe swallowed past the tightness in her throat. 'That is how it feels,' she admitted. 'And yet maybe that's all it ever was, ever will be—a dream.'

'Do you really believe that?'

'I don't know. I haven't found the fairy tale yet and I'm thirty-one, so…' She shrugged, spreading her hands. 'Maybe this is as good as it gets. My best offer.'

Aaron gazed at her steadily. 'Only you can decide that.'

'Well, thank you for that,' she said a bit tartly. 'At least you're not trying to emotionally blackmail me into doing the right thing for the baby.'

'I want you to be sure. This would be a permanent arrangement, Zoe. I won't sanction a divorce a couple of years down the road.'

'Too bad New York is a no-fault state,' she answered flippantly, and Aaron reached out and curled one hand around her wrist.

'Don't joke,' he said in a low voice. 'It's true I couldn't keep you from divorcing me if you really wanted to, but I could make it hellish for you.'

A chill entered her soul; this was an Aaron she hadn't seen before, at least not since their first encounter over the stupid phone. This Aaron was cold, calculating, even cruel. This was the Aaron she'd wondered at when they'd first met, the Aaron that had given her a faint frisson of fear. Now she felt it in full.

She yanked her arm away from him. 'Nice way to threaten me.'

'Just stating facts.'

'And is this supposed to help me decide in your favour?' she snapped, still unsettled by the low, deadly note she'd heard in his voice, seen in his eyes.

'It is what it is.'

'What if you want to divorce?' she threw at him and he barely blinked.

'Won't happen.'

'You can't say that.'

'Yes,' he answered. 'I can.'

Zoe let out a breath. 'Were your parents divorced?'

'No, but they probably should have been.'

She let out a sudden, wild laugh. 'A funny thing for you to say, considering how against it you obviously are.'

He shrugged. 'If you can't keep your vows, you shouldn't get married.'

Who in his parents' marriage hadn't kept their vows? she wondered. His father? Was that the cause of his mother's depression? She swallowed, forcing herself to ask the next question. 'So you would keep your vows?'

His nostrils flared, his eyes narrowing. 'Of course.' She'd offended him even by asking the question, she realised.

'You've been with a lot of women,' she pointed out. 'I can understand why you might be reluctant to give that up.'

'But I would.'

He hadn't denied that he was reluctant, she noticed. She glanced down at her tea once more. 'So this marriage—it would be real? I mean, consummated?'

'I don't think we have a problem in that area.' She looked up to see him smiling faintly, and she gave a rather silly smile back. Memories of that night tumbled through her mind again, not just the pleasure and excitement but the sudden intimacy of that moment when he'd driven inside her, looked in her eyes and she'd felt…

Complete.

'No,' she agreed. 'I don't suppose we do.'

They didn't speak for a moment, and in that silence Zoe felt her cheeks heat as memories flashed yet again through her mind, an incredibly vivid montage. She imagined that Aaron knew exactly what she was thinking, and with a thrill she wondered if he were thinking it too.

He turned away, setting his coffee mug down with a decisive clink. 'I need to get to work. Obviously, you'll have to think about it some more.'

'Yes.' She still had a thousand questions, questions that bubbled up inside her in an unholy ferment and other questions she didn't even know how to ask. So much uncertainty, unknowing…

'I'll see you tonight,' Aaron said. She watched as he reached for his blazer and briefcase, and then he was gone.

She spent the morning pacing the apartment, her mind buzzing, and then when she couldn't stand it anymore she went outside and walked through Riverside Park, ending up in a playground right on the Hudson. She sat on a bench in the drowsy early-autumn sunshine and listened to the creak of the swings and the squeak of the slide, watched toddlers with chubby fists chase butterflies and beg for ice cream from the stand by the gate. She tried to imagine herself in this same place in a year or two, with her round-faced child toddling along, and perhaps Aaron too, sitting next to her, smiling at the antics of their son or daughter.

She felt a smile bloom across her face as she pictured the scene, the three of them a family, a child drawing them together in ways she could only barely imagine. She wanted that. She wanted to belong to someone, to feel a part of something bigger than herself. She wanted to scoop a child up in her arms and tickle his tummy. She wanted to lift her head and share a knowing smile with that child's father: *Aaron.*

She wanted it to be reality—and yet, without love, would it be enough?

She was so tempted to say yes to Aaron's offer, even as another part of her acknowledged just how much she'd be giving up.

And yet perhaps she'd given up on it already... Four failed relationships, four men who had walked away from her without a backward glance, one of them who had utterly broken her. Did she really want to keep trying? Maybe if she made herself accept Aaron's lack of love it wouldn't bother her so much. She'd stop trying to find the fairy tale and settle for reality instead. A good reality. Dreams might not be the best foundation for a marriage, and at least she knew he would be faithful, committed...

Sighing, she rose from the bench. She knew this was not a decision she could make on her own. She needed to talk to Millie.

She called her from her mobile as she walked back to the apartment. Her sister answered on the first ring, her voice sharp with worry.

'Zoe? Where have you been? I haven't heard from you in over a week.'

'Oh.' Zoe sank onto a park bench and closed her eyes. 'Sorry about that. I should have told you...'

'Told me what? Where are you? What's happened, Zoe?' Millie's voice rose with each question. 'Are you in trouble?'

'No.' Zoe opened her eyes. 'Why do you think I am?'

'I—I don't.' Her sister sounded surprised, even guarded. 'But disappearing without telling me is kind of worrisome.'

'I'm living with someone.' This was not, Zoe reflected,

how she wanted to begin this conversation. She should have been up front with Millie from the beginning, she supposed; her news was now going to come as an almighty shock.

'Living with someone? But you weren't even dating someone at my wedding not so long ago!'

'I know.' *And I'm not dating someone now.* Even if she was contemplating getting married. 'It's…complicated.'

Millie let out a weary sigh. 'It always is, with you, sweetie.'

Zoe knew she shouldn't feel stung. She joked about her nightmarish love life all the time; when Millie had been in deepest grief, hearing about some of Zoe's dating disasters had been the only thing to make her smile. Yet now, with everything so uncertain and raw, Zoe did feel that sharp needling of hurt at Millie's assumptions—and she knew more was to come.

'So tell me,' Millie prompted. 'Who is this guy?'

Which part to say first? The pregnancy or the father? 'It's Aaron.'

'Aaron? Aaron who?'

Zoe almost laughed. 'Aaron Bryant, your brother-in-law.'

'What?' The word came out of Millie like an explosion. *'Him?* Zoe, he's such a—such a jerk!'

'Nice way to talk about family, Mills.'

'But you've met him! You've seen how he behaves. He's barely had the time of day for Chase or Luke for their entire lives.'

'He lives with a lot of pressure.' Zoe spoke instinctively, knowing it was true. She'd seen it in the taut lines of Aaron's face, the set of his shoulders and the shadows in his eyes. And, while she didn't know what the source of the strain was between Aaron and his brothers, she couldn't help but defend him.

'He's so not your type,' Millie said helplessly, and Zoe almost smiled.

'My type hasn't been a runaway success before.'

'Your type,' her sister answered tartly, 'has always been a guy who screws with you. Don't do it again, Zoe. Aaron will break your heart and he won't even care.'

She blinked at this blatant truth. 'He would care,' she said softly. But he would still do it.

Millie was silent and Zoe could almost hear her sister's mind spinning. 'When did this happen?'

'The night of your wedding, actually.'

'The night—? You mean—?'

'I'm pregnant, Millie.'

Another long silence, and this one was awful. Zoe wondered if Millie was thinking about her own daughter. 'I'm sorry,' she finally said and Zoe stiffened.

'I'm not. I want to have this baby.'

'You do? But—'

'But what?'

'Well, I'm surprised,' Millie said carefully. 'Your life isn't exactly—'

'That's just what Aaron said.'

'So you've told Aaron that you're pregnant?'

Zoe blew out a breath. 'Well, since I'm living with him, yes.'

'Why *are* you living with him? I mean, he doesn't seem the kind to—'

'He asked me.'

'Really.' Millie sounded completely disbelieving and, even though Zoe knew her sister's scepticism was certainly warranted, she still felt a stab of irritation. Was it so hard to believe that Aaron might want to be with her? That something between them could actually work?

'He wants to be involved,' she said stiffly. 'As a father.'

'Okay.' Millie was silent again, clearly processing this.

'You know we'll help you, Zoe—Chase and I. You don't have to rely on Aaron. I mean, if you need money or whatever.'

'I don't need money.' Zoe swallowed. This conversation was going all wrong. She felt wrong, like Millie was ruining something she hadn't even realised was precious. 'Actually, Aaron's asked me to marry him.'

Millie said nothing, which somehow was worse than if she'd exploded again. 'Millie?' she finally asked. 'Aren't you going to say something?'

'I don't know what to say.'

'You sound like Mum.'

'Sorry.' Millie let out a sigh. 'I mean, marriage—and you barely know him.'

'How long did you know Chase before you realised you loved him?' Zoe retorted. She knew it had been less than a week. She and Aaron had more history than that now.

'That's different,' Millie protested. 'That was Chase. And this is Aaron.'

'So? They're both Bryants.'

'Yes, but Chase is— Well, he's a good person, Zoe. He's funny and charming and I knew right from the beginning that he would never want to hurt me.'

'Well, guess what?' Zoe answered, and heard her voice shake. 'I know that, too. Aaron doesn't want to hurt me, Millie. He wants to do the right thing. Desperately.'

'I'm sorry. I know I must sound terribly judgemental—'

'Yes. You do.'

Millie sighed again. 'I just don't want to see you hurt, Zoe. I love you, and I've seen too many guys put you through the wringer. Guys with a lot less money, power and arrogance than Aaron Bryant.'

'I'm not going to get hurt this time.' Zoe knew she was speaking with more conviction than she truly felt. 'I'm walking into this with my eyes open.'

'What do you mean? Does he—does he love you?'

And there was the hollow heart of it, Zoe thought, the bitter root. 'No.'

'So why—?'

'It's best for the baby.'

'And you believe that? When you know we'll help you—Mum and Dad too?'

'I don't want to be my family's charity case,' Zoe said quietly. 'But that's not why I'm thinking of marrying him. I want my own life, Millie. My own family. I've spent the last ten years chasing the rainbow and I'm starting to believe it doesn't exist.'

'It *does,* Zoe.'

'For you, maybe. But, knowing the way I am, the way I always insist on falling in love with the wrong guy, maybe it's better to have a relationship where that isn't even an option.'

'But how do you know that's how it will be?' Millie asked in a low voice. 'How do you know you won't fall in love with him?'

'I'll just have to keep myself from it,' Zoe answered, and she knew her sister heard the aching bleakness in her voice.

She was still mulling over the question when she went to her session at the community centre. She had Robert again today. Over the last few weeks he'd made a little progress, and had opened up a bit about the anxiety he felt at not seeing his father.

'He's just so far away,' he said quietly as he carefully coloured in a huge, endless ocean of blue on his paper. Zoe nodded in understanding. Robert's father had moved to California, farther than the little boy could even grasp, and yet he'd still feel the separation if his father lived in Brooklyn. Sometimes distance didn't matter. The orientation of your heart did.

And, whether Aaron was in California or on the Upper West Side, she might always feel as if he were an ocean away, Zoe thought as she cleaned up after Robert had left the centre. Could she live with that kind of emotional distance?

'Hello, Zoe.'

She turned in surprise to see the man in question standing in the doorway of the art room. 'What are you doing here?'

'I thought I ought to see where you worked.'

She smiled, unaccountably thrilled that he'd made the effort. 'Well, here it is.'

He took a step into the room, seeming to dominate the space, and glanced around at the child-sized tables, the buckets of markers and crayons, the spills of glitter and paint. 'Any breakthroughs today?'

'It's more about little steps.'

He nodded. 'I'd agree with that. I saw you working with that little boy.' He nodded towards the table. 'He seemed sad.'

'He is sad. Life's been tough for him lately.'

'And the drawing's helping?'

'I think so. It helps him to accept the way things are, and that it's okay to be sad.'

He nodded slowly. 'That's a big one, isn't it?'

Her heart lurched; she knew how difficult it was for Aaron to talk about his emotions. With a smile to show she was sort of teasing, she gestured to the tub of crayons. 'You could have a go.'

'Maybe I should. It seems to work.' He didn't move and Zoe waited, sensing he wanted to say something more. 'Zoe, I don't think I handled our conversation well this morning.'

'You don't?'

'I only mean to say…I *will* try.'

He gazed at her, looking both vulnerable and determined, and Zoe's heart squeezed. 'Try what?' she asked softly.

'Try to make this work between us. I'm not— I don't think

I'm capable of loving someone. I've never...' He shook his head with a touch of the old impatience. 'That's never been a part of my life. But I want to make a marriage between us work. I want to make you happy, if you agree.'

'Oh, Aaron.' She blinked back sudden tears. His reluctant confession and barely made promise should hardly have moved her to tears, but it did, because she knew how much such intimacy cost him. How much he meant it.

'You've already decided, haven't you?' he said, and she knew from the flatness of his tone he thought she was turning him down.

'Yes, I have.' Zoe took a breath. 'I'll marry you.'

'You will?' Aaron looked so slack-jawed that she let out a trembling laugh.

'Surprise.'

'I—I thought you'd hold out,' he said. 'For love.'

'I've been holding out for love for ten years and I haven't found it yet.'

'I didn't think you were one to give up.'

I'm not. No, she could not think like that. She absolutely could not think like that, not if she wanted to have any chance at all of making this work. She needed to accept just how little Aaron thought he could give. She smiled and arched her eyebrows. 'Are you trying to convince me *not* to marry you?'

'No.' He took a step towards her. 'No, of course not. I'm just surprised.'

'Good surprised, I hope?'

'Yes.' He took another step towards her, and then another, and then he stopped, like he couldn't go any farther, or maybe because he felt he'd gone far enough.

A kiss would have been nice, Zoe thought. A touch. But Aaron stood on the other side of the room and just stared. 'We'll work out the details,' he said and she rolled her eyes.

'Just another business contract?'

'There are some similarities.'

She laughed, or tried to, because the tangle of emotions had knotted in her chest and suddenly it hurt to breathe. To think. What had she done? What had she agreed to, committing her life to this man?

'Well, we have time,' she finally managed. 'I'm just over two months along. We don't have to rush.'

'No, of course not.' He cracked a smile then, a real one. 'But I'm glad, Zoe. Thank you.'

And just like that the knot dissolved and her heart started to melt. Dear Lord, she was in trouble.

But trouble felt good, she decided later that night as she slept once more in Aaron's arms. He'd surprised her by asking her to sleep with him again, and she'd accepted with rather alarming alacrity.

Still, she slept better than she had in weeks, only to wake in the middle of the night, the room drenched in darkness, a stabbing pain deep in her middle. She curled her legs up to her chest and then gasped as the pain knifed her again, worse than ever before.

Aaron stirred, his arms tightening around her. 'Zoe?' he murmured sleepily. 'Are you okay?'

'No!' she gasped as pain knifed through her again. Something was wrong. Something was really, really wrong. 'Aaron…'

He was up immediately, the covers rucked around his waist as he went to switch on the light. Zoe's vision swamped and she thought she might vomit. Aaron stared at her, his face stark-white, his hand already reaching for the phone.

'Aaron!' she gasped again, and that was all she could manage as she fell back against the pillows, unconscious.

CHAPTER EIGHT

'IT WAS AN ectopic pregnancy.'

Aaron stared at the rumpled-looking doctor and tried to make sense of the words. 'Ectopic,' he repeated. He'd heard the word before, but he didn't know what it meant. All he knew was the last four hours had been hellish, from the moment Zoe had woken up in his arms, gasping with pain, and then fallen unconscious.

The call to 911, the ride to the ER in an ambulance, the endless wait in a fluorescent-lit waiting room—all of it had felt like a mindless blur until now, when he was finally going to find out what had happened to Zoe—and to his child.

'An ectopic pregnancy is one in which the embryo implants outside of the uterus,' the doctor explained. 'In this case, in Miss Parker's fallopian tube. The tube ruptured, and we had to operate to remove the damaged tube as well as the embryo.'

The embryo. Aaron blinked. He meant the baby. Their baby was gone. Swallowing, he asked the question he knew mattered most. 'Is—is Zoe all right?'

'She'll be fine,' the doctor said with a tired smile. 'She's lost a lot of blood, and we're giving her a transfusion. She needs rest to recover, but she will. In a few weeks, a month, she should be fine.'

A *month*? Aaron passed a shaky hand over his face. 'May I see her?'

'She's sedated, but you can have a look in if you like. If you come back tomorrow, she should be awake and able to receive visitors.'

Aaron nodded and wordlessly followed the man down a long corridor to a hospital room. Zoe lay in bed, looking pale and small and so unbearably fragile. Her lashes feathered against her cheeks, and her breathing was slow and even, but faint, so faint.

Aaron reached out a hand to the wall to steady himself. He felt as if his whole world had shattered, exploded, in the course of a single night.

He barely remembered the ride back to his apartment; his mind was numb, blank. He stepped inside the penthouse and felt its emptiness, which he knew was ridiculous because Zoe had only been living with him for a short while. He was used to being alone. He *liked* being alone.

Except now he found he didn't. Now he found he felt empty and wretched, *lonely*. This was what loneliness felt like, he thought as he poured himself a double shot of whisky. It felt as if his whole world had collapsed around him and there was absolutely nothing left.

He tossed back the whisky and strode towards his study. Sleep would not come tonight. He powered up his laptop and stared resolutely at the screen. At least now he could focus on work; he could remain alone, he could do what he needed to do. He need never see Zoe again.

The thought made emptiness swoop through him, air whistling right through the place where he should have had a heart.

Eight hours later Aaron was back at the hospital, gritty-eyed and dressed for work. He'd bought some flowers; originally the florist had suggested a subdued bouquet of white chrysanthemums, but Aaron didn't want flowers meant for grief, and he didn't think Zoe did either. He chose lilacs, like the ones in her painting. He'd stared at it this morning as he'd drunk cold, black coffee, looked around his apartment and realised how she'd made it a home. Their home. The thought made that empty space inside him ache.

Now he stood in the doorway of her room, the bouquet in hand, words bottling in his throat. She was sitting up in bed, the hospital gown emphasising the sharp bones of her clavicle. Her face was turned away from him.

'Zoe.' He spoke softly, but he could tell she'd heard him. She stiffened slightly, but didn't turn towards him. He took a step in the room. 'How are you doing?'

'Fine.' She faced him then, her face pale so the spattering of freckles stood out on her nose and cheeks. She smiled and shrugged, jolting Aaron out of his cautious approach. 'Why wouldn't I be fine?'

'A lot of reasons, I would think.' He put the bouquet on the table next to her. 'These are for you.'

'They're very pretty. Thank you.'

He gazed at her and tried to figure out what was going on in her head. He had no idea. Her eyes were dark and fathomless, her smile fixed. She folded her hands in her lap across the starched sheets.

'Admittedly, I feel a bit weak,' she told him. 'But overall I'm okay. And, really, this is probably the best outcome, don't you think?'

'Don't say that.' He spoke with instinctive sharpness, a gut-level reaction.

'Why not? We were making the best of a bad situation, Aaron, and now we don't have to.'

He shook his head, the tightness in his chest taking over his whole body, making it impossible to speak. Finally he managed a few words. 'You wanted this baby.'

'Even so. You said it yourself—my life wasn't really set up for a baby. I wasn't really sure how it was going to work.'

You were going to marry me. He just shook his head. 'Zoe…'

She cut him off, her voice turning hard. 'There's no point pretending that this isn't the best thing for both of us.'

He stared at her helplessly, because even though he knew there might be truth to her words he didn't feel it. He didn't feel it at all. 'Don't say that, Zoe,' he said quietly and she lifted her face to stare at him with a blankness that made him ache all the more.

'Why not? It's true.'

'It's not true.' His voice was a low throb. 'I might have said we were making the best of a—a situation, but you're still grieving. And I wish this hadn't happened.' He sat down next to her and reached for her hand. She pulled away. 'Zoe, please.'

'Do you?' she asked dully. 'Do you really wish this hadn't happened, Aaron?'

He blinked, cut to the quick by her question even as he recognised its validity. 'Of course I do. You almost *died,* Zoe.'

'And the baby? Aren't you a little bit relieved that you don't have to deal with that anymore?'

'No.' He blinked hard and swallowed past the tightness in his throat. '*No.* Zoe, whatever you think, I'm not that heartless, I swear.'

She lowered her head, her hair falling forward to hide her face. 'The doctor told me I might not be able to have any more children.'

He froze, fresh grief sweeping coldly through him. He couldn't think of a single thing to say. 'There must be ways,' he finally managed.

'Maybe with IVF, but I have a lot of scarring. The whole reason this happened in the first place was because of a burst appendix I had when I was thirteen.' She spoke dully, as if none of it really mattered. 'All the scarring *severely limits* my fertility, according to the doctor.' She held her fingers up in claw-like quotation marks, a horrible smile twisting her face.

'We can think about that later,' Aaron said steadily. 'The important thing now is to get you feeling better.'

'I'll never feel better.' Her voice tore on the words and she turned away from him. Aaron felt his control slipping away from him, if he'd had it at all.

'You will, Zoe, with time and rest. You *will*.' He took a deep breath and decided they both needed to focus on practicalities for a moment. The emotion in the room was palpable and thick, choking him. 'The doctor has said you need to rest for at least a couple of weeks.'

'I know. I can go to Millie and Chase's.'

'I have another idea.' She just stared, her face as blank as ever. 'I thought a change of scene might be—welcome. Get away from everything here. You could spend a few weeks on St Julian's. It's my family's private island.'

'In the Caribbean? I know. It's where Chase and Millie met.'

'Right.' He'd forgotten that. 'I have a private villa on the grounds of the resort. You could stay there, enjoy some sunshine, recover.' She didn't speak and Aaron continued awkwardly, 'I could stay with you for a few days. I'd have to get back to work eventually, but I could take some time off.' Still nothing. 'Zoe?'

'Fine.' She turned to face the window. 'Who am I to turn down a free vacation?'

'All right.' He felt gratified yet uneasy, because he knew Zoe had to be drowning in an ocean of grief. He didn't know how to access it, how to help her. He felt like he was drowning himself. 'I think you can be discharged tomorrow, so I'll arrange a flight.'

'Fine.'

'All right.' He hesitated, wanting to say something more,

something of the grief inside him that he didn't like to probe too deeply, didn't even really understand. She was still stubbornly looking away from him, and with a little sigh he headed for the door. 'I'll see you tomorrow.'

No response. Yet as he started walking down the hall some impulse made him turn around, head back. As he came round in the door he saw Zoe holding the bouquet of lilacs to her face, her eyes closed, and something in him twisted. She let out a ragged sob, and without even thinking he started towards her, his arms outstretched.

'Zoe…'

She looked up, her eyes sparkling with both tears and fury. 'Go away,' she hissed. 'Leave me alone, Aaron.' She turned away again and, both shocked and hurt, Aaron dropped his arms. Without another word, he turned and left.

Hold it together. It was her mantra, her prayer. *Hold it together, because if you don't you will completely fall apart and there might be no getting you back together again.*

Drawing a deep breath, Zoe shoved the bouquet back on the bedside table. She blinked back the tears that had risen so readily to her eyes and felt a cold calmness seep through her once more. Good. This was what she needed. She was glad Aaron had gone. She needed him to leave her alone, because she could not keep it together with him near her, trying to be kind.

Twenty-four hours later, still feeling weak, achey and incredibly tired, Zoe boarded Aaron's private jet for St Julian's. They had barely spoken since he'd picked her up at the hospital and taken her in his limo to the airport, and Zoe was grateful for the reprieve. His attempts at kindness felt like salt in a raw wound, every smile or worried frown hurting her.

It hurt that he was now practically giving away the kindnesses and thoughtfulness she'd craved when she'd been pregnant and planning to marry him. And why? Because of his wretched sense of duty—or a labouring guilt?

Either way, she couldn't stand it. Her only defence was to feel numb, empty, even though she knew all those awful emotions—grief, rage, despair—lurked underneath that emptiness, like freezing water under the thinnest ice, and she did not dare touch the surface for fear those tiny hairline cracks would appear and she would drown in the depths below.

She'd become like Aaron, afraid of her own emotions. Hiding from them, because it was the only way she could cope.

'It's about a four-hour flight,' Aaron said as he took her elbow to help her manage the stairs up to the plane. 'There's a bedroom in the back,' he added as she stepped inside, distantly amazed by all the luxury: leather sofas, teak coffe tables and a sumptuous carpet that came up nearly to her ankles. She could hardly believe she was on a private jet…and she didn't even care. 'Do you want to rest?'

Zoe nodded. Rest was good. Rest meant sleep, which meant not talking, not even thinking. 'Yes, thanks. I'm still feeling pretty wiped out.'

'Of course you are,' Aaron murmured and, still holding her elbow, he led her to the bedroom in the back with a king-sized bed and en suite bathroom.

'It's like a hotel,' Zoe managed as she sank onto the silk duvet. 'A hotel in the sky.'

'And perfect for moments like these,' Aaron said lightly. 'Let me help you.'

She watched, surprised and yet still numb, as he sank to his knees in front of her. 'You don't have to,' she began as he slipped off her shoes.

'I want to,' he said in a low voice, and she wondered what this was. Atonement? Did he feel guilty, as if somehow he'd brought this on her, on both of them? He hadn't wanted their baby, and now they didn't have it anymore.

Illogical, she knew, and yet it was a thought that had crept into her mind all too often. With effort she slid her legs up onto the bed. 'I'm fine.'

'You keep saying that.'

Because, if I keep saying it, maybe I'll believe it. Maybe it will be true. 'I just want to sleep.'

'Okay.' She watched as Aaron peeled back the duvet and then, before she could protest, he lifted her as gently and easily as if she were a doll and placed her beneath the covers, tucking them over her with a tenderness she hadn't even known he possessed. She wished he didn't, because he was making everything so much harder.

She turned her face away, felt the starchy coolness of the pillow against her cheek, and closed her eyes.

'I'll let you sleep now,' Aaron said. 'I'll wake you up before we land.'

And then he was gone, the door clicking softly shut, and Zoe let herself tumble into blissful oblivion, the only thing she wanted now.

When she woke the room was dim, the curtains drawn against a blazing blue sky. Although she couldn't see him, Zoe could feel Aaron's presence in the room, knew he was watching her. She blinked, stirred, and he leaned forward, coming into her vision.

'We'll be landing in about half an hour.'

She nodded, and she felt Aaron's cool fingers brush a wisp of hair from her face and tuck it behind her ear.

Instinctively she turned away. 'Don't.'

'I'm sorry. Did I hurt you?'

Your kindness hurts me. She could hardly say that, couldn't explain even to herself why it did. Only that Aaron's thoughtfulness, his sudden sensitivity, felt like a knife twisting in her gut, in her heart.

'Do you want something to eat or drink?' Aaron asked when she hadn't replied to him.

'Tea,' Zoe managed and closed her eyes again. 'Please.'

Aaron brought her tea a few minutes later and left as soon as he'd handed it to her, which made Zoe feel both relieved and disappointed. How, she wondered, was she going to manage the next few days with him? Even those first days in his apartment hadn't been as awkward, as painful, as this.

Perhaps she should have gone to Millie and Chase's, yet even now that prospect made her insides sour. After her argument with Millie, she could hardly bear to slink back to her, a screw-up yet again. She knew Millie would have been kind, understanding, and would have never even have thought 'I told you so'. Yet even so…

Zoe couldn't do it. She would rather be here, even if it meant this unbearable awkwardness and tension with Aaron.

She finished her tea and tidied herself up, brushing her hair and even managing a bit of blusher and lipstick. She looked awful, she saw as she gazed in the mirror: pale and haggard, with vivid purple shadows under her eyes. Sighing, she turned away. Her appearance hardly mattered now.

Aaron was seated in the main area of the jet and Zoe came in and sat across from him. 'The airstrip is on the edge of the resort,' he told her. 'We'll have a car waiting for us. You should be settled in the villa within the hour.'

'Thank you,' Zoe murmured. He was making everything so easy for her.

Twenty minutes later they'd landed, and just as Aaron had promised a luxury sedan was waiting on the tarmac. He helped her inside, sliding in next to her, his thigh brushing hers before he murmured an apology and moved away.

Tears stung her eyes and she blinked hard. She hated how stupidly emotional she was being, how everything felt sad, like an ending, even that little, courteous rejection.

The villa was utterly amazing, as Zoe had known it would be. Set a little apart from the rest of the resort's lush grounds, its living room had sliding glass doors leading straight to the beach on one side, and a private terrace and pool on the other. There were three bedrooms, all luxuriously appointed, and a gourmet kitchen already stocked with food.

'I tried to order what you liked,' Aaron said. 'Tea, dairy-free ice cream… And, of course, you can order anything from any of the hotel's restaurants and it will be delivered.'

'It all sounds amazing.' And thoughtful, yet she supposed that shouldn't surprise her. Aaron had, in his own way, always been thoughtful. He considered every angle, every possibility. And now his kindness stung. *It's too late,* she wanted to cry. Scream. *It's too late. There's no future for us now; making me love you will tear me apart even more.*

'I think I'll just change,' she said, because her loose fleece and sweatpants—she'd needed comfortable clothing for the plane—felt too warm in the sultry tropical air.

'Of course. There are clothes in the main bedroom.'

He'd given her the master bedroom, and the wardrobe was full of brand-new clothes: sun dresses and swimsuits; shorts and capris; silky, expensive-looking T-shirts, all in the bright colours she loved.

A few minutes later she'd changed into a T-shirt and capris and came out to see Aaron at the dining-room table with his laptop. He'd changed into a polo shirt and cargo shorts, the most casual clothes she'd ever seen him in. He looked as good in them as he did in black tie, the shirt hugging the sculpted planes of his chest, the shorts riding low on his lean hips.

'Sorry.' He closed his laptop. 'I just needed to check in with the office.'

'It's fine.' When had Aaron ever apologised for working? It was what he did, who he was. She didn't want him to change—couldn't let him, because it would hurt too much.

Everything about this hurt. 'I'll just go outside and relax by the pool for a bit.'

'It's after lunch time. Shall I bring you something?'

Zoe shrugged. She was a little hungry, although she couldn't rouse herself enough to do much about it. 'Sure. Thanks.' She turned her back on him deliberately, not wanting him to follow her out to the terrace.

He didn't, and as she stretched out on a sun lounger, the sound of the surf a pleasant background noise to lull her to sleep, she hated the confusing mix of disappointment and relief she felt yet again.

She must have dozed off, for she woke when Aaron came out onto the terrace with a tray of food.

'I got a little bit of everything,' he said, and set the tray on the table. 'Coconut shrimp, avocado salad, sliced pineapple and some grilled fish. What would you like?'

She leaned back against the lounger and closed her eyes; the sun was bright and white-hot against her lids. 'It doesn't matter.'

Aaron didn't answer, but she heard him serving the food, the clink of cutlery and porcelain and then the gentle press of his hand on her shoulder. 'Here.'

She opened her eyes and saw him looking at her with such blatant concern that her throat went tight. She took the plate.

They ate in silence, and even though the food was delicious Zoe only picked at it. Eventually she pushed it aside and rose from the lounger. 'I think I'll have a nap.'

Aaron gazed up at her, his own lunch only half finished. 'All right.'

Without another word, Zoe escaped the terrace and Aaron's overwhelming presence for the sanctuary of her bedroom—and sleep.

Yet lying there in bed, with the bright tropical sunlight filtering through the curtains, she found she couldn't sleep after all. She kept seeing Aaron in her mind's eye, that surprising tenderness softening his features, lowering his voice, making him someone she couldn't stand. Because it would be so easy to turn to him for comfort, to fall even deeper in love with him. She'd been halfway to it when he'd been hard and cold, and she knew if she let herself weaken now it would seal that awful fate.

There was no baby, and therefore no future for them. Aaron was only acting out of solicitude and maybe even guilt; nothing else bound them together. Nothing at all.

It would be better if he just left, Zoe thought. Left her alone here, to sleep away the days, and somehow eventually try to forget everything that had happened.

She finally drifted into a doze and when she awoke it was evening, the light through the curtain now violet and hazy. Zoe rose from the bed and took a shower, hoping to rouse herself from the grogginess that had overtaken her.

She felt only a little better as she came out into the living room and saw Aaron stretched out on the sofa, asleep. She stopped, her heart juddering in her chest. He looked so much softer in sleep, the lines of his face smoothed out, a day's stubble darkening his chin.

She had a sudden, insane impulse to go to him, to curl into his solid strength and let him put his arms around her. Let him offer her the comfort she so desperately craved.

She didn't move.

His eyes flickered open and he stared at her, their gazes holding for a long, silent moment. Suddenly Zoe couldn't think, couldn't even breathe. She just stared and longed and finally Aaron spoke.

'Zoe,' he said quietly. 'I'm sorry.'

She froze, then forced herself to move past him into the kitchen. She poured herself a glass of water, her hand shaking.

She heard Aaron rise from the sofa and walk towards her. 'Aren't you going to say anything?'

'There's nothing to say.'

'I disagree.'

'Why would there be something to say, Aaron?' She heard her voice rise on a trembling note and took a deep breath. 'There's nothing between us anymore. We have no relationship, no future, nothing to talk about.'

He was silent and she didn't dare turn around. She didn't have the strength so much as to see the expression on his face, much less have this conversation. She *wouldn't* have it.

'I don't even know why you're here,' she continued, her voice rising again. 'Unless it's out of guilt.'

'Guilt?' Aaron repeated neutrally. Zoe turned around.

'Yes, guilt. Because you got what you wanted, didn't you? And you didn't even have to pay me a cent, never mind fifty grand.'

She saw Aaron flinch and knew she'd hurt him; she felt a savage twist of both remorse and satisfaction. She wanted to hurt him, wanted to push him away, even if she knew she was hurting herself in the process. 'You must be celebrating,' she continued, her voice turning into an awful sneer. 'Or at least you should be.'

'Do I look like I'm celebrating, Zoe?' Aaron asked quietly, his voice turning raw and ragged. 'Do you honestly think I'm happy about this?'

She scrunched her eyes shut and shook her head. She couldn't manage any more. She felt his hands curl around her shoulders and he slowly, purposefully drew her to him.

'Zoe, please stop fighting me. Please stop pushing me away. I want to help you. I want to see you through this.'

'Why?' she demanded, her voice choked with tears. With heaving effort she pulled herself away from him. 'So you can walk away with a clear conscience?'

'Because I care about you!' His voice rose in an almost-roar that had them both blinking in shock.

'It's too late, Aaron,' Zoe said after a moment, her voice flat. 'After everything…' She shook her head, a cold numbness thankfully stealing over her once more. 'It's too late for anything between us now.'

CHAPTER NINE

WHEN ZOE CAME out of her bedroom the next morning, having endured a sleepless, endless night, Aaron was dressed in a business suit. He shut his laptop and slid it into his briefcase.

'You're going,' Zoe said flatly, and he nodded.

'It seems for the best.'

Which of course it was. It was what she wanted, what she had been pushing him towards last night. Yet in the unforgiving light of day it still hurt—far more than it should.

'I'll have someone from the hotel check on you every day,' he continued, still busy with his briefcase. 'At least twice a day.'

'That's not necessary.'

'It is.' He cut her off, his tone relentlessly final. 'You were very ill, Zoe. You still are. You could have died, you know.' She heard a faint tremor in his voice and she closed her eyes, fought against the impulse to offer him her own apology, to beg him to stay.

'Even so.'

'Dr Adams said you shouldn't be alone,' he continued flatly. 'The only reason I'm leaving at all is because it's obvious I'm doing more harm than good by staying.'

Guilt speared through her, an awful, sharp-edged thing, lacerating everything it touched. She opened her mouth to say something—but what? How could she explain her own actions without telling him the truth—that she cared too much for him already, that her grief was so overwhelming she didn't how to deal with it, how to deal with *him*?

'Goodbye,' she finally whispered, and she knew that hurt him, too.

The rest of the day dragged endlessly, a monotonous paradise, before the lull was broken by a phone call from Millie.

'St Julian's is beautiful, isn't it?' she said lightly, although Zoe still heard the thread of anxiety in her sister's voice.

'How did you know I was here?'

'Aaron called me.'

'Aaron? I didn't think he was even on speaking terms with you.'

'He wasn't,' Millie answered wryly. 'But he's desperate, and he thinks you need someone to talk to. He's worried about you, Zoe.'

Her throat closed up and she swallowed with effort, forced herself to speak. 'He has a guilty conscience.'

'What do you mean?'

Too late she realised she'd revealed too much. She would never tell anyone, much less her sister, about Aaron's initial offer. 'Never mind. It doesn't matter.'

'How are you doing?' Millie asked softly and her throat tightened again.

'I'm fine.'

'Oh, Zoe. You remember when I kept saying that, after Rob and Charlotte…?' Even now Millie had trouble talking about her husband and daughter. 'You're not fine. You're never fine when you suffer a loss.'

'A miscarriage is hardly the same,' Zoe answered. 'You've suffered far more than I have, Millie. I've always known that.'

'Is that what you think?' Millie asked quietly. 'That my grief is more than yours?'

It was always how she'd thought. How could she talk about

her paltry problems—being dumped by her fiancé—when Millie had lost everyone and everything?

'Zoe,' Millie said, her voice gentle, 'grief is grief. And pain is pain. I would never presume to think my experience somehow trumps yours.'

But it did, Zoe filled in silently. It always had. It had been silently and implicitly understood in her family that nothing she ever endured would compare to what Millie had happen to her. She had never attempted to try, had armoured herself with insouciance instead. It was how she'd handled life: lift your chin and laugh it off. Except now she couldn't. Now she was raw, exposed and vulnerable, hating how much weakness was on display.

'You shouldn't be there alone,' Millie said when Zoe hadn't said anything—couldn't. 'Don't close yourself off, Zoe. I know how that goes. It's okay for a little while, and sometimes it's what you need. But you can't hide forever.'

'This is hardly forever.'

'How long are you planning on staying on St Julian's?'

'I don't know.' She didn't have any reason to return to New York, she thought. She no longer worked at the café, and Aaron had arranged a month's leave of absence from the community centre.

And, even when she was able to resume her work as an art therapist, what about her life? Her friends? She'd kept so much from them over the last few months, and now she felt so changed from the carefree, insouciant woman—*girl*—she'd been before.

'Zoe?' Millie prompted gently. 'Maybe you should come back to New York. You could stay with me and Chase.'

'No.' The word came out too quickly, involuntary and immediate. Instinctive. 'That's very kind of you, Millie, but I'm a grown woman. I need to stand on my own two feet.' Even if she wasn't doing that now.

'Then perhaps you should reach out to Aaron,' Millie said after a moment. 'I wouldn't have said this when we talked before, but he cares about you, Zoe. I could tell. He's really worried about you.'

'I can't.' It was all she could manage.

'Is there something I don't know about, something about your relationship?'

Zoe closed her eyes. 'We don't have a relationship.'

'I thought you were thinking of marrying him.'

'That was when there was a baby.' She dragged a breath into her lungs. 'When there was a reason.'

'And now?' Millie asked quietly.

'There's nothing.'

'It didn't seem that way when I talked to Aaron.'

'All right then, there's not enough.' He would never love her. Strange, how she'd convinced herself it hadn't mattered when she'd been pregnant. Now, with the nothingness that had replaced her hope, she realised how much it did. How much she needed it.

'Maybe you should give him a chance,' Millie suggested.

'You're the one who said he was a big jerk,' she snapped. 'And that he'd break my heart and not even care.'

'Has he?' Millie asked quietly.

'No!' *Because I won't let him.*

'Oh, Zoe…' Millie sighed. 'I just don't want you to be on your own. What if—what if I came down? Spent a few days with you? It could be… Well, I won't say fun.' She let out a wobbly laugh. 'But it would be good to see you. I feel like I haven't seen you properly since I got married.'

'I know.' And, even though she'd been deliberately avoiding Millie for most of that time, Zoe knew then that she missed her sister. The thought of seeing her again, having her sweep in and somehow rescue her was tempting—but impossible.

'I miss you, Mills,' she said. 'And I'll see you when I get back. But I need to be alone right now.'

'I don't like the thought of you out there by yourself.'

'You came here by yourself,' Zoe objected. 'Remember? And met Chase.'

'Are you hoping to meet a Chase?' Millie teased gently.

'There's only one Chase.' And there was only one Aaron. With a pang Zoe knew which one she wanted to be with.

Aaron spent the flight back to New York focused on work. He forced himself not to think of Zoe, of the accusations she'd spat at him like bullets. And like bullets they'd wounded him, made him bleed. *Did* he care about her now because he felt guilty? It almost seemed like the easy answer when the truth was far more damning.

He cared about her. Full stop. Forget about what they'd been planning before. He cared about her, and it terrified him.

Resolutely he turned back to his work. A mysterious shareholder was quietly buying up stocks in Bryant Enterprises, and Aaron had no idea who it was. Still, he sensed the danger; he'd always sensed the danger, always felt as if he were teetering on the edge of the precipice of disaster. Bankruptcy. Ruin. Shame.

The legacy of his father, the inheritance he'd been given and hidden not just from the world, but his own family. The shame he didn't want anyone to discover.

Halfway through the flight, he broke down and called Millie. It was an awkward conversation, but a necessary one. He didn't want Zoe to be completely isolated and alone. She needed someone, even if it wasn't him.

His mobile phone rang as he landed in New York. Glancing at the luminous screen, Aaron saw that it was his brother

Chase, no doubt checking up on him after his phone call to Millie.

'Chase.'

'Hey, Aaron. How's Zoe?'

'Not all that great, as you probably know from your wife,' Aaron answered tersely.

'Millie's worried about her.'

'Of course she is. Zoe has gone through a very difficult time.'

'She thinks she shouldn't be alone.'

Aaron gritted his teeth. Like he needed to be told. 'I agree.'

'So?' Chase prompted. 'Why aren't you there?'

Aaron felt his fingers ache from gripping the phone so tightly. 'Because she doesn't want me there.'

'I don't think Zoe is in a position to know what she wants.'

Aaron felt a tiny flicker of doubt—or was it hope? 'She seemed pretty sure,' he said gruffly.

'You said yourself she's going through a tough time. She's grieving, Aaron. She's probably not making sense, even to herself.'

'I don't know,' Aaron said after a moment, and he heard how uncertain he sounded. And he never sounded uncertain, never showed any weakness or doubt. 'Look,' he said in a stronger voice, 'it's none of your business anyway.'

'Zoe is Millie's sister, so that makes it my business,' Chase answered. 'And you're my brother. Aaron, go back. Help her.'

Aaron closed his eyes, felt his throat thicken. He swallowed and forced himself to speak. 'I don't know how.'

'Then tell her exactly that,' Chase said gently. 'I think she'll understand.'

One of his staff had come into the main area of the plane, ready to assist. Grimly Aaron tossed his phone aside. 'We'll have to refuel,' he said. 'And then we're heading back to St Julian's.'

* * *

Zoe sat curled up in an armchair in the living room of the villa, the sliding glass doors open to the beach. A gorgeous sunset was streaking across the sky in technicolour glory, sending melting rays of gold and orange over the placid sea, yet she barely noticed it.

She'd spent one day alone and she was ready to climb the walls. Climb out of her own skin, because she couldn't stand it anymore. Couldn't stand herself. She drew in a shuddering breath and forced the emotion back. She couldn't deal with it, would never be able to deal with it.

She heard the door open and looked up, expecting one of the staff returning to clear away the dinner she'd barely touched. Instead her heart seemed to stop right in her chest, for Aaron stood in the foyer looking tired, rumpled and utterly wonderful.

Zoe swallowed, half rising from her chair. 'What are you doing here?'

Aaron's gaze narrowed in on her and he tugged at his tie. Funny, how he always wore suits yet he always took his tie off as soon as possible, shed it with a flicker of relief as if he was finally just a little bit free.

'What am I doing here?' he repeated as he came towards her. 'The real question is, why did I ever leave?' He dropped to his knees in front of her. 'I'm sorry, Zoe. I never should have left you alone, not even for a minute.'

She stared at him incredulously, longing to touch him, yet afraid to. 'You must have flown to New York and straight back again.'

'That's exactly what I did.'

She shook her head, her throat thick with tears. 'I was trying to make you leave.'

'I know you were.'

'Then why—why did you come back?'

'Because I'm not going to let you push me away. Because I want to be here, with you, working this out together.'

'I shouldn't have—I shouldn't have said those things to you.'

'Why did you?' Aaron asked quietly. 'Are you angry at me?'

Zoe opened her mouth to deny it and then realised she couldn't. 'I don't know,' she whispered. 'I know I shouldn't be.'

Aaron shook his head, his eyes dark. 'Maybe you should.'

'Why?'

'Because,' he said bleakly, 'I didn't want our child at the start. At least, I convinced myself I didn't.'

'That has no bearing on what happened,' Zoe answered, her voice wobbling noticeably despite her effort to sound reasonable. To feel it. 'It's not—it's not like you caused the pregnancy to be ectopic, Aaron.'

'I know that.' He let out a long sigh. 'But logic doesn't always trump emotion.'

'I thought it did with you,' Zoe said with a small, watery smile.

'I always meant for it to. But lately...' He shook his head again, his eyes dark and full of shadows, yet Zoe saw more honesty reflected in them than she'd ever seen before. 'I don't know what I feel, Zoe. And I don't know what you feel. Maybe you want me to go, but I want to be here. With you.'

She felt her throat thicken with tears and she blinked hard. 'I want you to be here,' she whispered. 'But I don't even know why, or what that means. I don't know anything, Aaron.'

'I wouldn't expect you to,' Aaron said, his voice rough with emotion. 'You're still grieving, Zoe. You're keeping it all inside, bottling it up. Trust me, I know how that goes. But you've got to let it out.'

Her throat was so tight now she could barely speak. She

blinked hard, willing the tears back. She might have admitted more to this man than she'd meant to, but she would not cry in front of him. She would not fall apart, because she knew there would be no putting herself back together again. At least not the way she'd been, the way she wanted to be again.

The way she knew she could never return to.

'No,' she finally said, the word strangled on a sob. *'No.'*

'Zoe.' She felt Aaron's hands on her shoulders; she still wouldn't look at him.

'Don't,' she whispered. 'Please don't. I can't.'

'Why not?' he asked gently. His hands were still curled around her shoulders and he was slowly, inexorably drawing her towards him. Zoe didn't have the strength to resist.

'Why are you doing this?' she protested brokenly. 'You're the one who told me you hated all that emotional stuff. Quantifiable results, remember?'

'Maybe I've changed.'

'You *haven't*.' She didn't want him to change. Didn't want to consider what that meant for her, for her heart.

He had drawn her to him, and now he pulled her onto his lap. Zoe went woodenly, unable to resist, yet still possessing enough strength not to curl into him as she wanted to, accept the comfort he was offering.

'Zoe,' he said quietly. 'I'm sorry.'

'No.'

'I'm sorry I hurt you when I offered you that money. I'm sorry I didn't give us more of a chance when I should have.'

'No.'

'And most of all I'm sorry for the loss of our baby. I wanted that child, Zoe. I didn't even realise how much until—' He stopped, his voice choking, and the tears she'd only just managed to hold back finally fell, coursing down her cheeks in a hot river as she shook her head, still trying to deny his words, the effect they were having on her.

All her defences were crumbling. Her heart was laid bare, weak, trembling organ that it was—defenceless, vulnerable.

'I'm sorry,' he whispered, and he wiped the tears from her cheeks, his arms around her, holding and protecting her. 'I'm so sorry,' he said again, a plea, a promise. 'I'm so, so sorry.'

Zoe didn't answer. She couldn't, for now that the tears had fallen the grief she'd locked deep inside came pouring out; her body shook with sobs and she buried her damp face in the warmth of Aaron's neck as she let her sadness overtake her.

She didn't know how long she cried. Time ceased to matter or even exist as Aaron held her and she poured out her heart. Eventually she stopped, utterly drained, yet feeling more replete than she had in a long time. She pulled away from him a little, wiped her face. 'I suppose I needed that.'

'I think you did.'

Yet now that she'd let the sadness out she didn't know what was left. She felt empty and, while it didn't feel too bad now, it still scared her. The future scared her, stretching endlessly ahead, and even though she craved the warmth and comfort of Aaron's arms she knew she couldn't stay there. Didn't even belong there.

'Thank you,' she said. 'For—for understanding.' She tried to slip off his lap, but his arms tightened around her and he wouldn't let her go.

'Don't, Zoe.'

'Don't what?'

'Don't push me away again.'

She forced herself to say the truth. 'It's not as if there's any future for us, Aaron.'

'Isn't there?'

She stilled, too shocked to form words. 'What do you mean?' she finally managed in a whisper.

'I know we came together out of expediency.'

'Making the best of a bad situation,' Zoe reminded him, her voice sharpening just a little.

Aaron acknowledged this with a nod. 'But I still feel something for you, Zoe, just like you told me I did. I haven't been able to admit it even to myself, but you saw it. You saw the truth in me.'

'Wishful thinking on my part,' Zoe managed and he shook his head.

'No, it's the truth. I care about you, and I don't want to walk away just because things have changed.'

Zoe didn't answer. Her mind whirled with this new information, because in all the scenarios she'd foggily envisioned she had never once imagined this. She was the one who fell too hard, too fast, who threw herself into relationships, desperate to make them work, to prove she could make them work. And Aaron had made it all too abundantly clear that he didn't do relationships. Didn't do love. Had he really changed that much? Had she?

'Say something,' Aaron said softly as he brushed the remnants of tears from her eyes. 'Tell me what you're thinking.'

'I don't know what to think. I never expected you to want more from me. Frankly I thought—I thought you'd be relieved.'

'Which is why you were angry at me,' Aaron surmised. 'Well, in all honesty, I expected to be relieved. I even wanted to be because, hell, that's easier. But I'm not, Zoe.' He touched her chin with his fingertip and angled her face towards him. 'I can't promise you anything, because I don't know what I'm capable of. I haven't had a serious relationship with a woman—ever.' He let out a shaky laugh. 'That sounds rather grim, doesn't it?'

'Honestly? Yes.' Zoe managed a smile. 'But I'm glad you're admitting it.'

'But I want to try,' he said softly. 'With you.'

Zoe thrilled to hear the words yet, whether it was a thrill of excitement, joy or just fear she didn't know. Probably all three. She knew herself, knew that if she entered a relationship with Aaron, a proper one, she'd fall fast and hard as she always did. Faster and harder, even, because already this man had stirred up way too many emotions inside her. Already she knew she felt more for him—far more—than she'd ever felt before.

And if she fell and Aaron didn't? If he tried and failed? He hadn't even mentioned love, and Zoe was feeling too raw and exposed already to bring it up. Could she survive that all-too-likely scenario?

'I'm afraid,' she said quietly. 'I don't want to get hurt, Aaron.'

'I know.' He said nothing else, made no promises, just as he had said he wouldn't.

She couldn't do this. Couldn't risk so much, not when she'd lost so much already. She might be healing, but the scars were livid, fresh and still so very painful.

'I always have such bad timing,' Aaron murmured as he touched a fingertip to her eyelash, where another tear was already forming. 'I shouldn't have said all this now, when I just got here and we've barely talked. I'm sorry.'

'Stop apologising,' she said with a little smile. 'I think you must have said more sorries tonight than you ever have in your whole lifetime.'

'I have,' he admitted. 'I never say sorry. I never admit I'm wrong.'

'Why not?'

He thought for a moment. 'Because admitting it is showing weakness and I don't want to be weak.'

'Telling someone you want to be with them could be seen as weakness too,' Zoe pointed out. Aaron met her gaze steadily.

'I know.'

Her heart seemed to turn right over. He really was trying. Really was laying himself bare. How could she turn away from that? How could she keep her own heart intact when Aaron was trying to offer his own? Or at least as much of it as he knew how to.

She took a shuddering breath. 'Aaron...'

'Don't answer me now,' he said, pressing a finger against her parted lips. 'You need to think. Rest. Recover. All I ask is that you let me stay here with you.'

She nodded, his finger still against her mouth. With a small smile he traced the outline of her lips with the tip of his finger. Zoe felt a little pulse of longing deep in her belly, a jolt to her system, reminding her that she was awake, alive.

'Then we should both rest. Together, if you'll have me. I've missed sleeping with my arms around you.'

She smiled, blinked hard. 'I've missed having them around me,' she whispered.

Silently Aaron led her to the master bedroom. As they got in bed Zoe hesitated for a moment, frozen in her loneliness and fear, before Aaron's arms came around her and her body reacted, instinctively knowing what to do. What she needed. She nestled into his embrace, her legs twining with his, her arms coming around his middle, glorying in the feel of him, hard muscle and hot skin.

Once again she was home.

CHAPTER TEN

AARON WOKE UP with Zoe's hair trailing across his bare chest, his hand cupping the warm fullness of her breast. He went immediately and painfully hard, even as he felt a thrill of both terror and joy.

This was so unbearably unfamiliar, so out of his control, and yet already so necessary and even vital. Nothing he'd said to her last night had been planned or expected. Every word out of his mouth had shocked him as much as he thought it had her: *All I ask is that you let me stay here with you... Maybe I've changed... I want to try...with you.*

He wasn't sure if he believed any of it, if he *could*. He'd lived his life in determined solitary independence, had wanted and needed to. The lessons he'd learned from his father went soul-deep: *don't trust anyone. Don't need anyone. Don't be weak.*

And yet his father had broken all his own rules, rules he'd drilled into his oldest son from the age of five—a realisation which had made Aaron only more determined. He wouldn't be like that. He'd take his father's lessons to heart and he'd live them. Perfectly.

Yet now he was breaking every rule spectacularly—and why? Because the few weeks he'd spent with Zoe had been the most awkward, intimate and wonderful of his whole life— and he wanted more. Even if it terrified him.

He felt Zoe stir in his arms and he glanced down at her, saw the fog of sleep in her eyes replaced with a wary smile. She wasn't sure of this either. Last night had been intense, with the tears, the honesty and the grief, but this was something else entirely. This was a beginning—but of what?

'Good morning,' he said, his voice a morning rasp.

'Good morning.'

'Sleep well?'

'Actually, yes.' She stretched and then curled back into him, sending a kick of lust ricocheting through him. He knew, what with the complications of the ectopic pregnancy, sex was out for at least a few weeks. His body, however, didn't seem to have received that memo. 'Did you?'

'Yes,' he admitted, because honestly he'd never expected to like sharing his bed, for it to feel so good. So right.

'And now?' Zoe asked softly, and he saw all the uncertainty in her eyes. Uncertainty about him.

'I thought you might be tired of kicking around the resort,' he said.

'Okay…'

'So we could go sailing.'

A smile tugged at her mouth. 'You have a boat?'

'Yep.'

'That sounds wonderful,' she said, and Aaron's heart swelled with an emotion he could not name.

An hour later they were on the water, the sea placid and shimmering with a brilliant morning sun. Zoe sat on the cushioned seat in the stern of the boat, her legs tucked up to her chest, her face tilted to the sun. She'd pulled her hair back into a ponytail but tendrils and wisps had escaped, turned wild and curly by the sea air.

Aaron loved looking at her, loved seeing her relaxed and happy. He felt his heart swell again, and this time he knew it was with hope. She must have felt him gazing at her, for she lowered her head, raising one hand to shield her eyes from the glare of the sun, and turned to him with a smile.

'Do you know, I've actually never been on a sailing boat before?'

'Never?' They were in for a good run and so Aaron took the opportunity to join Zoe in the stern. 'How come?'

She shrugged. 'I was never a very sporty girl. Books and art were more my thing. But I have to admit, this is pretty amazing.' She glanced at him, curiosity flaring silver in her eyes. 'Did you Bryant boys all learn to sail at around the age of two?'

'More like six.' He sat down next to her, his thigh nudging her hip and sending a painful flare of awareness through him. It was going to be a tough day for his libido. 'We had a house out in the Hamptons, right on the Sound.'

'Had?'

This was somewhat dangerous territory, he realised. He didn't like talking about his childhood, the mistakes his father had made. 'It was sold when my father died.'

'When did your father die?'

'Ages ago, when I was twenty-one.' Just old enough to take the reins of Bryant Enterprises and realise how tightly he'd have to hold on to them.

'I'm sorry,' she said quietly. 'It must be hard, not to have either of your parents alive.'

He shrugged. 'It's been a long time.'

'A long time on your own. Why aren't you close to your brothers?'

Another shrug; he really didn't like talking about this. Was this what relationships were, all this honesty and intimacy, like peeling back your skin? No wonder he'd avoided them for so long.

'Aaron.' She laid a hand on his arm. 'I'm not trying to pry, you know. I promise I won't psychoanalyse. I just want to get to know you. And I want you to get to know me.' He could think of ways of getting to know her that did not involve such messy questions or any conversation at all.

With a sigh, he nodded. 'I know. I'm just not used to… talking about things.'

'I realise.' She gave him the glimmer of a smile. 'You can ask me some questions, if you want.'

'What made you go into art therapy?'

'The practical answer is that I knew I would never make it as an artist professionally, but I still wanted to do something related to art. The emotional one is that I like helping people, and being useful.' She gave a little laugh that sounded to Aaron like it had a bitter edge. 'Funny, really.'

'Why is that funny?'

Now she was the one shrugging, her gaze sliding away from his. 'I don't know. I suppose I'm not considered to have lived a very productive life.'

He frowned. 'Says who?'

'Put me next to Millie, with her super-important career and her completely together life, and I look pretty—useless.' She let out another quick laugh then shook her head, the movement almost frantic. 'Which is a terrible comparison to make, I know, because Millie's been through a lot and I can hardly discount—' She stopped suddenly, pressing her lips together. 'Oh, it doesn't matter anyway.'

Aaron stretched his legs out. 'Obviously it does.'

'Obviously?' she repeated, arching an eyebrow. 'Are you going to play psychologist on me, Aaron? Because that so does not seem your style.'

'You're the therapist,' he answered with a smile.

'Right. Maybe I should draw myself a picture.'

'Now you sound as cynical as me.'

She laughed, the sound ending on a sigh. 'No. I suppose I've always had a bit of an inferiority complex when it comes to my sister. Millie doesn't make me feel that way—not for a minute. It's more my parents. And myself.' She lapsed into silence, frowning as she gazed into the distance.

Aaron knew he should get up and tack but he was reluctant to abandon this conversation. Zoe was sharing more with him than he'd expected, and to his own surprise he found he wanted to know. 'So your parents wanted you to be a hedge-fund manager?'

'Didn't yours?' she flashed back, and he tensed. So they were back to him. He should have known he couldn't avoid personal questions for ever, or even for ten minutes.

'They certainly did.'

'Were you always meant to take over Bryant Enterprises?'

'Always.' He did not have a memory in which that expectation had not weighed heavily on him; it had nearly crippled him.

'What about your brothers?'

'They were meant to have responsibilities, as well. Luke was in charge of the retail division until a few months ago.' He still felt a frisson of shock that Luke had just given it all up, walked away from Bryant Enterprises and all that it meant. He was free. 'And Chase was disinherited by my father when he was nineteen.'

'Ouch. Why?'

'He screwed up one too many times. He was a bit of a wild kid.'

'And you?' Zoe asked softly. 'You were meant to be in charge of it all?'

'That's about it.' He tried to speak lightly but somehow his throat became constricted and he felt a welling of emotion in him that he didn't understand. Why did this woman wrest emotions from him, like drawing out poison? He felt it seep out of him, infecting everything, leaving him weak.

Zoe laid a hand on his arm; her skin was soft and warm

from the sun. 'You don't like your job, do you?' she asked quietly.

'I hate it.' The words slipped out before he could stop them, and the vehemence with which he spoke surprised them both. It shocked him, really, and he felt a scorching rush of shame that he could have been so weak to admit such a thing, or even to feel it. That he could have betrayed his father, his family, so easily—and to a woman. Hadn't he learned anything from his father's mistakes?

Quickly Aaron slipped from the seat and walked back to the bow of the boat. It was time to tack.

Zoe watched Aaron walk away from her, every muscle in his body taut with tension. He'd said too much, she thought with a sigh. At least, he felt he had. She sat there, the sun still streaming over her, and let him go. Maybe he needed a little distance.

She knew her fatal tendency in relationships was to push. Demand or beg, it didn't matter which, but she got desperate and needy and no one liked that, not even herself. It was a legacy from Tim's betrayal, that she insisted on believing in love even as all her history said otherwise.

She watched Aaron do something with the sail—she really didn't know a thing about boats—and admired his long, lean torso, the wind pressing his polo shirt hard against the muscles of his chest. He squinted in the sun, his dark hair ruffled by the wind, and Zoe felt a surge of longing so deep and powerful it left her aching. The no-sex thing was going to be hard.

Dr Adams had told her she needed to have a check-up before he gave the all-clear, and since her surgery Zoe hadn't given it so much as a thought. Sex had been just about the furthest thing from her grief-stricken mind. Now, however, even though the grief was still there and always would be, she felt a fresh desire roll through her and remembered just how good sex with Aaron had been. Making love.

Would it be different, now that they cared more about each other? The thought sent another thrill ricocheting through her. It would be even more intense, more wonderful, more everything.

Smiling at the thought, she rose from the bench and joined him at the sail.

'I have no idea what you're doing,' she remarked and Aaron raised his eyebrows.

'Do you want a lesson?'

'Not particularly. I like watching you, though. You look all manly and heroic.'

He let out a short laugh, shaking his head. Zoe was surprised and a little bit touched to see a faint blush tinge his cheekbones with colour. He was a man of authority and power, yet also one unused to receiving compliments, even teasing, lighthearted ones.

They kept the conversation casual as Aaron managed the sail, and eventually navigated the little craft to a sheltered cove on the other side of St Julian's.

He brought out a picnic basket and laid a blanket on the sun-warmed deck of the boat. Zoe stretched out on it while Aaron served her delicacies from one of the resort's restaurants—calamari and coconut shrimp; plantain accras; fritters; baked goat-cheese. They washed it all down with champagne, and ate succulent slices of fresh guava, papaya and passion-fruit for dessert.

'So how did you end up with a whole island to yourself?' Zoe asked as they ate, gazing out at the secluded side of St Julian's, the dense foliage fringing a white sand beach.

'Not exactly myself,' Aaron answered. 'The island is owned jointly by my brothers and me.'

'Even Chase?'

'Even Chase. The island belonged to my grandfather and he left it directly to the three of us.'

'Has it been in your family forever?'

'Hardly. The Bryant fortune isn't that old. My grandfather made most of it.' He lapsed into a sudden silence, his eyes narrowing as he gazed into the distance.

'And you and your father just added to the coffers?'

A pause, telling in its length. 'Something like that.'

Zoe took a breath, wanting more. Wanting to understand this man she was just beginning to realise was unsettlingly complex. 'Why do you hate your job, Aaron?' she asked quietly.

He tensed but said nothing. Zoe waited. She really didn't want to press, but neither was she willing to let it go. If they were going to attempt some kind of relationship, she needed more. She needed to know him.

'Hate was probably too strong a word,' he finally said— his voice deliberately mild, Zoe thought. 'I didn't choose it, put it that way.'

Zoe considered this. When he'd said he hated it, she'd felt those words come from somewhere deep inside him, somewhere she didn't think he accessed all that often. And she was just about a hundred percent certain they were true.

'If you hadn't been born a Bryant,' she asked after a moment, 'what career path do you think you would have taken?'

Aaron shrugged. 'Who knows. I never thought about it.'

'Never?'

'Never,' he said flatly.

'Is that what you don't like? The lack of choice?'

'What I didn't like,' Aaron said, the words coming sharp and sudden, 'was being lied to. Over and over again, so my whole life was built on nothing but deception.' He shook his head and then began clearing up the picnic things. 'Enough about this. I don't like to talk about it.'

'About what—Bryant Enterprises? Your family? Your life?' She heard the sharp edge to her own voice and realised that somehow they'd started arguing.

Aaron shot her a narrow glance. 'I told you I didn't know how much I had to give, Zoe.'

She felt her inside freeze, like he'd tipped a bucket of ice water straight into her soul. 'And, less than one day in, you're already tapped out?'

'I don't know.' He pressed his fists against his eyes, his expression one of almost physical pain. 'Damn it, I don't *know*.'

She'd done it again, Zoe thought. Pushed and pushed for more, because she didn't know how to stop. Because she couldn't let things take their natural course. This was day one, for heaven's sake. She could have been a little more patient.

Gently she reached over, put her hands over his and drew them down from his face. 'I'm sorry, Aaron.'

'Sorry?'

'For pushing you into talking about yourself when you're not ready.'

He glanced away. 'I'm sorry I'm not ready.'

'I have this terrible tendency to push,' Zoe confessed with a shaky laugh. 'I should tell you about it right up-front, I suppose.'

'Push?'

'I always ask for more out of a relationship.' She let out another laugh, just as shaky. 'You should see the expression on your face. I know, it's pretty much poison to most commitment-phobes.'

'Are you calling me a commitment-phobe?'

'You and every other man I've dated.'

'And you think it's them—or you?'

'Both.' She hugged her knees to her chest, half amazed that she was admitting this to anyone, much less Aaron. She only hoped he didn't run a mile when he heard about all of her craziness. 'Have you ever been in a high place and had a weird urge to jump off, just because you could? Like in a tower or on a mountain or something?'

Aaron's mouth quirked in a small, surprised smile. 'Umm…sort of.'

'Apparently it's fairly common. Well, I have that urge when it comes to relationships.'

'To jump?'

'Exactly.' She sighed, knowing she needed to explain everything. Even Tim. 'I've had four serious relationships, which at my age may not seem that many, but in some ways it was four too many.'

'How so?'

'I flung myself into each one without really thinking things through, wondering if the guy I was with was right for me, or even right at all. Honourable.'

'Honourable?' Aaron frowned, the effect quite ferocious. 'What kind of guys did you date, Zoe?'

'Jerks, mainly, but I convinced myself I loved each and every one of them. Maybe I really did love them. I'm not sure I know the difference.'

'I can't help you with that one,' Aaron said quietly and she felt her heart twist because, really, what was she doing here with a man who had already told her he would never love her? That he couldn't?

'I rushed into each relationship, determined to make it work. And of course it didn't.'

'Of course? Is it so obvious?'

'Well, Millie always joked that I picked the absolute biggest commitment-phobic toe-rags to date, and she's probably right. I think I actually did it on purpose, on a subconscious level at least. If the guy wasn't that good to begin with, it wasn't my fault if it didn't work out.' She paused, took a breath. 'That part's probably because of Tim.'

Aaron stilled, as if he sensed the importance of that confession. 'Tim?'

'My fiancé.'

He didn't move, his expression didn't even change, but Zoe still felt his shock. 'You were engaged?'

'For about two weeks.' She smiled ruefully, although even now, three years later, the memories still hurt. 'We dated for a year before that, though.'

'What happened?'

'He dumped me.' She tried for insouciance and knew she didn't quite manage it. 'Because his boss told him to.'

'What?'

'Yeah, I know, right? In the twenty-first century and everything.' She shook her head. 'Tim was in finance, some kind of investment thing.'

'Hedge-fund manager?' Aaron guessed with a ghost of a smile and Zoe laughed.

'No, but same ball park. To tell you the truth, I never quite got what he did. That was probably part of the problem.'

'So what problem did his boss have with you?'

'I wasn't right for Tim's image. He was going places, you see, within the firm. Lots of international travel, hosting dinners, that sort of thing. I didn't quite fit in that picture.'

'And so this Tim listened to his boss?'

'Pretty much.'

'He sounds like a total waste of space.'

'Well, I loved him—or at least I thought I did.' Yet she knew that what she felt for Aaron was even more than she'd ever felt for her former fiancé. How scary was that?' 'Anyway,' she resumed, 'when he broke it off, I was devastated. I hadn't even told my family yet—I was waiting till we picked out the ring.'

Aaron cocked his head. 'And you never told them, did you?'

Zoe blinked, surprised that he'd guessed. That he knew.

'No, I didn't. Because two days later Millie's husband and daughter died in a car crash, and the last thing anyone needed to hear about was my sorry little drama.'

'And after, later? Did you tell them then?'

Her throat tightened and she shook her head. 'No.'

'And you weren't going to tell anyone about your pregnancy, were you? About what happened?'

'You did that,' Zoe said, an edge entering her voice again. 'When you phoned Millie.'

'I was worried about you and I wanted someone to be with you even if it couldn't be me.' He paused, his eyes dark. 'Are you angry that I called her?'

'No, I'm not angry. How can I be, when I know you just wanted to help?' She sighed, shaking her head. 'I'm just… embarrassed, really. Angry at myself for screwing up everything in my life.' She blinked, nearly brought to tears by the raw admission.

Aaron was silent for a long moment, and then Zoe felt his hand wrap around the back of her neck, warm and strong. 'You're not screwing this up,' he said softly. 'This is something good.'

'Yes,' Zoe whispered, because she knew it was, even though she was still so afraid that it might all go wrong. That she would push too hard and Aaron would walk away. That he wouldn't have enough to give and she'd be left empty-handed and broken-hearted.

'I think you're too hard on yourself,' he whispered as he drew her inexorably closer. 'And I think you don't like admitting weakness or failure to anyone, even the people who love you. I know how that feels.'

'I bet you do.' He laughed softly, his lips a breath away from hers. And then he kissed her.

It was the first time he'd kissed her since that one night, and this was infinitely sweeter and more precious than anything that had happened before. His lips moved gently over hers, a reassurance that this *was* good. They were good together. Zoe put her hands on his shoulders and then slid her arms around his neck. Her breasts pressed against his chest and the contact was achingly, agonisingly pleasurable. Aaron deepened the kiss.

Gently he pushed her back onto the blanket, his hand sliding along her middle and then up to cup her breast. Zoe pushed back against him, craving the contact, their legs tangled amidst the detritus of their picnic. She could feel his arousal pressing against her, felt his fingers teasing her, sending arrows of pleasure shooting through her. And frustration, too, because she knew this couldn't go anywhere—or at least not as far as her body desperately wanted.

'I feel like a teenager,' she murmured against his mouth. 'You know I'm not cleared for sex yet, right?'

'I know,' Aaron admitted with a groan. 'But I can't resist touching you.' He slid his hand from her breast down to her middle and then to the pulsing warmth between her thighs. 'Okay?' he murmured and she nodded, because it was more than okay. The pressure of his hand against her was exquisite, and as he moved his fingers with knowing and gentle precision she arched against him and gasped out a sudden, intense climax.

'That was quick,' Aaron said, a smile in his voice as he kissed her mouth.

'It was, wasn't it?' Zoe agreed shakily. She felt dazed by her intense and immediate response to him, more than she'd ever experienced with anyone before. It almost scared her, how much she wanted him.

How much she loved him.

No, she couldn't think like that. Not yet—maybe not ever, no matter how much she wanted to. How much she wanted him to think the same way.

With a smile she pushed Aaron onto his back. 'Now your turn,' she said softly, and his eyes widened.

'You don't have to…'

With a throaty, knowing laugh, she skimmed her hand down the length of his erection. 'Oh, yes,' she said. 'I do.'

And then they didn't talk any more, for there was nothing but the giving and receiving of pleasure, until they lay sated—mostly, anyway, Zoe thought wryly—in each other's arms while the sun shone benevolently overhead.

CHAPTER ELEVEN

'I'D SAY THAT physically you're just about a hundred percent now,' Dr Adams said with a smile. 'But tell me how you feel.'

Zoe slid off the examining table. 'I feel a hundred percent,' she said firmly. She'd been back in New York for three days, and the doctor's clean bill of health was music to her ears. At last she could be with Aaron as she wanted to be…as she was desperate to be ever since their precious few weeks on St Julian's.

'Have you considered counselling?' Dr Adams asked. 'Or therapy? The experience you had was traumatic, and there will be ongoing—'

'I know that.' She nodded, although she really didn't want to talk about that now. 'I work in therapy myself, so I understand that and I'm looking into it. I know it will take a long time to heal emotionally.'

'We have resources, if you need them. A support group meets here at the hospital.'

'Thank you,' Zoe said. 'I'll look into it.'

As she left the hospital she had a spring in her step—and a fear in her heart. As pleased as she was about the doctor's all-clear, she couldn't help but feel nervous for what lay ahead. The last few weeks with Aaron had been wonderful…but it hadn't been easy.

They'd spent two weeks on St Julian's, which Zoe knew

was an enormous amount of time for Aaron to be away from his work. He'd checked his phone and email often, and spent most afternoons tele-commuting while she'd lounged by the pool. But even with the constant pressures of work, there had been times—wonderful times—with just the two of them. Walks along the beach and candlelit dinners; long nights wrapped in each other's arms and endless kisses and touching that just didn't go quite far enough.

It had all been wonderful, but at the same time Zoe still sensed a distance in Aaron, a place he didn't allow her—or anyone—access. In exasperation she'd once asked sarcastically, 'Do you have any *hobbies*?'

To which he'd replied flatly, 'No.'

The man was a machine. A machine who still didn't want to be known or understood, at least not completely. How could a relationship survive in those kinds of conditions?

Millie had told her to give it time. Upon returning to New York, Zoe had moved in with Millie and Chase rather than go back to her lonely apartment. She wasn't ready to move back in with Aaron—not that he'd even offered.

The night she'd got back Chase had made himself scarce; Millie had made margaritas and nachos—their snack of choice—and they'd both curled up on the sofa and had the kind of heart-to-heart they hadn't had in years.

'I'd be the first one to say I wasn't sure about Aaron,' Millie said bluntly. 'About you and Aaron. From what Chase has told me, the guy seemed like a complete jerk—arrogant, autocratic, totally controlling.'

'But?' Zoe said, trying to smile. She knew there was a different man underneath that authoritative facade, but she didn't know if she could trust him—or if that man could love her.

'He clearly cares about you. And he obviously has wanted to do the right thing for you.'

'And the baby?' Zoe filled in. 'That hardly counts now. And doing the right thing isn't a foundation for a relationship.'

'No,' Millie answered. 'But it shows the nature of his character. He's honourable, Zoe. He's good.'

'That only goes so far.' Zoe swallowed, her fears seeming to crowd her throat, making it hard to speak. 'Anyway, maybe he just wanted to do the right thing because he felt guilty.'

Millie frowned. 'You've said that before. What did he have to feel guilty about?'

Zoe hesitated, then decided she needed someone to confide in completely. 'When I first told him I was pregnant, he offered me fifty thousand dollars to have an abortion.'

Millie was silent for a long moment. 'I guess he changed his mind,' she finally said.

'I probably shouldn't have even told you. He regretted it, and he said it was a bad decision. But—'

'It's hard to forget.'

She nodded. 'I can't help but think that it's part of who he is—to leap to that conclusion, to even want that. And, even though he's shown he's different with me, he *can* be different, I'm not sure if that's enough. If he can be different enough. Who's the real man—the one who made that offer, or the one who said it was a mistake?'

'You need to give him time. People don't change overnight.'

'I know that. And I'm trying not to push but—I'm scared. I don't want to be hurt again, and worse this time, because I care more for Aaron than anyone else—even Tim.'

Millie frowned. 'Even Tim?'

Zoe thought of what Aaron had said: *I think you don't like admitting weakness or failure to anyone, even the people who love you.* He was right, she knew; he was right because he was the same. *I know how that feels.* 'I never told you about

Tim,' she said, and then slowly she began to tell the story of her ex-fiancé.

'I wish you'd told me when it happened,' Millie said when Zoe had finished. 'I know the timing was bad, but still…'

'I didn't tell anyone.'

'There's something I never told you,' Millie said quietly. 'About Rob.'

'Rob?' Millie didn't talk much about her former husband; as far as Zoe had ever known, they'd had a great relationship.

'When I was pregnant with Charlotte, he wanted me to have an abortion.'

Zoe's mouth dropped open. 'So you know how that feels.'

'It wasn't the right time, he felt. We still had so much to prove in our careers. I almost went along with him.' She was silent for a long moment. 'I even made an appointment. I walked out of it at the last minute—I still feel guilty about it sometimes.'

'Oh, Mills.' Zoe shook her head. 'Aaron told me I was too hard on myself, and I think you are, too.'

'That's what Chase says,' Millie admitted with a small smile.

'Those Bryant brothers. They know what they're talking about.'

Millie leaned forward, her face turning serious. 'Do you love him, Zoe?'

Zoe swallowed, the question reverberating inside her, as well as its undeniable answer. 'I'm afraid I do.'

Now as she walked towards the subway to go to her art-therapy session, she wondered why she'd said it like that: *I'm afraid I do.*

Was love that scary? Yes, it most certainly was. It was terrifying…especially when Aaron had made no promises. He'd already told her he didn't know how much he had to give, that he wasn't even sure he could love. When there had been a baby to consider, Zoe had thought she could accept those conditions.

But now…now she knew she'd been fooling herself. Those conditions were terrible, and she could never accept them. Never live with them, day after endless day. Maybe she'd convinced herself before that she could because part of her had already been falling for him, was already desperate.

But now, for once, she wanted to be strong. She didn't want to make the same mistake over and over again—falling for a guy who was all wrong for her, who would never love her back, and this time so much harder.

If I was stronger, I would end it now.
Give it time.

Yet how much time? How much possibility for pain? She took a deep breath, let it out slowly. She had no answer to those questions.

Aaron drummed his fingers against his thigh as his limo sped towards Millie and Chase's townhouse on Central Park West, where he was picking up Zoe for an evening out.

He felt as if there were bands of steel wrapped around his skull, tightening with every second. The two weeks he'd spent on St Julian's had been costly, perhaps more costly than he'd ever know. Someone was continuing to make a move on Bryant Enterprises, buying up shares, skulking in the background. Meanwhile the uncertain economy in Europe and Asia was wreaking havoc on the funds Aaron managed. He felt as if he were teetering on a precipice of disaster, and his only salvation was Zoe.

Had his father felt like this, with his legion of mistresses? Had he only been able to find peace and even sanity with the women who had controlled and ultimately ruined him?

And would Aaron be the same?

During the last weeks with Zoe, he'd fought against that

fear. His father had led his business, his family and even his life into disaster because of his attachment to women—and one woman in particular. When Aaron had discovered his father's weakness, he'd vowed not to share it. Not to give anyone control over him, not to need anyone that much, and certainly not to love.

Yet Zoe was breaking through all those boundaries, breaking him. He needed her, maybe even loved her.

No.

The denial was instinctive, necessary. It was how he'd lived his life. Could he really change that much? Did he even want to?

The limo pulled up in front of Chase and Millie's brownstone. 'I'll just be a minute,' Aaron said tersely, and with his mind still in a ferment he went to fetch Zoe.

She was still getting ready upstairs when Aaron arrived and he spent a few awkward moments with Chase, conscious now of Zoe's question: *Why aren't you close with your brothers?*

He never had been, even as a child. He'd been set apart from an early age, too early for him actually to remember. He was the oldest, the most responsible, the one who had to be in charge. And when his father had died and he'd realised just what that meant, what it would cost, that had driven him and his brothers even further apart.

Now Chase smiled easily and cracked open a beer. 'How's it going?'

'Fine,' Aaron said tersely. He could not relax. Not with Chase, and perhaps not even with Zoe. He felt the pressure build inside his head, inside his heart. He wanted her, needed her—and that terrified him.

Chase arched an eyebrow. 'You sure about that?'

'I'm sure, Chase.'

'Everything's good with BE?'

Aaron's mouth twisted. He did not want to talk about Bryant Enterprises with Chase, or with anyone. He did not even want to think about it. 'Everything's fine, Chase.'

Chase shrugged and nodded. 'And you'd tell me if it wasn't.'

No, of course he wouldn't. 'What is this?' Aaron arched an eyebrow sardonically. 'It's not like we've had heart-to-hearts in the past, Chase.'

'Always a good time to start.'

Aaron shook his head. 'I have nothing to say. I'm fine. Bryant Enterprises is fine.' He felt his throat constrict and silently cursed. What was *wrong* with him? Zoe was making him weak, needy. Desperate. 'Damn it, everything's fine,' he said hoarsely, and turned away.

Chase, thankfully, didn't reply, and a few minutes later Zoe came downstairs. Aaron viewed her as if through a haze; he felt his temples throb and the pressure inside him intensify. Yet still he could acknowledge how beautiful she looked: her hair was swept to one side with a sparkly clip and she wore an off-the-shoulder gown in a deep blue that made her eyes shine. She smiled as she came down the stairs, but dimly he registered there was something tentative about her smile, something almost wary. Then he realised he was scowling.

Damn. Already this evening felt like it was going wrong. Somehow he forced the corners of his mouth up into a smile. 'You look beautiful.'

'Thank you.' She still looked uncertain but as Millie joined Chase in the foyer Zoe lifted her chin and took his arm. With a nod to his brother and sister-in-law, Aaron stepped out into the night.

Zoe could feel the tension in Aaron's body, his arm like a steel bar under her hand. She waited until they were in the limo, speeding downtown towards the exclusive club where

Aaron had been invited for a cocktail party, to ask the question that hammered inside her heart.

'What's wrong?'

'Nothing.'

'Aaron.' She turned to him, tried to make out his expression in the shadowy darkness of the car. Streetlights washed his face in pale yellow every few seconds. She saw how tight-lipped and hard-eyed he looked, and felt her heart quail. Surely it—they—weren't starting to unravel already. Yet, looking at Aaron's hard profile, she felt as if they were. 'Something's obviously wrong,' she said quietly. 'And if you don't want to talk about it, just say so.'

'Fine,' Aaron answered tersely. 'I don't want to talk about it.'

Well, she'd asked for that one. Zoe felt her nails dig into her palms. 'Fine,' she said, trying to sound calm, but a petulant note crept into her voice and she turned to the window.

Don't overreact, she told herself. *Don't assume it's just like every time before. Give it time, like Millie said.* Yet she desperately craved reassurance, for Aaron to say anything that would bridge the chasm that was widening between them. He didn't speak.

'I went to the doctor today,' she said after a few minutes when they'd been stuck at a traffic light on Park Avenue for a while. Aaron turned to her.

'Is everything okay?'

'Yes.' She took a breath, plunged. 'I've been given the all-clear.' She waited and Aaron just stared. 'You know.'

'I know?' he asked, and to her amazement she thought she heard a teasing note in his voice. She felt a tidal wave of relief crash over her.

'Don't you?' she teased back, and in the wash of the streetlights she saw Aaron's smile.

'I hope I do.' She felt his hand on her shoulder, then stealing around her neck. He drew her to him and kissed her softly on the lips. 'Tonight?' he whispered. 'If you're ready?'

Dear lord, she was more than ready. Even if she was still scared and uncertain and so desperately wanted this to *work*. Her mouth still brushing his, she nodded.

Zoe thought she would enjoy the party more than she did: champagne and fancy appetisers; amusing and glamorous people; and, best of all, Aaron by her side, his hand on her elbow, his body so tantalisingly near…which was why she could hardly wait to leave.

All she could think about was what would happen after the party. She imagined them riding home in Aaron's limo; going up the lift to his penthouse, and stepping into that darkened penthouse, the lights of Manhattan spread all around them in a glittering map.

And then…

'So you're a therapist?'

Zoe jerked her mind back to the conversation she'd been having with several socialites. 'An art therapist.'

'I didn't know there was such a thing.'

Briefly she described her work, sensing their scepticism, and then to her surprise Aaron jumped in. 'It's especially effective with children. They're much more likely to be able to communicate their feelings through pictures than words.'

Zoe stared at him in surprise while the two glamorous women nodded. 'I guess that makes sense.'

Only because a gorgeous billionaire had told them, she thought cynically. When she and Aaron were alone, sipping champagne, she gave him a teasing look over the rim of her crystal flute. 'You sounded pretty certain back there.'

He shrugged. 'I guess I'm converted.'

She gave a little laugh. 'Really? How?'

'You're very passionate about what you do and believe. I admire that.'

'Passionate,' Zoe repeated, and saw Aaron's eyes flare with heat.

'Passionate,' he agreed huskily. 'Now, how about we get out of here?'

She could only nod. Her heart had started thudding and her palms were slick. Now it would happen. *Finally.*

Aaron took their glasses and deposited them on a waiter's tray. Then he was taking her by the elbow and whisking her out of the party into the crisp autumn night. The limo was waiting as always, and as Zoe slid in she felt her first attack of nerves. Stupid, maybe, when they'd already slept together. This wasn't the first time.

Yet it felt like the first time, because it was so different now. At least, she wanted it to be different. She wanted it to feel like more, to mean more.

Yet she was still afraid it might not.

'You look nervous,' Aaron said and took her hand.

Zoe tried to smile. 'I am,' she admitted. 'Maybe I shouldn't be, but—'

'I'm a bit nervous, too.'

Zoe let out a shocked laugh. She could hardly believe Aaron could ever be nervous about anything. He certainly looked relaxed sitting there, his legs stretched out, one arm resting on the seat above her head. 'You are not,' she said.

'Well, I must admit anticipation trumps any nervousness. I feel like I've been waiting a long time for this.'

'So do I,' she whispered.

They didn't speak again as they arrived at his building, and just as she'd imagined they rode up in the lift in a silence that was tense with expectation. Zoe could feel her heart beating so hard she wondered if Aaron could hear its thud, or see the pounding underneath the thin silk of her evening gown.

The doors swooshed open; Aaron took her by the hand and led her into the darkened apartment. Her dress whispered against her bare legs as he drew her to him, his hands framing her face in a way that was so achingly tender, infinitely gentle.

He kissed her once, softly, barely a brush of his lips against hers. Zoe sighed in surrender.

And then his phone buzzed in his pocket.

It almost seemed like a joke. It was certainly fitting, considering the nature of their first meeting. She felt Aaron tense, felt his hand leave her face and reach for his pocket.

'Aaron,' she said desperately, because she had a terrible instinct that if he took that call their night would be over. And maybe she should be understanding; he had a high-pressured job and this was, after all, only one night.

But it was an important night, a defining moment, and Zoe felt all her uncertainties and fears rise up in her as she put her hand over Aaron's, trapping it before he could reach his phone.

'Don't.'

'Zoe, it could be important—'

'Could be,' she repeated, her fingers twining with his. 'And this is important, Aaron, isn't it? What's happening between us?'

His voice was low and rough with want. 'Of course it is.'

'Then please, just leave it for a few hours. Surely it can wait?'

'And you can't?' He spoke tonelessly, but she knew what he was asking her. Was she giving him an ultimatum?

Zoe hesitated. She didn't want to be demanding; she wanted to make this work. But neither was she willing to accept what little Aaron had to give, or set a precedent where everything but her came first.

'No,' she said finally. 'I can't.'

Aaron hesitated. Zoe held her breath. Had she just made a huge mistake? Had she ruined everything already by pushing yet again? And yet it had been necessary…hadn't it?

The phone buzzed again.

After a tense and endless moment Aaron removed his hand from hers. He took his phone out of his pocket and without looking at it tossed it onto a chair. 'There.'

'Thank you,' Zoe said, and she stood on her tiptoes to kiss him, another brush of the lips, but Aaron took it and made it his own, deepening it so his tongue thrust into her mouth and Zoe felt as if her soul had been set on fire.

There was a raw urgency to Aaron's kiss, to his hands, as he unzipped her dress and slid it from her shoulders. He kissed her mouth, her throat, and then moved lower to kiss her breasts, slipping aside the scrappy lace of her bra.

Zoe gasped at the feel of his mouth, so cool and hard, hot and soft all at once, on her bare flesh. She rested her hands on his shoulders to steady herself as he moved lower, slipping the dress down her hips and legs, his mouth following a blazing trail.

'Aaron…'

'I need you, Zoe. I need you so much.' The words were raw, a guttural confession that Zoe knew Aaron meant—even if he didn't want to. And, while need wasn't love, it was something. It was a start.

She kicked the dress away from her high-heel-shod feet as Aaron sank to her knees in front of her. She swayed where she stood as her hands clenched around his shoulders and his mouth found the hot, pulsing centre of her.

'Aaron…' she said again, amazed at how quickly he could bring her to that precipice of pleasure. Already she felt the first waves of her climax crashing over her, and she was helpless to stop it. Her knees buckled as she cried out and Aaron swept his arm under her legs, carrying her easily to the bedroom.

His eyes were dark, his face almost savage with intent desire as he stripped off his tuxedo so he was gloriously naked, all hard, taut muscle and sleek skin. Zoe reached for him.

The press of his naked body against hers had her gasping aloud from the sheer, intense joy of it, and as he kissed her, his hands moving over her body, his fingers finding her secret, sensitive places, Zoe found her body straining towards another climax.

'You're going to kill me,' she gasped and he laughed low in his throat as his fingers slid inside her.

'It would be a good way to go.'

'Yes, it would,' she agreed, and with a superhuman effort—because what he was doing felt so amazingly good—she slipped out from under him and pushed him onto his back. 'But this isn't a one-man show, you know.'

'No?'

'No.'

And then it was her turn to explore him, every kiss and caress evoking a shuddering response that had her thrilling with seductive power—and a far greater emotion. *Love*.

She loved him. She'd been fighting against it, lecturing herself not to, and yet here it was, pure, simple and so very right. The doubts fell away and as Aaron finally rolled her over and entered her in one pure stroke, Zoe felt tears come to her eyes.

Just as before his gaze locked with hers and she felt the moment of raw need stretch and grow into something greater, something more powerful than pleasure.

'I love you,' she whispered and Aaron tensed above her, his face a mask, but Zoe didn't care. She felt, in that moment, that her love would be enough. She put her arms around him and arched upwards as he drove into her again, filling her up into completion. 'I love you,' she said again, and Aaron didn't answer.

He buried his face in her neck as he moved inside her, and

then Zoe couldn't think or worry about his silence because she was swept away on a tide of pleasure too great to resist, too wonderful to worry about anything else.

Aaron lay in his bed, his arm around Zoe's shoulders, his heart thundering in his chest.

I love you.

The words had humbled him, felled him, because no one had ever said them to him before. Not his father, who had lectured him about responsibility and duty; not his mother, who had been too wrapped up in her own misery. Not a woman, for the women he'd been with before, if they'd deluded themselves that they cared about him at all, would certainly have known better than to say as much.

But Zoe was different. And he was different with Zoe, because when she'd said those three words he'd wanted to hear them. He'd received them with a kind of dazed joy, even if he wasn't sure if he could say them back. He still didn't know if he had that depth of emotion in him.

'You don't have to say anything,' Zoe said quietly, and although she sounded calm he still heard a faint thread of hurt in her voice. Of course she was hurt. Generally, when a woman said 'I love you', the man was supposed to say something—'I love you, too' being the preferred option. He knew that much at least.

'I'm glad you love me,' he said, pulling her close, and she let out a little laugh.

'Well, that's something.'

'I'm glad you think so.'

She rolled over, her hair brushing his bare chest as she kissed him. 'You're glad about a lot of things, aren't you?'

'Yes, I am.'

She smiled softly and from the other room Aaron heard a

sound that had him tensing, a sound he'd blanked out in the last hour. His phone.

He needed to answer it. Part of him wanted to ignore it, wanted to stay in the safe and warm cocoon of Zoe's embrace, but he knew how much unrest there had been in both the economy and Bryant Enterprises. He needed to check his messages.

'Just a minute,' he said, and slid from the bed.

Zoe propped herself up one elbow. 'You're going to check your phone, aren't you?'

'It's been an hour.'

'I didn't realise you'd set a timer. Or is it just your internal clock?' She sounded waspish, and Aaron felt the first flicker of anger.

'Be reasonable. It could be something important.'

'Fine.' She rolled over, her back to him, and with an impatient shrug Aaron slid on his boxer shorts and stalked to the living room.

He reached for his phone, his heart seeming to freeze within him as he saw how many messages he'd missed. He listened to the first voicemail with a numbing sense of disbelief.

'Aaron, there's been an emergency meeting of the board of trustees. Apparently, it's allowable when there is a majority shareholder...'

The mystery man who was trying to buy up his company. He listened to the next message, and then the next, as his second-in-command detailed the events of the meeting.

And then the verdict—stark, impossible: 'You've been voted down as CEO.'

He'd lost Bryant Enterprises. And all because of a woman.

CHAPTER TWELVE

ZOE LAY IN bed, her body still tingling from Aaron's love-making even as she berated herself for being so bitchy about him taking his messages. Honestly, would she ever learn anything from her past relationships? It was just that she was so desperate and afraid. Neither were admirable qualities, and certainly not ones she wanted to possess in any relationship—especially not this one, the most important of all. She hated feeling like the person who gave more, who needed more, who cared more. Who loved.

She'd told Aaron it didn't matter if he didn't love her, but she knew it did. Of course it did. If he loved her, she'd hand him his stupid phone herself. She'd understand, she wouldn't care about such trivial moments. It was because she knew he didn't that those little moments became far too important. Defining.

Sighing, she stared up at the ceiling. Only moments ago she'd felt so joyously certain, yet now the doubts crept right back in. She took a deep breath and forced herself to stay calm. She'd be honest with Aaron. She'd apologise to him for being stupid about the phone. She'd tell him what she needed.

It seemed like a good plan and Zoe had sat up in bed, the sheet wrapped around her, when Aaron strode into the bedroom, his face as frighteningly blank as it had ever been.

Still, she had to try.

'Aaron, I'm sorry I was obnoxious about you checking your phone. I know it's such a small thing, and I clearly over-reacted.' Aaron didn't answer. He sat on the edge of the bed, his back to her. 'Aaron?' she asked uncertainly. 'Is something wrong?'

'Is something wrong?' he repeated tonelessly. 'You could say that.'

A cold, creeping fear took hold of her heart. 'Was it the phone? Was there a message—?'

'There were twenty-two messages.' Aaron cut her off, his voice still flat.

'Oh.' She hugged her knees to her chest. 'I guess it was something important.'

'You guessed right.' Aaron raked his hands through his hair, his body in the grip of some terrible emotion. Then he dropped his hands and Zoe had the horrible feeling that he'd just come to some major decision—and one she didn't want to hear.

He scooped her dress off the floor and tossed it to her. Zoe caught it instinctively, the sheet slipping from her breasts. 'You should go.'

'*Go?*'

'This isn't working. It never could have worked. Every-thing between us has been a mistake.'

It was as if he were saying every fear her heart had whis-pered, turning them into terrible realities. 'You don't mean that, Aaron.'

He turned to her, his eyes hard and cold. 'I mean it ab-solutely.'

'You're just going to end it like this? Kick me out?'

'A clean break is better.'

She shook her head slowly, still numb with disbelief. Ten minutes ago he'd been inside her. 'Who the hell was on that phone?' she asked and Aaron didn't answer; he just gathered her underwear and shoes and deposited them on the bed.

'I'll have my limo drive you to Millie and Chase's,' he said, and left the room.

Zoe sat frozen in the bed they'd just shared, her crumpled dress between her clenched fingers. Her mind spun uselessly, for she had no idea what had just happened…or why. Had a single phone call really made such a difference, or had Aaron been stringing her along the whole while? In either case, she had judged badly—again. And now she was left reeling and hurting more than ever before.

She dressed quickly, feeling sordid and shamed as she put on her crumpled evening gown. She slipped on her heels and did as much repair as she could to her face and hair. Then she took a deep breath and headed for the living room and Aaron.

She didn't know what to expect, but when she emerged from the bedroom he didn't even look at her. He'd dressed in a business suit, which seemed odd at this time of night. It had to be nearing midnight.

She walked to the lift doors and still he didn't say anything. In stunned disbelief she realised he was just going to let her walk out of his life for ever. In fact, that was what he seemed to want.

Emotions tightened in her chest and clogged her throat. 'I think,' she managed after a moment when he still hadn't so much as turned his head, 'I deserve an explanation at least.'

'There's no point.'

'Really?' Her voice choked and she strived to even it—then wondered why she wanted to hide how much he'd hurt her. Devastated her. 'And how did you come to that conclusion?'

Finally he looked at her and then Zoe wished he hadn't. He was the same man she'd first met at Millie's wedding, cold and pitiless, arrogant and hard. A man she hadn't liked or respected. Was that the real Aaron, and the rest had been no more than a facade? 'It doesn't matter, Zoe,' he said flatly, and he sounded impatient, as if he could barely stand to give her these few seconds of his time. 'All that matters is that this—us—was a mistake.'

'A mistake.'

'Yes.'

She stared at him, searching for some crack in the mask, some sign that he still was the man she wanted and loved underneath. There was nothing. Even so, a part of her longed to try to reach him, to cross the frozen silence between them, take his face in her hands and kiss his lips. To insist that she knew him now and he wasn't this man. He was someone kind, tender and good. He was the man she loved.

The words were there, clogged in her throat, on her lips. A flicker of impatience crossed Aaron's face like a shadow, and with it came Zoe's defeat. She'd done this before—tried and begged and believed when she shouldn't have. When Tim had ended it, she'd insisted she could change for him, that it could work. She'd begged him not to give up on her. The memory now was unbearably shaming; long ago Zoe had promised herself she would never debase herself so again. Then she'd gone on basically to do the same thing in three other relationships.

She wouldn't do it now.

Lifting her chin, she met Aaron's gaze straight on. 'Goodbye, Aaron,' she said with as much dignity as she could muster. He didn't answer, and as the lift doors opened and she stepped inside she couldn't keep from some of the awful hurt spilling out. 'I hope you go to hell,' she spat, the words ending on a sob, and the doors closed on his stony, unchanging expression.

Two days later Aaron sat in his former office and stared at the remnants of his life. A few boxes of confidential files were pretty much all he had. There were no photos, no mementoes, no personal items beyond a spare suit to remove from the executive office of Bryant Enterprises. The high-rise office building in midtown had been in the Bryant family since it had been built back in the 1930s.

Now it belonged to someone else, some techno-wizard from California who had masterminded the hostile takeover of his company. Today was Aaron's last day.

The newspapers' business pages had been full of his failure: *Bryant Enterprises Crumbles!* And *No More Bryant in BE* He'd read every article, punishing himself even as he refused to give into the pulsing pain that coursed through him unrelentingly. He would not succumb to self-pity. How could he, when this was all his fault?

He knew it wasn't the simple matter of not taking a phone call. He wasn't so paranoid as to believe the course of his fortune had changed overnight. No, it had happened long before that; it had started at Millie and Chase's wedding when Zoe Parker had taken his phone and he'd let her. He could have got it back sooner. He could have handled that whole situation differently, but instead he'd given her control because he'd been so in lust with her right from the beginning. Enthralled and excited by her daring, by her playful smile and the spark he'd seen in her eyes.

And from that moment on he'd lost his focus—asking her to move in with him, coming home early because she'd asked him to, spending two *weeks* on a remote Caribbean island. All of it added up to a perfect opportunity for someone to step in and sweep away all his work like so many flimsy dominoes. And he'd allowed it to happen.

Enough. Aaron rose from the desk. Self-recrimination was almost as bad as self-pity and a waste of time. What was done was done. He was hardly destitute; he'd received a substantial pay-out and St Julian's, owned jointly by all three brothers, remained in the family. His apartment was his own, without a mortgage, as was a summer house he owned in the Catskills. He had some personal investments. Everything else was gone.

He'd practically given it away.

Shaking his head, Aaron reached for his coat and the brief-case he wouldn't need any more. He'd have one of the errand boys bring down his boxes. He'd have to take a cab; the limo was a corporate perk.

'Hello, Aaron.'

Aaron jerked his head around to see, to his surprise, his brother Luke standing in the doorway. 'Come to gloat?' he asked, hearing the bitterness mixed with gallows humour in his voice. 'I suppose I deserve it.'

'I'm not gloating.'

'I know I never gave you the control you wanted.' For fifteen years Luke had worked for Bryant's retail arm, but Aaron had still initialled every decision. It had been a de-liberate choice, because from the beginning everything had felt so perilous. Losing control would have meant losing the company...just as he'd done now.

'It's true you didn't,' Luke said, stepping into the office. 'Why didn't you, as a matter of interest?'

'What do you mean?'

'I always thought it was just because you were a control freak. Or that you didn't trust me.'

'I didn't trust you,' Aaron answered bluntly, and Luke let out a short laugh.

'So it really was that simple.'

No, nothing had been simple since his father had died and he'd discovered the empire he'd inherited was rotten to the core. He'd never felt so betrayed in that moment, abandoned by his idol, alone at twenty-one to resurrect a business bank-rupted by his father's folly. And he'd succeeded...for a while. Until his own foolishness had cost him everything.

'I didn't trust anyone,' Aaron said. 'Not even myself. And I was right, wasn't I?' He let out a bitter laugh. 'I lost everything.'

Luke was silent for a long moment. 'And don't you think that was a choice?'

'A choice?' A bad one, then, to follow his libido rather than his brain. His heart rather than his head.

'Aaron, I know you're piling the guilt on yourself now, but you are one hell of a sharp guy. I don't think an upstart computer geek could steal your company from under your nose without you knowing about it.'

Aaron stilled, his gaze narrowing in on his brother. 'What are you saying?'

'I'm no shrink, but I'm saying that some part of you knew this was happening—and allowed it.'

'No.' The denial was immediate, instinctive.

'Father always put far too many expectations on you, even when you were a little kid. I think you knew you were going to be CEO when you were about six. Is it any wonder you might want to rebel against that?'

Aaron didn't answer. His mind was spinning with this new knowledge, this sudden realisation that Luke was right—that he'd known about the possible takeover for weeks, maybe even months, and had in some secret part of himself wanted it to happen. Had wanted to lose Bryant Enterprises because for once he wanted to be his own man, free to chose his own path.

A path that would have included Zoe…if in the first shock of loss and fear he hadn't pushed her away and destroyed any chance they had together.

'How do you feel now?' Luke asked quietly. 'Now that it's all gone, and none of it matters anymore?'

Aaron considered the question. He'd been numb since it all started unravelling three days ago, getting through the mechanics of each day, of taking a life apart. And now? 'I feel…

free,' he admitted in a kind of hesitant wonder, and then he looked away. The confession felt like a betrayal.

'That's how I felt too,' Luke said. 'When I walked away from Bryant Enterprises. I didn't realise what a shackle it had been until it was gone.'

A shackle. Yes, it had chained him, maimed him: the end-less attempts to rebuild a company teetering on the edge of disaster; all his beliefs about his father; his family destroyed.

'Bryant Enterprises has been in our family for a hundred years,' he said in a raw voice. 'You can't just walk away from that.'

'That was the problem, wasn't it?' Luke answered, his mouth twisting sardonically. 'It was damn hard for me to walk away. I can only imagine how difficult it's been for you.'

'Even so.'

'That company was killing you, Aaron. Maybe you can't see it, but I can from here.'

Aaron blinked hard. He knew Luke was right, even if he hated to admit it. Even if his freedom felt like weakness. 'Still,' he said with a ragged sigh, 'I made a huge mess of things.'

Luke remained silent for a moment. 'You mean Zoe.'

'How do you know?'

'I don't, really. Chase told me a little. Do you love her?'

Yes. The admission, made in the silence of his own heart, stunned him. He knew it was true. And it was too damn late. 'It doesn't matter.'

'How can you say that?'

'Because she won't forgive me,' Aaron snapped. 'Even if I wanted to be forgiven.'

'And you don't?'

Did he want to go back to Zoe a defeated, ruined man? No. He wanted to return to her on his terms—proud, in control. Arrogant. Autocratic. A control freak, just as she'd once called him.

Was he capable of change? Was he capable of going to Zoe and admitting his weaknesses, his failures? The thought was abhorrent…yet necessary.

Perhaps this was the only way. He gave his brother a wry smile. 'This is tough.'

Luke let out a laugh and shook his head. 'Don't I know it.'

'You're happy, though, with Aurelie,' Aaron said, and he nodded.

'Absolutely. And you can be too, Aaron, but you're right, it's not easy. That doesn't mean it's not worth it.'

As he left the building for the last time Aaron felt that shackle finally slip off. Strange, how liberating it truly was. He had no idea what he'd do now, but the realisation that Bryant Enterprises was no longer his responsibility, his burden, almost made him giddy with relief…instantly followed by an instinctive disgust.

What kind of man did that make him?

A free man, a man at liberty to make his own choice. Zoe had been right when she'd asked if it was the lack of choice he'd minded. Now he'd made his choice, even if he hadn't realised it at the time. He'd chosen freedom, independence. Possibility.

Shaking his head, Aaron knew it would be a long time before he could reconcile his conflicting emotions. Before he could be at peace with what had happened.

And as for what had happened with Zoe…regret lanced through him. He'd treated her so very badly, hadn't even been willing to give her an explanation, a chance. He'd been reacting on instinct, out of fear. And not just fear, but disgust; thinking he had acted just like his father. Been as weak as the man he'd once idolised.

He'd been wrong.

Would Zoe give him another chance? He felt his heart thud at the thought of confronting her, asking for her forgiveness. He'd been able to say a few careless sorries to her before, but this was something entirely new and different, and all too risky.

And yet necessary.

He hailed a cab and told him to head uptown, to Millie and Chase's brownstone.

Millie answered the door when he arrived, her face pulling into a ferocious frown.

'I should slam this door in your face.'

'Is Zoe here?'

'If she were, I wouldn't—'

'Millie, please.' He held up one hand to stem her tirade, and she sighed.

'The only reason I'm *not* slamming this door in your face is because I happen to know that Bryant men can be rather stupid about women and love.'

'Phenomenally stupid.'

'That was the right answer.' Millie smiled, but it quickly faded. 'Don't hurt her, Aaron. She's been hurt before. I didn't even know how badly.'

'I know.'

'She told you?'

He nodded. She'd been honest with him. She'd been vulnerable. And he hadn't, not really. Now was his chance—and it frightened the hell out of him. 'Where is she?' he asked, and Millie told him.

Zoe smiled at Robert, the little boy who had been coming to the community centre for several months now.

Today he had made some encouraging strides; he'd drawn a picture of his family, including his father, taking care with the minute details: the sun shining, the smiles on their faces, the buttons on their shirts. Then he'd stared at it for a long moment and said quietly, 'I wish it was like that.'

Zoe's heart had contracted inside her and she laid a hand on Robert's shoulder. *I wish it was like that too, Robert,* she thought. At least acceptance was part of the grieving process, and both she and the little boy were grieving.

Now Robert had gone and Zoe was just clearing up the art supplies scattered across the table. The centre would be closing in a little while. She felt someone watching her and, stiffening slightly because the centre's doors were open to whomever chose to walk inside, she turned to glance at the doorway to the art room…and stopped in shock when she saw it was Aaron.

She should have nothing to say to him, she told herself numbly as he came forward. She shouldn't even acknowledge his presence, not after the way he'd treated her. She turned back to the table and scooped up a handful of crayons, her fingers shaking, and dropped several.

Aaron reached over and put the dropped ones in the basket. 'Hello, Zoe.' She didn't answer. Couldn't. She concentrated on the crayons and Aaron finally said quietly, 'I'd like to talk to you.'

'There are no words you could say that I want to hear.'

He was silent for a moment and Zoe didn't dare look at him. 'Perhaps I could draw a picture,' he finally said, and she sat back, folding her arms.

'A little art therapy? It can work wonders.'

'Then let me have a go.' He sat down at the table, looking incongruous in his business suit. Zoe watched as he took a piece of paper and a couple of crayons. As with everything, he worked carefully, diligently, his brow furrowed in concentration as he drew a couple of stick figures.

'Very nice,' she said, sarcasm edging her voice. 'Who are those supposed to be?'

'Me.' He pointed to the sad-faced stick figure in the centre of the picture. 'You.' She was another sad-looking stick figure in the corner of the picture.

'I'd say that's about right.'

He glanced up from the paper. 'I'm no artist, Zoe, but I would like to talk to you. I sincerely regret what happened between us the other night.'

'What happened between us? That suggests shared responsibility, Aaron—and, as I recall, it was all you. I just sat there like a lemon.' Bitterness spiked her words. If she had to have her heart broken, couldn't she have acted a little stronger, a little more in control?

'You're right,' Aaron answered. 'I acted like a complete bastard and I want to apologise. And explain. Will you please let me?'

She stared at him for a long moment, indecision warring within her. She'd never been in this scenario before; no one had ever come back, wanting to explain or apologise. Part of her wanted to stay strong and another part desperately wanted to hear what he had to say.

'All right,' she said at last. 'But the centre is closing. Let me clear up and we can go outside.'

Aaron helped her put away the art supplies and mop the floor, neither of them speaking beyond the basics, and a few minutes later they stepped out into a beautiful late October afternoon.

They walked in mutual, silent agreement towards Washington Square, the leaves above them crimson and gold.

'So,' Zoe said when they'd reached a park bench. She sat down, her arms folded, legs crossed, her position one of defence. 'What do you have to say?'

'I shouldn't have asked you to leave the other night.'

'*Asked* me to leave?'

'Kicked you out,' Aaron amended. 'That phone call—the

one I took—was a voicemail message calling an emergency meeting of my board of trustees.'

She frowned, not really getting it. 'Why?'

'Someone has been secretly buying up shares in Bryant Enterprises for a while now. I've been trying to keep an eye on it, but the other night he called the meeting and basically had me fired.'

She straightened, her mouth nearly dropping open in shock. 'Fired?'

'Basically. He replaced me as CEO. I no longer have a role in Bryant Enterprises, or a majority of the shares.'

'But…' She shook her head, still stunned. Aaron spoke so flatly, without any emotion at all, yet it sounded like everything had been taken away from him. 'What did that have to do with me?' she asked at last. 'Were you just angry?'

'Ashamed,' Aaron corrected quietly. 'But to understand why I need to go back a little further. I told you a bit about my father—how he singled me out from an early age to take over the company. My whole life was oriented towards that— every exchange, every conversation was a lesson in duty and responsibility. I had to be tough, above petty things like relationships.'

'That's what he told you?'

Aaron shrugged. 'That was my life. My brothers went to boarding school, I went to boot camp—military school starting at age seven. They had skiing and beach holidays. I went to training courses and had extra lessons. It was the price of being the oldest son.'

'But that's awful.'

'It is what it is. In any case, I idolised my father. I wanted to be like him: confident, in control, powerful.' He paused, his expression darkening. 'And then he died and I discovered it was all a lie.'

What I didn't like was being lied to. Over and over again, so my whole life was built on nothing but deception. Now she was starting to understand why he had said that.

'How was it a lie?' she asked quietly.

'He wasn't in control at all. The business was bankrupt and he'd given away money and shares to a bunch of mistresses—one in particular who took everything she could.' Bitterness roughened his voice. 'I promised myself I would never be like that. Never let a woman—or anyone—take my focus away from the business. Never be weak.'

Zoe sat back against the bench, realisation rushing through her. 'And when I asked you not to take that phone call, that's what you felt you were doing.'

'Not just the phone call. Everything—asking you to move in with me, to marry me, going to St Julian's to see you and be with you... In that moment it all felt like weakness.'

She blinked, her throat tightening. 'I see.'

'I don't think you do.' Aaron took her hand. 'I've been fighting weakness all my life, Zoe, trying to be strong, to seem strong. I never told anyone about the company's troubles, not even my brothers. I took it all on myself when I was twenty-one, which in retrospect was a ridiculous thing to do.' He shook his head. 'And today, when I left my office for the last time, I realised I felt relief. I'm glad to be shot of it all, to finally be free. To be free to be weak.'

'You could never be weak, Aaron,' Zoe whispered. 'You're the strongest man I know.'

'I'm weak with love,' he said. 'I'm in love with you, and it took me a long time to realise it. To accept it. Maybe I fell in love with you the first time you stole my phone.'

She laughed, the sound wobbly. 'I doubt it.'

'But I love you. And I'm not afraid of it now.' He paused, squeezing her fingers. 'I can only ask you to forgive me for treating you so terribly. I knew you'd been hurt before and I acted just the same. I'm so sorry, Zoe.'

Her throat was so tight now she could barely speak, and yet her heart was full, so wonderfully full. 'I forgive you,' she whispered.

'And do you think you could take another chance on me? This is new territory for me, Zoe, and I admit it's still scary. The honesty, the emotion.' He gave her a shaky smile. 'The love. But I want to try...with you.'

Zoe swallowed. She could hardly believe she was hearing Aaron say these words. Yet she did believe them, so very much. And she want to try again, even though trying and loving were scary—for both of them. 'I love you,' she said softly. 'And, yes, I want to try with you. I want to more than try, Aaron. I want this to work.'

'It will work,' he promised as he took her in his arms. 'As long as you give me lots of chances to make mistakes and say sorry.'

She smiled as he kissed her. 'I promise,' she said. She kissed him back, stopping as his phone buzzed in his pocket. 'Are you going to get that?' she asked, and he smiled.

'Not a chance,' he answered, and deepened the kiss.

EPILOGUE

Three years later

ZOE STOOD NEXT to Aaron in the church and watched with a swell of both love and pride as he cradled their tiny daughter. Camilla Anne Bryant was three months old, and today was her christening.

Summer sunshine spilled into the church, gilding Aaron's hair in gold. Zoe's gaze moved from her husband—they'd been married a year ago—to the other couples in the room. Luke and Aurelie stood next to Aaron, their fingers laced. They hadn't yet started a family, but Zoe knew they were thinking about it. Love brimmed over in both of their eyes, and as Aaron handed Camilla to the minister she saw them exchange a small, secret smile.

She turned to look at Millie and Chase, who also stood together, Millie's hand resting protectively on the small swell of her baby bump. Zoe knew it had taken a long time for Millie to risk trying again, and she was so happy her sister and Chase were expecting a cousin for Camilla—this time a boy.

She let her gaze rest once more on her husband, the man she loved more than anyone, the man who had both changed himself and changed her. He must have felt her gaze on him, for he lifted his head and smiled. She knew he was thinking what a miracle this was, to have them all together, united, happy. And Camilla was a miracle; it had taken four attempts at IVF before Zoe had fallen pregnant but the heartache and frustrated hope had finally turned to joy.

Stepping forward to take her husband's hand, Zoe knew she had everything she'd ever wanted.

* * * * *

Join Britain's BIGGEST Romance Book Club

50% OFF your first parcel

- **EXCLUSIVE offers** every month
- **FREE delivery direct** to your door
- **NEVER MISS a title**
- **EARN Bonus Book points**

Call Customer Services
0844 844 1358*

or visit
millsandboon.co.uk/subscriptions